The GUARDIAN of TIME

C C CHAMBERS

STEP
THROUGH
BOOKS

The Guardian Of Time Copyright © C C Chambers 2002

Published by Step Through Books

Cover and illustrations © C C Chambers 2003

The right of C C Chambers to be identified as the author of this work has been
asserted in accordance with the Copyright Designs and Patents Act 1988.
A CIP catalogue record of this book is available from the British Library.

ISBN: 0-9545953-0-0

Printed and bound in England by Bookmarque Limited.

To those who don't know what day it is.

CHAPTER ONE

Plan A and Plan B

Friday 13th March 3.15pm

"ROBERT GRAFELD TAYLOR! STAAND UP NOWWW!"

Ms Gibben's voice exploded from the back of the classroom with all the ferocity of a volcano, and quickly brought a deathly silence to Form 3B. Bob felt like the attention of the entire world was suddenly upon him, and any second now a clamouring news crew would come bursting in through the door. Heads turned in eager anticipation of the fate that was about to befall him, and he slowly stood up. For a moment, he wondered if his great strategy wasn't going to work out quite as planned, because judging by the tone of Ms Gibben's voice there was a very good chance she was going to kill him.

She marched with slow and deliberate steps towards Bob's desk, and her piercing click-clacks came to a halt beside him. Her question was short and stupid, which was entirely appropriate for her.

"What is this?" she snapped.

A familiar piece of paper gently floated down onto the open book in front of him. It showed a large monkey with enormous glasses and wild hair, dancing on a huge cream cake - and she appeared to be wearing a very full nappy. The words "Be Quiet Form 3B Or I Will Go Ape!" were written in a big speech bubble, leaving Bob to wonder exactly what Ms Gibben needed to know. It was, in his opinion, one of his finer efforts.

"Well, Ms Gibben," he began, extra careful to pronounce the 'enn' of her name as the more ape-like 'unn' in order to start on her wrong side, "I would have to say that, err.. someone is being disrespectful and mis-using their talents.. disrespectfully. Frankly, I'm appalled."

Andie, sitting at the desk next to him, tried to draw enough of her chestnut hair forwards to not only hide her grin but also to stifle a laugh. She had suspected that he'd been secretly doing something all day, but hadn't seen the masterpiece until now. The resemblance was pretty good, and assuming it didn't wind up in the bin, might be one worth keeping. She stared at the floor while suffering her silent agonies, keeping her eyes well away from just about everything.

"If, Bob, I thought this was your work, I would slam you in a detention this very evening SO hard that you would leave an impression on the Detention Room door," she said, pushing a grey curl up out of her eyes, "But I have to assume that even you are not stupid enough to actually sign a piece of filth like this!"

She pointed a chubby finger at the bottom right corner, just next to the second cream bun. Someone, somewhere in the room, was actually dumb enough to have scrawled 'R G Taylor 3B' and had therefore wrecked the credibility of his near-foolproof plan. Disappointed, he figured that whoever had handed it over to Der Führer was most likely the same one who had added the signature. They must have thought it was the final nail in the coffin.

"I believe you drew it, Bob, but maybe you didn't - perhaps someone is very eager to see you in trouble. Although it's nice to know there are those amongst us who long to see you reigned in, I will not tolerate any 'entrapments'. Such behaviour only escalates and before too long we could have the police involved. Yes, the police.. and then perhaps regional television reporters.. possibly documentary makers or a few journalists at the very least. As such, I will let it go - this time."

Having delivered her uniquely-bizarre verdict, she positioned her glasses back at the top of her nose and turned to face the room, casting a suspicious gaze that absolutely no-one dared to meet. With a sharp clap of her hands the class resumed their preparations for the second half of the double English lesson. Plan A had failed, but Bob was ready with the almost-guaranteed Plan B.

Once Andie had totally regained her composure, she edged over onto Bob's side of the desk and pencilled 'I know what u r up 2 - stop it now!' on the front page of a piece of work entitled 'My Grandfather' - or as Bob knew it, Plan B.

The school horn signalled the end of the first English lesson with four long blasts, and Ms Gibben stood beside her immaculate desk, knocking on it twice with a ruler.

"Right class, you have now had long enough on this project, and I will call some of you to read your Elderly Citizen Appreciation essays during the next forty minutes. Those of you who are not called this week can be sure they will be called next week, and I will keep hold of their papers in the meantime. Now then, who will start the proceedings for us, Bob?"

Bob looked up, ready to throw a little more petrol on the fire.

"Umm.. I don't know, Miss," he said, trying hard to look wide-eyed and genuinely stupid. Andie snorted and gave his foot a kick, and he struggled not to laugh.

"You know very well I meant YOU, now move!" she bellowed.

A wave of murmurs and sly sniggering spread around the room. Bob didn't particularly like this class. The year before had been okay, but school policy put everyone in new classes each year and if, like Bob and Andie, you lived nowhere near the school, you could never quite fit in. And if, like Andie, you only had partial hearing in one ear and practically none at all in the other, school life could become very difficult at times.

Bob went and stood next to Ms Gibben's desk and watched her waddle to a spare chair at the back of the room. Plan B simply could not be allowed to fail. Confronting his audience, he took a deep breath and began.

"My Recently Deceased Grandpa - His Life, Times and other favourite magazines and newspapers."

Just as expected, total silence met the first deliberately bad joke, and Bob was pleased to see Andie's second big grin of the day appear. He met her eyes and was lost for a moment while a million butterflies took flight in his stomach, instantly spreading the most wonderful chaos all through him. As usual, they came to rest somewhere around his brain before disappearing as quickly they had arrived. He carried on with his performance before they could come back again, and hoped he wasn't blushing.

"My.. my Grandfather was born in the small town of Blandford at the age of nine. He moved.. oh hold on, bad handwriting and a full stop in the wrong place. Can I start again, Ms Gibben?"

"Bob, you are on thin ice.." she growled.

"Thank you. My Grandfather was born in the small town of Blandford. At the age of nine he moved to Lymington, not through choice but because he got on the wrong bus and didn't have enough money for the return fare. You see, life was much harder back in those days - especially for him. He was named after his father, which made his childhood very difficult indeed - can anyone here imagine having a name like 'Dad'? As if that wasn't bad enough, he suffered from a rare form of colour blindness and had no concept of black, which meant he thought it was really sunny even at night time. How tough can life be?"

Ms Gibben was beginning to look dangerous. She lowered her Assessment Sheet onto her lap and pointed her Assessment Pen towards him. Her left eye gave a slight tremble as her eyebrows edged closer together.

"Bob! I am warning you.."

"I hear you, Ms Gibb-un..enn," said Bob, respectfully. Andie's shoulders gave a small judder as a giggle escaped her, and a group of girls nearby tutted their disapproval.

"Eventually, Gramps joined the Royal Navy and served on the good ship HMS Why The Hell Won't This Bottle Break. He only lasted a mere three hours before running ashore like a shameless coward. He avoided.."

Bob was aware of Ms Gibben's intense glare burning into him, and he sensed victory was within reach.

"..avoided the Naval authorities for two whole weeks by seeking refuge behind a friend's settee, but was duly arrested and thrown back on board. He gave forty of his best years to King, Queen and country on that ship, and kept those toilets clean enough to eat your dinner off. Just 'cause no-one ever chose to didn't mean they couldn't. Mind you, plenty of dinners did end up all over them occasionally, 'cause those seas could be very rough at times. Ironic, in a way."

Bob paused, ready for the big finale. He raised his right leg onto Ms Gibben's highly polished table. All except two of the room's twenty eight faces stared blankly back at him. One at the back glowed red with rising rage, and one at the front was half-hidden behind the raised neck of her jumper, giggling.

"He gave blood, sweat and tears - yes tears, for his beloved England through many, many conflicts around the world, but alas his bravery on the bloodied battlefields.. sorry, battleseas, of Europe went sadly unrewarded, and like so many of his compatriots, he died a poor man. So poor in fact, that in his Last Will And Testament all he could leave me were these, his old war wounds.."

Bob rolled his trouser leg up to just beyond his knee, revealing a series of hideous scabs and gruesome scrapes which had actually come from a game of rugby the previous week. With elaborate hand gestures like a presenter on the 24-Hour SellyVision Channel, he started pointing at different lumps and bruises while mentioning the various wars where the damage had been done. Nauseated groans and wobbling cries of "Ms Gibb'nnn.." rose up from the class right on cue, while Andie began falling into gales of helpless laughter. Mount Gibben was ready to explode again.

"THAT DOES IT! Detention tonight you obnoxious, foul, immature and wicked creature! I will not tolerate such disresp.."

Ms Gibben's words were all but lost on Bob, who was triumphantly making his way back to his desk. Andie's shoulders were still rocking as he sat down, and she buried her laughter into her forearms.

"Ah, my work here is done," Bob thought to himself in true superhero style, as he tried desperately hard to look innocent, apologetic and sheepish all at the same time. He failed dismally, but that didn't matter because he had landed one of the school's more severe punishments, and thus Operation Don't Let Andie Have A Detention By Herself was a complete, resounding and unequivocal success.

CHAPTER TWO
Earlier That Day

Friday 13th March

Friday morning had started badly. Bob's 6.15am alarm had failed to deliver its usual frantic volley of high-pitched bleeps, and only the wailing of a mad cat somewhere outside his window had woken him up. Well, that and his mother shouting loudly up the stairs. He practically fell out of bed and a mad panic followed in order for him to be in the back of his dad's car and heading to Andie's house by 7.00am, to pick her up on their daily trek to the bus station. The dark skies, rain and more rain hadn't helped him to wake up on the way, and Bob was sure that his brain was going to spend the entire day tucked up and cosy, back in bed.

Andie was fine as ever though, and as they stood at the empty station waiting for the rusty crate of a school bus to turn up and cart them off to the King Olaf Trygvason School, she began showing off a new trick with her yo-yo. Not only could it now flash while walking up her arm, but it could also return to her hand complete with all its string expertly wrapped-up out of sight. Bob had always encouraged Andie to practice her yo-yo manoeuvres, because apart from making her a figure of interest amongst other kids for all the right reasons, she was also lethal when a situation demanded it. He had no doubt at all that her yo-yo could stop a charging rhino dead in its tracks if necessary. That wasn't very likely to happen, because the small not-quite-a-town of Barton On Sea wasn't famed for its roaming wildlife. Or any wildlife, really, other than loud seagulls or the occasional squashed hedgehog in the road.

The bus arrived at 7.15am, cold and empty except for a grumpy driver and a stubborn smell of old cigarettes. Ten minutes into the journey Andie was asleep, as usual. How she managed to do that was a mystery to Bob. Almost every single day she would be fast asleep until the second stop, when some kind of internal alarm would wake her up in time for the rest of the world to get on. The first stop was hardly worth bothering with. A short pudgy kid from the Junior School - who was named 'Short Pudgy Kid' by Andie in her own special way of naming people, would clamber up the steps and drop things, get back off and pick them up, then scramble up again and sit behind the driver. Every day, he went through the same routine. But after half an hour or so, the second stop would arrive and a storm of insanity would take over.

In every school in every country, there are kids whose sole purpose in life is to cause trouble. Some do it unintentionally, some do it on purpose, but most do it because they're totally unhinged and need medical treatment. This was the sort that Bob and Andie had to deal with twice a day, to and from school. All the psychos and loonies at King Olaf's seemed to travel on the school bus. It was almost as if the school had a Government target, a 'Quota For Deviants & Social Misfits' that it had to achieve, and needed to bus them all in. Heaven help the poor souls who sat too near the back.

By the time the bus had reached its fifth and final stop, shouts, yelps and general chaos were drowning out the radio, and a small group of soon-to-be-leaving thugs known to Bob and Andie as The Psycho Fifth were ruling the roost and inflicting damage on anything or anyone who deserved it. Over the previous few years they had caused Bob far too much grief, but recently even the Loony-in-Chief, Thombert 'Wart' Stubbs, had eased off in favour of terrorising fresh new batches of smaller kids. Bob had always hoped that Andie was unaware of the jokes they made about her, the faces they pulled and the nasty impersonations that they occasionally tried. She never mentioned it, so maybe she didn't know. Maybe.

Her own particular nemesis joined the bus at the final stop. Dertha Lynch lead a cell-block (or whatever the collective term is for a group of deranged Fourth Year girls) who were each slightly more unattractive than the next, in any order. They believed that if somebody was going to be picked on, the victim ought to know about it - name calling behind someone's back was far too subtle for them. Around Easter of the previous year, outside the School Library, they took one step too far and put a tearful Andie in a situation where two things could have happened. Option One would have involved Bob delivering some well-planned put-downs in Andie's defence, the kind that he spent ages thinking up and crafting for those moments when needed. That approach sometimes worked. Option Two was the safe option and involved both of them walking away (one feeling very hurt and one trying not to show it.) But Andie chose Option Three, a previously untried form of defence which hadn't been discussed with Bob. She plunged a hand deep into her bag and drew it out fully-loaded with a yo-yo, and unleashed a barrage of lightning fast shots to pummel the loudest and widest one of the girls in front of her. Cries, squeals and a few peculiar words echoed through the Library Corridor as Andie taught five unpleasant girls a valuable lesson. Other than Bob, no-one saw the attack but news of where Dertha's bruises and red marks came from spread very quickly. Suddenly Andie was no longer the subject of any direct teasing, and even strange looks from others were briefly replaced with admiration.

Since then, life had been easier for Andie, and the five had stopped being thorns in her side for a few months, but they eventually worked out that as long as they stayed beyond yo-yo range they could keep up with their entertainment. Andie didn't seem to mind too much, as she knew that her point had been made and that they were scared of her. In a way, she was proud of being 'Deaf and Dangerous', as they kept reminding her.

But on this particular Friday morning, as everyone was spilling out of the school bus, they fancied levelling the score. They waited just inside the school's huge gates before grouping around her, and while Bob was sidetracked by a dimwit who had borrowed a cd and now wanted to keep it, they began hissing and then shouting 'Pesta', which in a school like King Olaf Trygvason was a particularly vile name indeed. It was an insult that reared its head every now and then, depending on which creative genius had stayed awake for long enough in a History class to realise that such a word had a lot of abusive potential. The reasons why were deeply rooted in the school's heritage.

The early history is rather vague, and the few existing records of its founding briefly refer to the bitter midwinter of 1813. A travelling Norwegian businessman was in a great hurry on his way to the docks at Southampton, and stopped at The Round Barrel Inn - a lowly tavern near the small rural town of Ringwood. As the snow fell that evening, he regaled the townsfolk with tales of his journey from northern lands, and even claimed regal ancestry dating back to one of Norway's great kings, Olaf Trygvason. The local Priest, Father Magnus (who was there as he was every night, trying to save wayward souls over a few flagons of ale and some odd versions of hymns) immediately offered him a place to stay for the night. By morning, the Norwegian businessman was gone, never to be seen or heard of again. For reasons never established, he had deposited two vast trunks full of money and gemstones with the Priest, and according to Magnus' housekeeper, he had even left his gold fillings behind.

Rumours soon started racing around the locale, and suspicion quickly fell upon the Priest who vainly tried assuring the townsfolk that this was a gift to the church from a repentant sinner and had nothing at all to do with any kind of gambling or murderous shenanigans. Very little was ever known of Father Magnus, but history does show that after numerous meetings with town dignitaries and leading church figures over a two week period, he pledged the windfall to be put to good use. Before retiring in December of 1813 to run a goat farm on a remote Welsh island, he wrote and signed the Magnus Charter, the original parchment of which was still proudly on display in the school's Library.

Translated from its original Latin, his Charter states: *"I hereby pledge, bequeath and give sufficient monies that a school shall duly be built to strengthen the rich and historic ties forged between Norway and England by.. King Olaf Trygvason, many centuries long past. Who could want for better reason, may such never be forgotten, and so on. Here, have all the ..... money."*

A blotch of ink obscured a long word immediately before 'money', no doubt the result of a grammatical oversight. A carved stone copy of this adorned the base of a marble bust of the great man outside the entrance to the school's Nordically titled main hall, The Hov.

So in July of 1817, after almost four years of planning, building, and rebuilding, the magnificent King Olaf Trygvason School became the very first Anglo-Norwegian educational establishment in the town of Ringwood, and perhaps the first in the whole of England. The local people were rightly proud, if not a little bewildered.

Staying true to the spirit of the school's origins, Norwegian history and culture played a significant part in the day-to-day lives of the pupils, much to the despair of consecutive Governments since the 1819 Minister Of Education first realised what was going on. Despite countless predictions of its imminent demise, the school went from strength to strength and over the years had sent thousands of Nordically-aware students out into the world.

The group who were taunting Andie had just covered the 14th Century in their Scandinavian History class, and found that for a few decades the Black Death had wiped out thousands upon thousands of people in a rather horrible way. The very best medical minds of the day concluded that the disease was being spread by an evil, ugly Plague Woman called Pesta.

Armed only with this solitary new line of abuse the five girls decided that the time had come to let the school know who Andie really was. The taunts around her grew louder, and Bob stepped in.

"Hey witch-freaks, your bus is leaving!" he shouted over and gestured towards the back end of the school bus, which was chugging towards the traffic lights.

"You'll be late for the labs - the doctors are sorting out faces today, and there's free cakes afterwards! Hurry up!" he added and began heading over to guide Andie away. But this time was different. This time she was crying, and the jeering seemed to be cutting straight through her. As Bob came nearer, the name-calling moved on to new and nastier areas, and dense collections of kids in the playground were grinning. He was fuming more with every step but held his anger back for Andie's sake, and as he reached the crowd he gently took her arm, picked her bag up, and began to lead her away. They hadn't taken more than two or three steps before Andie spun around and unleashed a whirling fury of double-barrelled nickel-plated yo-yo shots. This made last April's yo-yo defence look like a genteel demonstration of beginner's tricks. Bob grinned like someone who'd just found out that large portions of chips were good for raising IQ levels.

Hefty thuds and cracks were met with squeals and screams, and before Andie had even warmed up properly, Mrs Fynne-Bunche, the stick-like Chemistry teacher, intervened. She cast her narrow eyes over the bawling group of Fourth Years, noticing that two had serious nose-bleeds, two were barely able to stand, and the remaining one was semi-conscious in a hedge. She immediately drew the conclusion that Andie was a danger to the entire world, and therefore a First Degree Detention was called for. A detention of that variety was rare. It meant the accused had committed a crime of such staggering evil that whatever was planned after school on that day, such as going home for example, would have to wait. Instead, there would be almost two hours worth of Nordic poetry to copy out - in its original Old Norse. Nobody wanted to do that. Not even the Skalds who wrote the verses down in the first place could have been too pleased about writing them in Old Norse.

So for the rest of the morning Andie had been very quiet and Bob knew her well enough to understand that she was hurt, very deep down inside. The prospect of her spending two hours alone feeling bad about herself was something that he knew had to be avoided at all costs, so before the start of the day's lessons he made a quick phonecall home to arrange for his dad to pick them both up in the evening - and he then began working out a plan of such supreme cunning and genius that he almost felt like telling Andie about it. Of course, she would have gone spare if she knew, so it became his top secret Plan A. Even the emergency back-up Plan B was a work of calculated tactical magnificence. On the downside it would involve getting no marks at all for an essay that he'd actually spent quite some time preparing, and also landing himself in a First Degree Detention of course, but that wouldn't matter in the slightest, all things considered.

And by the end of the day, as the school horn gave its five short blasts and everyone else began leaving for the weekend, Bob felt on top of the world to be staying.

CHAPTER THREE

Dark Skies

Bob and Andie sat in the small Detention Room, high up on the top floor of Vige Tower, at a double desk by the room's only window. Vige was the third of the five towers which cornered the Old Building, and had to be the least-worthy of them all to be called a tower. Only its pointed roof raised it above the height of the main building, and the rounded walls had something which very few tower-designers throughout history had ever thought to include - a single flight of narrow stairs running up around the outside, rather than the inside. That had been caused by a technical error on the original plans, so they had been closed off with a carved 'Danger - Don't Be Stupid' plaque since the day their construction had been completed in 1815. Hardly surprisingly, the sideless Steps Of Death had become a test-of-bravery for many students ever since. Bob and Andie certainly didn't fancy having a go.

Their desk gave another ominous wobble - or maybe that was the building? Either way, the Distress Rating neared Level 10. The room hadn't been used for teaching for around a hundred years, ever since an unfortunate incident involving a First Year and Sigurd (the last ever School Parrot) back in 1905. School folk-lore was full of such stories, one or two of which might even be true, and that was supposed to be one of the true ones. As such, the room had become nothing more than a graveyard for desks that needed fixing, and Bob and Andie's battered relic needed a major overhaul.

Mr Scrimley, who was the world's oldest, frailest Maths teacher (and self-proclaimed King Of The Abacus) settled down behind his desk and took out his pen at the official Detention Start Time of 4.15pm. Slowly and pedantically he began working his way through a teetering pile of Sixth Form Maths books, giving each and every point his fullest consideration before awarding a small and neat tick, or an equally small and neat cross. Bob watched for a few moments, amazed that anyone could move so incredibly slowly and yet still manage to be alive. Andie sighed and opened up their first book.

In between copying verses from a compilation volume of Halfred Vandredaskald's greatest hits, the two of them passed doodles and the kind of messages that no-one else could possibly understand, in a bid to fend off the intense boredom. But with half an hour to go, as the clock crawled past 5.45, Andie's head touched the table and she was, in Bob's medical opinion, spark out. Mr Scrimley looked over and raised his eyebrows in a seen-it-all-before manner, and carried on marking.

The clouds outside grew threatening once again, and an extremely heavy thunderstorm seemed to be developing somewhere on the horizon. All day long the dull, grey sky had merely threatened rain, but the black clouds that were now gathering high above a very unfortunate place were simply awesome. There was, Bob figured, a depressingly good chance that the storm of all storms was located right over Barton. Hopefully it would hold off until after his dad had come to pick him and Andie up. That was the only benefit of being in a two hour detention - the timing was really convenient. His dad would close the chemist shop for the night at about six o'clock as per normal, and would take less than half an hour to drive over to the school - which meant that by the time the detention was over, they wouldn't have long to wait for their chauffeur.

The clouds seemed to be darkening by the minute, and looked so much like a bad painting that Bob felt he ought to nudge Andie awake just so that she could see them. He resisted the temptation and instead leaned his head against the lead lattice of the windowpane and looked down into the school kitchen's delivery yard, six floors below. A few more tiles had blown off the roof during the afternoon, leaving a mass of black and red fragments in the centre of the yard. All the towers were booked for a long-overdue summer of restoration ahead, and Bob sighed a hope that the old structure would last long enough to see out the detention. Dying in a detention had to be the all-time worst way to go.

The seven huge cylindrical metal bins were overflowing with a thousand kinds of junk. Protruding cardboard panels waved and dangled in the wind while stray papers and empty boxes were beginning to be cast about over the old cobblestones. Yes, a storm was coming and it would no doubt be coming soon, sighed Bob. Just as his eyes began to drift back over to the clock, he noticed a black shape disappearing behind one of the bins. He kept his gaze directed there, because now that he had time to think about it, he'd been noticing a black shape in the corner of his eye all day. There was one occasion at the bus station, at least three on the way to school, a couple after lunch and maybe even one on the way over to the Old Building. And now there was another one.

"Freakishly bizarre," he thought to himself.

After a few moments a jet-black cat strolled out from between two of the bins, sure-footed and with a baying tail high in the air - and unless Bob was unbelievably mistaken, it seemed to be staring straight up at him. Eventually the cat settled in the very centre of the yard, oblivious to the wind and the increasing amounts of rubbish dancing all around, and continued to keep looking up at the window. That was odd, but there was something else that wasn't quite right though, and the more he looked, the more he struggled to think of what it might be - but no words really fitted. The cat was.. was..

"Weird-Factor Nine, I reckon.." said Andie, snapping Bob out of his staring contest.

"Yeah, it's been sitting there looking up at me for ages - definitely a Factor Nine," he replied, trying not to sound too disturbed by the experience.

"No not the cat, I mean you! C'mon it's time to go now."

Andie went back to packing her things away and Bob was surprised to see that almost an hour had passed since he'd first noticed the dark clouds over Barton. He was not in the least bit surprised to see that the cat had gone when he looked out again.

"Ahem?" coughed Mr Scrimley, who was already holding the door open. He pointed to the bin before they could leave.

"Please place your transcribed writings of Halfred's works along with your jottings into the waste-bin if you'd be so kind, not forgetting numerous games of Hangman and a veritable gallery of artwork. And do try and avoid having to come up here again, would you? All these stairs are so tiresome, they really are."

The door echoed shut a long way behind them as they hurried down the wide flights of stairs, passing a dozen empty classrooms before racing along two long, old fashioned corridors. Eventually the heavy reds and blacks of the small tiles gave way to slightly more modern greys and blues, and Bob and Andie arrived at the front of the school - or the side of the school, depending on how you looked at it, as both had enough ornate decoration to warrant the term. A small 'U' shaped staff car park next to the The Hov's corridor lead onto the main road, and Bob and Andie sat on the short wall between two of its slender stone pillars and waited for their ride home. It had been a long day, and the entire week was starting to feel very, very long.

"Thanks for doing all that, Bob, you didn't have to. It was really nice of you.." said Andie, sounding tired and a little unsure how to phrase herself.

"Aah, 'twas nothing m'lady," he replied, trying to keep her spirits lifted. More than anything he wanted to put his arms around her and hug away the bad feelings she must have been carrying all through the day, but the moment was hardly right for attempting that. Besides, she'd probably think he was a loon and might shove him over the wall if he tried, so he decided to do the usual Bob Thing and keep the conversation light and harmless instead.

"You were awesome with those yo-yos, and everyone, and I mean everyone, saw you. Totally awesome. Everyone's going to call you 'Sir' or maybe 'Your Majesty' from now on. When you say jump, those kids are gonna jump, you'll see. Yoo owns dis joint, yeah?"

Andie laughed and Bob continued, staying on safe ground and trying not to say anything that would make her think he was a professional idiot.

"But enough of that - I've been meaning to ask you all day, right, how much practice have you been putting in? You made last time look like a kiddie show."

Andie beamed back, and for a moment Bob felt like he was on top of the world, but suddenly he leapt to his feet and squinted into the failing light.

"Did you just see that, over by the entry? I think that cat's back again, y'know," he said pointing towards the main road.

The light was now so dull that neither of them could see anything much. Andie poked Bob's knee with her foot and looked in the opposite direction, which was her usual way of suggesting he should stop being so bothered. Bob soon forgot about cat-watching and a few minutes later the car park was thrown into yellow brightness as two huge Volvo headlights appeared at the gates. There was just one more hurdle to get over, and then Bob and Andie's long day would be almost over.

Bob's father formally touched the front of his flat driving-cap as they piled into the back seat. Whoever thought of giving those caps away free with a new Volvo needed shooting, and Bob felt more than willing to be the one to do it. Their previous cars had come with useful free extras like a sun-roof or air conditioning, but this one had a truly horrendous grey flat cap (and mini-scarf) tucked into the glove compartment. Inexplicably, Mr Taylor had decided this was the world's greatest fashion item, the perfect accessory to go with absolutely anything. Even worse, Bob's mother approved of it - but that might have been her way of guaranteeing that no woman on the entire planet would go near him.

"Evening Andrea! Robert tells me you sorted out some bad types today? Well, well. Detentions are not to be taken lightly but I must say 'good for you' although two wrongs of course do not a right make, unless of course you're unable to draw the line as to the precise start or initial cause of the first wrong, by which I mean an objective analysis of any given situation can be entirely subjective at the time, therefore.."

Bob and Andie looked at each other, resigned to one of those endless monologues that they had both become so used to. Andie swapped sides so that she was seated behind Bob's father, because that way he'd be less able to aim any carefully mouthed sentences at her. He might even give up after twenty minutes of not getting any responses, if they were lucky.

The steady rain had gradually become a heavy rain as they approached a very dark Barton, and by the time the car pulled up on the pavement outside Andie's mum's café-home, the turbo-charged raindrops were bouncing high off the pavement.

"See you tomorrow then Bob, and you have to think of your birthday prezzy tonight! Thanks for the lift M'stuhtayluh!" said Andie as she prepared to race up to the front door. They waited until she was inside, and then half a mile later Bob and his dad made a similar run into 46 Corsair Avenue.

"..but it was a Sacrificial Detention dad, I had to get one so that she wouldn't be on her own - that wouldn't have been right for a minute.." said Bob, as they stepped under the small cover above the front door, carrying on a sentence that had started just after Andie had left the car.

"Yes Robert, but Machiavellian bravado serves only to.. damn it!" Bob allowed himself a small grin as his dad dropped the front door keys. Interruptions like that could sometimes bring the most pompous speeches into a nutshell. The rain seemed to get heavier and louder as he looked for them.

"Look, in some ways you did the right thing, but.." he fumbled around near a plant pot, "..aha found them, err.. just don't tell your mother or she'll never leave it, okay?"

As the word 'okay' started, the door swung open and Bob's mother stood before them, with an eyebrow already raised. As usual, Bob gave a very brief highlights-only version of the day's events. He had learned long ago that both his parents could win gold medals if ever Interrogating & Over-Analysing became Olympic events. The two of them were a lethal combination and any of their conversations, no matter how trivial, could easily escalate into a fully-blown battle of knowledge, with long words of too many syllables thrown in for good measure. They could even argue about things they agreed on, so Bob tended to keep quiet most of the time - life was so much easier that way. It was highly possible, he suspected, that nobody knew their first names. Absolutely everyone called them by their formal titles, even on social occasions, and Bob had always felt as if he was being a little too casual when calling them 'mum' and 'dad'. If he really strained his brain, he could probably remember what their names actually were, but there was really no point trying as he knew that he'd never, ever use them.

Tonight, Mrs Taylor was annoyed. During dinner she hadn't risen to any bait thrown out by Mr Taylor, and had been dangerously quiet. By the time they had almost finished, Mrs Taylor could hold back no longer.

"Look at that phone," she said, gesturing towards it a little too enthusiastically with her knife.

"I had to listen to twenty three-ee consecutive messages from one of Agatha's lodgers when I got in! Ooh, she's a snooty one whichever it was. Her tone! You should have heard her you should, it was all.." at this point, Bob's dad carefully stepped in.

"What did she want perchance, Sweetness?"

Bob's mum fetched a notebook from by the bread bin and sat down at the table again. She slipped her reading glasses on, pushed her auburn hair behind her ears and sat bolt upright, thus marking this a special occasion and worthy of everyone's fullest attention.

"Well, the first one was nice enough and she even sounded nice enough, and her verbatim message was as follows - 'Hello the Taylor family, would you like to drop in for coffee here with your Aunt Agatha as soon as possible please? She'd love to see you as it's been so long, how about half past ten t'morrow, bye byee'. She actually said 'byee' - can you believe that? Byee!"

Half an hour and twenty one accurately documented messages later, the caller had degenerated into, 'Look who cares what time you get here - if you don't want to come then fine, be like that. How about anytime tomorrow instead, or maybe tonight? Just send Bob along if you don't feel like it. Madame Ag.. your Aunt.. look she's trying to be nice to her family and that's you in case you've forgotten. So do you want to make it eight thirty tooonight for a coffee then? Just call me back!'

Although she was becoming very agitated, Bob's mum seemed to be enjoying herself, and getting into character. Why she didn't just let the answer machine tell the story was beyond Bob. This must be one of those Parental Quirks that Andie had mentioned, which she'd been reading about in last month's SavvyGrrrl magazine.

The final message, the twenty third, involved a couple of words that were supposed to be unrepeatable, but the description given in their place left Bob in no doubt as to which ones they were.

"The little madame. Who does she think she is?" concluded Mrs Taylor after her performance. She folded her arms and looked indignantly to her captive audience for their support and outrage.

"I say we'll go when we choose to, if we choose to," she continued, "..and you two don't need to bother with ties. We won't make an effort for that kind of invitation," she declared, then tore up each page and firmly pushed them into the overloaded pedal bin. Bob felt decidedly uneasy and dared to make a suggestion.

"It does sound like it's important - maybe Great Aunt Agatha's not well? She is getting on a bit.."

"Politeness isn't expensive," she slung back.

"Manners," mused Bob's father aloud, "..shall reveal paupers as Kings, and Kings as paupers, Robert. Was that Shakespeare or one of Wordsworth's colleagues, I wonder?" he added, seeing if his wife was finally ready for an intellectual joust. She was.

Bob left before it could start properly, and soon flopped onto his bed, relishing the sound of his door clicking shut. The voices downstairs became dulled to the point of almost not being there at all. Raindrops were still falling as if the gravity in Barton was far too strong, and he spent a few minutes just looking out of the window alongside his bed, watching the water pouring down the pane. His room was as dark as the world outside, which for the time being felt pretty much ideal.

Almost an hour later the rain began easing a little and Bob's attention was drawn away from his tv by the faintest sound of a cat meowing. Or maybe that was just the wind playing tricks out there? Had it not been for all those near-miss sightings throughout the day, he wouldn't have bothered looking. He kneeled up, leaned on the windowsill and looked out - but there was nothing there. No cats, no dogs, no people, no cars, nothing but rain and huge puddles, and some clouds illuminated in the moonlight, which looked as if.. Bob stared in disbelief as the huge black clouds seemed to be drawn up and into the moon, like thick black smoke slowly being drawn into a luminescent extractor fan.

"How weird is that? Totally off the Bizarro Scale.."

It went even further off the scale when the process reversed itself, and the clouds began re-appearing. There was no sense or perspective to what was happening, and Bob watched transfixed for a long, long time. A sharp meeow snatched his attention to the end of the driveway. There at the top of the concrete gate-post sat a black cat, maybe the same one from the school, or maybe one of its friends from the journey into school. Or maybe all of them were the same one? Bob didn't want to think about that. It appeared untroubled by the rain, which at last seemed to be easing off to a light drizzle. The penetrating eyes stared straight at Bob, who looked back with a puzzled expression.

"Has anyone ever been stalked by a cat?" he wondered, "..and can I get a Restraining Order put on one?"

The cat began making more and more noise, meowing with such intensity that she was soon practically squealing up at Bob. A well-aimed boot from Mr Thompson, who lived two doors down, missed her by inches and clattered off the top of the gate and landed in the road. With an air of nonchalance the cat slinked onto the pavement and wandered out of sight, closely followed by a barrage of insults and a hearty belch from Mr Thompson.

9.30pm rolled around on Bob's clock, and he went downstairs to make a coffee for everyone, as usual. This particular chore had started many months ago, as a discrete bid to cool-down a heated argument between his parents regarding the most influential Chinese Emperor, and who forgot to call the plumber for the downstairs toilet. Somehow, it had become a commitment to be honoured on most nights ever since. He soon returned to his room armed with a huge Homer Simpson mug of coffee plus half a dozen biscuits, planning to just settle down in front of an old Marx Brothers movie - and something struck him as being different. But what, exactly? Nothing in the room was out of place, the rain was still drizzling outside, the purple lava lamp from cool Uncle Mike last Christmas was still doing its freaky lava lamp thing over in the corner, and no shelves or walls had collapsed in the previous few minutes. Yet something was definitely not right..

Bob looked around and eventually realised that the moon had moved. In the ten minutes that he had been in the kitchen, the moon had gone right across the sky, from being way over on the left side of the window out above the sea, all the way to the window's other side, far over land.

As the opening titles of A Night At The Opera began rolling, Bob dunked the night's first biscuit and wondered if there might be something on the news tomorrow about all the odd happenings.

"Now that would take some explaining," he thought and promptly lost most of the biscuit in the mug.

The black cat returned to the gate-post, and patiently watched the upstairs window.

CHAPTER FOUR

Always Have, Always Will

Saturday 14th March 6.15am

As if apologising for missing the previous day, Bob's alarm clock filled his room with frantic bleeps at a time on a Saturday morning when the entire universe should be asleep. By the end of the fifth barrage, a muffled groan emanated from somewhere beneath Bob's bedsheets. It was similar to the kind an Egyptian mummy would make after being disturbed from a 5,000 year slumber.

Dark, tousled hair appeared first, slowly followed by a bleary-eyed Bob. He allowed another burst of unwelcome bleeps to escape while he tried to figure out what day it actually was.

"Wuh.. yeah's Staddurday.. lousy clock.. swine you.." he mumbled while trying to press the shut-up button with any part of his hand.

After spending a few minutes accepting the fact that he wasn't likely to fall asleep again, Bob sat up in his bed and leaned an arm onto the windowsill. The early morning sky over his part of the world was already starting to become light. There was a good possibility that the storms had all but gone and today might just be fit for venturing outdoors, which was convenient as he was supposed to be going on a major shopping trek with Andie. His 14th birthday wasn't actually until next Friday, but he was under orders to think of something to be bought today. Previous years had never been too tricky, but this year he was drawing a complete blank. If anything, he wanted to buy Andie a whole truck-load of presents to make her feel special, but she'd probably think he was some kind of loon if he did that. Her birthday wasn't until the end of April, which felt like absolutely ages away. He'd spent so long since Christmas making a Brilliant Things For Andie list that he was going to have real problems narrowing it down to just one present, or even three or four. It could easily get embarrassing. Last year had been so much easier, and seemed like such an incredibly long time ago.

Bob lay back on his bed and thought about absolutely nothing for a while, and just listened to the waves rolling steadily onto the shingle beach. There was always something reassuring about that special sound, and Bob couldn't imagine ever being away from it. Birds joyfully began returning from wherever they go to at night, briefly pausing for a song on the telegraph poles and thick telephone wires along the street before launching themselves off to their next important place. He kept his eyes closed and carried on listening.

Corsair Avenue was about a third of a mile back from the cliffs, which at the current rate of collapse, according to the Council, meant that Bob wouldn't have to be worried about waking up with the fish for anywhere between ten years and five hundred years. Apparently that was good. Bizarrely, Andie had even less reason to be concerned. She lived with her mother above their café, The Coffee Pot, which was a mere fifty yards from the cliff tops. According to the Council, this would be fine '..to beyond calculable figures..' for all kinds of geological reasons which could only be understood by people with unpronounceable degrees and far too much hair.

Barton's beach was not a world-famous beauty spot. If beaches could be fined for being ugly, this one would be in debt for the next three or four thousand years. The huge unstable cliffs leaned backwards from the shingle banks of the shoreline, and stretched along the wavering coast for as far as the eye could see. The shingle disappeared every now and then to make way for enormous plains of clay and mud. It was hardly surprising that not too many holiday-makers were drawn there - this was more of a fossil hunter's paradise. Occasionally one of their ranks would appear on the local news - not because of any great find, but because they had sunk up to their neck in a clay pit and had needed to be rescued. They never seemed to realise that the reason there were so many bones and fossils on Barton's beach was because dinosaurs, just like themselves, also had a tendency to get stuck in the clay pits.

The sun began its steady rise and by half past seven Barton On Sea was about as awake as it was ever likely to get. Elderly folks walked small dogs to the newsagent down the road, and then the small dogs walked the elderly folks back home. If it hadn't been for one of these small yappy dogs wanting to examine a boot lying in the road outside the front gate, Bob wouldn't have given a thought to the black cat from last night. But now that he did, he had to think for a while as to whether or not he'd dreamed all the weird cloud movements.

With a few words of encouragement from Mr Thompson, Eddie, the eldest of his identical non-triplets, ran out to retrieve the boot. Although it was biologically impossible for the young Thompsons to really be triplets (they were aged 9, 8 and 6), the three of them were unnervingly similar. Eddie, the most intelligent of the bunch, picked his dad's boot up and happily threw it back towards the house. A window shattered, and Mr Thompson loudly expressed his dismay to the world. Bob laughed and clambered over his bed and switched on the Breakfast News, fully expecting to see something resembling a major report on the strange events of last night. Nothing was mentioned, so he decided it was time to get dressed and go and see Andie for breakfast. She would probably know what to make of it.

As he reached the foot of the stairs the front door closed firmly behind his father, who was heading off to open up the shop for the day. Bob checked his watch - unbelievably, Mr Taylor was actually ten minutes late leaving the house. That was a rare event, and if Bob still kept a diary it would have been worthy of a whole line in capital letters.

For the last twenty or more years, his parents had owned and run Taylor's Corner Chemist, a small business just a few miles away in Highcliffe. It used to occupy a corner site, but around the time Bob was born they had moved to a larger property which was in the very centre of the main street. Neither of them seemed to have noticed the problem with the shop's name, but then again, it could just be one of their who's-going-to-mention-it-first battles which had spiralled out of control. Bob certainly never mentioned it.

As always, his mother was rushing around whilst trying to put on her make-up, do her hair and complain to herself about the mess everywhere. Trying to talk to her before, during or immediately after work was a seriously bad idea, and in many ways she reminded Bob of Saxon, cool Uncle Mike's enormous Rottweiler. No matter how friendly or distant that dog seemed to be, Bob never really knew if the beast was just sizing up which limb he wanted. So rather than risk getting into a conversation with Mrs Taylor, Bob backed into the safety of the hallway.

"I'm off round Andie's now, okay?" he called, while something clattered onto the kitchen floor and rolled across the tiles, soon followed by the sound of a chair toppling over. Bob took a step further back.

"When are you off to Andie's then? Shouldn't you be going now? Honestly if you could only get your brain into gear once in a while. I'll be off in five minutes and remember I'll be back at half twelve with some lunch for you both," she shot back, oblivious to any voice but her own. Bob sighed and headed out into a refreshingly bright and sunny morning. He wandered from Corsair Avenue and along the imaginatively named Sea Road, and stopped off to buy a newspaper and next week's tv guide for Andie's mum. She never asked for them, but it was just something he always did simply because she always liked it. He carried on to where Sea Road drifted left and became the start of Marine Drive, a long road which ran parallel to the cliffs. The houses along the left side were in a constant state of demolition and renovation, so almost two miles of road was gradually turning into a millionaires' parade. In Bob's opinion, that made the area very good to look at but probably a little tricky to move into.

A wide stretch of grass ran all the way along the other side of the road, reaching thirty or so yards from the pavement over to the cliff-tops. It was a bad place for dogs to chase sticks, but that didn't put them off trying. He noticed that one of the eight Scenic Barton Benches which fronted the cliffs had disappeared along with a triangular chunk of land again. The loss hadn't made the news, so nobody could have been sitting on it at the time. Some brave Council workers would probably soon arrive and put a new one as close to the edge as they dared. Locals never went near any of the benches - only blissfully ignorant visitors would ever take a few minutes to admire the view of the Isle of Wight, unaware that they were only attached to England by grass and a few carefully placed poles. During summer, the older Bartonians would gather like a geriatric paparazzi, ready with their cameras just in case something unfortunate happened.

Half a mile further along Marine Drive on the the cliff-top side of the road stood the small parade of shops, with Andie's at the end. The Coffee Pot, June's Gift Shop and The Barton Deli offered an oasis for those who had become lost in the maze of twisting dead-ends, one-ways and muddy tracks that made up Barton's roads. No map had ever been right, and most people in Barton were proud of that. Bob waved between the array of promotional stickers in the huge Deli window to Mrs Reid, who briefly stopped sweeping around a customer and waved back. The gift shop was still asleep, and wouldn't wake up for another month or two.

Despite years of steady tweaking, The Coffee Pot still looked like a large conservatory waiting for a huge house to be added. It was as if the builders had only ever got as far as the kitchen and a few rooms above it before losing interest. Visitors liked its odd design, but Andie found it embarrassing - especially the huge 'FANCY A CUPPA?' painted on its roof. There was enough space inside for about forty people, and maybe a couple of dozen more outside in its fenceless garden - the 'Landscaped Dining Area' as it was called. There was a certain charm to sitting outside during the summer and just watching the world go walking or sailing by, and if customers didn't want to see nature taking her toll on the ever-changing coastline there was always a view of Barton's nine-hole golf course - but not too many ever fancied standing on a chair placed on top of the tallest table in order to see it.

The bell gave its customary tinkle and the floorboards joined in with a chorus of small creaks as Bob arrived in the empty café, and was immediately engulfed in the welcoming aroma of coffee and toast. He turned the door's Closed sign around to show Open, and even before the ringing had died down Andie's mum appeared clutching a bundle of fresh tablecloths.

"Hello Bob! Andie's just through the back - how are you then?"

Andie's mum was very different to Mrs Taylor. She was remarkably easy-going and tended not to be dangerous. Even when Andie's dad was visiting, hostilities never really seemed to take off and the air was rarely filled with arguments. Everyone called her Mags, except her latest boyfriend who called her whatever he felt like.

"I heard about yesterday, and you're a shining knight, you are. That sort of thing means a lot," she said, dropping her words and smiling at Bob in the way she always would whenever he had done something very right.

"I didn't do much.. neither did Andie, I mean no-one died or anything, I think," he replied, and she gave a laugh. He handed her the papers and she sat him down at one of the tables by the long run of tall windows that occupied the two cliff-end sides of the café.

"So, are you after some nosh then?" she added, brushing her highlighted fringe from her eyes before quickly wiping two table tops in preparation for any real customers who might arrive. Before he could reply, the door's bell rang again as a man with an unforgivable beard came in. A much younger woman in a bright orange coat followed close behind, and Bob figured they deserved each other. Even before the bell had stopped ringing, Andie's mum had already breezed over and was guiding them to a table.

Andie emerged from the kitchen carefully carrying an over-loaded tray that contained enough breakfast to feed an army - a very large and very hungry army.

"Hiya.." she grinned widely and began unloading cups, teapots, cutlery and finally a plate piled high with everything good about breakfast on it. There was even a bowl of his favourite cereal, Crunchy Munchy, with a serious dribble of honey laced over the top. Bob could see she'd made a real effort, and he was going to have to push himself hard to climb this huge mountain of food. Andie's own breakfast was quite sensible in comparison, and talking took second place for a while. Steadily more people began arriving, and the general hubbub of conversations mixed with the radio to create enough background noise for Bob to feel more comfortable about mentioning the previous night. She watched him intently while he told her about the weird cat from school turning up again, the even weirder clouds, and then the really exceptionally weird moon. Her eyes didn't wander away once, which was always a good sign. Andie gave it her deepest consideration for almost an entire cup of tea.

"Hmmmm.." she pondered, gazing intently towards a small ship a few miles out at sea, "In my opinion, I think you're a loony. Dr Andie has spoken."

"Huh? I'm not winding you up or anything - it really happened, honest," said Bob, lightly drumming his fingers and hoping she wasn't going to leave it at that.

Her eyes remained fixed on the ship, only breaking away when she poured herself another tea. Conversations with Andie worked on two levels. Level One was the simple use of words, and Level Two was the far more important and revealing level - what the rest of your body was doing before, during and after Level One. She had always read lips, and over the years had developed this ability much further. She could read eyes, eyebrows, cheek muscles, head posture, shoulders, hands, in fact just about anything a person could possibly move was there to be analysed and understood. Bob knew about this, and tried it himself a few times before finally admitting that he was generally hopeless at it, except for those few occasions when something was nice and obvious. Like now, for example. Andie was on her second cup of tea, and still looking out into the great beyond. That meant she was still thinking about everything, preparing some carefully chosen words for him.

He watched her for a long moment, and a wave of butterflies took flight again. He began wondering precisely when she'd become so different, so.. something.. whatever the word was. Or maybe she'd always been like that and he'd always known it without actually knowing that he knew it, until now when he knew that he KNEW that he knew and.. his brain fell over as the sentence rambled on and on in a great big circle - again. He gave the bacon an excessive layering of tomato sauce to try and get his mind working again. Andie finished her tea, and he decided to prompt her for her deeply considered opinion.

"So.. are you really sure I'm a loon, or is there something a bit weird happening?"

"Huh? Oh sorry, I was miles away. What's bothering you again?"

"Oh please.." despaired Bob, "..that cat and the clouds and the moon and all that stuff - it really happened Andie, and it's way off the Freaky-Things Spooktrometer and.."

"D'you mean that cat over there?" she said, and pointed to a black cat sitting impassively on an outside table. Bob flinched, and nodded.

"Come on Bob, you can break fears by facing them, can't you? So if dat likkul puddytat is bothering you, let's go and say hello then, shall we?"

Andie stood up and pulled Bob's sleeve to make sure he followed. Rather than struggling to open one of the big window-doors, they went back out through the front of the café and then round to the outside tables. As soon as the cat came into view, it launched itself from the table and tore at full speed towards them, hissing as it jumped up towards Bob. Andie stuck one hand in the way and reached for her Emergency yo-yo with the other. She squealed as a trio of red scratches appeared from her knuckles to her wrist. The cat stopped briefly by the road, and looked back as if taunting them, daring them to follow.

While Andie was having her hand attended to by her mum and Sandy The Saturday Girl (and a small party of concerned pensioners, plus the man who'd come to fix the dishwasher), 46 Corsair Avenue was receiving a visitor.

A metallic blue Audi screeched to a halt outside the front of the house, more on the pavement than off. An anxious looking woman stormed out of the car and rushed up to the front door, with her mane of black hair billowing behind her. She rang the bell and hammered over and over again on the frosted glass panels as if her life depended on it. After a few minutes of desperate silence, she peered through the lounge windows and then through the side windows, knocking and pushing each one. The side gate proved too high and awkward to climb so she ran back to her car, wildly revved the engine and sped off.

Andie felt shaken after having her hand covered in antiseptic and far too many bandages, and certainly didn't feel like embarking on a grand window-shopping tour of Christchurch or Bournemouth like they had planned to do. Instead, Bob suggested a quick bus ride and a wander around the nearer and smaller New Milton, because that was the ideal place to go if you didn't really feel like going anywhere.

They wandered up and down the main parade of shops, calling into certain ones which were guaranteed to make Andie feel good and put her back on track. Dashin' Fashin, Top Tops and This Miss had become regular ports of call, and just for once Bob was glad to be going near them. It didn't take long for the clothes to work their multi-coloured magic and by the time they dropped into TasteBuds for a well-earned ultra-frothy Happy Cappyccino, Andie was full of the joys of spring again.

"You know what?" she said, dipping her Chocky Flake into the foam, "My hand feels fine now - it hasn't been sore or anything for ages. I'm taking a look," and after flexing her fingers a couple of times to prove her point, she unwrapped the great swathe of bandages to reveal a smooth, unmarked hand. Apart from a few patches of dried antiseptic ointment, there was no sign that anything had ever been wrong. She hurried to the Ladies to wash it off, and quickly returned, smiling.

"You didn't take my Chocky while I was gone did you? Are you sure you didn't?" she said as she edged her chair back up to the table.

"Ahh, Sherlock, you've rumbled me again. As a matter of fact I did take it, and you didn't really eat it all in one go, apparently that was me doing it all the time. Here, would you like mine as an apology? Note complete absence of bite marks or melty bits."

Bob handed over an untouched Flake, just as he always had done since the age of six when he really had committed the sin of finishing something of Andie's without asking her first. Exactly what it was had been long-forgotten, but the principle had survived and was still alive and kicking, regularly.

"But apart from that," he continued, while Andie scooped up the last of the froth in her huge cup, "Now do you think there's anything weird going on, Andie? You almost screamed the entire cliff down when the antiseptic went on those scratches, but now it's like nothing happened. Mix that with the whole spooky cat thing, throw in the freakish clouds and moon, and you must be raising an eyebrow by now, aren't you?"

Andie nodded.

"Yeah, I am. My eyebrow's been raised way above the normal level since this morning. I didn't doubt you - I just couldn't think what to make of it, that's all. You saw things that nobody else appears to have seen last night, my hand's been through a minor miracle, and there's a barmy cat out to get us. What could be less normal than all that? I say we sit back and see what happens for a while, you know. And if I could think of an appropriate cliché to throw in right now, I'd say it. How about.. red sky at night, shepherd's alight, or something like that.."

"That makes sense, probably. I prefer 'softly softly catchy Monkees'. That works for just about anything."

"And I say you're Cappyccino's gone straight to your head. Shall we go now?"

They paid an absolutely, definitely final visit to This Miss, followed by a quick rummage through the CD Megatastic Bargain Bin in The Store Next Door, and Bob found one that might hopefully be a genuine megatastic bargain. He was glad that searching for his birthday present had been forgotten, and felt even better now that he'd stumbled over something good for Andie. The day had improved so much that they even felt like wandering down a side street to call into Helen's Melons, the greengrocer shop. Helen was a rotund and friendly woman, who laughed at just about everything. She'd known Bob and Andie since they were both in pushchairs, and always had time for a quick word with them. Today was no exception, but as she spoke Bob wasn't listening to a word she said - his eyes were darting around for any signs of black cats.

The journey back was very quiet, and apart from a fat tabby, no cats appeared or disappeared, and by the time the bus pulled up to the small stop on Sea Road, Bob and Andie weren't too bothered about them anymore.

"..so maybe I should have asked to try on the blue one instead, what do you think? I'm sure it's miles better than the green, isn't it? Next time I'm definitely doing.."

Andie stopped in mid sentence, and pointed thirty yards ahead to the front of Bob's house.

"It's back!" she announced.

They hurried over to the corner of Corsair Avenue, and paused for a moment to stare warily at the black cat who was sitting on the concrete gate post.

"That's the one it was sitting on last night. What d'you reckon? Should I borrow Saxon off Uncle.." wondered Bob aloud. But Andie had carried on walking and had already stopped a few feet before the gate. He hurried after her and nervously stepped a little way ahead, dangerously close.

"It's got a name tag - cover me Andie, I'm going in.." he said like a Hollywood hero. Andie duly drew two Rapid Response yo-yos from her pockets, primed and ready for immediate action. Bob hovered just close enough to read the silver tag. The cat stared at him, composed and very still.

"My name is Jinx. Hello." read Bob, while Jinx continued to stare.

"Ask her if she's hungry, now you've been introduced!" called Andie, with a hint of sarcasm in her voice.

"You hungry? Fancy Andie's other hand for lunch, maybe?"

Jinx remained motionless and merely carried on staring at Bob as if he was deliberately blocking her view of the entire world. Andie made her way past, and Bob stayed in front of Jinx just in case she really was on the menu. He then hurried to the front door, and if he hadn't been fiddling with the locks he would have seen her launch three shots at Jinx, each one close enough to ruffle her long whiskers. The cat didn't even blink, but Andie felt that she had made her point and went to join Bob. Jinx leaped down to the pavement and began walking off towards the cliffs.

"Maybe," Andie began, "..her owners are on holiday and she lives nearby? Or maybe, in a past life she was murdered by me or you and now she wants revenge so we're.."

"You've been recording daytime chat shows again, haven't you? They're all actors on those things, I read about it.. here, grab a Coke and let's try to stay on planet Earth."

They raided the fridge, put the PopStyle channel on the satellite-tv unit, and headed up to Bob's room in a one-sided conversation about the merits of This Miss compared to Top Tops. Neither of them noticed the red answer-message light flashing on the phone.

Bob had always known that despite Andie's limited hearing, she could really get into certain songs as long as they had the right depth of sound, and Saturday mornings before his mum would return for lunch usually provided the chance for some serious musical appreciation. Andie went around the house closing the double glazing in order to avoid annoying the neighbours, while Bob sorted out the growing pile of 'Andie Tracks' beside the mini hi-fi. He lined up the Bass and Middle sliders with all the analytical precision of a NASA engineer. Levels 8.3 and 6.8 were safely within the Optimal Audio Ranges, and would do just fine for a test-run on the latest cd. He'd heard it a few days earlier on the radio above the cacophony of the school bus, and thought it might just have some potential. Andie lay on the floor in front of a speaker, and as soon as 'Always Have, Always Will' began thumping through the sub-woofers Bob knew he'd picked a winner. Andie immediately started feeling the depth of the beat and grinned as she stood up and started moving to it. Now some good mindless fun could start, and despite their unique approach to dancing and the vibrating of the floorboards, the room survived intact. The song definitely met with Andie's approval, and Bob felt like a king.

Strangely, every week whenever Bob would be prompted to either fetch more drinks or to go and change the satellite tv channel, elaborate moustaches would appear on his posters by the time he returned. Andie always denied any knowledge of how they got there, but occasionally her hands would have felt-tip marks remarkably similar in colour to the ones on the faces of the actresses and pop princesses. The mystery had never been solved, until today. The sixth replacement poster of Bob's all-time favourite singer had been criminally defaced. She now had cross-eyes, a Hitler moustache and a tattoo that had obviously gone a little wrong. Andie stood before it, still with the smoking gun in her hand, laughing uncontrollably at her latest artistic triumph. Being caught just made her laugh more, and spurred her on to the next logical step and Bob soon realised he was in the wrong place at the wrong time.

Downstairs, Mrs Taylor walked through the front door at precisely 12.30 after having spent the morning charming money from customers at the shop. She usually spent Saturday lunchtimes at home, before heading back to the grindstone with Bob in tow. She called something up the stairs on her way to the kitchen, where she began putting out three of Barney's Big Baguettes for all of them on the table.

"Oh Robert, just look at your face! Go and wash it off, go on now! You know how unhealthy.. hello Andrea.. it is for a person's epidermis with all those alcohol-based pigments in the.."

Bob missed the key phrases of the lecture as he stood at the kitchen sink attempting to wipe off a particularly heavy Groucho moustache. Instead of emerging clean-shaven he made matters worse and now had the kind of five o'clock shadow that Fred Flintstone would have been proud of. Andie, the picture of innocence, copied his mum's disappointed expression and tutted loudly at him. Mrs Taylor bent down for a loud word with her.

"Yooo musst stop-puh himmm frommm doooin-guh thaaat - yesss? Funneey no-no!" she instructed, mouthing each word clearly a few inches in front of Andie's face, before patting her on the head. She turned to Bob just as Andie's tongue made an appearance.

"You know Robert, there are times when I'm almost sure she understands every word I say. Wonderful, truly wonderful. So clever."

She turned around with some teacups, and Andie was once more the picture of innocence.

"Oh no, I see we've been getting more messages again - that little red light is flickering away like nobody's business. It can't be good for the phone, getting so many. I expect it's that frightful lodger from Aunt Agatha's on our backs. Well she can wait - I'll call her this evening, perhaps, but only if I feel like taking that course of action.."

Bob and Andie shared a despondent glance and pretended to be interested.

For Bob, Saturday afternoons always dragged. He never quite knew if his parents were giving him a taster of the real world, or just having some free help. Andie would be with her mum and the staff at the café, enjoying herself preparing gastronomic delights and generally being both useful and appreciated. Bob, on the other hand, would be creaking his way through creepy old store-rooms above the chemist shop trying to find replacement cosmetics for empty display units down below. Or if he was really lucky, he could spend hours putting child-proof caps onto different sizes of small brown tablet bottles, replenishing the supplies for the week ahead. After all, as he'd been told many times over the years, the manufacturers hadn't yet thought of supplying them ready-fitted so someone else had to do it instead, and that was a job for a very responsible person.

The afternoon wore on. He sat on the floor underneath the heavily fortified Dangerous Drugs Cabinet trying to fend off pins and needles in both feet, and looked out past the mountains of empty plastic bottles, gradually becoming more and more bothered about the phonecalls. Something must be wrong with Great Aunt Agatha, and even though his parents had no real affection for her, they should have gone around last night or early this morning, or even just phoned her back. Bob sighed. He knew that there was no way he'd ever change their minds regarding rights and wrongs, and couldn't really go and visit Agatha without them being there as well - that would be a major family faux-pas. So he flung another trio of capped bottles into the wrong saggy plastic bag, and figured that all he could do was to wait until whenever. And then he froze.

Was that a noise coming from the main store room, or just his bored imagination? Nobody was upstairs with him, and he'd been alone for at least an hour or two. Admittedly, the narrow curved stairs were out of sight so he couldn't see anyone who might have come up anyway, but they creaked so much that even mice couldn't climb them without announcing to the world that they were going upstairs. And mice frequently did do exactly that, much to his parents' irritation. Bob stood up, trying hard not to make any noise.

The shop was built in the late 1600's, and showed it. The upstairs floors were wildly uneven, perfectly matched by the wildly uneven walls. Rooms must have been added just for a laugh rather than to serve any practical function, so the retail stock of the shop had to be spread between two large rooms, three peculiar smaller ones, and a grim side room. They were all very creepy, and the biggest, creepiest one of them all was where the noise had come from.

Bob waited for another sound, but there was nothing but silence, save for the dull hubbub of voices below.

It was tempting to ignore the noise completely and go back to the mundane process of bottle-capping, but Bob felt obliged to go and have a look. This had nothing to do with bravery, and everything to do with avoiding parental wrath. A few years earlier he'd ignored a noise which turned out to be his elder brother becoming trapped under a pile of shelving units and huge boxes. This was unlikely to be the case again because he had moved to Melbourne (far away from his second wife) last year. However, for Bob the memory remained very fresh and so with some trepidation he wandered past the supplies of health food and took the single step down into the main store room.

He could hear and see nothing. Total silence in almost total blackness. He tugged the frayed cord and four strip lights began spluttering and blinking into life, and he looked out at three broad and long rows of badly-lit shelving units, and piled wooden tea chests. Everything seemed normal. No intruders, no crazy people, no trapped morons, no.. black cats. Bob shivered at the thought of seeing Jinx concealed somewhere, staring at him. Suddenly it felt like a very real possibility. For a fraction of a second, the idea was laughable but that was wiped out by a wave of paranoia, and he didn't fancy wandering up and down all those rows with so many hiding places. Instead he settled for a quick glance from the top end, down along each row.

"Nope, nothing in this one, and nothing in this.. and.."

An economy bag of cotton wool lay on the floor, near the far end. Had it fallen by itself like so many bags before it, or was it a trap, put there to entice him further inside for reasons that would become apparent just before his painful death? He paused for a moment, to weigh up the odds.

"Okay, reality check. I'm in a room which I've been in a million times before, looking at something I've seen a million times. Things fall over because these floors are weird. That's why, that's all.."

A black blur disappeared around the far edge of the row, and Bob's heart jumped.

"Just my mind playing dumb tricks.. imagine Andie's here seeing me getting hopeless.. imagine Andie's here.. so don't be hopeless.."

A shuffling noise from the furthest corner of the room proved beyond doubt that something was there, and it probably was that wretched cat, ready for another session of weirdness.

Bob's mood shifted to one of annoyance and also embarrassment for having been so edgy. He looked around for something to throw at Jinx, if it actually was her. If the culprit was only a mouse or two, they could carry on doing their mouse-things because the dozen or so Squeaki-Gone mousetraps would get them sooner or later.

A promotional Rimmel lipstick as high as his waist leaned against the wall. He picked it up and held it in front of himself, as if he was brandishing the kind of light sabre that Luke Skywalker wouldn't be seen dead with. He slowly began walking between two long shelving units, listening for the slightest noise.

He approached the area where the shuffling sounds had come from, gave the floor a few taps with the glittery end of the lipstick, and then nudged a few suspicious boxes on the Orthopaedic Shoe shelf. Nothing. He gave an empty box on the floor a good whack, dropping sequins and a bow from the Rimmel prop, and started to relax a little. The shelves were stacked solid, the tea chests were full of impulse-buy paraphernalia, and there were definitely no cats of any kind at all.

"Stupid mice.."

Then the shuffling noise came again, but louder and from the opposite corner this time. Bob slipped back into being paranoid and slowly creaked his way over the floorboards to where he thought the sounds were coming from, but again there was nothing strange, just piles of boxes, sprays, packets, cartons, and maybe..

The lights gave a big flicker and that was Bob's cue to leave. For a few seconds the room was plunged in and out of darkness while he tried to make his way back to the door. His foot hit something soft and he fell forwards, landing against a wall of tightly stacked anti-perspirants. Whatever he stumbled over scurried off into the darkness. The lights came back on and his mother stood in the doorway looking down at him.

"Oh Robert, what are you doing? Don't be wasting time in here when you should be helping us with the bottles! I try to keep any instructions so easy for you, don't I?"

She pulled the cord a few times, and tutted loudly.

"These lights still need sorting out.. now you run along and cap those bottles because it does help us a lot, you know. Falling over and making a mess in here doesn't help anyone. The staff might notice, and tell people things about you.."

Bob sighed and dusted himself off. This would need careful planning and practising before mentioning to Andie.

By six o'clock, Bob and his mother pulled into the driveway back at home. His father always stayed behind to cash-up, lock-up and generally sort things out, and tended to turn up by the time dinner was usually ready. They both stood before the front door and stared in amazement. It had been almost completely covered in small yellow Memo-It notes, each bearing one word of a sentence, with longer words spread over two Memo-Its. Bob stepped forwards and read out the message.

"Would you please come visit.. Agatha. I mean how diff-icult can it be? In case you have forgo-tten, the address is Pierp-ont House, Becton Lane, and it's still only about a mile or so from this door here! And do bring Robert."

That wasn't good. Bob sneaked a look back at his mum.

"Ooh that cheeky mare! As if we've forgotten!" she seethed and began plucking each note from the door. Bob dared to put the other point of view, and stayed a few feet away by the fuchsias.

"Well, we haven't been there for almost a year, have we? Maybe she's ill and.. well nobody else is likely to visit her, are they?" he ventured, nervously.

"Oh, enough. This has been a right week, and I've been run off my feet for most of it - and that mouthy-piece doesn't help one bit.."

"Well could I go then? I'll say you're busy and feeling really tired and then at least she'll have had a visitor."

Mrs Taylor looked as if she'd just detected a foul smell.

"Oh, and won't you be the saintly one? How will that make me look, or your father? We go as a family or not at all, and we'll go tomorrow to get it out of the way. Obligations are best carried by many, like in that play.. I'll think which one it is later so don't mention that to your father, yet.."

Bob was pleased that a visit was on the cards, at last. According to his father, Agatha was the world's oldest living battle axe. In many ways that was true, because her narrow range of emotions were all frightening ones, and she did look ancient. However, the biggest plus-point in her favour which elevated her way above anybody else who Bob knew, was that she could catch either of his parents out on any subject at all, whenever the mood took her. That required linguistic skill, real nerve and a huge encyclopedia for a mind.

Without even listening to the flashing answer-phone, Bob's mum pressed 'Erase' and muttered something to herself before striding up the stairs. She reached the top and called back down to him.

"Stick the kettle on while I'm having a bath and see if there's anything in the fridge, okay? God, what a day.."

Bob wandered into the kitchen, and felt relieved that there was very little to eat in there. This meant a trip to The Friendly Plaice and Bob's favourite delicacy, Barton's greatest contribution to the culinary world, deep-fried mushy peas. The day wasn't going to turn out too badly after all.

CHAPTER FIVE
Great Aunt Agatha

Sunday 15th March

Bob felt good when he woke up on Sunday morning. There had been no sign of cats (black, demonic, or any other sort) at all during the night and nothing strange had happened up in the sky. A small laugh escaped as he looked over at Andie's creative flair adorning the posters on the opposite wall.

"Maybe they don't need replacing," he thought, and wondered how many more posters he could pin up for her to improve.

Somewhere in the house, his mother was on the phone. Her voice was raised by at least an octave, which was entirely normal for when she was talking to anyone outside the immediate family, especially over the phone. However, she sounded excessively polite, which was always a worrying sign.

"Yes, yes, we'll be round for coffee then. Lovely.. yes, it'll be wonderful to see her again, I'm just so sorry she's not well.. yes, yes.. bye then."

Bob heard the phone clatter back onto the receiver and then clang against the radiator, ending in a short curse. That meant she was in the hallway. The receiver on that particular phone had broken a few weeks earlier during an Oscar-winning disagreement between his mother at one end, and his father up at the shop. It was an odd one to have been getting angry about, even by their standards, regarding who was the shortest-serving Prime Minister, and who was supposed to have paid the car insurance. Since then, the handset always fell onto the floor unless it was placed back perfectly balanced in the cradle, which Mrs Taylor rarely ever managed. After three more attempts, the phone started behaving itself.

"Right, we'll be there for a quick coffee, say a few pleasantries and then go, okay? Aunt Agatha's unwell, so let's get it out of the way," she announced to the house in her normal voice.

Trips to see Great Aunt Agatha were always very formal, and had the kind of tense atmosphere usually reserved for end-of-year exams. Even though the house was barely two miles away and the sun was shining brightly outside, Bob's father insisted on taking the car. Mrs Taylor agreed, and very little else was said all morning.

They passed the small Post Office and newsagent on Sea Road and sedately joined Marine Drive. Bob gazed over to The Coffee Pot and saw Andie carrying a tray of something to a group of people sitting outside, and once she had drifted out of sight he turned around to silently admire the increasingly larger and newer houses opposite. Eventually the road curved away from the cliffs and towards the heavily wooded area between the golf course and the not-quite-so-expensive estates.

Pierpont House was set at the end of a long driveway, protected from view by masses of huge firs, pines and conifers. The car soon emerged onto its forecourt from a narrow tunnel of over-hanging and interwoven branches. Bob felt a knot beginning to form somewhere in his stomach and hoped the next couple of hours weren't going to be too awkward.

The house looked like a small hotel, which was practically what it was. Agatha rented out most of the six suites to a very select band of occupants, and they seemed to keep themselves to themselves - which is another way of saying Bob's mother had never been able to find out who was there and what they did.

They walked up the broad steps and through the large, open double doors into a spacious reception area. The layout had changed a lot since their last visit. A heavy-set desk now occupied the far end, contrasting starkly with the cream and white of the new paintwork, and a staircase curved off to the left behind it. Mr Taylor scratched his head, sure that the stairs had been on a different side before, and quickly decided that he couldn't care less.

There were no bells to ring or buttons to push, and nobody seemed to be around so Bob went to have a look at the two doors on either side of the reception. The signs on them were painted as white as the woodwork, and gave no indication as to what lay beyond - and the door that they'd been allowed through for their last visit wasn't there anymore. Meanwhile, Bob's father began to walk around the desk to have a look up the stairs.

"Do try not to go up there, it's private."

A slim woman aged somewhere around 30 appeared from one of the doors that Bob had just been examining. She had a friendly and yet firm expression, and long black hair which flowed over her shoulders.

"I'm glad you could make it, my name is Feiya and your Aunt Agatha is in the North Room upstairs and ahaa - you must be Bob?" she said in one rapid breath.

Bob felt honoured to be singled out. He nodded, and silently wondered if Feiya was of Indian or Pakistani descent. He'd spent the long winter months watching their respective cricket teams slaughtering England during the Asian Humiliation Tour, and had been glad when it was all finally over and the beleaguered squad had skulked back home. He decided that if he had to say anything at all to her, he'd start with cricket. She was bound to like that.

"I do stress that she isn't very well at all, so maybe you could see her in two groups, instead of all at once? Her strength fades easily," she added, at a slightly slower pace.

"Ah, Fay-aaahr, you'll find that you cannot divide a group of three persons into two groups, as such. You would get a two and a one which makes one group plus a single, if you like, but not two groups," Mr Taylor pointed out, helpfully. Mrs Taylor seemed to enjoy that moment, as if it made up for some of those phonecalls and Memo-Its. Feiya's eyes narrowed.

"Correct, but presumptive. I was going to go in with Bob, thus making the second group. C'est complet," she replied, using a French expression in an English context - something that was guaranteed to annoy Mr Taylor immensely. Bob hid a grin, and Mrs Taylor straightened her back even further.

Feiya lead them up to the first floor, and then along a broad sun-filled corridor. Large photographs from far away places around the world hung at regular intervals on the walls, and Bob had a strong urge to spend some time looking at them.

After three gentle knocks on the end door, Feiya ushered Bob's parents in to see Great Aunt Agatha, and the door quickly swung closed behind them. Bob sat midway along the corridor on a long white leather chair, and was soon joined by Feiya. He couldn't help but feel embarrassed, and knew he had to say something.

"I'm sorry we took all this time to get here.. my folks are very busy all the time and.. uhh.. it's a tiring time of year I expect. What's wrong with Great Aunt Agatha?"

"Mr and Mrs Taylor think she's about to croak and leave them a pile of cash. How desperately shallow," she responded, in the same friendly-yet-serious tone.

"We don't need them anyway, Bob," she said, nodding in the direction of the door, "..it's you that had to get here, and if they'd taken an hour or two longer we would have had to come to 'borrow' you. Those two would have been dealt with."

Bob shivered.

"Huh? Why me? What have I done wrong? I haven't been here since last time we came and that was ages ago.."

"One year, two weeks, three days, two hours and.." she paused while looking intensely at her watch, "..one minute precisely. I do love it when a Fourth Dimensional line of contra-symmetry crops up. You're not in trouble Bob, it's everyone else who's in trouble, and by that I really do mean everyone. Including you. So.. yes, technically you are in trouble."

Bob was coming to the conclusion that Feiya needed to get out more often.

"Oh. Any suggestions why? Or would it be dangerous for me to know?" he said, trying to follow the advice he'd seen on a documentary about loonies a couple of weeks earlier - 'Whenever you are confronted by a dangerous headcase, try to become friends in order to live longer' - and in Bob's opinion, that was good advice.

"I'm not able tell you anything. Rules exist for a reason, and I am unwilling to offer any more information at all due to the fact that I was the one who insisted that you shouldn't know anything until a time of greater appropriate..ness presented itself. And such a time is pretty near, I'd say."

Bob felt like he was teetering on the very edge of a diving board, way above a tiny pool. He decided to jump.

"Do you have a black cat? A scary one by the name of Jinx? Can't sing to save her life and enjoys making me paranoid?"

"Jinxy? Oh yes she's mine, more or less, and I've had her for years and years. She likes you. If she didn't, you'd know about it. You should have tried following her, you know. Life can be so simple if you just look around yourself."

"Yes, I suppose so. Err, why was she was trying to get me to follow her, or would that be classified?"

"Correct yes, classified, I'm afraid. You can ask me about these pictures though," she said, and waved her hand towards the rest of the corridor.

Bob made polite comments and said 'ahaaa' every now and then as Feiya lead him on a tour past each one. She'd snapped famous places in different climates, exotic people, strange animals and impressive buildings from mind-boggling angles, and created a truly bizarre gallery. Bob acknowledged to himself that she seemed to be a dab hand with a camera.

"You must've been everywhere.." he said, staring at one of her more striking images. It was the kind of photograph that could turn anyone's stomach upside down. At first glance it looked like a picture taken near the top of a very tall skyscraper while it was being constructed, high above a black and white city. The vague horizon looked a very long way off and created the most incredible sense of vertigo. But on closer inspection, it became a far worse feeling altogether..

"Were you being craned-up on a girder to take this? You must have been forty feet out from the sides!"

Feiya laughed a very short and very loud laugh, and Bob started to change his mind about her. She was way beyond a mere loon.

"Yes, I had to ask nicely but they let me ride a huge steel girder up a few floors. Worst elevator ever! Great shot though, isn't it? I was going to send it to National Geographic, but I wasn't officially supposed to be there, so some nice folks would have been in trouble.. and I disapprove of trouble."

They returned to the long chair and no sooner had Bob settled into the seat than his parents emerged from Agatha's room, locked in a whispered bicker about the origins of pasta. Feiya couldn't hide her impatience.

"About time too! How long does it take to say 'hello' and then 'goodbye'? Why not spend all day in there, Mr and also Mrs, Taylor?"

Feiya glared at them, and although Bob was impressed to see someone so completely unintimidated by his parents, he was relieved there were no sharp objects lying around.

"You two may sit here and wait for us, once Bob has stood up and followed me in."

They all did as she said, and Bob nervously stepped into Great

Aunt Agatha's shaded bedroom. Agatha had always been a powerful figure, tall with regal features and an austere demeanour, but today she was small and pitiful, looking lost in a huge and very neat bed, propped up against a wall of pillows. Her pale, wrinkled face made her look close to death's door, and just about ready to ring the bell.

While he tried to think of something to say, Bob noticed that the furniture and general decor looked very modern, not at all like the room of a lady who must be on the wrong side of 200. He went back to trying to think of something friendlier than saying 'Hello, Great Aunt Agatha' and quickly gave up.

"Hello, Great Aunt Ag.."

"Oh spare me the formalities Robert," she said in a whisper that was as harsh as it was tired, "I wanted you here days ago. Those two opinionated fools never seem to change.. they know nothing worth knowing. Come along, stand up here where I can see you properly."

Bob edged around the bed and stood a scared-but-polite distance away from her.

"You look healthy, that's good. You're awake as well, that's also good.. such a shame you don't know day from night. Ohh, there is so much that you need to be told, but I'm feeling so.. damn it all.. tired again. Where's Feiya? Where did she.." she trailed off as her words became much weaker. Feiya reached over and held her hand, and Agatha breathed deeply before continuing.

"Robert," she said, much quieter, "..come closer. You have to do something for me, but first you have to trust me with all of your heart.. will you do that?"

She held him in the kind of gaze that could crack granite. Those penetrating steely blue eyes did not belong in such a frail body.

"Yes of course I will, of course, anything," replied Bob, nervously glancing to Feiya before looking back to Agatha.

"Liar. I don't blame you though, child.." she hissed back.

"Feiya, fetch him the keys would you, dear?"

Feiya went over to a vast dressing table, nestled between two huge decorative wardrobes.

"They're in the fourth drawer, third column.." said Agatha, but her voice was so weak even Bob could barely hear her words. Feiya came back over to the bed with a long-necked silver key.

"There was only one there, this one!" she said, waving it a few inches in front of Agatha, who gave a small nod of acknowledgement, allowing Feiya to draw a thin length of gold chain through a hole in its top. Much to Bob's surprise, she placed it around his neck. He tucked it away beneath his shirt, to avoid a parental grilling later on.

A door near to Agatha's bed clicked open, and Jinx hurried in and settled on the other side of the bed near Feiya, and stared at Bob in a disdainful manner that he somehow expected. Either someone had opened the door for her, or she was a whole lot weirder than he had imagined. Feiya smiled to herself and stroked Jinx's head. Agatha gave a small cough and forced herself to carry on.

"Robert, that's the key to so much.. the other place.. on Lincoln Drive. Go there, go and find me back then.. go today.."

She raised her finger to emphasise the point, which seemed to tire her far too much. Her head sank back into the pillow, and her eyes rolled inside a slow blink. Feiya looked concerned, and raised her voice.

"Madame Agatha! Madame Agatha! Shall I tell him the rest? You have to tell him more - I can't tell him all those things I don't know about! You can't sleep now!"

"Hey, steady on Feiya, she's ill," said Bob, trying to sound firm. Feiya looked at him, and for a fleeting moment her eyes betrayed all the anguish she was going through. Agatha stirred slightly, and tried to speak. Her voice wavered.

"Where is my Robert? He was here.. and now he's.."

Bob leaned closer.

"I'm here Aunt, right where I should be, it's okay, everything's alright. Uh.. I've got your key now?"

"Don't humour me, it is not alright.. far from alright.. you know nothing.. nothing of any consequence.. Jinx will let.. let you in.. to the Lexington buildnn.."

Her eyes closed again and she slipped away into a deep sleep. Feiya looked at Bob, who was looking straight back at her.

"I know what you're thinking, Bob," she said after a few moments of very heavy silence.

"You do?"

"Yes, it's in your face. You're thinking 'How can I go to the house on Lincoln Drive if I don't know which one it is?' to yourself."

"Where?"

"Yes, my point exactly. Well Madame Agatha's very weak and therefore she's allowed to forget certain things. Such as that. It's still number a hundred and seven, 1-0-7, for your information."

Bob wondered if there was something strange in the water around this part of Barton. However, in an attempt to avoid the scene turning even more uncomfortable, he played along.

"Well, what's lexington then? And that bit about finding her? I think I already know where she is.."

Feiya thought for a moment, and kept stroking Jinx who seemed to be ignoring her attention.

"It's all so simple, Bob. I can't believe I'm telling you this. Listen, Number 107 is like an unofficial collection of doorways to a few different places in time, and it's hardly ever used by anyone because it's so secret. Only Madame Agatha and one or two other High Level Guardians know about it - or even where it leads to, which is where you come in. All you have to do is go there and into the Master Bedroom and then you might be in the building at Number One, Lexington Avenue in New York - or at least somewhere near it, anyway. Did I say it's somewhere in the past? Yes, I did, I'm sure I did. I did just now. Anyhow, that's where we all used to be and you'll find Madame Agatha there, only she'll be younger and healthier and everything.."

Bob waited for a moment, expecting canned laughter to come from somewhere and a mad tv-host to enter the room. But nothing happened.

"Oh, of course. Who's 'we'?" he said.

"People you don't know. Maybe me, I'm not sure."

"Ahh. And the reason it's me who has to go, and not.. umm.. let's say you?"

"I wish it was me, but I'm not you and neither am I a Guardian or.." she gestured to Agatha, "..or The Guardian Of Time."

Agatha gave a small snore, and Bob dropped his voice to barely a whisper.

"My Great Aunt Agatha's a guardian of time?"

"No, not 'a' - she is 'The' because there's only one of each kind. More than one would be ridiculous."

"Oh, of course. And this is the Time Department, I take it?"

"No. It's the Department Of Time. A Time Department is where they sell clocks and watches in large stores. You really have to be careful before speaking, Bob. Saves trouble."

"Okay. And speaking of trouble, why are you roping me into this?"

"You're the only person who can use the doorways without being detected, because you don't officially exist - so technically you're not using them, when in reality you actually are using them, do you follow? It's something to do with you being born twice and that means that no-one can track your movements, and that's how you'll get ALL of the Mirrors back!" she said, spreading the fingers of one hand out.

Agatha gave a weak moan, and they both looked at her until she fell silent again.

"Born twice? Look, if I was born twice I'm sure by now my mum would have mentioned it, or at least used the whole 'two agonising labours' thing to get me doing more stuff around the house. And what's so special about some mirrors?"

"You're not making this simple, Bob, and it really is so simple. I don't know how she.. how Madame Agatha swung it, but because she did you are the only person who can do this. Troub.. bad people took all five Eternity Mirrors."

"And those are.."

"They're the official access points through time. Because of her position, Madame Agatha can intervene in any past event in order to prevent future events being awful, okay? The Mirrors reveal everything to their Guardian, deny her nothing, and let her step through to whenever - and they've been taken by the.. bad people."

"Right.."

"Yes! That's better, now. You're starting to understand. See, we don't have much time.." she said, and wiped a tear from her cheek. Bob could see that she was a potential straight-jacket case, and went into psychiatrist mode.

"It's okay, keep telling me what's on your mind."

Feiya nodded and hugged Jinx, briefly.

"Yes. Well up until just after midnight on Thursday night stroke Friday morning, everything was fine but something went really terribly wrong - I had no idea it could happen and we must have been wide open to get raided because of the wretched Andromedan Fault."

"Who's that? Some kind of alien?" said Bob, hoping Feiya would allow him a moment of bewildered humour. Fortunately she did.

"No.. it's to do with planets. The Andromedan Fault happens every few centuries and weakens all the complicated special security forces around the Mirrors.. but that's not my area so I don't really understand any of that. Anyway, Madame Agatha will explain it all when you get to her.."

"I see, I see.. and this is causing great stress for you?" Bob asked, and immediately wondered if he'd just taken the agony uncle psycho-analysis too far. Feiya nodded, rather than damage him with the cat.

"So much so, you wouldn't believe. We have to have the Mirrors back by midnight on this coming Thursday because that's when the Sirian Alignment takes place and.. I can't say right now because you'll get so crushed by all the responsibility that you'll just die or jump off the cliff, or something."

Bob furrowed his brow as much as possible.

"Hmm.. is there more you want to tell me about?"

Feiya nodded, and wiped another tear away.

"It's actually quite simple. If we don't get them back, the Mirrors, that is, by the time of the other alignment at midnight on Thursday like I just mentioned, the entire balance of power in the universe changes to the Troublers, and everything that's ever happened and ever will happen will change for ever! The very nature of existence shifts! No rules, no accountability, no responsibility, no committees, no.. no nothing. Do you get it?"

Bob dropped the psychiatrist approach now that she had thrown a question at him.

"Err.. almost. How exactly does the word 'simple' fit into this?"

"Look, anything can be simple Bob, as long as you don't ask questions at the wrong time. See? Just do as you're told and things can start moving. You go to the house, find the doorway that leads to where younger Madame Agatha will be in the past and she can help you, and you simply can't not go today and get things happening!"

The intensity in her voice increased as she spoke, and Bob felt as if he had stepped into a very weird dream, one where common sense and double negatives didn't matter. Jinx raised her head and fixed her eyes back onto him.

"So.. err.. who'd want the mirrors?" he ventured, trying to bring her back into a friendlier mood.

"I just told you not to ask questions like that - you're not keeping it simple and right now you have to keep it simple!" she despaired, losing her temper. Agatha drifted into consciousness, and in a faint whisper muttered Feiya's name and something about Manhattan.

Feiya began repeating half sentences to Agatha in an increasingly distraught voice. In moments of extreme stress or confusion, Bob's mind tended to take a running jump into the refuge of any number of pop videos. The one he chose at this point involved a slightly over-made up actress-turned-popstar who was currently at number five in the charts, looking unbelievably gorgeous and singing about..

"Bob! Bob! Are you listening to me?" Feiya called while prodding his shoulder. Bob nodded, convincing no-one but himself.

"The Main Bedroom is where you go, okay? If Jinx is around, you can go into the house, okay? And you tell no-one and trust no-one except Madame Agatha, you promise me now! There's other travellers around but don't trust them, you trust no-one!"

"Okay, I promise, really I do. Well, it's been nice meeting you, and we mustn't leave it so long till next time, shall we? Perhaps it's time for me to be going away, as everyone looks a little tired and so on and so forth.." said Bob in the most understanding daytime-tv voice he could manage. Feiya was on the verge of tears again.

"Yes, you go and start doing everything - it'll all become a lot clearer Bob, there's just so much that I can't tell you and so much that I can't not tell you, so just go would you? Now?"

Her request was more of an order, and her mood shifted in just one sentence from being upset to almost too controlled. Bob was happy to oblige though. His very high tolerance level for crazy-talk had been reached quite some time earlier, and there was only so much he could handle in one day. He went back into the hallway and sighed with relief as the door shut behind him. Escaping from Feiya and Agatha's barmy world felt good, and also a little disturbing. They genuinely seemed to believe what they were talking about, which was very sad indeed. He made a quick Mental Note to always make an effort to keep a tight grip on reality, and to only drink bottled water.

His parents had progressed onto a disagreement over migratory patterns of barren-ground caribou, and also why the living room did not need redecorating. His mother stood up quickly.

"Oh so you've decide to join us! Perhaps we'll go now while our one day of the week at home is still here? We took five minutes to say all our 'hello's - honestly Robert, you've been over an hour - what did you ever find to talk about?" she said, exaggerating every third or fourth word.

The prospect of trying to repeat even the tiniest part of his actual conversation didn't feel like a good idea. Bob managed to bluff his way through their questions on the way back home, blaming his long stay on Agatha's poor health, and in an inspired moment of side-stepping he roped in Feiya, who had '..been talking about all kinds of stuff and things'.

Nothing more was said of the visit until they were all sitting around the kitchen table, working their way through a rather tense lunch. Bob's father broke the silence.

"Look, if she's planning on leaving you her fortune, you should give away anything over fifty thousand to charity, Robert. You earn your money in life, not have it handed to you on a plate. Short-cut to ruin, that is. We started with nothing, your mother and me, so.."

"No dear, that should be 'I' not 'me'. You should say to him, '..your mother and I'. But do carry on.." interrupted his mother, in her most teacherly voice.

"No dearest, you're quite wrong, I believe you'll find it's definitely 'me' because.." replied his father, and their on-off Battle Of Grammatical Perfection was about to recommence.

Bob finished his lunch quickly and left his parents to lock horns. He hurried upstairs, lay back on his bed and let a DVD start playing in the background. The theme to The Return Of The Pink Panther wiped out the rising voices below. Bob felt miserable. He turned the silver key over in his hands. It was heavy enough to be real silver, polished to an unbelievable shine, and had probably been an old 18th or 21st birthday present for someone many years ago. He sighed. Meeting two such unstable and deluded people as 'Madame' Agatha and the over-stressed fruitcake called Feiya was a very depressing experience. Maybe there was no-one else living at Pierpont House, and life had become a bit too much for just the two of them? It was a huge place, after all. He decided that Andie didn't really need to know about any of this.

As he mulled things over in his mind, he began to wonder about the house on Lincoln Drive, a dead-end road that ran the other way along the cliff top.

"Fancy Great Aunt Agatha owning a place along there.." he thought, and contemplated perhaps taking a look one day, if there was nothing on tv.

Bob had rarely ever turned right onto the other road at the curve where Sea Road starts its cliff run as Marine Drive. There was no good reason to go along there. Lincoln Drive consisted mainly of dull and largely forgotten guest houses, reaching for well over a mile. The first property was the appropriately named Cliff House Hotel, which was always popular by Barton standards and had a 'Three Crown' rating proudly displayed outside its car park. However, as the road progressed the properties steadily became increasingly dilapidated and neglected. The absent owners didn't seem to care, and two or even three years had passed since Bob and Andie had bothered to cycle that grim and pointless route. But if Number 107 was Great Aunt Agatha's 'other residence' then it would definitely be worthy of a visit, someday.

Bob sat bolt upright. A penetrating and unmistakable cat-like noise had come from somewhere. He looked over at the tv in the hope that it came from there, but Inspector Clouseau was merely having problems with an accordion player and a monkey. Nervously he looked down from his window, and there was Jinx sitting on the gatepost looking straight back up at him. It was time to go.

CHAPTER SIX

107 Lincoln Drive

"I'm off now for a wander," Bob nervously announced to the house, failing to give the impression that he wasn't nervous.

"What about your brother's chemistry notes? Have you studied any of the valency ones yet? It's so important to be ahead of the class.." his mother called from the living room, and his father grunted in agreement. Revision was becoming an increasingly heavy burden that Bob had to carry. He was supposed to improve on the high-flying performance of his brother at school, and his parents figured that by surrounding him with mountains of text books and exam papers, success would be practically guaranteed - unless he chose to do badly by being deliberately lazy, of course.

"I'll get back to them this evening," he half-groaned, and gladly escaped into the driveway. An hour or two being lead around by a mad old lady's equally mad old cat would be far preferable to ploughing through yawn-worthy theories about molecular things that nobody could even see.

Jinx kept sprinting a few yards ahead, staying close to the walls and hedgerows and then waiting for Bob to catch up before racing off again. They made their way along Sea Road, and branched onto Lincoln Drive. As he looked at the buildings with more interest this time, Bob thought how strange it is that you can live somewhere all your life and yet not know an area that's almost on your doorstep.

After a couple of minutes walking, the widely-spaced houses began to look more unkempt. It started in small ways, with peeling paint on some window sills, a few missing roof tiles here and there, or a garden that was overgrown in certain parts. After a few more minutes the large houses stopped being merely untidy and became neglected, and then finally abandoned. Roofs had collapsed, vast areas of plaster had fallen from front walls, windows were either missing or broken, and the only occupants seemed to be small gatherings of birds.

Bob figured that this stretch would be completely bought-up and developed pretty soon, just like Marine Drive, and if he had the money to buy everything right now, he could make a fortune. He made a Mental Note about that and added a few suggestions as to what he could do with all the huge profits. When he snapped back into the real world, Jinx was no longer waiting ahead of him.

"Jinx? Jinx.. eh, where you go, hombré?" he said, expecting the entire world to start laughing at him for talking to thin air. He'd come far enough along Lincoln Drive to justify going the extra few hundred yards with or without Jinx, and it probably would be interesting to see Agatha's house, or at least what she claimed to be her house.

"Bless her," thought Bob, "she probably saw it once and thought it would be nice to live there, or something."

The houses were becoming so ramshackle that even cockroaches would turn their noses up at living in this area.

"Or they'd turn up whatever cockroaches have instead of noses," Bob corrected himself, and paused for a moment to find out how much further he needed to go.

"Ah, Number 71, more or less," he declared, noticing that more of it was lying on the ground than was actually standing. He carried on walking, trying to convince himself it was definitely 107 that he was heading for, and not 110, 101, 171, 177 or something completely different. And it was absolutely definitely Lincoln Drive not Lincoln Road, Street, Avenue, Terrace or Cul-de-sac Under The Sea.

The houses ended with a total wreck marked by a 97 hanging from its weather-beaten fence. The mess was succeeded by a long, long expanse of rubble, tall weeds and defiant remnants of walls and pipes which created a morbid wasteland all the way up to the side of a large and appropriately sinister two storey building. Bob soon found himself standing outside its low front wall, straining his eyes to make out the chalked numbers scrawled across the front door.

"A one, a dodgy zero, and then a seven.. marvellous," he said under his breath, regretting having come this far. A sprawling, leafless elder tree stood between him and the house, and rustled to give the residence an even more sinister air.

A black conical peak sat high on top of a hexagonal tower on the dominant left side, giving the entire house a low-budget horror movie feel. The rest of its front was hidden beneath twisted masses of dark green ivy, clearing in a few places to reveal cracks running up, down and along the brickwork, where the brick-red colours had been replaced with shades of dull brown and turquoise moss. Yet bizarrely, eight near-perfect windows ran along the front of the upper floor, looking very dark and not even so much as cracked. Above them, the house was crowned by a steep granite-grey pointed roof which, Bob mused, was the kind that Santa would have a really tough time landing on.

The six ground floor windows now appeared to be fine as well, and even the frosted glass arch above the front door looked undamaged. Were they like that a moment ago? They were near perfect, and seemed to be completely out of place. He tried to ignore the logic, but couldn't stop wondering why this house wasn't as ramshackle and wrecked as the ones before it. Or even the ones after, and there weren't many of those before the road merged into the mud and grass. Number 107 was definitely a place he wouldn't suggest bringing Andie to, even if it really was going to be his one day soon. It was a big weird mess, and there was no way that he felt like going inside, not even if Jinx was somewhere in the grounds and waiting for him to catch up.

"Of all the stupid things I've ever done, following a cat to a dump like this is the.. uh oh." He stopped in mid whinge and his heart jumped as he noticed Jinx silhouetted in an upstairs window.

"Oh great," he lied to himself. After a very long moment, he decided that there would be absolutely no harm in just taking a quick look inside the old place, and that being nervous about going into a big, deserted, creepy old mansion was pathetic.. but also entirely understandable.

Dense tufts of grass reached up through cracks and gaps in the driveway, joining up in some areas as if the cliff tops were patiently reclaiming their land, blade by blade. As Bob stepped closer towards the front door, he expected a bad-tempered reclusive psycho to appear at any of the windows - or maybe all of them - to hurl gibberish and furniture at him. Even though the driveway was no longer or shorter than an ordinary driveway, it felt like a double-marathon course by the time he arrived at the heavy oak front door. It was wider than a normal front door, but that might have been due to the style of a bygone age, perhaps. He took some comfort from the fact that there was no catflap by his feet - because that meant Jinx must be genuinely familiar with the property in order to have found her way up to the window so quickly. She must know another way in, and she couldn't have just stumbled over that by chance in the last few minutes. He admired the elegantly carved 107 in the dark wood panel beside the door, and wondered for a moment if it had been a little different a minute or two ago.. but no, he had to be mistaken. He was good at being mistaken, and any number of teachers could vouch for that.

Feeling less intrusive, Bob unpopped the top buttons of his denim shirt and lifted out the key. It was an awkward and cumbersome thing, but that didn't matter too much because he was starting to feel excited about whether or not it actually worked. The lock gave a solid clunk which shook all the way along the key's neck and up through his arm. The door swung open, leaving Bob standing in the doorway and holding the key in mid-air.

"That's a rare Freak Factor Ten, a definite Weird Event Moment, a Special-Reserve Abnormal Happening of the highest order, and also a very worthy Not Altogether Expected Incident," said Bob, listing the Andie Awards that the front door had just earned.

Bob hesitated a moment in order to take in the scene before entering. He'd sat through far too many Friday Fright Night movies to fail to do that. A formal, deep-red carpeted hallway stretched out before him, perhaps ten feet wide to start off with, and maybe fifteen yards long. It quickly narrowed due to an elaborate staircase occupying almost the entire length of the left side, which gradually disappeared from sight up into darkness. The pinewood door near the foot of the stairs, which Bob figured should lead through into the hexagonal tower, seemed to be resting at a slightly odd angle from a weak hinge.. but no, it wasn't. He looked away, then back, and it was fine. Another mistake, a trick of the odd lighting, of course.

Directly ahead of him at the far end of the hallway, stood a closed door with a diamond shape in its large frosted glass panel. And that panel definitely couldn't have been cracked a second or two ago, because it definitely wasn't cracked now. It was perfect.

"Nothing too spooky so far.." he thought aloud, and took a step inside - and suddenly noticed that there were two evenly spaced doors along the hall's right wall, the nearer one much darker than the other. He could almost hear his father pointing out that they were both in desperate need of a good sanding and a new coat of varnish. That could wait for some other time.

Bob didn't fancy taking a look in any of the rooms, and certainly didn't feel like embarking on a trip up the stairs. But despite himself, he took a few steps further inside and immediately became aware of a loud and obtrusive ticking which was coming from a tall grandfather clock over by the furthest door. For a moment Bob felt that the ticking didn't start until he actually set foot in the house, but soon pushed the idea to the back of his mind, because those kinds of thoughts were way off the Paranoid Dimwit Scale.

Considering Number 107 had such a depressing exterior and was in such a dismal area, the interior was certainly well looked after. The carpet wasn't worn, the minutely patterned wallpaper wasn't peeling in too many places, and a whole series of paintings were all still hanging - most of them straight. He took a few steps further into the house, and as he looked at the old-fashioned paintings of nameless buildings and people, he began to relax a little.

"Maybe," he thought, "this really is Great Aunt Agatha's, and Feiya looks after it so that they can make the odd visit? That'd fill up an afternoon for her, every now and then.."

With that thought in mind, Bob began to feel like trying one or even two of the rooms before going home. He wandered back past the paintings to the dark door - which by pure coincidence happened to be the one nearest to the front door and therefore ideal for a quick getaway, just in case there were any freaks behind it. He turned the round brass handle enough times for it to make a weak click, and went into the living room - and felt as if he'd stepped back at least a hundred years.

The dark wood panelling and heavily patterned wallpaper gave the room a sombre atmosphere and another grandfather clock in the near corner didn't help, but plenty of lace and china brought an uneasy kind of balance. Two tall rubber plants reached high from their squat brass pots either side of the magnificent fireplace in the far wall, which looked as if it had been used within the last day or two. A heavy-set oval table occupied the front end of the room, fitting neatly into the bay windows, with an intricately ornate chandelier hung high above.

"No wonder Victorians always looked so glum," Bob murmured.

The retro effect was spoiled a little by a widescreen television over in the corner, and helped even less by a series of small flat speakers dotted along the walls, but despite that, Queen Victoria would probably have approved. The house was becoming the kind of place he might bring Andie to, after all.

Bob stepped further in, and wandered over to the pair of vast double doors which occupied the central section of the wall on the left. They opened with the slightest touch to reveal what must have been the dining room.

Eerily life-like portraits hung on each of the walls, and elegant glass cabinets stood in each corner of the room displaying everything from cracked old pottery to sparkling jewel-encrusted figurines and egg-like ornaments. A long rectangular table took up the centre of the room, with places set for at least a dozen people, four of which had gold cutlery instead of merely silver. Bob couldn't think of a dozen people to have round, and figured four was a more realistic number. Actually, two places would do just fine. Still, the important thing was that there were no psychos or deviants in these two rooms, no dead bodies, no spooky floating objects, and no sinister footsteps running around upstairs.

He wandered back into the living room and tried the door near the fireplace. It opened into a library which ran the entire length of the other two rooms, and he drifted aimlessly up and down dozens of rows, amazed at the age and size of some of the books.

"Smells even older than the stock rooms up at the shop," he thought to himself as he ran a finger along the dusty tops of some of the more ancient-looking volumes.

Bob suspected that he might have walked along the same rows more than once without realising it, because there seemed to be far more rows than there was enough space for. So after meandering through a maze of books covering almost any subject, plus endless volumes of collected works and countless illegible one-offs, he wandered back into the hallway and decided to try the door down at the very end. It would probably lead out to the back garden or maybe a patio, or perhaps just the kitchen. But he didn't find out. His mind must have fogged over on the way, and instead he found himself opening the door at the foot of the stairs.

"Aha.. so this must be the parlour, howww civiliyyz-duh," he whispered in his best upper-class voice, looking at six cream-leather chairs placed around a triple-layered glass coffee table. Each chair had its own rack of magazines alongside, and he began wondering just how sudden Great Aunt Agatha's illness must have been, because she obviously seemed to have quite a social life. Part of the room was hexagonal, which proved it was the lower portion of the tower and therefore wasn't quite how he expected it to be. No instruments of torture, no mad people chained up, no weapons on the wall, no echoing drips from the ceiling, nothing. He barely noticed that the decor was far more simplistic and modern in style than the other rooms, as his attention was taken by a stag's head on the right-hand side, up near the ceiling.

"People actually have those?" he wondered aloud, and tugged the handle of the deep-set white door beneath it, which opened up a truly bizarre mess. A large old-fashioned writing desk faced him, the kind that had lots of shiny wooden drawers running up to a large flat writing area, rows of pigeon-holes and a pull-down protective cover that formed an arc over the top. Or a partial arc, in this case. The entire desk was covered in Memo-Its, hundreds of them, layer upon layer, all written in either appallingly bad handwriting or an obscure foreign language.

Dozens of clocks hung from the walls, all of them frozen at different times which made the room feel sinister and worthy of a good shiver. A huge door occupied almost the entire end of the narrow room, which opened with the slightest of touches to reveal a chaotic office almost the size of the library, consisting of three long desks surrounded by hundreds and hundreds of reference books. Huge sheets of paper were pinned to the walls, each covered in arrows and bizarre squiggles. If a few test tubes and fizzing glass beakers had been lying around, this would be pretty much how Bob imagined an extremely mad scientist's study ought to look.

He picked a random path through the piles of books, trying to piece together just who would need to refer to all of them at the same time. Volumes of political discussions about Prussian War Campaigns were piled on top of a thick Monet study, which stood on top of a history of the Ford Motor Company, above a biography of Karl Marx and so on, for pile after pile. Countless coloured bookmarks and torn notepaper poked out of the sides, patterning and adding to the mess.

Without disturbing anything, he left feeling more bewildered than he'd felt in a long time, which was quite an achievement. He closed all the doors behind him as he went back to the hallway, and sat at the foot of the stairs to take a moment and weigh up everything.

"Okay, okay, Unavoidable Fact A," he decided, "Great Aunt Agatha isn't entirely barmy. Unavoidable Fact Number B is.. that she really does own this place, and probably comes here quite often. Unavoidable Fact Number Three.. I've got a dilemma time.." he moaned, as he realised that if this much of Agatha and Feiya's story was completely true, was there even a tiny chance that the Master Bedroom was not just a Master Bedroom? He looked up towards the dark landing, and felt sure there would be a few interesting rooms up there - but could there possibly be something like a huge swirling vortex waiting to suck him through to a parallel dimension, perhaps?

"Or maybe I'm just too gullible and a bit too dim to recognise when I'm being too gullible and a bit too dim.." he whispered to himself, and started climbing the steps.

Surprisingly, the upstairs was a lot brighter than it looked from the hallway. The walls and doors were made entirely of the same wooden panelling of the living room, but there was no drab wallpaper to weigh it all down. Bob stood at the top of the stairs, not entirely sure which way to turn. A broad corridor ran across the width of the house, a shorter one ran straight ahead, and a slightly longer one ran back behind him, above the hall. By Bob's reckoning, that one ended somewhere above the front door. He decided the shortest corridor was a good bet, and walked up to a locked door at the end. He tried his key in the lock and it smoothly opened out onto a grey, stone-clad balcony which ran all along the back of the house and around the left side of the house to the tower.

"Nice for an ice-cream on a summer's afternoon.." Bob thought with more than a hint of sarcasm, looking out at the neighbouring relics. Somehow they all looked even worse from on high.

He stepped back inside the short corridor, and opened the door on his right to reveal a mundane Victorian bathroom, complete with a florally decorated bath and sink. He closed it with a grimace, and went to the room opposite. This one was little more than a compact and neat bedroom, completely out of step with its surroundings. It looked as if it had received a tv make-over, but only as a last-minute item at the end of a programme. Pastel blue walls, matching bedspreads, obsessively neat bookshelves, smart wall-lamps, a plasma television.. and a host of colour co-ordinated extras running along steps of glass shelving from one wall to the next. Nothing was out of place, probably because nothing dared to be out of place. That wasn't even remotely likely to be a Master Bedroom, so he turned left at the main corridor and went up to the far end, where another grandfather clock was ticking steadily and loudly. He suspected that if the Master Bedroom was going to be anywhere, it would be here, opposite a wide expanse of windows which overlooked the rear of the house.

"Ladeez and jenullmennn, we have a winner!" he announced to the corridor as he looked into the much larger and very Victorian bedroom that lay before him. This was far more how Bob thought it should be. Big double bed, dark floral wallpaper, wide wardrobes, brassy chandelier, big oval rugs, stretched out tiger skin on the wall and elegant, shiny ornamentation. It had to be.

Bob's nerves disappeared. The room looked so uninteresting that he didn't have any second thoughts about stepping inside. Nothing weird could possibly happen in such a mundane 'old lady' kind of room, and he even wondered why on earth he'd ever worried about finding himself stumbling into the middle of nowhere.

"Here we go, then - one small step for an idiot, a giant leap for idiot-kind," he announced, and he..

CHAPTER SEVEN

The Middle of Nowhere

..didn't lay a single foot on the bedroom floor. The first thing he noticed as he came to a heart-stopping halt was that he was standing in a much darker room with a table right in front of him, and he was surrounded by the smell of new wood. The only light came from a vertical window on the far wall, and wasn't helping to reveal very much at all. He turned around to see where the house on Lincoln Drive had gone, and stared at the dark void that had replaced the bedroom door. He could make out vague steps in it which lead upwards, but they were soon lost in the darkness.

Suddenly he felt very sick, far sicker than he'd ever felt before. This time the feeling went right from toe-level all the way up to the top of his head and just kept on going and going, making his entire body feel as if four huge demolition balls had all collided at the same point, with him caught right in the middle. A thousand questions blew around in his mind, and he could see why Feiya insisted on not asking too many of them at once. Some questions would take a lot of explaining, and some questions were almost impossible to phrase in the first place.

He sat on the floor for a few minutes to try and gather some thoughts together - or even just one or two would be fine. A faint chorus of twittering birds drifted through the still air, so Bob covered his ears for some serious Thinking Time.

"Okay, right, so I've established that Aunt Agatha and Feiya aren't entirely barmy. Or if they are, then I am as well. So let's say they're not, and therefore I'm not. That's good. I need to be looking for Number One Lexington so that a previous version of Aunt Agatha can explain everything about this, and also those mirrors as well.. so I need to find her before I do anything else. That's the plan. Find Aunt Agatha. So simple even Feiya would approve. Yes. Ask no questions, just find old young Aunt Agatha. Good."

While Bob was deep in thought, more daylight had gradually started to fill the room and as he stood up armed with his plan, he could see that he was inside a very basic wooden kitchen that was mid-way through being built. An old-fashioned granite-grey stove stood on the far side, with a tall pipe leading up through the roof. A sink and draining board were nearby, and importantly, a doorway without a door in it was just on his left.

He leaned on the table, then the wooden chairs, and finally sent some small ripples through a basin of cold water as he convinced himself that he was unquestionably in a real place, rather than caught in an epic of a bad dream. He stood at the window and looked out at mile upon mile of rolling fields of greens and pale yellows, which were interrupted only by small clusters of trees and a few short hedgerows. Birds darted through the air and sang loudly, just like normal birds should do in a normal world. Everything was most definitely real.

After a few minutes of staring numbly at a trio of birds flying further away, Bob started to calm down and looked back over to where he'd come in, and saw that the staircase was steadily fading away and leaving behind a solid wooden wall in its place. For a moment he thought the only way out had just vanished before his eyes but as he stepped nearer to the wall, the arched doorway gradually returned and he could see the steps again.

"Nice one Aunt Agatha, freakish but definitely nice.." he croaked, and waited for his heart to start beating again.

He went out of the kitchen and along a partially decorated hallway, not daring to take a look around any of the other rooms just yet. He creaked his way to the front door, and without thinking, gave it a push. Despite its flimsy wooden appearance it was as solid as a wall of steel, and didn't even wobble. He guessed the walls of the entire house must be equally deceptive, and tried his key in the lock. It glowed warmly, and the door withdrew sideways into the wall. He would have been impressed by that, if he hadn't just traversed the time-space continuum by passing through a multi-dimensional portal in the kitchen - that experience had raised the bar rather high. He stepped out onto the porch, and a mild early-morning breeze welcomed him into an open landscape which was almost entirely lacking any other buildings.

Bob wandered onto the dust-track of a drive, and stood for a while to simply take a look at where he was. The place where he'd turned up appeared to be a partially-built farmstead rather than a house, and was much larger and more complete (in places) than the kitchen had suggested - its wooden verandah had even been half-painted. A huge barn stood about a hundred yards away to the right, and from then on there was absolutely nothing but fields and a few more clusters of trees, rising gently to a broad hill on the horizon.

"This must be New York before the architects got hold of it," he said to himself, immediately aware of the silence he'd just broken.

He carried on for a couple of hundred yards down the dusty track to where it joined onto a main road. As roads go, it was a pretty hopeless one. It was as dusty and rough as the path he'd just walked along, only a lot wider and ravaged with deep grooves, ruts and pot-holes. All in all, it was the sort that would be next to impossible to cycle along. He looked to his right and saw nothing but empty roadway, hedges and trees all gradually disappearing into a distant corner. However, in the other direction towards the rising sun, he could just make out something resembling a sign, way off in the distance. He took a deep breath, tried to convince himself he was more than up to the task of finding any Mirrors, and began his search by tripping over a ridge of baked mud.

Fifteen minutes later he stood before a post with a split plank of wood nailed at the top. The words 'Town ahead. 3 or 4 mile, maybe' had been written in the kind of large red letters that suggested the sign had been raised before the paint was dry.

"Ah, brilliant. Now I know exactly where I am!" he declared, and carried on walking. He soon began leaving the scrawny clusters of trees behind and began passing dense thickets, separated by long rows of bushes. Birds kept singing, leaves kept rustling in the gentle breezes, and Bob figured this wasn't too bad at all. He felt like he might as well be in the past, the present or the future, because some things simply never changed.

Half an hour later there was still no sign of a town. However, a huge pond which seemed to be trying desperately hard to be a lake had appeared to the right of the road, and a lone cow wandered away from its shoreline to join him, and stopped a few cow-lengths away. There are very few cases recorded in history of cows attacking people, but Bob had a morbid fear of them. Until he was about four or five, Taylor family holidays involved towing their small caravan to a dis-used airstrip for the weekend, which was owned by a farmer who was glad of the extra money. Part of the reason for the low price was the fact that every now and then he would lead his cows from the fields on one side of the air strip to the fields on the other side, and for up to an hour there would be a massive bovine exodus. Even eight years later Bob was convinced that nobody knew what fear was until they'd been on one side of a thin caravan door while a cow on the other side went 'Moooo' repeatedly. And the overpowering cow-smell just made it so much worse.

So Bob was very pleased when this particular cow let him pass by without even so much as a half-moo.

After a further hour he was nearing a town, which according to another make-shift sign appeared to be called 'The New Town'. A side-road branched off in a gentle and very long curve, past a series of narrow wooden houses and into the town's main street. With a slightly nervous feeling in his stomach, Bob headed for civilisation.

Gradually the houses gave way to small shops, with larger ones soon taking over. By comparison, The George Washington Hotel looked enormous. It stood proudly at a corner of the central junction, dominating the town centre. The clock above its entrance showed that the time was now almost nine o'clock. According to Bob's watch, the time was slightly after six o'clock in the evening, so he reset it and simply stood opposite the hotel for a while, with only a mannequin from the Shuer's Gent Outfitter Co. for company, and looked at the different people who were starting their day. A few women walked past in long dresses and wide hats, and one or two even had parasols. The men were either in odd-fitting suits, or braced-up trousers that were baggy enough to lose a herd of buffalo in, and most had moustaches that were obsessively over-groomed.

Part of his brain desperately tried to figure out how he could be seeing and hearing people who had lived and died many, many years ago, and how they could be going about their lives for (as far as they were concerned) the first time. Bob knew that when he returned to Barton he could probably find out who any of these people were, where they lived and where they raised families, and of course, where and when they died. A shiver ran down his spine and didn't stop till it reached his knees. He decided Feiya's advice was worth following, and tried burying all the questions somewhere in the back of his mind - after all, Agatha would be able to explain all of this, and then everything would make perfect sense.

The people passing by in the bright sunshine didn't seem to be in any great hurry to get anywhere at all. Most gave Bob a strange glance or two, and he soon realised that black jeans, a denim shirt and a spacious grey Next jacket with far too many pockets wasn't the ideal disguise for blending into the surroundings.

He looked further up the street and noticed a very well-dressed woman outside a small parade of shops, and a spark of recognition instantly made him think of Andie's mum. There was a certain something about her that was vaguely similar - maybe it was her shape.. or perhaps her hair.. or something else. From such a distance, he wasn't really sure what it was, but she certainly seemed like a good enough choice to be his first Past Person to talk to. He nervously waited as she came closer and closer, casually wandering her way down the main street towards him. He was amazed to see that the resemblance wasn't just her size, but in her face as well and for a very confused moment he wondered if maybe, just maybe, Mags was here with him and he wasn't really completely alone.

Her eyes fell on him, and she paused momentarily. Bob took his chance, and stepped towards her.

"Err, hello there M'ame, nice morning isn't it? I'm new here, and.."

"Well you sure are! What kind of gittup is that? Is there a circus in town? Or maybe someone's payin' you?"

She carried on along the sidewalk, laughing the most ridiculous trill laugh Bob had ever heard. If a banshee ever thought of something really amusing whilst hammering its head against a rock, its laugh would be nothing compared to the one made by her.

"So much for similarities.." he thought, anxiously scanning the small groups of strolling people for someone else to talk to. After a minute or two his stress levels were rising wildly, and he knew he needed to slow down and try to settle in, rather than trying to sort out everything all at once. He sat down on the window-ledge of Millicent's, a milliners near to the hotel. After ten minutes of people-watching, the odd glances he was attracting didn't really bother him anymore, and even the mind-numbing shock of being in such a place began wearing off - and at long last the butterflies in his stomach calmed down.

"Have to pin a year on this.." he thought, and let his eyes wander from one end of the street to the other. However, he knew absolutely nothing about vintage transport, fashion or architecture, which made it difficult. A few horse-drawn carriages trotted along the street, and every few minutes very shaky black cars would go past with their spindly comedy-wheels wobbling under their sputtering engines. They looked even less well-designed and reliable than the ones in his early Charlie Chaplin films, which meant that he must be somewhere around the year 1914. That lead him to think hard, back to a book about silent movies that Andie had given him for Christmas, and he tried trawling his memory for any other facts or pictures from that time. He couldn't remember any at all, but being equipped with this little knowledge of the era made him feel a lot easier about being there, and he decided that the search could now start properly.

A blonde middle-aged lady in a ruffled purple dress came out of the doorway of the milliners.

"She must be Millicent," deduced Bob.

"Young man?" said Millicent, "Would you mind heading away off'ah my window? I think you're putting folks off from comin' in, see?" she said with a wary smile, and gestured to her empty shop before going back inside. Bob gave his best diplomatic grin and wandered over the road in a weak attempt to look as if he had somewhere else to be.

He arrived in the shade outside a long row of shops, and took a look through the window at the empty tables inside Delaney's Tea Room. It wasn't open, and neither was the Fine'n'Dandy Store next to it, nor the next few after that. But fortunately the owner of one shop had just opened his door for the day, and the small bell was still ringing as Bob walked past. He took a moment to look through the window of Phingley Parr's Cornucopia and watched an elderly man making his way between mountains of junk. The man paused to straighten the fur on the head of a badly stuffed bear, as if that would stop anyone noticing that the poor creature only had one ear and a surprised expression. He ambled into a back room, carefully rearranging bric-a-brac and doing a little dusting on his way, and seemed harmless enough to Bob.

As soon as he stepped inside, Bob was struck by how old the shop felt. It didn't look particularly old, but it had a very old atmosphere and an even older smell. It was as if aged wood, tobacco, and varnish had all been mixed together and somehow used as an air-freshener. Bob decided he ought to give the right impression by pretending to examine an item or two, perhaps look at the bases of small things, and generally browse with an air of antique-expertise before making any enquiries about Lexington.

Rows upon rows of shelves ran along the walls of the shop, each crammed with an entirely random collection of bits and pieces. Elegant figurines that could easily be added to the list of Potential Andie Prezzies nestled amongst ugly dolls, tacky jewellery, shoes (some even in pairs), stuffed animals, portrait photos, containers and dulled ornaments. Everything that could possibly fit onto a shelf was there, and he quickly decided against picking anything up or even looking too long at anything in particular, in case the entire lot might come crashing down.

There was still no sign of Mr Parr, so Bob kept on browsing and trying to appear perfectly normal. He gradually made his way between the piles of magazines, tall lamps and top-heavy tables, and reached a dead-end by a precariously balanced pile of books. This particular pile stood between a damaged hat stand and a chest-high china elephant, neither of which really belonged so close to the main window where the public could see them. He prodded the elephant, letting it rock on its uneven feet. And then he jumped.

Had that been a sharp rap against the window? It sounded too harsh and deliberate to be an accidental knock. He looked around and caught a brief glimpse of a tall, thin man in a black hat turning away, disappearing into a passing crowd. Bob had the eeriest feeling the man had been watching him for a while but let the idea go, because Mr Parr had appeared by the counter. He was ticking things from a long list, humming and tutting to himself. Bob picked up a worn-out book from the top of the pile, and flicked through it as if he was genuinely interested.

"Well, I have seen some things.." said Mr Parr, a short man with grey hair and sideburns that merged into a dense moustache. He had a friendly voice, and raised his eyebrows expectantly while hooking a thumb into his waistcoat.

"Oh, I'm uh.. with the theatre," said Bob, thinking quickly, "This is a costume for a new play and you'll have to come along in a week or two.. we're rehearsing until then. It's all the way from England."

"All The Way From England? I'm 'fraid I've not heard of that one. Still, if it keeps you young folks busy.. I take it you like that book? It's a fine one I'm sure, and ought to be worth around.. nine cents, unless it's signed. Depending on who's signed it makes the price a bit more, or a bit less.."

Bob gave a polite laugh, and felt relieved that he'd found someone approachable. The poor stitching on the book's outer cover gave way and most of the cracked spine dropped off, and came to rest beside an old riding boot.

"Hmm.. best make that seven cents," added Mr Parr.

"Oh, uhh.. great, thanks. This is quite a shop you've got here. There's loads of.. all kinds of stuff. I might come back for that parrot over there," Bob said, and pointed to a multi-coloured hunch-backed parrot which had obviously been stuffed by someone with a grudge against parrots. "But first I'm supposed to be meeting a friend around here, and I've got no idea where to go. Do you know where Lexington is? It's a street, apparently, or a road.. or a drive. But it might be an aven.."

"Lexington? That rings no bells, no bells at all.. I got a map through the back. How 'bout I fetch it and we'll have a look-see? And if you find any other books while I'm gone, maybe I'll do you a real fair price? Keep on browsing as there's no harm to be had from browsing, that's what I always tell people.." he laughed.

Some shuffling noises and occasional clatters came through from the back room, and as the minutes passed Bob grew more anxious and restless. How difficult could it be? This was hardly the biggest town on earth, after all. He looked at the book he'd picked up, and grinned as he read the title from the remaining part of its torn cover.

"The Concise Compendium Of Modern Knowledge by Dr Hermann F Buntz, ARF CRA. Most Eloquently Translated by Lord Philliponte Bagshaw-Philliponte," he whispered, noticing the frontispiece illustration of a Victorian gentleman staring imperially out from behind the long rip.

He began flicking through its excessively-wordy pages, soon arriving back at the illustrated portrait of His Lordship on the coffee-stained first page, and held back a laugh at the mouth-obscuring moustache. He looked old and friendly, as if he was some lucky child's favourite grandparent. A series of small medals ran across the left side of his smart jacket, and a watch chain linked one top pocket to a lapel. A leaky signature ran underneath, dated 'This Twenty-ith day of March, in the Year of Our Lord 1902'.

"Well I doubt you'll be any help, will you Lord Bagshaw Phipple..

Philli..ponte," muttered Bob through a sigh, noticing the peculiar spelling of Twentieth.

"Oh, I don't know, old boy. There's absolutely no harm in trying, is there? Does depend rather on what you need, of course."

Unless Bob was more mistaken than anyone else in the entire history of the world, Lord Philliponte Bagshaw-Philliponte had just spoken to him. His moustache had even moved with the words. Bob looked around the shop, but it was most definitely empty. Nobody was hiding anywhere to deliver the world's cleverest prank, nothing looked particularly weird (apart from the parrot and maybe the bear), and nobody outside the window was laughing and pointing. Even corny musical birthday cards weren't due to be invented for a very long time yet, so what on earth was he holding? Bob opened the cover again. Lord Philliponte was casually re-adjusting his monocle, and gave a regal wave. Bob felt as if he had just been elected as the new Mayor of Crazyville by a massive landslide majority, with a 100% turn-out and absolutely no votes against him. Maybe stumbling into the past had left him a lot more shaken up than he thought? He opened the cover again.

"Aha, young fellow m'lad, greetings! I don't believe we've been properly introduced? I am, as the penned line suggests, Lord Bagshaw-Philliponte of the Bagshaw-Phillipontes, world-traveller and occasional lecturer in Classical Languages, Afghan Camel Herding, Gregorian Cutlery and.."

Although it now appeared impolite to do so, Bob closed the book. Then just to prove to himself that he had finally lost his weak grip on reality, he immediately opened it again.

"..and all manner of Middle Eastern to-do-ments, as I was saying, at the acknowledged Universities of Oxf.."

And then he closed it again.

Mr Parr emerged from the back room, struggling with an unruly and heavily-creased map in front of himself, before eventually managing to spread it out over the items on the main counter.

"Well, this covers the whole area for roundabouts here and I can't see anythin' as to a 'Lexington'. Mind, they do keep buildin' those new buildings apace so this'un might be too old already.. which way'd you come in?" he said, tapping his chin.

Bob's heart was racing and shaking his entire chest, and he tried to keep his voice steady.

"Thuh.. this book - how much is it, did you say? It's really.. different, isn't it? I've never seen anything like.."

Mr Parr squinted closely at the cover.

"Hmm.. it's torn 'cross there, bad too. Say I'd need to see seven cents for it.. no, call it six, it's been here a long time. It's a little old, but it's full of knowledge and that's always worth having. You'd like that?"

Bob rooted through all his pockets and found a few pound coins, a front door key, one of Andie's emergency hairgrips, a snapped yo-yo string and some popcorn. That wasn't good.

"Yes, I could really do with this book, but I don't have any money, I err.. I'm from England.. but would you trade for it?"

He pulled out three biros from an inside pocket and put them down on the map. His heart sank as he realised they were the cheap see-through kind which wouldn't impress anyone. Mr Parr held each one up to the light and examined them very closely, turning them around a few times before making a series of wavy lines on the map.

"Are these takin' regular ink?" he said, looking at the one that was almost empty. Bob cringed inside.

"Well, no.. they can't. But you can have my watch as well!" he said in a moment of inspiration, and put it down on the map.

"Your watch as well? Son, you'll not make a Rockefeller! Sure take the book with my compliments. But tell me, where d'you get these pens - I don't know that they'll catch on, but I could sure use them. Save buying new shirts and cuffs so much!"

Bob could tell that his watch was perhaps a trade too far, and Mr Parr showed no interest in it at all as he slipped it into his waistcoat pocket. However, it was a worthy sacrifice as he now had a talking book. He side-stepped trying to explain where the biros were from, and instead tried to get back to the issue at hand.

"So there's no Lexington on the map then?" he said, and moved closer to have a look for himself.

"No, doesn't look so, not round here.." replied Mr Parr, as Bob leaned over the counter. He could soon make out the farmstead area and the long road where he'd come from. No other towns lay anywhere near by, just small dots representing places that were too insignificant to have a name yet. Even the town he was standing in was only shown as an oddly-shaped grey area with a few streets and a town square. Finding Agatha was going to be very tricky, unless of course Lexington was simply an extremely new road, like Mr Parr had suggested. Some serious wandering was called for, so Bob thanked him for being helpful, but was really thanking him for simply being friendly. He left the Cornucopia and found the day outside had grown considerably warmer.

He kept his book out of sight and firmly tucked away in his official Talkative Literature pocket, feeling impatient to open it up again but far too self-conscious to risk doing so in public. Instead he decided to concentrate on searching, and began walking back past the shops on the main street, most of which still hadn't quite opened up yet. Over the road, Millicent's remained empty which made him feel like the jury had delivered a Not Guilty verdict on him, and therefore he could go and sit there all day long if he felt like it. Which he didn't.

The street progressed around a gentle right corner, and after a few minutes of walking Bob noticed that the shops were becoming small hotels, houses, and many works-in-progress. Unfinished side roads trailed off to nowhere and road names became all but non-existent, so he wandered through a few short streets towards the large white Town Hall, which was set in the centre of a well-maintained open area resembling a park. A town Official would be a good person to ask about new roads and developments, and the Town Hall ought to be crawling with them.

Bob paused on the long pathway dividing the lawns to look at a dark statue of a very fat and dignified man. This was a good chance to have a quick word with his new book, without feeling too obvious. He opened it up to the image of Lord Philliponte, who was drinking a cup of tea. Bob, feeling like the world was watching and laughing, felt an apology was called for.

"Hello, Lord Philliponte? I'm sorry about closing the cover on you earlier, you see the moment wasn't quite right for a conversation - I was in a shop."

"Oh I see, perfectly understandable, yes, most inappropriate place indeed, I must say. Not to worry though, closing the old cover makes little difference to me. Have you noticed there's a great tear across it, old boy? Had a nasty encounter with a Corgi once, dreadfully unpleasant it was. Always keep your eyes open for the little blighters. But isn't today simply glorious? I'm so pleased to be out in the fresh air again! I've been languishing in that shop and far, far too many others for so long.. but not anymore! Perhaps you might care to introduce yourself?"

That made as much sense to Bob as a talkative illustration was ever likely to make.

"Well, I'm Robert Taylor but call me Bob, and I'm looking for a relative who lives somewhere around here, and I've never spoken to a book before. Do all you books talk to each other, then?"

"Well of course! It would be the height of bad manners not to speak to one's neighbours. I once spent two happy months next to a collection of poetry by Ms Emily Dickinson. Oh bliss, how divine her words! Unfortunately she was soon bought and I've had a very long time practically shackled to a literary halfwit who wrote one book concerning seasonal crop-farming in southern Poland. Such a frightful dullard."

His Lordship paused for a moment, lost in a fond memory.

"Perhaps one day I might find Ms Dickinson again - I dwell in possibility.. however, here we are in the great outdoors surrounded by joyous fresh air and sunshine! No more dust and no more farming anecdotes about beetroot! Ah, how wonderful!"

"But how can you be talking to me? This doesn't normally happen does it, so why is it happening?"

"No idea at all, old boy. Unable to help you there, not even one little bit. I was rather hoping you might tell me?"

Lord Philliponte's monocle dropped from his eye as he raised his eyebrows, and he ducked out of sight to find it. Bob sat down on the grass, resting against the shaded side of the statue's stone plinth. He felt that he needed a friend, even if that friend happened to be conclusive proof that he also needed strong medication. His Lordship re-appeared, complete with monocle and trying to look unflustered.

"Found it, troublesome little thing.." he said, looking pleased.

"Should I be calling you Lord Bagshaw-Philliponte, or is there something a bit less.. umm.. of a mouthful?"

"Hmm. I usually insist on my full title, but I was always Bagshaw in the old school days, so you may use that if you like. Ah those school days, how amusing.." he added, with an air of whimsy. "Can I strongly emphasise that now we are acquainted I think you'll find me a worthy colleague, nay companion, and not one who ought be left.. gathering dust, as it were?"

"No, I won't leave you anywhere, don't worry.."

"Thank you, that's something of a relief.. and the encyclopedic endeavours of Dr Buntz can never be a waste!"

Bob felt obliged to ask an encyclopedic type of question, and he found a good one on the bronze plaque next to him.

"Okay then Bagshaw, who was this gent? Mr Halden J Kolvereid III, 1817-1898."

"Ooh, you've got me there, haven't you? Never heard of him. Maybe Dr Buntz's Expanded Compendium Of Modern Knowledge might help you - this volume is the Concise Edition. Limitations of space prevail, you see."

"Ah, I should have known. How about Lexington? Have you ever heard of Lexington?"

"Leck Sington? Haven't the first clue, old chap. Anything else you want to know?"

Bob had a think. He didn't want to get off to a bad start with his new friend.

"Maybe you could just tell me who Dr Buntz is, then?"

"You don't know who.. well old boy, Dr Hermann Friedrick Buntz is a most highly educated gentlemen of the Austrian persuasion who's earthly gifts to the common man are mainly of the written variety. Really, I'm most surprised that you have never heard of him or his works. Still, you Americans never did take to him.."

"Huh? I'm English like you, and why didn't they like him?"

"Following a series of unspecified incidents in Europe, he chose to travel your fine country giving a series of lectures, educating American society with his wealth of knowledge. His intention was to enable all types from the very wealthiest to the most frightfully common of people to lead rich and full lives. He even supplied them with a beverage for the mind, known as Buntz's Brain Elixir and kindly provided consumers with the first bottle free of charge. But there were certain unforeseen problems with the very foundation of the tour."

"Amaze me.."

"Alas, his accent meant the public could barely understand a word he said, and his Tour Of Enlightenment ended after just two cities. So sad. And the batch of Brain Elixir must have been contaminated during production in some way. I ask you, there were only six deaths from over a hundred people admitted to hospital, and is that so dreadful? At least ninety four recovered. Your American government very kindly paid his travelling expenses back to his native town of Klagenfurt where he began to write enlightening books in his native tongue, and I had the rewarding task of adapting this very one into the King's English. What an honour, no less!"

Bob was having difficulty accepting the fact that he was talking to a book - and even worse, talking to a book where normal people could actually see him talking to a book. A few dozen were strolling around the grounds of the Town Hall, and at least three or four were looking over in his direction. After a polite 'See you later' Bob put the book back in his newly re-titled Weirdy Talking Book pocket, and let Bagshaw get back to happily translating into Latin a pile of notes about African tribal rituals and late-Mongolian weighing devices. Apparently, he had been working on it since being sandwiched between two such books during the previous Christmas, and had been challenged by the author of one book (who was a dreadful bore of a Boer, apparently) to attempt such a feat. However, it was 'most entertaining' according to His Lordship, and after much hard work, he had very nearly finished it.

Bob set off along the path again, towards the entrance to the Town Hall. It was certainly an impressive sight compared to the buildings of the main street. There were four stories made of white wood and white stone, with countless tall windows running around the sides and a few rooms with pointed tops up on the roof. An American flag waved proudly from the top of a tall flag pole, reaching a long way above the chimney stacks, and Bob couldn't decide if there were fewer stars on it or fewer stripes than usual.

A lot of people were now milling around and about, all of them looking very important. Bob stood at the foot of the steps leading up to the double doors, and failed to catch anyone's eye. Now that he actually wanted to be noticed, they all seemed to ignore him very easily. One woman over in the reception area looked vaguely friendly, so Bob stepped inside to go and have a word. Before he had even taken three steps, two security guards clasped a hand each around his arms, and lead him straight back outside.

"Now jus' what business could you have in this Government Building here, son? You look t'me like you're from out'n town, and we get paid t'be careful who sets foot in these walls here. You got an appointment or anything, Mr Mayor?" the broader and no doubt more dangerous guard drawled to him. The smaller guard laughed in such a way that Bob figured the bigger guard must also be the slightly more intelligent one.

"No, I'm just looking for a street called Lexington, that's all, and I can't find it anywhere. I thought someone here might.."

"There's not any Lek-sing-tunn anywhere here, boy. Now take your circus voice and run back to momma, else me and ol' John L here might not forget we ever saw you."

Puzzled by the strangest threat he'd heard in a long time, Bob went down the steps and wandered back over the grass towards the main street. He needed a moment to think about things.

If he returned to Pierpont House without having found the past's version of Agatha, Feiya might have a complete nervous breakdown, and what would the stress and disappointment of such a failure do to Great Aunt Agatha? And he also wouldn't be any closer to finding those Mirrors, so maybe the whole world would really get messed up in whichever way was bothering the two of them. Plus there was a good chance that the devil-cat-beast Jinx might rip him to shreds, so all in all, this was becoming a very bad day. He knew that presenting Agatha and Feiya with a talking book wouldn't really make up for letting the entire universe come to an end.

As he wandered the same streets over and over again, a knot that could win prizes started making his stomach ache terribly and as the afternoon wore on it turned into a sick feeling that was almost unbearable. He was going to have to go back and own up to failing dismally. He opened Bagshaw's page for a quick word, but he was still gone - no doubt figuring out the correct gender and declensions for an obscure African grunt, or insane Mongolian war-cry.

Bob eventually wound up leaning outside Mr Parr's shop, and spent a moment or two looking over at the George Washington Hotel. If only someone would walk out and see him, and say something like, "Ah Bob! You're here! Aunt Agatha's been expecting you.. cup of tea.. well done and so on, and all that."

But no-one did. People simply kept on going about their daily business, doing their important daily things. He started walking again, and before too long he was treading the long road back to the farmstead. He tried not to think about what might happen when he got back to Barton, which lead him to trying not to think about how he would actually get back. A whole load of questions suddenly began leaping around in his mind. How did that portal work in the first place, anyway? What if it wasn't there anymore? And how was it possible for him to be walking along a dusty old road so long before he'd even been born? And what was all that 'born twice' stuff about? Bob groaned.

Around half an hour had passed and the questions still wouldn't leave him alone, so for a while he tried thinking of a subject to start a conversation with Bagshaw, but somehow the prospect of talking to a drawing in a book just made him feel worse.

Suddenly Bob felt a hand on his shoulder, and almost jumped out of his skin. He turned around to find himself looking up into the face of a very tall, very thin man with long whisps of white hair reaching out from under his black top-hat. The man's eyes were as cold and narrow as his grin.

"Why hello, young sir - I'm sure it's a pleasure to meet you. The name's Salesman. Mighty convenient name for a travelling salesman such as myself, most folks say. Happens I agree."

His light voice seemed to move like a snake, slowly twisting beneath his words. Bob looked at him, and recognised the man from outside Mr Parr's shop. Behind him was an overloaded wooden handcart piled high with pots, pans, tins and so many small household essentials that Bob was amazed he hadn't heard him approaching. The man drew his face closer.

"What's wrong, son? Cat got your tongue?" he said slowly, and his eyes narrowed even more. His grin widened, revealing the kind of mangy teeth that belonged in a dentist's journal.

"No, sorry, I was miles away - you gave me a bit of a shock.."

"Miles away? Miles away from where, son? Oh not to worry, I know how your feeling. From the clothes you got on, I'd say you were a travellin' feller. Travellin' takes a man a long ways from home, and maybe he forgets where home is. Is that man you, son?"

Bob had no idea what to say. He was more concerned that the man hadn't blinked yet, or taken his vile bony hand away from his shoulder.

"Never mind, never mind.." he wavered, stroking his stubbled chin with a long finger. He stood up to his full height.

"I like out-of-towners, I do. See, I'm what you might call a perpetual out-of-towner. I see a lot of towns, selling things to a lot of people. Somedays I swear I walk almost a hundred miles. You'd be amazed at the differences between the towns I visit, so you would. Why, some towns have things that other towns ain't likely to see for a long, long time to come yet, oh yes. You follow?"

Bob began to get the impression that this man wasn't a particularly scary loon, but was actually a time-traveller just like himself. After all, Feiya had mentioned something about other travellers being out and about, and this one probably had a screw loose, just like her. Bob decided to proceed with caution.

"Yes, I think I follow you. I'm looking for somewhere in New York, but I just can't find it. I don't seem to be doing much good."

Salesman walked back to his cart, teasing a long strand of white hair while looking over his wares. He laughed quietly to himself.

"Did you think that small town yonder is New York?" he called back to Bob, who nodded.

"Son, I'm going to help you. You like that? We travellin' folk have to help each other an' be in the right places at the right.. times. See, if we don't, then who will?"

He laughed to himself as he rummaged around the back of the cart, and eventually stood up holding a pale wooden whistle. It seemed to glisten for a moment in the sunlight. Bagshaw muttered something in dismay about having confused a dative ending with an ablative, and was therefore going to rewrite some chapters, but Bob missed it completely. He was staring at Salesman's gift, which was now being held an inch or two in front of his face.

"See this? If you're ever in some kind of trouble, just blow on this wherever you might be, hard as you can, and I'll be there quicker than you think. Like I'm sayin', we look after each other.."

Although Bob was pleased to have found someone to help him, the feeling was more than matched by one of wariness. He took the whistle, and ignored the rough craftsmanship and split corners. This thing would never go anywhere near his mouth, and he put it in his Stuff To Bin pocket.

"That's really good thanks, but it's New York I really need to be sorting out."

"Ah, you're a man of real determination, I can see that. Well for the time bein' I suggest you stay put, son. It's getting late in the day and you're most likely a long way from wherever you came, and certainly a long way from where you need to go, so you'd best be staying here courtesy of a fellow traveller, such as myself. You'll find night falls quickly, and these times ain't so safe that a body should be wanderin' roads alone. Without saying too much young feller, I think we understand ourselves, do we now? Tomorrow we'll make it to New York, I'm sure of that, so shall we go see the folks at The George about a room for you? It's such a fine an' peaceful resting place, it is."

Bob was too confused about what the right thing to do was, but he did know it would be another hour or two's walk back to the farm. Feeling very unsure of himself he agreed to tackle New York early the next morning, and walked back to the town alongside Salesman. Very little conversation passed between them, which didn't help Bob feel any easier about the situation. All the time the cart rattled and shook loudly on the uneven road.

Salesman instructed Bob to wait by a tall wooden pillar just inside the entrance, while he went over to the reception desk. The clock above a door near the desk showed that six o'clock had rolled around. Bob figured he must have been in the town for ten or twelve hours without a single thing to eat, but he certainly didn't feel like asking Salesman for any more help. The tall man lightly rang the bell on the desk.

"Are you the manager, sir?" he said in a particularly superficial manner, looking down to a smartly dressed man who was completely bald except for a small tuft of hair on the very top of his head. Before he could reply, Salesman continued.

"The young man over there requires a room for the night, not the best but not the worst. We all watch our pennies don't we? Sensible is sensible, I'm sure you'd agree?"

He cast a creepy smile back at Bob, and then exchanged some very quiet words with the manager, who offered up a number of keys for him to choose from. The bald man looked past Salesman and over at Bob with an expression similar to the one perfected by any of the Psycho Fifth whenever a teacher was passing by. Bob felt there was a secret in the air, but had no idea why he thought so and figured he was probably being suspicious for no reason. The manager summoned a portly man in an ill-fitting uniform over to the desk, and Salesman turned to Bob.

"Now then, this gentleman will show you to your room, and I will be here not a minute before nor after seven o'clock tomorrow morning, you care to write that down? That's not a minute before.." he announced, in an unnecessarily loud voice.

Bob declined, feeling embarrassed as people turned to look. He gladly left Salesman in the lobby and followed the porter up three flights of stairs. They wandered along the corridor to a small room near the end, marked by an early 1900's version of a drinks dispenser. A dented metal water barrel the size of a pedal bin stood outside the door, balanced on a small wooden table. A tower of filthy glasses teetered next to it, and the breathless porter merely waved a finger at them, rather than risk having a heart attack by trying to speak. Bob could tell that he was trying to say the barrel was empty, or perhaps highly toxic.

The room was definitely not the best in the hotel, and if it wasn't the worst then it must have been a very close second. It was barely larger than the bed, and had a very odd smell. The porter closed the door with an insecure click, and Bob stood at the window, watching the last arc of the sun disappearing somewhere over in the general direction of the farmstead. He leaned out and looked down at the near-empty street below, and soon found that if he leaned out even further and looked left to the main junction, he could see Mr Parr's shop. He started to think about how lucky Mr Parr and everyone in the town was. They could just go home and put their feet up, have dinner and worry about nothing in particular, living in ignorant bliss.

"How fascinating," he thought, and immediately considered the pros and cons of leaning a long way out of a high window to look at nothing important.

"Huzzah! Finished at last! Two volumes of perfect prose. I'd like to find that uncouth Dutchman and show.." bellowed Bagshaw, startling Bob and making him cling to the side of the window frame for dear life. He inched himself back into the room, and waited for his heart to stop pounding. He congratulated Bagshaw on his literary achievement, and lay down for a moment or two. Eventually the tiredness of the long day began quickly catching up with him, and he tried working out what time it really was. It must have been about three in the afternoon on Sunday when he went into the bedroom at Lincoln Drive, and then suddenly six in the morning when he arrived up at the farm, on.. one of the days of the week..

"So Barton Time is about nine hours and any number of years

ahead of wherever I am now. So if it's six or maybe seven in the evening here, it's three or four in the morning back at Barton, so that's Monday already.. oh my God - Andie's going to kill me!"

Bob sat bolt upright as everything in the entire world paled into insignificance, and he became buried under an avalanche of stress-filled thoughts. The first and biggest thought involved sudden and painful Death By Andie.

"Something bothering you there, young Bob? You'll never get to sleep with unfinished business on your mind. If you have a look at page 316, there's a whole section on Psychological Unpleasantness, and very good it is too."

"Thanks, maybe later.. but Andie's going to kill me a whole load of times! I haven't finished writing my half of our King Harald Hardrada Visits Warmer Climates presentation yet! If I'm still here tomorrow she'll have to do it on her own in front of everyone, and she's always hated that more than anything!"

"Oh, I see, trouble with the wife, is it? Oh well, we've all been there, haven't we? Can't really help too much, I'm afraid. Domestic troubles and so forth, best left to those involved. Anything else then?"

"Huh? No, she's not my.." he began before another thought, almost as bad, emerged. "Oh no.. killing me is nothing compared to what my parents are going to do to me! They'll already have most of the police out looking high and low! Mum's going to pick out a hideous smiley-face photo of me when I was six years old for the news! Major Embarrassment Factor Ten, maybe an Eleven! Oh please, no.."

After a few moments he slowly came to terms with the shock, and soon realised that he was also very hungry and very tired. All those factors combined and meant that facing Feiya and Great Aunt Agatha wouldn't be so bad after all. Plus he really didn't fancy spending a whole day with a smarmy stick insect who wore a hat that was even worse than his father's. So Pierpont House was promoted to the top of his list of priorities, and for the first time that day Bob felt like he had some kind of control over what he was doing. At last, he had a decent plan.

"Bagshaw, we're going home, okay? I'll be in so much trouble when I get back, but I'll be in worse trouble if I get back even later!"

"Aha, a damage limitation exercise. They're always a good idea. I remember once in the foothills of Ash-Ahmahabad.. or was it Edinburgh.. anyway, there we were in the midday sun completely surrounded by giraffes.."

Bob left Bagshaw to his recollections and swung his legs off the bed, causing something by his foot to give a loud clang. He looked down to see a fairly flat, white metal bowl which was shaped like a square with rounded corners. He picked it up to see if it was part of something he'd broken, and started silently examining the label on the inside rim.

"Templeton Brothers Deluxe Bedpan Corporation, Illinois.."

A sharp smell hit his nose and the bedpan made another loud clang as it hit the floor, and suddenly Bob was very pleased he hadn't eaten anything that day. He quickly went back over to the window for some fresh air.

Salesman had been right about night falling quickly. The early evening was already pitch black, interrupted only by the orange glow of a few lamps flickering in the main street. Bob decided a very discrete exit from the hotel was called for, to avoid the attention of the strange manager on reception. He spent a while preparing the old 'pillow down the bed' ploy, much as he used to do a few years earlier when he and Andie had discovered the fun to be had by simply wandering around Barton and its beach at ridiculous times of the night. Using his fingertips and trying not to breathe, he positioned the bedpan at the end of the line of pillows to where his feet should be, and the set-up was complete. He placed the whistle on the table by the bed, fetched an empty glass to put next to it, and stood for a moment trying to figure out why he'd gone to all the bother.

"You total flatline idiot.." he whispered in despair at himself.

He spent a few minutes judging if the coast was clear in the street below, and tentatively poked a leg out onto the wooden slats that made up the outside wall. Compared to climbing from his bedroom window at home, this was a breeze. The slats were broad and ridged, and didn't make all those give-away scraping noises like bricks did. The only problem was the height, but Bob knew that if he could manage a house as a 10 year old, he could manage something a bit larger by now. After a couple of minutes of careful climbing he was down on the sidewalk, dusting off his knees and waiting for his foot to stop hurting before heading away as quickly and as silently as he could. By the time he had passed the houses at the start of the town, he was breathing hard and feeling dizzy. He made a Mental Note to carry emergency rations from now on, because going an entire day without eating was definitely a bad idea.

Remembering how Salesman had silently appeared before, he stayed close to the hedgerows along the main road, and kept turning around every few yards to look through the momentary bursts of moonlight to see if all the shadows were really just shadows, and not lurking weirdos. After a while he passed the huge silvery pond, and knew he must be getting closer to the farm, even though he didn't feel as if he was making any progress at all. It seemed to be at least a hundred times further away than before.

The faintest smell of burning drifted on the night air as Bob arrived at the almost invisible track up to the farmhouse. As he reached the front door, his feelings of triumph and relief were immediately obliterated by a far stronger sense of dread. What if someone was in the house? Maybe some kind of low-life was there, or maybe Salesman was a headcase and was hiding in a room, or maybe he was cloaked in darkness and watching him right now? Bob's heart didn't slow down, and he had to summon every ounce of courage to open the door. The door creaked all the way.

"It slides sideways when I go out, swings open coming in.." he whispered under his breath, surprised and yet somehow not surprised, and added it to his List Of Insane Questions for the younger Agatha. Although he couldn't see the kitchen door ahead of him, he knew it was there. He couldn't remember if he had left it open this morning or not, so he shuffled around in his pocket to find his keyring light.. which was back in his bedroom at Barton, awaiting a new battery.

"Marvellous.." he breathed, and took a nervous step inside, convinced that there must be hundreds of armed loons at the top of the stairs. He slowly took another step, then a slower one, and then an even slower one.. and eventually nudged the kitchen door. It silently crept open. A break in the clouds allowed moonlight to suddenly flood the kitchen, and he bolted towards the emergent black void in the wall, gritting his teeth as he leaped through..

CHAPTER EIGHT

Retrospective Disorders

..arriving in a sprawling mess on the upstairs corridor back at 107 Lincoln Drive. He lay still for a moment, making sure that he was really there. The first thing that struck him was that it was still daylight here. The clock was ticking steadily and loudly, showing the time to be almost.. he straightened his head to work it out.

"Five past three? Oh no nonono, it's Monday afternoon already - I'm in even huger trouble.."

He stood up and looked around. Much to his relief the door to the bedroom was closed again. If anyone was going to chase him from way back whenever at the farmhouse, they would have a hard time getting through that. As he went down the staircase, he felt the book in one of his coat pockets bumping against his side. That was Exhibit A, the conclusive proof that he hadn't just dreamed the last few hours - but a talking book would take an awful lot of explaining. So rather than rush to meet whatever fate the world had in store for him, he went through the living room and into the library and opened the compendium to His Lordship's page.

"Here you go, Bagshaw, you fancy a chat with any of these? I'll come back in a while for you, don't worry."

"Jolly decent of you, old boy!" he exclaimed, and replaced his monocle with another one. Bob carefully wandered along a few rows of baffling gibberish so that Bagshaw could see all the titles.

"My word, what an extraordinary collection.. surely these aren't yours, Bob m'lad?"

"Not exactly, they're.."

"Ah, just here will do! A fine example of Biblical texts, and they're all in.. oh my.. they're all in stupendously ancient Aramaic - oh happy day! I'll have a chance to brush up on the old squiggles and whatnots. It's been a while you know.."

Bob left Bagshaw on top of a tall series of cracked, leather-bound books and grudgingly acknowledged that the time had come to go home and meet the first part of his doom.

He looked back at the house from the road, and saw the curtains of the upstairs window shake slightly as Jinx disappeared from the sill. Bob was stunned that she could have been sitting there for such a long time - no cat was that patient.. or weird. He was already feeling tired and the walk back home felt like it took hours, so he decided that next time he ventured out he would definitely take his bike. Anything that would make dismal old Lincoln Drive pass by more quickly had to be worthwhile.

Considering that this was now Monday afternoon, there were a lot of cars parked on driveways and along the pavement of Sea Road. Some people were even flying kites over on the grassy stretches by the cliff tops, which was really strange. But none of this registered with Bob, who was trying to think up plausible excuses for having been 'dead, presumed missing' for a whole day.

He wandered across to Corsair Avenue and wasn't surprised to see both his parents' cars in the driveway. The absence of a police squad was a big relief though. He let himself into the house, with absolutely no useful defence prepared. His mum poked her head out of the kitchen.

"Oh, you back already? I've just made a pot of tea, and there's some of that nice treacle cake from Chewton's but your father's asleep in his chair so don't go putting the telly on in the lounge."

Of all the greetings Bob was expecting, that one hadn't even made the lower reaches of the Top 200. Without saying a word, he ran upstairs to his room and flicked on the tv. One of the sports channels showed Liverpool playing Chelsea, with the small words 'Sunday Sports - LIVE' in the top right corner. He pressed the teletext button, and at the top of the news headlines page was the date, Sun Mar 15, and the time, 15:31.

Bob sat on his bed, too relieved that he'd only been gone for about an hour to even begin worrying about how. The answer would probably lie at Pierpont House, and that could wait a little longer. For the time being he was only too pleased that there were no police, no tv appearances, no hysterical mother, and even better than all of that added together, he hadn't let Andie down. There was still time to finish off the presentation, so the safety of the entire universe could wait another half an hour for him to do it. Even though he was feeling fit to drop and could really do with a shower, he took out his King Harald Hardrada reference books and began sorting out the consequences of the 1031 journey to Palestine.

"It's boring, but at least it's not in freakishly old Aramuhic.. Arameaai.. or Latin," he thought, sparing a moment to marvel at Bagshaw's mind-blowing enthusiasm for the kind of languages which lined the very bottom of history's barrel.

His mum soon came into his room with a cup of tea, along with a slice of cake that was big enough to choke an elephant. She gave an approving smile when she saw all the books spread out, and left without a word. Usually that would annoy Bob, but this time he was quite pleased about it. He wolfed down the cake while a cat meeowed outside, which he found very easy to ignore this time. Maybe it was tiredness, or maybe he was just glad to be back in familiar surroundings, but some things were more important than chasing a cat. Jinx would have to wait another ten minutes while he kept himself in Andie's good books.

Just after four o'clock he went downstairs and leaned into the lounge. His father continued snoring, and his mother looked like she'd soon be doing the same. He whispered across the room to her that he was going to see Andie to run through the presentation. She nodded, more or less, and yawned.

Instead of going to The Coffee Pot or even Number 107 again, he cycled after Jinx to Pierpont House, and walked into the reception area. As expected, nobody was around. Jinx ran from behind him and bounded like a small panther up the stairs. Almost immediately Feiya stepped around the corner, cradling her like a baby. She stopped as soon as she saw him, and stared in disbelief.

"Mirror? Mirrors? Between one and five, where? There's none with you!"

"And hello to you as well. Any chance of a quick word with Great Aunt Agatha?"

"Where the hell.. where is even one Mirror?" she growled. Jinx stared intently at him.

"Take me to your leader, comprendez?" said Bob, who was way past caring about being in trouble. "I need to speak with Great Aunt Agatha about everything - it's all been a bit mad."

She looked down her nose at him, 'hmmph'd a reply, turned around and went back up the stairs, and Bob followed behind. He sat on Agatha's bed, and tried to get everything straight in his mind before beginning, while Feiya sat on the other side anxiously stroking Jinx.

Agatha looked even worse than before.

"Robert, speak to me.. speak.."

Bob gave up trying to figure it all out, and tried not to think at all about what he was going to say.

"Well, I went through the bedroom door, and then I was in a farm in the middle of nowhere, sometime around 1910 I reckon. Nothing much happened except I couldn't find Lexington or even New York, so maybe it hadn't been built yet? But I did find a book that talks back - any idea what that's all that about?"

Agatha looked as if she would have cried, if she had the strength.

"Robert, you went through the wrong room. That wasn't the Master Bedroom, that was a secondary bedroom. You were in Arizona, a harmless place for discrete planning sessions.."

"Arizona? Ahh, so I was in France, then. But everybody who was there was American.. even the money was."

Agatha gave Bob the ultimate look of despair.

"It IS in America, for Heaven's sake. The places through 107 are important to.. to some of us, Robert. They were sites for confidential meetings.. dare I say holidays together.. we all have to get away at times.. and so.. it's all gone so wrong. You really must get to New York, you must. And forget the book, it's no use at all."

"I know, but he means well," said Bob, in Bagshaw's defence.

Feiya jumped in.

"Did you speak to anyone? Does anybody know anything about you or us at all?"

Bob thought for a moment.

"Well.. there's the shopkeeper who sold me the book, he's an old guy called Phingley Parr - honest, that's his name. Nice bloke, I gave him some biros for it. I didn't say anything much to him, and there were one or two others who didn't want to know me at all. And I'm sure there was a really creepy tall guy who let me stay at a hotel, and we were going to find New York tomorrow, but I think he was way off the Weird Ranking System. That's right.. strange character.."

Bob paused, feeling a little concerned.

"Isn't that odd? I can't remember much about him, or even how we met but we must have spoken a lot because of the hotel."

Bob shrugged, and looked from Agatha to Feiya and back again.

"Do you two know him, then?" he asked.

Agatha sighed deeply, and might have nodded. Her movement

was so weak Bob couldn't quite tell.

"Robert, they're onto you. There must be so many more of them than I ever feared. You get to Lexington, it's safe there.. the portals are safe for you.. some very bad people went through them during the Fault.. but.. I doubt they can return until the Security Fields grow weak again during the Alignment on Thursday.. I don't know what they're doing with the Mirrors.. or what they can do."

"Onto me? I thought I was in the clear, you know, born twice can't be followed, and so on?"

Feiya's eyes widened.

"No, Bob! They can't detect you moving through the portals to and from Lincoln Drive, that's all - everything else is normal!"

"Normal?"

Agatha touched Bob's hand and whispered.

"Robert, did he give you anything, something useful to carry around, or wear? This is more important than you can imagine.."

Her voice grew weaker, and she seemed to be struggling to keep her eyes open. Bob thought very hard.

"Yeeah, I vaguely remember he gave me a whistle, in case I was ever in trouble. That's it! He's a traveller too, a salesman!"

Agatha rocked her head slowly from side to side.

"The whistle isn't a whistle, Robert.. it's merely his property and would have acted like a tracking device for every single step through time that you take, whether you used it or not. Something like that is the only way they can trace you. Where is it?"

Bob checked his pockets.

"I must have left it in the hotel.."

Agatha relaxed, but Feiya could barely contain herself.

"Well make sure you left it there Bob! Check back home, check your pockets a million times, check everything! I told you not to trust anyone. Always go with your feelings - if you think someone's being weird, you can't afford to trust them! They might as well be firing a gun at you, it's the same thing. Well, except one's quicker, of course but you have to understa.."

Agatha glanced at her, and she stopped talking. She twisted a thick length of hair around her fingers, and only carried on speaking when she had calmed down.

"Look, you got the wrong room and you even got spotted which is unbelievably bad, so now you need to do two things. First off, try the

Master Bedroom this time, and secondly, do it now, okay? A badly trained chimp could have found the right one and.."

Feiya's words became lost as Bob's mind wandered off to join a stunning pop diva who was at number four or number three in the charts, Viva La Noche-ing her way through a..

Agatha touched Bob's hand again, bringing a halt to this particular interlude.

"Robert.. go back and you'll find me.. you have to, Robert.. Feiya.."

She drifted away into a deep sleep and looked just about ready for burying. Jinx stepped down off the bed, and made her way to the door, followed by Feiya who fumbled twice with the handle and then beckoned Bob to hurry along.

She disappeared into one of the other rooms to fetch her bag and he waited for her on the stairs, surprised that she was humming to herself when she emerged. She seemed to have cannoned to the far side of a mood-swing, and began talking in a pleasant way as they stepped out into the afternoon sun. Jinx had raced ahead and was already much further along the driveway.

"I'll walk with you if that's okay, Bob - I have to go up to the house anyway. The fresh air might clear my head a bit as well."

Bob really wasn't sure what to make of her, but if she was in better spirits he wouldn't mind her coming along at all. She might save him from dreaming up reasons to be even more confused and paranoid. He waited until they had reached the start of Marine Drive before daring to start up a conversation with her.

"I vaguely know what Aunt Agatha does, but what's your role in everything? And how did you get into this in the first place? I don't expect it's the kind of job that gets advertised much? After the kind of day I've just been through you can't imagine how many questions I've got, Feiya."

"One hundred and thirty three precisely, which is pretty poor. When I started off I had over a thousand, and then a load more occurred to me. I'm working my way through them, steadily."

Bob sensed she was avoiding the other questions, so he tried again.

"Ahem.. how did you get into this?"

"Can't tell you. It's classified"

"Okay, so.. the thing that you do each day is?"

"..is also classified. If I did tell you, I'd have to kill you which in this case would be entirely counter-productive, so I'm better off by not telling you."

"Thanks very much. I owe you a cup of tea sometime."

He noticed Feiya smile to herself, and for a moment she looked almost like a perfectly normal and attractive woman. He dared another question.

"Are there loads of different departments in Pierpont House? It looks a bit small for that.."

"No, it's only Time these days, plus our communication links to essential staff. There's hardly any of us there. We all used to be in the Lexington Building, you see. It was so good there. Then the whole Guardianship structure was decentralised a while ago, which is why we became so vulnerable. The rest is classified, of course. Madame Agatha will tell you lots more than I can, when you find her."

They walked past The Coffee Pot, and Bob looked over the road to see if Andie was in the café, or maybe at one of the windows.

"Special lady?" grinned Feiya.

"No! Well, you know, not really.. well that sounds bad, she is special to me.. ever so sp.. that's all classified."

Bob knew he had to change the subject before he started turning redder than a sunburnt lobster. It was probably too late for that, but he changed the subject anyway.

"Umm.. if I go to old New York and stayed with young Great Aunt Agatha in the past and tell her everything, she'll know what's going to happen and none of this needs to occur.. right?"

Feiya gave a long sigh at Bob's complete lack of understanding.

"Bob, you've not had any training at all in this, okay? Your level of comprehension is as basic as it gets. A little bit of time-hopping does not mean you should take any decisions on your own, or be tempted to work out your own theories, okay? This is a big spicy meatball and you have to chew it properly."

"Fair enough.." Bob replied, trying to avoid getting her cross. "Did she say meatball?" he wondered to himself.

"But let's say you do stay in New York, way back somewhere in the past. You tell the younger Madame Agatha everything and then settle into her world back then, whenever that was. The years pass by and the moment comes along when the theft happens. In the meantime Madame Agatha and the rest of the Guardians have had plenty of time to figure out how to stop the Mirrors being taken, so therefore they never actually get taken, and the world carries on like nothing's happened."

"But that's good, isn't it?"

"Almost. Tiny problem, though - Madame Agatha is the one who sent you back in the first place, and that's a BIG tiny problem. If the Mirrors are never stolen, modern you wouldn't ever have needed to go back to see Madame Agatha in the past, so how could you have warned her - and managed to have lived the rest of your life there - when she never sent you there in the first place? The loop in time would never close, and that'll be an 'oops' I do believe - and that's why it's modern you that has to get them back, rather than younger Madame Agatha acting on a tip-off regarding the future. Simple. Hence you have to 'retrieve' them, not 'prevent' them, from being stolen. Not un-interfering yourself into a hole would be stupid."

"Uhh.. what's that in English?"

"In even simpler terms? Umm.. you have to do it, not her. I think that all the younger Madame Agatha will do when you meet her is.. I don't know, maybe get you up to speed, hopefully. Understand?"

Bob was trying to unravel how he could do whatever Feiya had been saying.

"Uhh.. so I don't.. umm.. she doesn't.. and I have to.."

"Exactly. Think of it like this. Imagine you walk into a room and find a time machine, and travel back just one minute. You get out of the machine, and hold the room's door shut - preventing the other you from ever getting in."

"Uhh.."

"Yes. How could you be holding the door shut if you never went inside the room in the first place? Interfering with your own past is SO bad. But you can't avoid it in this case, can you? Your creating a past which could wipe out your own future - and Madame Agatha's, and.. people you haven't met yet, and me, maybe. Retrospective Disorders are the bane of my life. I wrote a book all about them.. passed a few laws as well."

Feiya stopped for a moment, and scratched her head.

"Or maybe that doesn't apply here, due to how you move through time.. damn it, I'll be up all night sorting that one out. The worst thing about Dimensional Theories is that the only way to find out which ones are right involves getting into such an awful mess in the first place.. which we hardly ever deliberately do, and this one is way too serious to try testing any out. But once you've got the Mirrors back, we'll have either not proved that some don't work, or maybe undisproved the others - so that's a silver lining, I suppose. Temporary Alternate Existence, Parallel Time Lines, all that stuff.. the big prob with this particular situation is that it's never happened before - so we're going to have to find out an awful lot as we go along. Major headscratch for everyone then, isn't it?"

She looked at him, expectantly.

"Uhhuh.."

"Quite. Oh, and here's something to be careful of - keep a low profile wherever you go, not just because of all those people who might want to kill you, but because of the Non-Existence Dilemma."

Bob managed a whimper.

"Yes, it's that awful. You might interrupt the chain of events that lead the right people to meet all the other right people which eventually allowed you to end up being born years later. There's a headache. How could you exist anywhere if you weren't born in the first place? Or in your case you weren't just not not-born once, you were also not not-born twice? Ooh, that's bad.."

"Uhhhh.." Bob said, like someone who'd been meditating for far too long. If Feiya kept on talking, his brain might spontaneously combust - but she was on a roll, and had even developed a spring in her step.

"You'll just have to cross your fingers and hope it doesn't happen. See, you really have no idea how fragile existence and its relationship with the whole passage of time can be. Once you start interfering, you can't undo that interference, not without spending years figuring out what happened and why, and even then all you can do is decide on a Best Case Scenario to try and improve a situation, or perhaps remove your fingerprints from it.. oh, I shouldn't have said that last bit. Forget that. Scratch it."

Bob nodded rather than saying 'Uhh' again. Feiya didn't notice though. She was trying to keep her balance while walking along the edge of the kerb.

"Where was I? Oh yes. Every single thing you do in your life has a knock-on effect somewhere else. I've spent over fifty years studying Analytical Cause & Consequence and I specialised in Advanced Domino Theory - and believe me, that isn't easy. There are some mind-blowing cases throughout history, and you don't know any of them yet. Some events that are historical facts to you at the moment are actually the result of hundreds of meetings and interventions, big and small ones, and there's no way you would ever know which ones I'm talking about, which goes to show how well we do things!"

"Yes," agreed Bob, pleased to have understood enough to offer a comment. But had she really said fifty years studying something? Maybe it was fifteen, and even fifteen years studying anything would be far too long.

"You just need enough discipline to realise that there are some areas in your life, like now for instance, where you have to spend a lot of time learning without thinking. You know why?"

"Umm.. no?"

"Because while you're doing that, you're actually learning how to think. It just takes a long time, that's all."

"I can handle not thinking, pretty much. But what if I do think of something? It happens occasionally, and might be the right thing.."

"Oh for Heaven's sake, Bob. Here's the simplest analogy I can manage and if you don't understand this I'll resort to using hand-puppets - and you do NOT want to see what I'll do with them," she said, and gave Bob the kind of glare which Agatha would have been proud of.

"In a very tiny nutshell, all I'm saying is that you shouldn't try running before you can walk. And at the moment you're at least twenty years away from realising you even have legs."

"Ohh, right.."

"So don't worry about anything except finding the right room this time - or who knows where you'll end up. Honestly, I wish it wasn't you doing this, 'cause I could sort it much.."

"Woah, rewind - don't you know where the doors lead to?"

Bob sensed a very heavy weight was about to land on him. Feiya tugged a leafy stem from a bush which had grown over someone's garden wall, and rubbed it between her hands.

"Mmm.. lavender. No, of course I don't know. I'm only allowed in a couple of the rooms on the ground floor if Madame Agatha is with any of us.. or me on my own with her - and those rooms are just normal ones that lead nowhere. Only certain Guardians, and people called Bob who don't exist - which is you - can go anywhere else. Not exactly fair if you ask me, Your Highness. I'm not like you because I don't not exist, as such."

The queen of the double negative had struck again. Bob's tired brain was slowing down, and he couldn't even begin to think how long he'd actually been awake. He stared out towards the sea. All this confusing time-talk wasn't helping him feel better about anything. A few moments of silence passed before he picked a new subject that he felt capable of handling.

"This road's a bit grim isn't it? Why would the portal house be somewhere like Lincoln Drive instead of having it at Pierpont?"

"It's the whole wretched decentralisation process. No joke, the bureaucracy's gone crazy these last few years, and us having two sites means the security's better, supposedly. It's like how Government Ministers never travel all at the same time in the same plane, just in case it crashes. Same principle, but in this case it's been done in a totally inappropriate way. Madame Agatha's spent years fuming about it.. and that's not pleasant.."

A slate tumbled from the roof of Number 57 which made Bob jump, but Feiya ignored it completely.

"But why this grotty stretch?"

"It's meant to be grotty. Neighbours can be so troublesome and inquisitive, and we tend not to approve of that so we encouraged the ones along here to leave. You know when bad dreams feel ever so real? Well sometimes there's a very good reason why."

She interrupted herself with another of those loud, short bursts of laughter that sent shivers down Bob's spine.

"So once they'd all gone away we got some of Angharrad's drones from the Department Of Nature to do the landscaping and turn this stretch of coastline into something of immensely hideous unappealing..ness, and then we fixed the house so that nobody can even see in, never mind get in. Even birds don't fly over! How good is that?"

Bob had no idea how good that was, so he just nodded. They arrived at the driveway of Number 107, and despite the stressful time just a few minutes earlier at Pierpont House, the walk had actually been a nice one. But now Jinx was waiting in the upstairs window, looking down at them. Feiya seemed very nervous and followed Bob to the front door, staying close to him. She stepped away a little while he fiddled with the key.

"I need to go in Jinxy - I have to check the Comms Desk! Bob will be with me, okay?" she called up to Jinx's window, who briefly glanced down at her. The door opened as soon as Bob's key touched the lock, and he headed straight for the library.

"Hey Feiya!" he called, waving the compendium in the air, "I left Bagshaw in here to make some new friends! He's that talking book I was on about - how far south of Jupiter is that? Unreal!"

Feiya had remained just inside the front door, on the small mat. Bob hurried back to show her his book, and was surprised that she wasn't in the slightest bit interested.

"How exciting for you, Bob. Come on, come onn nowww.." she pleaded, pointing towards the parlour door.

"None of these are locked, you know Fey. This key's just for the outside doors.. or aren't you allowed to open doors in here?" he said while giving the door a push. It smoothly and silently obliged. Feiya stayed where she was while he went inside.

"No.." she called to him, "..I can't even open the doors that lead to the rooms I'm allowed into, unless they're already open and then that doesn't count, in which case I can go through" she garbled, with a higher pitch creeping into her voice. Bob was beginning to wonder about her again as he walked through the parlour. She still waited in the hallway while he opened the white door to what he now knew to be the Communications Room.

"Excellent!" she cried with genuine enthusiasm, and even before the door was partially open she had run across and squeezed her way through the gap.

"I'll show you this, Bob, but only because I've been requested to by Madame Agatha," she said, raising her voice through the sentence as if informing the entire house of what she was doing there.

"Yeah, I meant to ask you about that.." said Bob, pointing at the mass of Memo-Its all over the desk. Feiya quickly scrawled another one, and after a quick survey of the other few hundred, stuck it carefully into place.

"These are meant to disappear from here and reappear on the Guardian Of Spatial Dynamics' very own personal desk. Not even his advisers, assistants or secretaries see them - this is as direct as it gets for me, short of standing in front of him and talking loudly - and I'm not allowed to do that.. anymore. But it's not working and I just can't believe they're not looking into it. Maybe it's too late, and they're all dead? Maybe the Troublers have taken over the most powerful and biggest department already? This would all be pointless, and far too late, no use at all and.."

Bob could see she was getting stressed again so he tried doing what he always tried to do with his parents, and calm the choppy waters.

"Troublers? They're the bad guys, I take it? Well maybe they have got a foot in the door of whatever that department is, but I would have thought they'd need control of Time first? Once that's sewn up, they're home and dry aren't they? I know I've got just about no idea what's going on, or how any of this works, or what I'm supposed to be doing.. or anything.. but we still have a chance to change things, don't we?"

Bob realised he was talking top-grade Utter Drivel. One more sentence and he might set a personal best. He took a deep breath and continued.

"I know enough to bring Aunt Agatha's old younger self in the past right up to date with all the things that are happening now, and she can sort out what to do because.."

Feiya wasn't listening. Her teeth began chattering as if she was freezing cold and her gaze was locked somewhere between herself and the door to the study. Her eyes began darting around the room growing wider and wider as a look of panic spread over her face. Suddenly she half ran and half stumbled back into the parlour, and then bolted for the front door. If Bob didn't know any better, he would have said she was being thrown out of the house by invisible things of a scary nature. But this was Feiya, and part of him expected her to be acting a little strange. After all, everything looked and felt fine to him.

The front door slammed loudly behind her, and Bob watched from the parlour window as she hurried past the front wall and back along the road. If there was one person in the entire world who needed a nice long holiday, she was the one.

As Bob climbed the stairs, he began to wonder just how many Troublers were out there waiting for him. Why were they trying to take over, and more to the point, what were they taking over? But the more he wondered about them, he couldn't help but wonder a whole lot more about Great Aunt Agatha and Feiya, and just what kind of organisation they were part of. His biggest ever knot began forming all around his stomach, so he stopped thinking about questions that he had no chance of answering and tried to remember which rooms he'd already looked into. The grandfather clock over by the expanse of windows now showed the time to be three minutes after five o'clock.

"Well that depends on how you look at everything, really," he said to himself, "..'cause it's all relative."

His unintentional pun made him laugh nervously as he went towards the end of the corridor, and shivered as he passed the Arizona portal, and he swung open the next door along from it. This looked a vaguely similar size to its neighbour, but had two single beds in it, each occupying a differently decorated half. One half contained very modern looking furniture, not a million miles away from the angular kind in trendy shops, while the other half was far more conservative. His mum would approve of that half. No Master Bedroom could look this bizarre, so Bob closed the door and tried the room opposite, the one just along from the windows. It was only another bathroom.

He wandered back along the corridor, and turned left to the short corridor before the stairway. Unbelievably, there was a room near the end, supposedly behind the wrong bedroom he had entered earlier. Stunned beyond words, he opened the door and looked into a huge drawing room complete with roaring fireplace, big old fashioned globe, book cabinets and a few portraits like the ones in the dining doom. Judging by the bay windows over on the right, Bob could tell he was above the living room but there was no possible way that such a large room could fit into the available space. This house was going to have the highest Freak Factor ever recorded, which was probably not a strong selling-point if Agatha ever wanted to put it on the market. He closed the door, and tried the small room behind him, which by his reckoning was immediately above the parlour.

Nothing. Nothing but pitch blackness. Where the door ended, there was absolute nothingness, just a darkness that felt like it was reaching out for ever. Bob was mesmerised by the feeling of incomprehensible depth until his knees gave way under the most awesome wave of vertigo. He swayed like the entire world was being turned upside down, then he keeled over backwards and the door closed itself. Bob lay on the floor waiting for his heart to stop pounding, and tried desperately hard not to think of what would have happened if he'd fallen forwards. He crawled most of the way back towards the main corridor that stretched across the house, and eventually managed to stand up straight again using the final short column of the banister. Once the floor had stopped shaking, or maybe that was his knees, he looked at the two remaining doors.

He walked past the top of the stairs and found that the remaining door across the corridor was yet another bathroom, and might even have been the same one that he'd looked at when he came in from the balcony.. but that was too confusing to think about. Instead, he closed it and turned to face a highly varnished, very broad door.

"How did I miss this?" Bob wondered, as he grasped the ornate handle and turned it downwards. The key around his neck gave a warm glow, the lock gave a solid 'ka-thunk' and the door slowly started to open, tugging itself away from his hand.

This should, by all accounts, have lead to a small room. The stairway down to the hall began less than a foot to the left of the door, and the large window at the end of the upstairs corridor was only a few feet to its right - but if ever a bedroom earned the title of Master Bedroom, then this one certainly did. It looked like it was twice the length of the house, at least the same width, with a long white arch dividing and spanning the room midway down. A huge four-poster bed draped in white and cream lay near the tinted window at the far end, just visible through a swaying veil of chiffon. White wardrobes ran along the entire left side, separated in the middle by a huge vanity table that could offer plenty of space for an entire troupe of beauty queens. Three doors ran along the opposite wall with large scenic paintings hanging between them, ending with an elaborate writing desk near to where he was standing. The soft light from three tastefully-designed chandeliers gave a warm glow to the room and Bob was stunned, yet again.

The grandeur of the room was so completely overpowering that for the briefest of moments, the prospect of entering another time and place simply didn't register with him at all. His tired mind decided he should try finding out what was behind each of the other doors, and as he stepped into the room, he suddenly remembered that he wasn't going to get there..

CHAPTER NINE
The New New Yorker

..and instead found himself standing in a large, warm and fairly subdued room instead.

He could tell that he'd changed one opulent place for another, but this one was shrouded in early-morning darkness and the kind of quiet serenity that he could almost touch. For a few moments he tried to make sense of the blurred and dull shapes around him, but decided he really ought to go and first open some of the curtains over on the other side. Their velvet folds must have been at least ten feet tall, and for a while Bob groped around looking for cords to pull. He soon drew open the first pair, allowing enough soft sunshine in through the net curtain to reveal a stylish room around half the size of the Master Bedroom. A single chandelier hung above the large central table, casting faint triangles of morning light onto the walls.

He picked up a triangular clock from a table near the window, and held it in the light. The time was two or three minutes past six, which lead Bob to figure that six in the morning must be the usual time for arriving anywhere from Lincoln Drive. He then figured that with all this sunlight it must be summer, not that it mattered - his brain was getting ready for hibernation, regardless. He yawned and looked over to the place where he'd just come from, but could only see a wide expanse of a subtle-patterned wallpaper. A framed door stood further along the wall, but he knew there was no way he'd entered from that far across. He hurried closer to the area where he thought he had arrived, and as he came to within a few feet of the wall a small trembling circle about the size of a golf ball appeared, and exploded into an elaborate archway with a blue staircase leading steeply upwards. Bob took a few steps backwards, and triggered the process in reverse, leaving just an ordinary hotel wall behind.

"Nice, nice.." he said, appreciating how far from completion the portal in the farmhouse must have been.

A few magazines were neatly fanned out on the oval table in the centre of the room, so Bob sat down and took a look at them. The top magazine was a copy of The New Yorker, dated July 23rd 1927. Bob felt fairly sure that this was new, which was a relief because that meant he was definitely in the right place this time. A copy of The New York Times from the day after was the icing on the cake. He picked up The New Yorker and sat in a soft high-backed chair and opened it up in the hope of finding something resembling a map, or to try and get himself prepared for a day in New York.. but he was too tired to sort out what he was trying to do. He stared at the cover illustration for a while. It showed an elegantly exaggerated woman sitting at a table underneath a starry Manhattan night sky, having a cocktail with her equally elongated boyfriend. Just as Bob started wondering if the drawing was based on a real place and whether or not Andie might like it there one day, the magazine began slipping from his lap and he was asleep before it had even reached the floor.

He woke up as the clock in a nearby room chimed for the eleventh time, and was pleased to notice that for the first time in far too long, he actually felt like he was awake. He opened the centre of the net curtain, and took a proper look out at where he was.

"I'm a very long way up, that's where I am. Mental Note: do not climb out of this one," he said to himself as he looked down about fifteen floors to the busy street below.

Vast black cars crawled along the wide roads, and trams and omnibuses hurried people to the important places that they all had to get to. Bob looked out in awe across the most amazing landscape he'd ever seen. Countless huge buildings towered majestically over their neighbours for as far as he could see, and even way off in the hazy distance a few peaks of the really tall ones were still visible. He took a few minutes to simply look out at the hustle and bustle of Manhattan, drawn into the incredible burgeoning energy of the city.

His attention wandered around and down to individual buildings, large stores, smaller stores and finally the tiny shops in the street.. and then back to the huge buildings again. His heart jumped for a moment and he had to look twice at one building just a few blocks away. A raised black spire similar to the one on the house at Lincoln Drive sat above the intervening few buildings - surely another 107 right here would be too weird by a mile?

"Could be anything, might be part of a church.." he said, trying to avoid any more stress - but he figured he'd have a look on his way to finding the Lexington Building, just to make sure. Unless of course, this already was Number 1, where he needed to be? But that seemed highly unlikely as nobody else was around. He figured there were two options. The first involved wandering around this grand apartment looking for Agatha, and therefore running the risk of meeting homicidal Troublers who might be waiting to hack him to pieces. And as if that wasn't bad enough he might also run the risk of stumbling across another portal and being zapped into another time and place entirely, which was even less appealing than being hacked. Slightly.

So Bob chose option two, which he knew would please Feiya. It involved leaving right now, going to find Agatha and worrying about this place later. Besides, he was starting to feel very hungry again.

He went over to the huge pair of double doors nearest him, and watched the two handles move towards each other. The doors swung open by themselves to reveal a wide circular room with a grand piano over on the far side with a series of Renaissance-styled chairs around it. Six huge windows ran from the right side around to a pair of doors next to an elaborate opening to a hallway - which was full of more doors. Simply getting out of this place looked like it would take a long time. Bob stayed where he was, and the doors closed again.

He opened up the other two curtains to let the full daylight in, and then crossed the room to try the framed door on the side which contained the portal. It opened easily and lead to a broad and ornately decorated corridor. A large diamond shape was stitched into the otherwise plain royal-blue carpet, which would be a good marker for showing which room he needed to come back to. Going right would lead to somewhere near the circular room, so he went left and walked past almost a dozen doors with intricately engraved emblems carved into the woodwork above each one. He reached the door at very end of the corridor, and opened it to reveal.. an even wider corridor running left and right.

"Great Aun.." he began, and looked at the gold-framed portrait of an elderly woman which hung on the wall ahead of him. She looked very important indeed, and her eyes were so similar to Agatha's that he had to pause for a moment and take a second look. There was another diamond shape in the rich green carpet beneath the picture which he tried to add to his growing list of Serious Mental Notes.

"Bagshaw, hey Bagshaw?" he said, and took out the compendium.

His Lordship had disappeared. The background was still there and so were the top leaves of the rubber plant, but he was gone. Bob tried looking at different angles to see if he could get a better glimpse into the picture, but that didn't seem to work.

"Bagshaw? Have you gone somewhere?"

A few moments passed before he returned into his picture frame, clutching a thick pile of loose papers in one arm and a quill-pen in the other.

"Ah, Bob m'lad! Thought I heard you. I've been scribing a gargantuan mountain of notes - those scholars were such company! What a collection, such knowledge. Did you know some of them date from the year 45AD? Their grasp of English leaves a little to be desired but oh, their command of.."

"That's great in a way, and definitely tell me later, okay? But in the meantime - do you know who this is?"

Bob held the book up to the portrait, and Bagshaw put a monocle up to his other eye.

"Bit closer.. bit closer.." he instructed, "Now then, to me that looks like.. Astrid Thoresein. Yes, definitely Astrid Thoresein, unmistakeable, no less. A most beloved lady, I believe."

"Good one! Who was she?"

"No idea at all. I merely read the name plaque underneath the picture. Any others you want reading, old boy?"

Bob sighed.

"No, maybe not just yet. Are you familiar with New York?"

"New York? Ah, I last came here in '93, by mistake. Long story and a little embarrassing really. Her name was Martha something or another, or maybe she wasn't? Anyway, I'm certain we were in New York though, or maybe Tarapoto.. wait a moment, let me see now.. it's the elephants with small ears that are from there, and so.." he muttered vaguely, and wandered off to check.

"I'll get back to you, Bagshaw old chap.." and Bob put the book back in his pocket.

The corridor lead off to the right, ending far away in the distance with a small window - which Bob figured would actually be huge if he went all the way along to it. Each side was lined by important-looking doors with portraits and landscapes hung between every second or third one, which he cast an eye over as he wandered along.

He passed a few side-corridors and two narrow lifts (which flatly refused to open) before arriving at a main junction which lead off to the left. It looked as if it joined up with a parallel corridor over on the other side of the floor, as if these three main passageways made a large 'H' shape. Bob's head was spinning. Despite all the smaller routes leading off from these major ones, there wasn't a solitary sign anywhere. Whoever designed this place must have been one of those flawed genius types - the kind who could create the world's greatest car and forget to leave space for the driver.

Bob took the joining corridor, the one that linked the two sides of the H, and soon gave a small triumphant cheer as he arrived in a kind of lobby area midway along. A wall of five doors, each with narrow glass windows, formed a barrier of panels which blocked the way to the other side. He peered through the glass to where six elevators stood at the top of a magnificent staircase. The panels were each locked in at least a dozen places, but before Agatha's key had even touched the first lock, a series of clicks and judders smoothly travelled around the central panel. It withdrew up into the ceiling, and the pairs remaining either side silently flattened themselves against each wall, in a concertina fashion. He went through and they firmly rattled shut behind him, forming an impenetrable wooden wall with a single, mundane door in the centre - even the glass sections looked like wood. Bob shivered at the latest weirdness, and added it to the list of Other Stuff To Ask About.

He opted for the stairs rather than take an elevator and risk encountering Otis's First Law, which states that the chances of being trapped in a lift with a deranged psycho-loon for company are directly proportional to your urgency to leave the building. The banister rail was more than wide enough for sliding but every now and then the iron-mesh safety grill would suddenly leave a sizeable gap, and the drop on the other side of the rail was such a stomach-churner that he decided to be conventional and walk.

The landing sections of alternate floors were resplendent with drinking fountains and chairs, probably for those occasions when the lifts didn't work. Climbing these stairs would be a nightmare, but going down them was a blast so Bob carried on swinging around the big right-hand corners, flight after flight after flight.. except when he could hear voices coming from below. People meandered to and fro on many of the floors, dressed in smart clothes that were far lighter and occasionally more colourful than those in Arizona. Times had obviously changed, but not by too much, he guessed.

He finally arrived in the reception area, stepping from the stairs onto a vast marble-chessboard floor, which stretched out twenty or thirty yards to an arched entrance away to the right. The chatter of a dozen or so people in small groups echoed above the light splashing of a central fountain, and filled the foyer with life. Smartly dressed porters helped some with their suitcases, and laboured for others with masses of shopping bags. This was a definite place for Andie.

He stood at the end of an excessively long reception desk, waiting to ask someone where he was. After a few minutes, the desk was still unoccupied so Bob craned his neck to look at one of the upside down note pads.

"Broadway's Finest, New York's Finest, The World's Finest - The Ansonia - 2107 Broadway," he said quietly. He was relieved that at last he knew what building he was in, the date, and according to the gold-rimmed clock supported by an under-dressed statue of a life-size dancing girl, he now knew the time as well.

"11.43am precisely. Time to go.."

Bob slowly walked down the dozen steps from The Ansonia and spent a moment just standing in the bright sunshine, looking out at Broadway and trying to take in the epic scale of the buildings, the roads, and the wild mixture of sounds - all wrapped up in searing July heat. He tried to cross the road while transfixed by the elegant enormity of The Dorilton just a block or so away, and was honked at by a cumbersome black and yellow taxi. That snapped him out of his daze, and brought him back to planet Earth with a bump.

He needed to get a good view of the hotel, to know which of the huge buildings around him he would have to come back to, so he took refuge at a crossing-island in the middle of the lanes. A sign pointed out that he was at an entrance to the IRT subway, and he narrowly avoided being caught up in a group of people who were going into it, and then another who were coming out of it. He turned around to look up at the biggest and most elaborate building he'd ever seen. It was seventeen stories of gleaming white limestone and countless shades of brick and terracotta. Each of its floors were decorated with hundreds of intricately worked balconies and windows, which all added up to make it look like a cross between a palace and an over-worked wedding cake - with a few turrets planted on the top for good measure. And for Bob that was a huge relief because The Ansonia wouldn't be too difficult to find again.

An overloaded tram rattled closely by and drew his attention to the black-spired building that he had thought was another version of Number 107. Down at street level it looked about a million times bigger, and much to his relief it actually was a church, with absolutely nothing unusual or creepy about it. He wandered past a few shops and stores, looking for a sign that would hopefully say Lexington. The one he found said Amsterdam Avenue, and a little further along this became Tenth Avenue. The street numbers were all in the high sixties and low seventies, and after a few minutes of random wandering, he stood at another sign, feeling puzzled at how the street numbers were still around the seventies.

He knew he'd have to ask for directions, but could he trust anyone? The bad guys might look as normal as anyone else, unless they were all a bit tall and creepy like the Salesman freak. The knot grew bigger as he wandered along the block, but quickly disappeared as the friendly aroma of coffee reached out and greeted him. Although Gerstle's Café and the few people inside were as unrecognisable as anybody else, the smells and the atmosphere were pure Coffee Pot and Bob felt like he was with friends. He noticed the woman behind the counter's cake display looking him over as he walked in.

"Hello, I'm with the theatre, don't panic. My clothes.." he began.

"It ain't your clothes, sweetie, it's you. You look like you seen a ghost! Have you eaten today?"

Bob was surprised that anyone was bothered.

"No, come to think of it. It's probably been a couple of days since I had a proper meal. But I'm from England and I haven't got any American money so.."

The woman laughed, and pointed at a seat.

"Take a seat an' sit down, you c'n have a bite and a coffee too - but don't go tellin' no-one!"

He settled on a tall chrome stool at the counter, and watched as the waitress leaned through the serving hatch to the kitchen. She made a loud request and quickly returned with a pile of thick pancakes dripping with golden syrup. Although they were some way past their prime, Bob demolished them.

"So you're with the thee-atre?"

"Uhh.. kind of. I'm looking for a relative who lives somewhere round here. Do you know where Number One, Lexington is? Do go easy, 'cause I can't sort out these avenue numbers and streets and everything.. they're all over the place.."

"Nahh, it's a pizza-cake here. Avenues go north and south, an' streets run east an' west so if you're looking for the start of Lexington Avenue, you just walk south down this one, Columbus Avenue, to 59th Street, which runs across it like streets do. There it's a good idea to head east, that'll be a 'left' for you, seein' as you're new here, and don't get mashed crossing Columbus Circle - wooh it's big. An' you keep going past Central Park till y'find a sign sayin' Lexington Avenue, head on down to 20-whatever street where that longboy starts, an' Gramercy Park stops you goin' too far anyhows. Easy!"

"Wow, you really know this place," said Bob, impressed.

"Nah, I'm cheatin' you, I grew up just a few blocks beyond - but you'll be a new New Yorker by the time you get there!"

Bob wrote the general points down on a serviette, and kept the conversation light just in case someone was listening. Bagshaw also made a note of the directions, translating them into Greek just for fun.

"Fun?" Bob whispered down to his Barmy Aristocrat pocket, immediately going red as a girl at a near by table gave him a quizzical look. After another coffee he was back on the asphalt and cramming an emergency muffin into his newly allocated Ration pocket.

He knew he was getting closer with every step to Agatha's residence, so he didn't allow anywhere near as much dawdling time for looking at the buildings, shops and people as he would have liked. Besides, there was so much hustle of daily life going on around him that he couldn't have dawdled even if he wanted to.

He soon arrived at a tall black signpost, one arm of which pointed along East 59th St, and within a block Bob was faced with a huge circular traffic island running around a tall monument of Christopher Columbus. He checked his notes, and they were still making sense. As he ran from street to street in the protection of other crowds of hurrying pedestrians, he looked back along tree-lined Broadway initially to see if his life was about to end, but apart from a car bumper he caught a view of The Ansonia far off in the distance. That made him feel less isolated, and spurred him on.

The journey then became a little surreal. For almost half an hour he wandered by the railings of a huge park that might just as well have reached all the way back to England. He turned around a few times, slowly taking in the contrast between a seemingly endless stretch of nature, and the towering facades of skyscrapers which were only separated by enormous jam-packed roads. Just as he was beginning to feel sure that he must have missed the sign and ought to turn back and check them all again, he gave his second triumphant cheer of the day, all be it a stifled one to avoid embarrassment. Lexington Avenue at last lay before him.. and judging by the street number he only had thirty or forty more crazy roads to cross.

"Marvellous.."

Most of the frenzied drivers didn't seem to realise that people weren't built as strongly as cars, so Bob was glad to be alive by the time he reached a signpost with East 21st St written on it. He looked around for a huge flashing neon sign displaying the words 'Over Here, Bob!' - but it must have been turned off.

In this area there were fewer shops, and the buildings were either large residential ones, or mundane offices. Gramercy Park appeared like an oasis amidst all the concrete and stone, so Number One had to be around there somewhere. He scratched his head and looked around. A fairly tall building, perhaps a dozen stories high stood at the end of the block opposite where he was standing. Its first two floors were pale stone, and everything above was a rich, red brick colour. The spiralling keystones above each of the dozens of windows and the intricate metalwork of the slim balconies made Bob feel that this building had enough subtle similarities to The Ansonia to be just the kind of place where Great Aunt Agatha should be.

A familiar knot started in his stomach.

CHAPTER TEN

No1 Lexington Avenue

Bob crossed over a couple more roads and leaned against the railings outside Gramercy Park for a while, watching smart people arriving, leaving and passing the entrance to the tall building. Hopefully one of them would look like a considerably younger version of Agatha, and maybe she'd be carrying a big placard with her name written on it.

Huge black cars that seemed to be only slightly less dangerous than the ones Bob had avoided for the past couple of hours continually pulled up outside, barely allowing people enough time to get in and out before roaring off again.

A few long minutes went by until Bob felt that Agatha probably wasn't going to walk past, so perhaps the time had arrived to go inside. He darted between the cars and ran to a short covered way which lead over a narrow dry moat. He heard barking coming from somewhere, and looked over the stone handrail and down at a pack of Alsations that were trotting by underneath, followed by a security guard. He was about to point them out to Bagshaw, but a group of serious-looking people blustered past behind him, probably en route to an important meeting. Talking to a book could easily give the wrong impression, so he nervously checked that his shirt was properly tucked in and the buttons were done up correctly, and made his way up the steps at the end of the covered way.

He knocked on the entrance doors. They were even bigger than the ones at The Ansonia, and felt cold and hard, as if they had been made of granite and simply painted to look like wood. Neither of them had anything resembling a handle or even a metal panel to push, which was worrying because his knocks were making practically no sound. After half a dozen attempts his knuckles had turned red, which wasn't the best of starts. He looked around for anyone who might be going in, but surprisingly there were very few people near, and the few who were within asking-range seemed to be locked in deep conversations. He stepped back and tried to find a hidden bell to prod or pull, but there was nothing. He tried knocking again, and then resorted to pushing instead.

"Hello there? That side's always locked, but this side's open.." smiled a young woman as she effortlessly opened the other half with the slightest of touches. She gestured for him to go through, and Bob went a hopeless shade of Dimwit Red before stepping into the reception hall.

Audacious, ostentatious, and dozens of other words ending in 'ious' that Bob hadn't a hope of either pronouncing or spelling were all entirely appropriate for this place. He didn't know where to look first. His eyes followed a dozen square columns which merged into high broad arches, and guided the way to a reception area at the far end. Instead of chandeliers, which Bob was half expecting to see, there were a series of wide-bladed fans lazily spinning at the ends of golden shafts. Back down at his level, a series of long Oriental rugs ran across the mahogany floor, and he tried to decide if he shouldn't be stepping on the carpets or shouldn't be stepping on the heavily polished panelling. Even the vases at the base of each pillar were taller than him, and he stood before one of them watching people rush, scurry and occasionally just walk by, and felt even more out of place than he looked.

He turned to the woman he'd come in with, but she had already begun trotting up Staircase One, which for some strange reason lay in between Staircases Two and Six. Staircase Four was much narrower and had its first few steps missing, but the others seemed to be almost normal - just all in the wrong order. He shook his head and walked silently to the reception desk, which looked more like an over-staffed and very large cinema-ticket kiosk. The principal receptionist behind the low glass finished talking into her old-fashioned headset and smiled professionally at him.

"Yes? An' yoowarrr.." she said in a high-pitched statement, rather than a question.

"I'm Bob, umm.. I doubt you know me. I'm here to see Great Aun.. uhh.. Madame Agatha over an issue of immensely important and urgent magnitude..inous..ness."

Feiya's habit of attaching new endings to words was highly contagious, and Bob hoped it would help.

"One moment please.." she said, without changing her expression. She pressed a series of buttons, and waited for the connection.

"The line's engaged.. I'll try again shawwtly. Please get seated.. ov'thayuhh," she said, with a vague wave.

Bob looked around and began wandering over to a row of court chairs against a short wall, which ended with a gramophone that had been playing light orchestral music. A uniformed old man, who was seated on its other side, snored gruffly and nearly woke himself up. Suddenly a voice driven insane with rage roared across the hall.

"NO! YOU SHOULD BE DEAD, DAMN YOU! WHAT IN THE NAME OF ASLAK ARE YOU DOING HERE?"

Bob felt as if a bucket of icy water had been thrown over him. He looked across the reception area to see a large red-faced man storming towards him from one of the staircases, waving a clenched fist. Bob knew the end must be nigh, as this headcase looked capable of taking on an entire police force, and maybe the ones from a few other states as well. He stopped in front of Bob, towering over him like a colossus, close enough for Bob to look up and see the loon's bloodshot right eye twitching far more than Ms Gibben's ever did. Bob's legs turned to jelly, and he knew he couldn't run anywhere so he looked around in desperation, but everyone seemed oblivious to the commotion. The receptionist behind the desk showed no interest at all, and moved a vase of flowers off her desk.

"OH, THERE'S NO ESCAPE NOW, NOT THIS TIME!" the man boomed, and Bob backed up against the wall, terrified. Surprisingly, the man didn't follow. In fact, he didn't seem to be looking directly at Bob anymore, but just off to his side. He tried to follow the man's gaze, but there was only a tall plant in a Chinese pot nearby, so he carefully edged away a little, barely a foot or so to the right. The man took a step forward and pointed straight at the top leaves, but before he could shout anything else, he noticed Bob. He paused, and looked down at him.

"Oh, hello small person. Is this a friend of yours?" he said in a voice bordering on pleasant, while pointing back at the plant. Bob slowly shook his head.

"That's good, because you have to choose your allies carefully - you never know when they'll turn on you. LIKE THIS ONE! DAMN YOU TO THE LOWEST PITS OF HELL! AAAAGGH!"

He clamped his huge hands around the yucca plant's stem and began shaking and strangling it for all he was worth. Bob watched as they toppled over onto the floor amidst a flurry of leaves and shattered pottery. Two breathless security guards emerged from the foot of Staircase Three. The one wearing a badge with Guard A written on it jumped into the melee, while Guard B prepared an injection which he administered straight into Guard A's thigh. Guard C arrived and stood for a moment leaning against a wall, trying to catch his breath. He dragged the now-sleeping Guard A off to the side, and began his own attempt at separating man and plant. Guard B casually took out another injection, flicked it a couple of times, and tried to get the correct leg this time. Guard C fell asleep almost instantly. Guard B looked over at Bob, shrugged and dragged his colleague out of harm's way. He walked back over to the fight, and tapped the man on the shoulder.

"Mr Alfons? Hey, Mr Alfons! I've kinda run out of your special medicine, so can you pretend like I gave it to you? I'll get a final warning if you kill another plant. You're scarin' the florists, y'see?"

Mr Alfons froze like a bizarre statue for a while, contemplating whether or not to release his grip. Bob felt like offering a few words of assistance, but decided that if this freak and the plant had fallen out, it wasn't really his problem. The guard helped Mr Alfons to his feet, brushing leaves and a few twigs off his suit and walked him past the other guards, who were beginning to show signs of waking.

"How 'bout we go back to the Fourth Floor now, huh? With the nice soft carpets and the comfy chairs and none of them plants nowhere?" he said to the big man, and they steadily began climbing up Staircase Two. The other guards were sitting on the first step of Staircase Three, dozily muttering about Union Rules and who gets to hold the injection next time. The busy sounds of different conversations and dozens upon dozens of footsteps returned, and brought something resembling normality back to the hall.

The old man by the gramophone woke up, turned the record over and went back to sleep again. Music crackled from the trumpet-like loudspeaker, and Bob noticed the receptionist waving him over.

"Mistuh Bawb, I have Madame Aaagatha awn the line. She says she's unaware uhf who you arrre so she'd like tuh know mawwwuh. Say somethin' mawwuh to me in your crayy-zee voyiss!" she said, and lifted her vase back up onto the desk.

Once Bob had translated the important parts of her sentence, he tried thinking of something that not only this Agatha and his other Great Aunt Agatha would both have in common, but also something that wouldn't involve mentioning things that might start a panic.

"Tell her that I'm here to.. clean some mirrors, and I've come a long way, from England. And then mention Arizona and also Feiya, 'cause that might mean something."

Bob's sentence was rephrased, re-packaged and delivered in a way that could perhaps only be fully understood in an obscure part of New York, and even then by only a few people.

"She still don't know you, she says Arizona ain't in Engerland, and she ain't nevah hoyd of no Fayble-ayahh. Try 'gain, or I press a special red buttuhn."

Bob tried his best to think calmly. Maybe subtlety wasn't the best approach to this, after all.

"Tell her I've got a silver key, there's Troublers everywhere, and a cat called Jinx meows at me a lot. That should do it. Oh yeah, mention she looks a bit like Astrid Someone."

"Thoresein, I believe," added Bagshaw.

"Yeah, Astrid Thoresein," hurried Bob, hoping that the receptionist wouldn't wonder who had prompted him.

Once again, the sentence was remixed into an unintelligible mass of long vowels and bonus syllables, and she absently examined her fingernails while waiting for an answer. The knot returned to Bob's stomach until she looked at him with her eyebrows raised high.

"Well wellll! Seems yoowarr somewann affterrall! She's even comin' down here fo'yuh. Bit young t'be the President, ain'tcha fella?" she said, and then added in a whisper, "C'n you tell her I was good t'you, would yuh? See, she gets annoy.."

The receptionist interrupted herself with a strange noise almost like 'a-hahaah', smiled again and pointed over towards an elevator door. The arrow on the semi-circular dial above it reached '0' and bounced a few times, and the doors slid open.. and Bob felt as if he'd been hit by a tram.

A truly stunning woman stepped into the hall. She was tall, somewhere around 40, and easily the most stylish woman that he had ever seen. There were no old-lady nightgowns for this Agatha. She had been poured into a slender, knee-length red dress with edges so sharp they could slice through steel, and her angular black jacket would be equally lethal to anyone who dared get too near. Her regal looks were no longer haggard and wrinkled, but striking, powerful.. and so undeniably beautiful. And he could feel that her steely blue eyes were fixed on him, burning straight through him and leaving absolutely nothing unscorched - or unseen.

He felt his mouth drop further open with every high-heeled step that she took. She couldn't possibly be the old woman he'd always known, the nearly-with-the-angels Great Aunt he'd seen just hours earlier, could she? The way she walked, the way she carried herself, the way.. the way she seemed to be scaring the living daylights out of everybody..

The entire reception hall had fallen deathly silent, allowing each self-assured footstep to echo endlessly around him. His brain had gone on strike by the time she reached him, and he completely missed the first thing that she said. She raised the angled, narrow band of netting from the front of her wide-brimmed hat and bent down to speak again, stopping only when the brim touched the top of his head. Her prey was trapped. For a few seconds she said nothing, rendering him helpless by staring directly into his eyes.

"We have to talk," she whispered, "Don't we?"

Bob nodded and tried to close his mouth, and then tried to blink. He failed to do either, and she pushed his chin up with a gloved finger.

"Shall we depart?" she said even more quietly.

Bob replied with a cross between a whimper and an 'eek'. She straightened up again and minutely adjusted the lie of her jacket, in a way that he remembered seeing her older version do during previous family visits to Pierpont. That easily-missed mannerism made this Agatha seem a little more like his old Great Aunt Agatha, and he followed her towards the elevator feeling a little less scared - the difference was infinitesimally small, but it still counted. A group of eager management-types started hurrying over to her, waving wads of paper and calling.

"Madame Agatha, could we talk.. an appointment.. issues regarding.. really we must.. arrange to.. immediately.. insist.."

Without breaking her stride, and with only the slightest turn of her head, she delivered the kind of look that could turn July into January. Suddenly they all seemed to change their minds and one of them looked as though he might even start crying. This was Great Aunt Agatha on top form, and Bob would have grinned - if his mouth had started working yet.

She paused at the panel next to the elevator doors. It was covered in small dark red buttons numbered up to 190, all except the top row which were a strange luminescent blue, and marked by odd symbols. Agatha pressed one of the blue ones, and the semi-circular dial above the doors dropped back down to '0'. The doors opened immediately, but instead of the usual kind of small compartment, a long corridor lay in front of them. She began walking into it and gestured for Bob to hurry along. He stepped through just as the doors began sliding closed, and still expected to feel the floor start moving upwards.

"You may go and wait in the department's reception until I call you through. Do not speak to anyone about anything until we have spoken about everything. Claudette will look after you."

She pointed to a door further down the corridor, and then went into a room marked by a diamond in the deep-pile carpet, similar to the ones at The Ansonia. The door shut firmly behind her, and Bob was left alone. He slowly began wandering along, looking at the etchings of New York that were hanging on the wall, hoping that Agatha might re-emerge and miss out the whole 'waiting in reception' idea. He made a Mental Note to keep an eye out for any drawings by C Nevinson next time he was drifting around the picture section of Highcliffe's Thursday market.. but forgot the name completely when he reached the end window, where he looked all the way down 198 floors to the ground.

When he regained consciousness a moment or two later, he clumsily stood up and kept his eyes well away from the outside world, and leaned against the nearest door until his stomach turned itself the right way up. The word 'Reception' was elaborately written on a small white panel, in gold lettering.

The door clicked open and Bob found himself stumbling into a short passageway, leading into a large room. An annoyed voice was coming from somewhere, so without intruding too far inside, Bob took a few steps along the passageway and looked around. The central part of the room was filled with a vast, perfectly-sized Chinese rug similar to the larger ones down in the reception hall. A table topped with a display of colourful flowers occupied the very centre, and the obligatory chandelier hung directly above them. A widely-curving staircase leading up to the next floor lay off to the left of the rug, just beyond a well-organised mess of papers, files, large books and a few jumpers, which were spread all over a desk and its surrounding cabinets.

Straight ahead, far beyond the flowers, stood some closed double doors made up of countless frosted glass panels, so the woman's voice had to be coming from somewhere over on the right. Bob took a few more nervous steps forward, and peered around the end of the passageway to see a large desk a short way in front of an arched window. It had an even bigger mess on it than the other desk.

A skewed pile of magazines teetered on its edge, while the last few drops of coffee from an overturned mug dripped into a dark puddle on the floor. A white phone cord ran from somewhere underneath two shopping bags, up and over the magazines and around to the other side of a dark leather chair which was turned away, facing the window. He went and stood a couple of feet before the desk, causing just enough disturbance in the air to make all but one of the magazines cascade down onto the carpet. A few landed in the puddle of coffee, and Bob cringed as the tall chair swung round.

A woman with eyes as dark as her hair looked straight through him and carried on talking as if he wasn't there. She wasn't quite as well dressed as Agatha, but certainly ran a not-too-distant second. At a guess, he thought she was probably somewhere in her early 20s.

"Isch ka bibble, Reuben, ish-kahh-bib! I don't need a moochin' shoe-shine herdin' dumb Janes who happen along in ab of YT! No way.. nuh-uh.. oh you wish.. you can go take a hike to Oxnard.. huh? You sayin' it? Well.. you sure got a stra-ange wayuhshowin' it!"*

For some reason, her mood shifted considerably.

"Okay then.. yeeah that's dee, eyeball seven at Soma's then.. gotta skate.. yeah, full house now.. hugs'n'shugs. Ba-ba. Mmmwáh."

She placed the huge white receiver back in its cradle, shuffled some papers in an important way, and looked at Bob as if she had only just noticed him.

"Hmm," she said, studying the top few sheets on a clipboard and flippantly discarding each one onto the floor.

"Nothing like you.." she said, and pointed at him as if pressing an invisible button in the air, "..is on my list."

---

* **Please note:** A translation of such dialogue is available at the back of this book in a rarely-permitted reprinted section of the document which was, in the late 1920s, thought to be responsible for causing widespread linguistic mayhem. Historians have since become convinced that it was indeed **entirely** responsible, and are not in the least bit surprised that most copies had been burned by mid-1930.

"No, I'm Robert Taylor, here to see.. the lady I came in with, Madame Agatha. She told me to wait in here," Bob replied. He felt that he couldn't introduce himself as a relative of Agatha's, considering he wasn't due to be born for a very long time yet.

"Ohhh.. you're you? See, your name was mentioned when she stormed past.. but you don't need to know that. Well hello then, Robert, I'm Claudie and the one who's not here yet is Naomi. She'd be over there, if she was," she said, pressing another air-button in the direction of the other desk. Claudie had an impish face which gave the impression that she was permanently amused by something, which in a peculiar way encouraged Bob to try and make the tone less formal.

"Hello, then.. Claudie. Just call me Bob, nearly everyone does."

"Ahh, like my hair, which you haven't complimented me on - I had minor surgery on it yesterday. No insult Bobs, but there's no way I'd have a style called a robert, whatever the niftyness. A bob yes, a robert, no!"

Bob began trying to help pick up the magazines while Claudie explained that she'd only just picked them up from the last time they'd fallen over. Naomi arrived in a bluster, hurrying down the broadening flight of stairs and then dramatically collapsed into the chair behind her desk.

"Oh, you wouldn't believe what the traffic was like," she exclaimed, fanning herself with a laced handkerchief.

"Hey Nay, this here's Bobs, express delivery courtesy of Madame Agatha - herself!"

"No! You're joking? She.. Madame Agatha fetched you up here - perrrrsonally?"

Naomi looked a little younger than Claudie, and was probably taller. She had longer, waved hair which seemed to be dark brown on one side and a few shades lighter on the other, and her clothes were much brighter. Bob tried to think of something to say.

"Yes, she did, Nay-omie, she came into the reception and.. and what's with the lifts round here? We stepped straight into the corridor out there. I've probably got a great big question mark above my head - and I'm sure this place didn't look so tall from the outside."

Naomi laughed and rooted through her shoulder bag for a compact before trying to explain. Claudie tutted to herself as she nudged a pile of small boxes off her desk with the last of the magazines.

"Well firstly, to the people on the outside there's only a dozen floors, but really there are 189 more above those, including the top one which might not really count because it literally is just a floor at the moment. This one is Floor 198, by the way. All the ones above Floor 12 are Inverted Solidity Floors, or something like that."

"Inverted Solidity Floors?"

Claudie handed him some of the boxes to hold, and took over.

"She means you can't see them and birdies don't bounce off them. Smartie Stuff, and that's 'Smartie' written in big letters. And don't ask about the lifts here because no-bunny except the Spatial Dynamics boffins has got a clue how they work. We just use them. Fancy a coffee?" she added and went into a sideroom, which was presumably the kitchen.

Bob pulled up a big chair and sat in front of Claudie's desk while Naomi disappeared behind her own desk, shuffling around and muttering about losing something. Bob took the chance for a quick word with His Lordship.

"Hey, Bagshaw.." he whispered close to the book.

"Ugh, not so close to the page old chap! What have you been eating? Your breath reminds me of the inside of A J Tibblie's confectionery establishment! Oh, are you in his establishment? Try the Peppermint Roundies, most delightful."

Bob opened the book more and showed him a quick panorama of the room.

"I'm in New York, remember? I ate my own body-weight in pancakes and syrup earlier on in that café place. But to get to the point, do you know anything about Inverted Solidity?"

"Is it an illness? Try and get hold of Dr Buntz's fascinating Home Treatments For Modern Ailments. It was withdrawn from the general public only a week after its release, so it can be tricky to find. Must have had some spelling mistakes, I expect.."

Bob was about to answer but dropped the book as Claudie suddenly emerged from the kitchen with three steaming mugs on a tray. Naomi re-appeared from somewhere beyond her desk, clutching a notepad. She tapped it with her pen as she walked towards him.

"Now Bob, we need to know a few things about you before we decide if you can have your coffee," she said, trying to sound very official.

"Uhh.. it's all classified till Madame Agatha says it isn't," he replied, hoping that a Feiya phrase might score some points.

"Fair enough, just thought I'd try," she grinned, and picked his compendium up off the floor. Bob had to say something, and quick.

"Umm.. don't be scared if that talks to you, it just does and I've no idea why. I found it in a junk shop quite some time ago. It cost me three biros and my watch."

Naomi looked at Claudie and they both started laughing. And then they laughed some more, and then a lot more. Once they had wiped away a few tears, Claudie started talking through a big grin.

"It only talks to yooo, Bobs, nobody else can hear it - that's the Rule of Three! Don't you know about that?"

Bob shrugged.

"Nope. You could write all I know on the back of a stamp, and still have room for the complete works of Shakespeare."

Claudie took the book and flicked through the pages, and didn't look very impressed.

"Okay, here goes," she said while briefly scrutinising Bagshaw, "Habso ages ago, The Committee For Traveller Safety & Welfare allowed any schmoe who winds up in a new playground to have a few perks to make their stay light on the freternation and dot dot vee gee, or something as close as. In other words, once you're in the club this and that can parlez as required, but there's only three invites. You catchin' my drift yet Mr Hayshakes, like comin' undumbnified?"

Bob stared blankly back, trying hard to think of a question that might imply that he had understood one or two words. Naomi came to the rescue, and stopped the silence becoming embarrassing.

"In other words, Bob, you've obviously done some time travel, haven't you? And time travel can be risky so the first three inanimate things you talk to can talk right back to you! Apparently there have been times when it's saved travellers' lives, you know. And assuming you don't abuse the privilege, you can do pretty well out of it. You're lucky to have spoken to a.." Claudie handed her the book, "..a Compendium Of Modern Knowledge, 'cause that must come in useful all the time! But you'll really need to be ever so careful with the other two things though, 'cause the powers-that-be don't like letting you change them. Takes ages for any appeals to get heard. One nameless person not a million miles away from here chose a drinks mat, then a cherry on a stick and then an ice cube.."

Claudie jumped in, "Yes Bobs, but her rootiest best friend who shall also remain nameless - who's called Naomi - chose a large whiskey then her left shoe and finally a chair which she immediately threw up all over.."

"I did not throw on the chair - I missed by at least a foot.."

"Yeah, Miss Prohibition 1927, and who's foot was it? My best steppers as well.."

"Well.. you can have my one that doesn't talk, if you want?"

They dissolved into laughter again, and for the first time in a very long time, Bob felt like having a laugh too.

CHAPTER ELEVEN

Troublers

Somewhere beyond the far double doors came the muffled sound of another door closing, and brought a serious mood to the room. Claudie's phone gave a polite ring.

"Hello Madame Agatha.. yes.." she said, and stared at Bob, "..yes, everywhere's tidy out here.. you'll see him now? Okay, I'll send him through."

She put the phone down and pointed to him.

"Madame Agatha will see you now, Bobs.." and then added in a whisper, "..and don't be scared, she's already eaten."

He crossed over the central rug, frantically trying to decide if he should knock on the door or just walk in. Walking straight in might give a bad first impression, but knocking on a glass-panelled door might make a far worse impression. He could almost hear the glass shattering on the floor already.

The doors opened by themselves and he walked into a room which was far larger than the one he'd just left. Agatha sat behind a well organised desk, in front of a window that ran all the way from the floor to the ceiling. She stood up and drew the net curtains closed as if she knew he was terrified of the view, and then leaned on the back of her chair. She didn't say a word, and stared at him for two very long minutes.

"Have a seat," she said eventually, and with the slightest of hand movements gestured for him to roll a chair around to her side of the desk. Her voice was warm, but defensive. Bob had no idea if that was good or bad, so he moved the chair to the end of her desk and sat down.

"And do stop being nervous, there's really no need. If you had anything worth being nervous about, you wouldn't be sitting here right now. You'd be somewhere out there.."

Agatha casually waved a finger towards the window, and Bob's chair rolled itself a few inches in that direction. He stopped feeling nervous, and started feeling petrified instead.

"Now then, I haven't been able to ascertain certain very important things about you, and perhaps you might help me? I can't trace you from any location or era whatsoever, and I can't even trace how you arrived here. And yet you say that you know me."

"Yes," squeaked Bob, before clearing his throat and managing a more normal pitch, "..yes. You see, in quite a few years time you live in Pierpont House, which is in Barton On Sea in England.. well, just about in England.. the cliffs keep on.. anyway, you're just down the road from me. You're my Great Aunt Agatha, Madame Agatha."

Agatha's expression gave nothing away. She sat down in the huge leather chair keeping her eyes fixed on him, and tapped the desk lightly with her fingers.

"I'm your Great Aunt? Well, how very surprising.." she said. The hard edge to her voice softened noticeably, even if her face didn't.

"Yes. And you looked after me for a week when I was really small.. mum and dad were having time apart.." Bob added, hoping to step further onto firm ground with one of his few memories of her, even if it did come from one of the more vague parts of his life.

"I'm enthralled, Robert," she said ambiguously, "We do move location when it's judged to be appropriate, and there are fools amongst us who favour the 'less obvious' backwater sites such as Barton. I would have hoped for somewhere a little more refined. Bermuda perhaps, or Prague.. but that's irrelevant. The only movement I've been able to trace of yours has been from the entrance of this building and up to that chair. Do go on, and try not to stare - it can be so impolite," she said.

"I can't help it, Great.. uh Madame.. Aunt.. you're very different, like this. I saw you.." Bob's brain almost imploded as he tried to think of how to describe the time of his meeting with the older Agatha.

"You see, back in Barton, today is Sunday, okay? My mum and dad and I were asked loads of times by your assistant called Feiya to come and see you because of your health, so we all went around and you kept me behind because of the Eternal Mirrors. The Troublers took them last Friday due to some kind of faulty alignment."

"That would have to be the Andromedan Fault. That's not good.. it happens occasionally, but for anyone to actually take the Mirrors, the Fault must have coincided with Saturn's bi-millennial polar reversal.. hmm.. and that would provide any Troublers with a few hours when the Security Field around the Mirrors is dangerously weakened, which would enable the theft. Well, at least I can place you somewhere in time now. But that doesn't explain why, or even how, you're the one to have come here?"

Bob only understood the final few words.

"I'm here because.. of all kinds of reasons that sound barmier every time I think of them. I was hoping you'd be able to tell me."

Agatha raised an eyebrow, and Bob shivered.

"You're not here to ask me questions. But having said that, I might tell you more when I'm a little more confident about you. People who can't be monitored simply don't exist."

Bob felt as if someone had switched a light on in his head.

"Yes! Feiya says that you and the uh.. Guardian of Space and Dynamite.."

"Spatial Dynamics," she corrected, leaning forwards in her seat and taking a more obvious interest.

"Well, you two worked it so that I was born twice, so now I'm the only person who can go through the doorways of Number 107 without being monitored."

"Born twice? Let me think.."

She gave a three-note 'hmm' and gazed out of the window deep in thought, making a temple with her fingers in front of her chin

"The first 'you' would have been automatically registered in the Library Of Existence, as is everyone else in the world.. but the second 'you' wouldn't have registered at all, and might even have negated the first 'you'. How did we manage that? Now there's a challenge.."

Bob shivered again as she fixed her eyes back on him. He figured that if she put her mind to it, she could have glared Attila The Hun into a career change, and Attila The Cake Decorator would never have troubled the pages of history. She continued in her steady tone.

"Do tell me more about Number 107. That greatly concerns me."

"That's your other house, which Ann Harrod and the Spatial Guardian helped with."

"Angharrad. Continue," she said, inching her chair a little closer.

"Well that place is right near me as well, and.." Bob knew the next bit would sound excessively crazy, even compared to everything else, "..a cat called Jinx lead me there and apparently let me in."

Agatha smiled discretely, which didn't strike Bob as being a sign of ridicule, or even impending death.

"I've got a silver key as well," he added, and lifted it out from under his shirt, "..which is totally weird. Anyway, the upstairs rooms are like doorways to other places in time, which is how I got here. Fey says that you needed these extra places for ultra-confidential meetings with other Guardians, and then sometimes just to get away for a while, without actually being away for any time."

"Ah, Immediate Absence! Well that is good to hear. At the moment it's just a classified theory, and the dynamics are way beyond anything else.. but do carry on.." she said, rolling her fingers in small circles.

"Well, the Mirrors were stolen from Pierpont House and have most likely been taken through Number 107 by the Troublers, so the older you in the future said I was supposed to come here and find you, and you'd put me straight about getting them back, which won't.. involve.." Bob could feel his brain slowing down, "..won't involve you doing anything to stop me being here now, and.. also there.. later on.. before.. ugh."

"Try not to think about it - that's my job."

"Well, after lunch on Sunday, which in my world is still today, still.. somehow.. anyway, I went there and got the wrong room, and ended up on a farm in Arizona a few years before even now. So I couldn't find this place, but I did get spotted by a freak in a hat.. and he offered to help me, but I can hardly remember him. He seemed pretty familiar with the whole travelling thing and booked me into a hotel, but he was a bit creepy so I didn't stick around."

"That's always a good idea," she quietly acknowledged.

"I just went back to the farm's portal instead, and through to Number 107. Then I went to see the old you but you were too weak and ill to say anything much, so you sent me here to see.. you."

He paused for a moment, expecting Agatha to either say something that would explain it all perfectly, or call for medical people. Instead, she stayed quiet and adjusted each of her black gloves without taking her eyes off him. The knot that was usually in his stomach moved up to his head, and a silence hung between them for too long, so Bob felt that he had to say something.

"Umm.. then you and Fey sent me back to get the right room, which I managed because here I am, and I would have been earlier but I dozed off in the apartment for a while this morning. And that's it, really. I don't know anything about anything, other than I have to get the Mirrors back by Thursday at.."

"..midnight," finished Agatha.

Bob sat back, hoping she wouldn't grind any more information out of him, but also relieved to have told her about what had been going on. He was even more relieved that she hadn't pressed a button to drop his chair through the floor. Agatha moved a little closer.

"And now I can place you exactly. Your Thursday, specifically midnight, would be the Sirian Alignment Time, which is an immensely important moment. It's the only time each century when a new Guardian can replace a retiring Guardian - I'll have had two hundred years by then, but from what you say I must have been granted another term in Office. That's good, that's very good. And before you ask me, Naomi and Claudette will explain how anyone can live that long."

"..I hope they write it down.. with pictures.." thought Bob.

"It's rare that the Andromedan Fault coincides with the Sirian Alignment, and even more rare for them both to coincide with Saturn's polar reversal - so whoever did this must be on the inside, with a vast knowledge of how such matters work - and that would take a long time to achieve. But they've managed it, haven't they?"

Bob shifted uncomfortably.

"Uhuh. Who'd do that?"

"In all walks of life," she said with a sigh, "there are those who choose not to see the bigger picture, merely their own small section. Usually such people want that section to be the entire picture, and they try to destroy the rest. Any who behave in such a manner within this organisation are termed Troublers.." she paused, to emphasise the word, "..which is a loathsome word. We remove them in a variety of ways, hence it isn't a term to be thrown around."

"Oh. I said it to the receptionist, I think.."

"Yes, you said quite a few things to her.. all of which she'll have been encouraged to forget within an hour" she said, and underlined the receptionist's name for the third time. She gave the gold pen a slight flick, spreading a series of blotches perfectly across it.

"Umm.. what kind of organisation is this?" Bob asked as a low cloud drifted past the window.

"Oh, Naomi and Claudette will explain the structure to you, or as much as they know of it. All you currently need to be aware of is that practically everything you know regarding existence, the universe and anything else you care to mention, is wrong - or at best, over-simplified. All those aspects of life which people take for granted happen because we do our job very well. But in your time, we seem to have slipped, don't we? Because if we fail to retrieve the Eternity Mirrors, and therefore allow a Troubler to be seated before them at midnight of the Sirian Alignment.. there will be a new Guardian Of Time, one who is unaccountable - and once that's happened, everything will change."

Bob tried to think of a question. And tried. And tried.

"Troublers aren't like aliens, are they?"

Agatha sighed.

"There are no aliens. They're just subversives who must have spent years infiltrating and weakening the whole system in preparation for their one big chance. They might be the ones who planned the decentralisation of the Departments in order to make the Department Of Time vulnerable, and that would have taken patience and a great deal of planning.. but this isn't all about those types though, is it?"

"Yes it.. isn't," said Bob, hoping that he had Fey'd the right answer.

"It's about you. You were explaining yourself," she said in a friendlier way, and granted Bob a smile which even looked pleasant.

"Well, that's pretty much it, really. Oh, I arrived here at six this morning, in a huge apartment up in The.."

"Don't tell me!" she snapped, making his chair rock, "I shouldn't know where it is. My future-self would have chosen the building because I would never have used it in the past, or been in that area. So I don't require you to tell me where it is. I'll trust my future-self's judgement, for now. Tea or coffee?" she said, changing the subject.

She leaned forwards to her ornate vertical telephone, lifted its white ear-piece and quietly asked Claudie to sort out some coffee, then rolled closer to the window where she looked out at the very distant skyline.

"The Mirrors." she said, running her fingers along the brim of her hat, "You need to see them, otherwise the importance of this will be lost on you."

She fixed him with another one of her granite-cracking stares.

"Shall we depart?"

CHAPTER TWELVE

The Eternity Mirrors

Agatha picked up a small clutch-bag and walked across the room towards a panelled oak door.

"You haven't been through a Blue Time-Shift before, so you might find this a little strange. You might even start to think you're a shapeless mass of ectoplasm - but that's entirely normal."

Bob whimpered.

"You don't need to worry about it, just follow me."

The door opened as she approached it, and then faded away completely to leave a pulsating metallic blue void in its place. She calmly walked into it, leaving Bob alone and feeling as if he'd put on a pair of boots that were a hundred sizes too big - and filled with concrete. She stepped back through, took his hand with a surprisingly gentle grip, and made sure he followed.

Bob found himself walking through a room with no definite walls, floor or ceiling, just a strange ever-moving shift in colours from blue to complete blackness, and then back again. Agatha gradually disappeared into a band of drifting blue nothingness even though Bob could still feel her gently holding his hand. He couldn't understand how he was keeping up with her, as there was no ground to walk on and he couldn't even feel his legs. Time meant nothing as he felt himself turn upside down, spinning clockwise and anti-clockwise both at the same moment. For some bizarre reason he decided to scratch his left ear, and watched as his left hand took the longer route around the entire world before re-appearing and delivering the scratch from the inside of his head. This was too weird for words. He couldn't even begin to list the Andie Awards that a Blue Time-Shift should be honoured with, and figured that even Andie would be hard-pushed to manage it.

Suddenly the rich blue faded away into a dense blackness, which was in turn replaced by a grandiose, and very real, room. Apart from the weird arm situation, Bob was pleased with himself that he had survived in one piece and didn't even feel sick.. but he did manage to fall over as soon as he could feel the ground beneath him again.

This room was almost twice the size of Agatha's office, far more ornate, and the ceiling was at least three times as high. The floor sloped gently downwards, past more than a hundred chairs which had been arranged in small semi-circles, leading to a Louis XIV chair facing a wide golden table. Five oval Mirrors stood on top of it, held together by elegant wooden frames.

Each Mirror was dark silver and didn't seem to be reflecting much at all. The central one was over five feet tall, the two either side were about a foot shorter, and the two at either end were a foot shorter again. Some music was playing quietly in the background, and Bob wondered to himself what it was.

"Chopin - I have my reasons. Now then, other than being your Great Aunt, I am the current Guardian Of Time, and therefore the High Overseer of all groups, committees and sub-departments which make up the Department Of Time, and my role is to control access to events throughout history. My word is final, as are my actions," she said, and lead the way down the slope.

She sat on the chair before the Mirrors, staring intently into nothing, for a while. He nervously stood by her side as she leaned towards the central Mirror, where she breathed a few words silently before it. All five slowly began to reflect the room's contents, and Bob felt very sick.

"Where.. where's my reflection? I can see you, but there's no me! Oh great, I'm a vampire.." he said, anxiously looking from one Mirror to the next.

"No, this is merely proof that you technically don't exist. Indulge me for one moment - here, hold your hand out," she said, and removed one of her gloves. She placed it on his palm and for a split second, Bob wondered what she was doing.. but her eyes gestured his attention to the Mirrors. In the reflected image, her black glove fell straight to the floor. Bob looked at the same glove which was definitely, undeniably, unquestionably still in his hand, and then looked down at the glove in the Mirror. Agatha slowly took the glove back from him, but her reflected image bent down and picked it up, dusted it - and then in perfect synchronisation, both Agathas put the glove back on.

"Hmm.. that's very disturbing, and in some ways I don't like it.."

"Well, it was your idea, apparently."

Agatha ignored him, and chose a Mirror to point at.

"Starting at the left, we have the Distant Past Mirror. All I have to do is speak a time, date and location ranging from a few thousand years ago, up to exactly one hundred years ago, and it shows me the scene. Think of it as a doorway through time. I break the Mirror's surface, and become drawn through to whenever, and wherever."

"You step through time?" said Bob, feeling his heart pounding, "But what if someone else speaks to it?" he spluttered, imagining how complicated this could all get.

"It will only respond to me, as I am the current Guardian. I'm a part of these, they are a part of me.. I could tell you why, but the reasons would make just as much sense to you in Arabic or Sanskrit."

Bob nodded, and wondered if Bagshaw would understand them if she did. Or at least translate them, perhaps.

"Because of your 'condition' I would prefer it if you didn't even speak in their direction, just to be on the safe side. You're an unknown quantity, in far too many ways."

Bob took an obliging step away from them.

"What if something bad happens to you in the past, like an accident, or you do the wrong thing?"

Agatha smiled her approval that he had managed two good questions on the trot. Bob was equally amazed.

"Various representatives from the Approval Committees and the Monitoring Organisations.." she paused for a moment, and a gave a sly grin, "..they occupy Floor 3 - a year ago I got them demoted 182 floors and I'm still amused about that.. but I'm digressing, aren't I?" she said, more lightly. "The chosen representatives all stay in this room observing my actions, and once the purpose of the intervention has been achieved, I return via a pre-determined 'gateway' which brings me back to this side of the Mirror. Others can go in my place if I give permission - which is infrequent, to put it mildly. I don't mind being accompanied by others if necessary, but I never trust anyone else to do my work for me."

"Why intervene somewhere?" asked Bob, gazing into the Mirror.

"To improve the world we live in, without radically undermining or destroying the future. Think of it as safeguarding tomorrow. It's not easy, and such privilege is a heavy burden."

"Re-writing history.. umm.. could future-you change exam results?"

Agatha hummed a reply which sounded like a blunt refusal.

"The larger Mirror next to the Distant Past is the Immediate Past, which shows and grants access to any moment from the last hundred years. The central one is for the Present, which allows us to keep an eye on anything happening anywhere, right now. The next one is the Immediate Future, you can guess how far that serves us, and the right one is the Distant Future."

"You change the future as well?"

"Bravo. Of course we do, but not by intervening - that would be tackling a situation from the wrong direction, and give rise to the most dreadful dilemmas - such as now, for example. Changing the past changes the future, and allows a high degree of control over the present, so the two Future Mirrors are only for reference. You see, before any historical interventions can take place, myself and other Senior Guardians have to assess the potential consequences of any proposed actions - and to do that we view the Future Mirrors. They give a 'best guess', if you like. If judged appropriate by myself, then by ourselves and then by a majority of the Approval Committee, we act accordingly. I'm not fond of the committees - I find that politics can bludgeon common-sense to death, but fortunately it's been a long time since they dared to oppose me. As I was saying, the Future Mirrors are vital, because blindly intervening in the past is akin to giving Pandora's Box a good shaking before opening it. So we're very careful."

"I see.. and what's Pandora the Guardian of?"

Agatha sighed.

"Nothing, she's a figure from Greek mythology. I'm giving you an analogy about solving one problem, but creating millions more."

"Oh.." said Bob, vowing to himself not to ask any more questions. If Pandora was Greek and old, Bagshaw would probably know all about her anyway. He might even have known her.

"Are you beginning to understand the purpose and power of these?" she said, turning away from the Mirrors and looking at him as if he ought to ask a question. Bob tried to think of something safe to say which would have nothing to do with Committees or analogies.

"It's awesome. How can mirrors do all that? They're just glass and that reflective stuff, aren't they?"

Agatha hid a sigh.

"Touch the Immediate Past Mirror, but don't break the surface. Heaven help you, if you do."

Bob touched it and drew his hand away very quickly. The surface shimmered like water, rippling in slow motion before turning into a deep and intensely black void. It filled with the reflected image of Agatha sitting down and talking to no-one. She sounded as if she was actually there, as real as the Agatha beside him. Bob felt that he could reach in and touch anything, or should at least be answering back when the reflection said, "Are you beginning to understand the purpose and power of these?"

The image faded while that version of Agatha instructed an invisible person to touch the Immediate Past Mirror. Bob looked back to the real Agatha, speechless. She gave a small laugh.

"Don't think of them as ordinary mirrors - their shape is just a functional design. Think of them as the tip of a multi-dimensional iceberg. What you can't see is all the 4th, 5th and 6th Dimensional workings behind their surfaces. And as for these frames.." she leaned forward and ran a finger along the in-laid wood surrounding the Present Mirror.

"They only look like frames?"

"And looks can be so deceptive, can't they? They're stabilising fields that create a harmony between each Mirror, or cross-dependency if you prefer. Without these.."

Agatha paused for a moment, and Bob could see that she was searching for words of fewer than ten or twelve syllables, and then for ones with less than two or three. She stared into the Present Mirror, adjusted the angle of her hat by a barely-noticeable amount, teased the band of netting into a sharper fold, and continued.

"..without these we're all in trouble. And if they've been separated from each other as well.. that's very distressing. And now we reach the heart of our problem - how you reclaim the Mirrors and prevent the wrong people from holding such power. How very irritating.." she said, tapping her finger against her chin, "..but credit where it's due, and I have to applaud the Troublers achievement - it would have been no easy feat."

Bob was surprised at Agatha's graciousness, but that feeling didn't last long.

"However, they deserve a fate infinitely worse than death for their treachery, and I'll work on some suggestions this evening. I'll ensure they pay.. and others will learn from their shameful behaviour."

"Well, you've already got one suspect's name, which is a good start. It was Anderomedan's fault, wasn't it?" offered Bob, hopefully.

"Do try not to think too much. The Andromedan Fault is a series of black holes in space which cause all kinds of problems with the way these Mirrors work. I suppose you want some idea of how?"

Bob nodded, in much the same way that someone would nod if they were in front of a firing squad, and the General had asked if they would like to be shot now.

"Time is linear," she said, as if that was obvious.

"I thought so.."

"Don't humour me. In other words, the past comes before the present, which comes before the future. Think of it as a long line with plenty of dates on it. Therefore, a line can be folded.."

Bob stared blankly at her.

"..so two points in time, such as today and any other day, can be placed alongside each other regardless of how far apart they may be on the line - and thus allow me to pass through from one to the other. That takes the kind of vast energy that simply can't be generated - it can only come from 'borrowing' and then converting gravitational forces from various planets - those which happen to be close enough. And then every hundred years, those planets line up.."

"The Sirian Alignment?" said Bob, scoring a few points.

"Good. They create an immeasurable surge of power that we can barely deal with - and that's the time when the person sitting in front of these Mirrors becomes inextricably linked with them, for all kinds of sub-atomic reasons which took me a very long time to understand. I can't make it simpler than that."

"I see.."

"No you don't. When the Andromedan Fault passes by, the flaws start to show. And if Saturn's going through a bi-polar reversal, it gets a whole lot worse.. imagine being too strong and too weak at the same time. All the dynamics around these Mirrors count for nothing and anyone can threaten the privilege of Guardianship. And if you haven't retrieved them all by the Alignment, or if they aren't held in a stable unit.. I suggest you change planets, because this one may become damaged, slightly. Wretched Troublers.. and please don't start thinking about aliens again because there still aren't any."

Bob tried to put images of huge space-weirdos out of his mind, and instead tried to give the impression he was actually listening. He tapped his chin in the same way she tended to do, thoughtfully.

"So couldn't we just bend the time-line and go into the future and stop these from ever being stolen then?"

Agatha shook her head.

"It's not just the 'fix one problem and create more' syndrome, it's all the security procedures and physical limitations. There are more rules and regulations about the future than for the past. It's not possible for any Guardian to move forwards in time through these, because we have to prevent Guardians being in the same place as their own Future Self so that the temptation and possibility of self-cloning in the quest for absolute power is avoided. Human nature is so flawed."

"So how come you're allowed back into the past?"

"It's in no-one's interests to duplicate yourself in the past, because if you interfere with your own past.. you can adversely change, or perhaps eliminate, your own future.. which is a major problem for both of us, now."

At long last, something made sense to Bob.

"How about me, then? Could you let me go forwards in time?"

"Hmm.. no. Although your traversal wouldn't be recorded.." she gestured towards his lack of reflection, "..the usage of the Mirror would be registered, so I would have to explain how an unrecordable activity had taken place, why no approval had been requested, why no Monitoring Committees were arranged, and why the specific destination had been chosen. That would rattle a few cages, and your anonymity would suddenly be worthless. Besides, if you were successful, you'd remove your own reason for being here in the first place - and I can't imagine where that would leave us."

Bob vaguely remembered Feiya mentioning something about that, but decided not to say so in case Agatha asked him to repeat any of it.

"..and is therefore not a good idea," Agatha continued. "All that you and I know is that a number of Troublers are intent on carrying out their raid in the future - and they might even be in this very building, right now, plotting and recruiting for the event. So we don't want to risk alerting them to the fact that we know of them, and we certainly don't want to give them an advance-warning to look out for you in the future - they'd kill you as soon as they find where you live. That would make this situation three or four times as complicated as it already is.. how inconvenient that would be."

Bob's mind began wandering and he stared into the Distant Past

Mirror, and moved around. This novelty would take a long time to wear off.

"You still won't be there next time you look, Robert, so tune into me again, would you? The only travelling is to be done through the Immediate Absence Portal - its very existence doesn't register in these Mirrors, so consider it a back door which is also a front door, side door, and also trap door. The technology behind it must be staggering, utterly staggering.."

Her voice drifted away and she became lost in awe of such a dimensional masterpiece. She drew a sharp breath and carried on.

"You were born twice for a reason, and I suspect this might be it. You're my safety net, in case anything went wrong due to Immediate Absence."

"It's nice to be appreciated."

"You're not yet, but there's always hope. Much as I hate to admit it, this shows why we were wrong to pursue the implementation of an Immediate Absence Portal. Without those gateways, I doubt this would have happened"

Bob's black-belt in the art of taking what someone says and carefully spinning it the other way was about to come in useful again.

"Or maybe not. Maybe it's because the portals exist that we can sort this mess out? And maybe if you didn't figure out how to create them, the bad guys probably would have - and then you'd be up a creek, they'd still have the Mirrors, and I wouldn't be here."

Agatha looked surprised.

"You may well be right. Regard yourself as part of my clan, at least while you're here. You realise you can't stay a moment longer than is absolutely necessary?"

"Fey's explained about that, I think. Closing doors before I get to them.. not being born even twice, something like that."

Agatha walked over to the windows and opened the long velvet curtains. Either the world's tallest firs were outside, or this room was on a different floor. Bob couldn't be sure without going for a proper look, but there might have been snow on them.

"That's enough for now, Robert. Shall we.." she began, and gestured with subtle elegance towards the Time-Shift door.

CHAPTER THIRTEEN

The Big Advantage

The second trip through the Time-Shift wasn't such a disturbing experience, and Bob felt it came to an end a little too quickly. It was weird enough to be fun, but that conclusion would probably need re-phrasing before mentioning to Agatha.

They sat down again on her side of the desk, where two coffees and a plate of biscuits were waiting for them. Bob had learned enough from Andie to know a thing or two about body language, and Agatha was showing no signs of wariness or controlled hostility any more. She had even slipped her jacket and gloves off, which was a particularly good sign. The hat stayed on, but that was no cause for alarm. She toyed with a biscuit, and Bob wondered if he ought to demonstrate the art of dunking.

"So tell me, Robert, how are you dealing with the differences in conventional time? By that I mean the time of day," she said, much friendlier than before.

"That's all a bit tricky, really. I traded my watch for that book," he replied, and pointed at the compendium which Claudie had placed next to the coffee, on its own small tray. He picked it up and checked that Bagshaw was still there.

"Ah, h'lo Bob m'lad!" announced His Lordship, who had brought a gentlemen's club style of chair into his panel and was sipping a cup of tea, "I've been on the desk of your young lady friend, a Ms Clawdeee. Delightful creature. Couldn't understand a word she said, though.. still, quite charming all the same. Fragrant as a bed of roses.. and bourbon, maybe a dash of gin. Fair reeks of it, actually."

Agatha smirked as if she heard him, and took the book from Bob.

"The Concise Compendium of Modern Knowledge.. hmm, I'm sure that's very useful. The name Buntz doesn't inspire any great faith, though. I read his book on healthy eating - I'll spare you the details. Now, you need a timepiece, I believe."

She left the book open on the desk at Bagshaw's page, who was cheerfully pouring himself another cup of tea. She leaned forwards to her elegant vertical white phone, lifted its Mother of Pearl earpiece and flicked one of its two switches.

"Naomi, would you nip down to Sigmund's floor for Robert? Sweet-talk a terribly hasty turn-around on a watch, if.. yes, he needs a comprehensive pan-dimensional.. yes, at the very least. With a touch of class, and whatever else you judge to be appropriate. Yes, you run down now, but do so with dignity. Cheers."

Without looking, she reached into her black handbag on the desk and took out a gleaming black cigarette case, tapped it once and slid out a very narrow pastel-blue cigarette. She held it up as if she was going to light it, but instead began twirling it through her fingers..

"Aunt Agatha?" Bob croaked. Offering advice to Agatha seemed unwise, somehow, "Where I'm from.. they're.. not so good for you."

She grinned over to him, and twirled it more.

"They're only dangerous if you light them, Robert."

Bob felt as if she was a lot more than one or two steps ahead of him - a dozen laps seemed far more likely. Without thinking, he demonstrated the art of biscuit-dunking and changed the subject.

"So.. how old are you right now, if you can be a Guardian for a hundred years at a time?"

Bagshaw choked on his tea, and gestured for Bob to stop talking.

"Oh my.. dreadfully unwise line! Indubitably dreadful.." he cringed, and hurried from his panel so quickly that the compendium closed itself. That surprised Bob, but Agatha seemed unruffled.

"A gentleman never asks a lady's age," she said, "but I will tell you that once you're accepted into the Guardianship System, even at the lowest levels, your age is the opposite to dog years, I suppose. You would age one year like anyone else, but it would take seven years and a few months to happen. Those of us at higher levels have one or two privileges beyond that of course, which can be very useful especially after a good Christmas."

She allowed herself a proper laugh.

"The reason for the slow ageing process is because of the amount of time required to reach senior positions of responsibility. Experience and understanding count for everything, and you can't rush that. Initial training is 107 years, and then Guardian Assistance runs for however long the Guardian remains in Office. That can be five full terms. You need experience."

"But if you were going for a third term, how come you were so frail and so.. you know.. why had you aged so much?"

"Well.. I would look elderly because that's appropriate for how you and your family need to see me, but as for the degenerative ageing.. that would be down to the theft mainly, but also the wretched Andromedan Fault and Sirian situation. Unless very careful steps are taken with the Mirrors at those times, a Guardian such as myself would find that time can take away all that it has given. If the Mirrors are back in one stable unit by Thursday's alignment at midnight and my future-self is seated before them, everything will be fine. So there's a job to be done, isn't there?"

"Looks like it - no wonder Fey was so stressed."

"You keep mentioning her, but you needn't. I haven't met her yet, and it's far better that I don't know about her beforehand."

Naomi knocked on the door, which swung open a couple of seconds later. She presented a small cyan bag on a silver tray to Agatha who shuffled around inside it and withdrew a shining watch, which she held up into the sunlight.

"You were very quick, well done. Hmm, a Patek Phillipe.. very nice, very sleek indeed.. either today or tomorrow fetch a Breguet for me, I fancy a change. Robert, put this on and do not take it off - ever," she said, adjusting the time slightly.

Bagshaw appeared in his panel again, and tried to be helpful.

"Ahaaa.. she's the other one, Bob! Your Clawdee-friend's friend. Didn't quite catch her name, but she seems equally engaging.. reminds me of a charming someone who I met in St Petersburg once, back in '68 or thereabouts.. hmm, long time ago," he trailed wistfully.

"Well you never know.." whispered Bob, wondering if Naomi might really have been there with Agatha for a quick intervention.

Agatha handed him the watch. The gold rectangular face spanned the width of his wrist, and the leather strap felt as if it was sealing itself. It didn't appear to have any lasers or amazing add-ons, but it was still the weirdest design he'd ever seen. An oval occupied the gold frame, with long numbers stretched out to the corners and squashed ones in between, which was odd but probably very trendy. The weird stuff lay in the extras. The day and date weren't surprising, but a panel along the bottom had small letters reading '1 LEX AVE' with another underneath stating 'MANHATTAN'. Beneath that was a smaller one, 'COMFY CHAIR'.

Naomi smiled and proudly handed over a slim grey book.

"I picked up one of these as well - I thought it would help," she said.

Agatha showed signs of being pleased as she flicked through it.

"Thank you and off you go, you have been very perspicacious, and that has been noted."

Naomi wasn't sure if that was a compliment or not, so she left looking puzzled. Agatha handed over the compact narrow diary, which had Bob's name on the front. For a moment he was impressed, until he realised it was written in ink and had a spelling mistake. It smudged as he opened the cover.

"You have to keep track of everywhere you go, everything you do, where you are at specific times of the day and most importantly of all, who you talk to. This diary will prevent you from meeting yourself or inadvertently causing a situation where you alter your own past, present or future."

"Oh, right.. of course...."

"It's important for you, and also for us. Either myself, or my two Assistants, will check and file everything confidentially."

"Okay.. does everyone who steps through time need one?"

"For the chosen few, a diary like this would be a simple personal reference file, a something to look back on. But in your case your movements aren't traceable, so you have to keep your own records to avoid.. any unpleasantness. Are you with me?"

The sound of softly padding steps came from across the room. Agatha ignored them, but Bob turned quickly.

"Is that Jinx? Oh, hang on, umm.. extreme moment of stupidity. Fey said Jinx was her cat, so that must be another black cat," he said, and promptly turned a shade of red.

"Yes that is Jinx," replied Agatha with no warmth in her voice, "and she belongs to who she wants to belong to. She was here before I joined, and I assure you Robert, that was quite a long time ago. I wouldn't be too surprised if she's still here long after we're all gone."

Agatha opened a white book, and much to Bob's amazement, started writing with a pen which seemed to lift itself to her hand. Meanwhile, Jinx had climbed onto his lap and was staring at him. He stroked her head and saw that she had closed her eyes. For the briefest of moments she was almost a normal cat, but ran off before there was any danger of either of them getting used to it.

"Now then, apart from a farm in Arizona and a site in Manhattan, what locations do the other doorways lead to, and how many doorways would you say there are?"

"I have no idea, and.. I have no idea."

Bob squirmed, feeling useless, but was then hit by inspiration.

"If your portal place in Barton is created by you and the Guardian Of Spatial Dynamics, wouldn't the destinations be important places to you both? If the doors exist to allow you to get away without actually being away, and also have a few meetings of course, they must be places that you both like for some reason?"

"Hmm.. that would explain the New York connection.." said Agatha, becoming a little whimsical for a moment. The slightest hint of a blush appeared across her face - this was even more bizarre and unimaginable than the Normal Cat Moment with Jinx.

"Major brainwave!" he exclaimed, and nearly jumped from his chair with excitement at having thought of something flaw-proof.

"Can't you just tell all this to the Guardian Of Spatial Dynamics now? You can both start getting rid of anyone who looks even slightly dodgy, and there you go!" he said, feeling intelligent.

Agatha spun her cigarette into another blur, and launched it towards a flowering cactus by the curtains. It embedded itself alongside others in the soil, and her gaze came back to rest on him.

"No. If the guilty ones are here now, we'd remove the reason that you came here - you really must stop thinking so much. Besides, there's over 7,000 in his Department. One swing of the axe wouldn't solve this, it would just let the Troublers know that we're onto them - and that we have no idea who they are. No, I refuse to involve him. We'll sort this out ourselves.. specifically, YOU will sort it out."

Bob whimpered, before a huge question sprang to mind.

"Hang on.. now I've told you all this, aren't you going to spend the next few decades knowing it's all going to happen?"

"We start to get Advanced at this point. Sure you want to hear it?"

"Umm.. okay?"

"You're really sure?"

Bob nodded, knowing he was going to regret it.

"The answer to your question is No, but with a slight Yes, because you've undermined the future. Would you like me to confuse you?"

"Well.. okay then. I might get it?"

"Time Lines. Normally they're not a problem. There can only ever be one Official Time Line, so when intervening in the past, we create a Temporary Alternate Time Line - which dominantly merges back with the Official Time Line when the intervention is complete, hence history has been changed."

"Okayy.."

"But the current Official Time Line results in you being sent back here to me - because the future has already happened, for us. However, it's my future-self who sent you to me - and that's where it gets very, very complicated. I must have been so desperately ill to break such a golden rule. Anyway, I suspect that from the moment when you told me of what lies ahead, the 'future' and the 'past' would start running alongside each other, causing what we call Parallel Time Lines. By 'future' I mean your time, and by 'past' I mean right now, yes? I suggest we've split from the Official Time Line, so a day in your life is a day in mine regardless of the decades between us - and the portal's 6am gateway doesn't help. What I'm saying is that the actual future is now far from certain - it hasn't definitely happened yet, even though it potentially has, because you're affecting the past and the future concurrently. Only you and I are aware of this fact, so let's keep it that way, shall we?"

"Yeah.. so there's two of you now? Official.. and alternative.."

"No. There's only one me and only one now, but a number of potential futures and pasts. You see why traineeship takes so long?"

Bob stared back, and must have nodded.

"Indeed. Now then, the Official Time Line continues as if you never came here, hence the Mirrors will still be missing when you return to Barton. Only when YOU remove the reason for coming here in the first place will history become definite, because my future-self, when re-instated as Guardian, will begin sorting out the aftermath of all this mess. Well, I will unless the Troublers get away with it, because if that happens this Line might submissively merge, which doesn't bear thinking about. Who's to say? You see, there aren't any reference cases, so theories are all we've got. And that one might be wildly inaccurate. Give me an hour and I'll have plenty more, all contradictory," she said, with a grin.

"Uhmm.. is there an un-Advanced version?"

"Yes. You have to get those Mirrors. It's going to be a long few days for all of us, and none of us knows where it might end up."

Bob could follow that one.

"Could your Mirrors here show where the stolen Mirrors are?"

"You're forgetting something. They're not small movie screens -

you have to understand that. Using these Mirrors to trace their own future-selves would be like driving a car along a mountain road while trying to change all four tyres. It can be done, but it's next to impossible and the risks are ludicrous. And instead of merely plunging to your death, you'd create a Finite Inversion Situation, in this case on your first visit to us. You wouldn't want to do that would you? It'd look bad, very bad. The Mirrors are out there somewhere, and the way they'll be retrieved is for you and ONLY you to find them and return them to Pierpont House. And much as I resent saying so, away from here you'll be on your own. This can be headquarters."

"On my own? But I know just about nothing.."

"If not less, but that's you're second big advantage. You're more likely to listen to me and also watch out for everyone and everything."

"My second one? I didn't know I had a first one?"

"Your first and biggest advantage over the Troublers is that you have freedom. No-one can monitor you, therefore I won't risk anyone else going with you through the Immediate Absence Portal - they might be able to track its activities."

"And that's bad then?"

Agatha sat all the way back in her chair and spoke to the ceiling.

"Very. Because if the Troublers are able to monitor who's using it, they're always way ahead of us. We just don't know what they can or can't do, either with the portals or with the Mirrors, and we have to respect those things that we don't understand."

"Oh.. have you got some kind of detector-gadget that I can have then? Otherwise I won't know where the Mirrors are, will I?"

"I wish I did. Nobody has ever been foolish enough to try taking them before. I'll mention it to the Guardian Of Spatial Dynamics.. and he can have a think about that. Incidentally, before you came here, had nobody in your time tried to contact him?"

"Well, Fey thought they might all be dead, because that desk over there," he said, pointing over to one of Agatha's many desks, "..is at 107 covered in notes that should have re-appeared on the Spatial Guardian's desk.."

Agatha leaned on her armrest.

"No communication? Now this gets more challenging.. hmm.."

She became lost in thought again while she slowly finished her coffee, and frowned as Bob lost another biscuit into his.

"You're going to need Encapsulation Fields. I'll sort those for you, immediately," she said, and quickly wrote down a series of bizarre squiggles on a pad. Bob wasn't keen to ask what Encapsulation Fields were, but his expression gave him away.

"They look like blue bags, but they're more complicated than that - I'll spare you the why's and how's. There's one for each Mirror, and they're vital for preventing.."

Agatha paused and struggled to find appropriate words for him.

"..in excessively simple terms, only a truly ruthless and very knowledgeable person or group could even begin to consider separating the Mirrors from each other. So I'm assuming that the people who have carried out this theft would know enough not to risk their own necks, and therefore they would get other fools to do the dirty work - people who don't have a hope of realising exactly what they're messing with.."

Bob whimpered, and felt some sympathy for the other fools.

"And their ignorance will benefit you, Robert."

She fixed Bob with one of her most intense looks, and then offered a re-assuring smile.

"A solitary Mirror is very dangerous, and a solitary Mirror that's been removed from its 'wooden frame' would be even worse. Either would interfere with the immediate surroundings, so the location of one might be indicated by the Contra-Dimensional Irregularities in its immediate vicinity, I'd suggest. Are you with me?"

The big words had made Bob's mind go on a walkabout. He stared at Agatha's hat, and wondered if its little red dot had swapped sides.

"Okay, I'll say all that again, but through a sieve. The Mirrors on their own might 'mess up' things around them, and I can't give any examples to look out for so just keep your eyes open. Follow?"

Bob glanced down at Bagshaw, who briefly stared back before wandering from the panel looking completely bemused.

"Yeah, I think so. Look out for weird stuff, because dimwits are probably the ones who nicked them in the first place."

"Right. Well we're both happier now, aren't we? I do believe this meeting is adjourned!"

Agatha spun her chair around and raised her arms in the air. Bob could see that beneath her incredibly cool exterior there was a real person in there, just like anyone else. Well, almost like everyone else..

CHAPTER FOURTEEN

Naomi and Claudie

Agatha's glass doors closed behind him and he felt as if the weight of the world had been lifted from his shoulders. Unfortunately it had been replaced with something a little heavier, like Jupiter - assuming Jupiter had been colonised by billions and billions of elephants.

Naomi and Claudie were hunting around their desks, trying to find notepads and pens. They soon hurried over to the doors, and stopped for a quick word on the way.

"We won't be a minute, Bob," said Naomi, resting her pad against his head and trying to find out if her pen worked.

"Yup, we're not giving you the icy mitt, Bobs," said Claudie, doing the same, "You're headline news in this office, and the delightful Dame A's in the mood for a convy, that's all. So don't go gettin' lathered 'cause if she didn't like you, she'd have high-tailed you long-ways ages ago, so you can park at mine and be a bunny while we're blowin' feathers. Java's courtesy Claudie's Hot-house so it's okay, you c'n hold with the baksheesh. Medium rare."

Bob tried hard to think of something to say. His options were very, very limited.

"Huh?" was the best he could manage, and looked to Naomi for a translation.

"She means Madame Agatha's going to tell us all about you, and there's a lovely cup of coffee waiting for you over there on her desk while we're gone. We'll only be a couple of minutes so don't start worrying or anything, because you obviously meet with her approval. Mind you, the 'medium rare' bit is a new one on me."

"It's how roasted he looks, and also how you like a steak. You should know that already, and.." said Claudie, as the doors opened.

Bob sat down in front of Claudie's desk and stared at the illustration of a rubber plant in the compendium, wondering where Bagshaw had gone off to again. Did he have a whole inky world to walk around in, or was it just an inky living room with a window for looking at Bob's world through? It was too weird to think about, so he spent a couple of minutes trying to think about nothing and settled for just eye-wandering around the room.

Everything about the reception-office was friendly, and also a little peculiar. He guessed there must be twenty or thirty calendars on the walls, and none of them showed any reference to a year. All the ones around Naomi's area were covered in blue arrows and scribbles, and Claudie's were in red. Big ticks and crosses stood out from all the indecipherable words, and some were almost completely obscured by too-conveniently positioned plants. A large spider plant and a solitary red shoe had fallen off one cabinet, and lay on the floor next to a toppled figurine of a long-limbed dancer. The ivory and gold figure lay forlorn near to Naomi's chair, so Bob went and straightened her up.

"I wish Andie was here," he thought for the millionth time that day, "..she'd really like this," and added the figurine to the Brilliant Things For Andie list, before wandering back to his coffee.

He imagined her walking down the curved stairs, wearing a hat like Agatha's, or sitting in Claudie's chair trying to look serious with a notepad. Everything would be so much better if she could just walk in through one of the doors and be with him. She wouldn't have to come up with any big plans, big answers, or big anythings - just being there would make all the difference in the world.

"She hasn't even been born yet," he thought, and felt a lump rise in his throat, "Nor her mum, or her mum's mum either. None of them exist for ages.. and ages."

A feeling of extreme loneliness crept over him and brought on a dull, pounding headache. More than ever, he just wanted to wake up, find that it was Sunday morning back home, and then forget all about the most realistic and awful dream of all time. He would have breakfast and then go with his parents to visit Great Aunt Agatha, the old lady who could scare anyone. That would do nicely. And then he would go and see Andie and she'd laugh at his latest Freaky Dream and everything would be.. normal again.

A copy of Crazin' Crosswords fell onto the floor from the top of a lop-sided wooden chest next to Claudie's desk. It was closely followed by Jinx, who appeared from nowhere and made Bob jump. She knocked over the rest of the pile, which seemed to trigger off some faint music, and she ran into Agatha's office through a glass-panel cat-flap. The rest of the magazines spread out onto the floor so much that Bob felt obliged to pick them up, and while doing so he had a look at the chest. It was about three times the size of a shoe box, with an elaborately framed metal dial embedded in the front.

"RCA.. Radiola 44.." he read from its lid, "Probably the 1920's version of cool Sony thing," he figured, and followed the wires to somewhere under a collection of bags, where its octagonal speaker lay buried. An orchestral version of Sweet Georgia Brown suddenly blared out, so he buried the loudspeaker back under the bags and tried to find the volume control on the box. He knocked the tuning dial off instead, and silence returned.

"Oops.."

He kept hold of the crossword magazine and sat down again, amazed that crosswords could ever have been described as 'the newest craze that's sweeping the nation!' He flicked through the pages to try and keep his mind off Andie, and also to try and find one which he could actually do, but they seemed to be entirely in Claudie-talk so he quickly gave up and dared himself to try looking out of a window again. He decided against doing that, not because he knew that he'd pass out, but because Naomi and Claudie were just about to leave Agatha's office. Very soon. Really, really soon. Any moment..

Twenty minutes later all three came back into the office and converged around Claudie's desk. Bob felt as nervous as a laboratory rat who'd suddenly been surrounded by scientists with scalpels, clipboards and cameras. He shifted uncomfortably in his seat.

"Naomi, in your opinion, tell Robert what he needs to do. You may consider this a test."

Naomi consulted her notepad, and Agatha took it off her.

"Umm, you ought to keep a low profile, I don't mean like a midget, but like someone who's not obvious, you know.. in the shadows, as if you've got one of those sunlight allergies like my cousin. And then find however many Mirrors you can but whatever you do don't touch them - you have to wrap them in that Tiffany Blue stuff in the other room and remember to tie the strings up at the end. Does that make sense? And then take it back to where you come from, otherwise all kinds of things will happen which are too 'Yikes!' for you to know about, because if you did know about them you might get scared off right at the beginn.."

Agatha's eyes went skywards, and she brought Naomi to an end.

"Yes, thank you so much, Naomi. We all get the idea. That was not a fail, but you could've asked how long he's been up today.."

"..and mentioned the spook-ola dimensional reeeepercussions of bringing a Mirror back here!" added Claudie, who flinched as Naomi threw her an excellent trainee-Agatha style glance. Agatha noticed, and looked pleased.

"Very good, both of you. Under no circumstances are you to bring any Mirrors back here. Having a duplicate near an original would very likely cause a Fluctuating Bi-Continuum Disorder, and that really is something to avoid."

Bob didn't like the sound of that at all, and dug up a good question. "Huh?"

Agatha tipped her head slightly in Naomi's direction, prompting her to answer.

"If you brought one here, then completely strange things would happen with the way that time, people, objects and.. well, everything really, interacts. Most likely."

"Most likely?" mouthed Bob, wondering where his voice had gone, and wishing he was there with it.

"Yes. No-one's ever been dumb enough to try this before. Anyway, do tell how long you've been up," she finished, trying to sound as if she had intended to ask him all along. Bob tried to work out when he was last in bed back at home, but couldn't even begin to guess.

"I was asleep for a few hours up at The.. the portal, but apart from that, maybe something like a day or more. I gave up telling the right time hours ago. Or maybe it was years ago.. in the uhh.. future?"

"Shoot sweety pie, yerr as confoozed as a babe raccoon," announced Claudie in a curling southern accent, twirling a pencil between her fingers.

"Are you tired?" asked Naomi.

"Yes, I think so.. "

"That's good enough for me. We've already sorted you're room out so you can stay here tonight."

Bob was almost going to ask 'What room?' but decided against it. The day had been incredibly long, and the previous few were catching up with him again. He stifled a yawn instead, and Agatha prompted Naomi and Claudie to start taking notes on what she was about to say.

"Tomorrow your two associates will sort out some appropriate clothes for you, and let you settle in around here a little more. And then the following day, you'll have an early start in order to go back to Arizona. There could well be something there, and I believe it has my name on it."

"How early is early?" Bob wondered aloud.

"You'll leave here around six o'clock in the morning, so that you arrive at the farmstead in closer time-sync with your surroundings. Now then, I have certain other work to attend to," she said, and handed a few papers to Naomi before going back to her office.

There was a knock at the front door and a friendly waiter brought in a trolley loaded with sandwiches and enough extras to make a buffet for at least half a dozen people, which Bob could have managed on his own. He underlined his Mental Note about getting a Supplies pocket sorted out, and they all descended on the dinner.

"So do you two live upstairs, like above the office? That must be convenient - it was really busy outside when I was coming here."

"It's trés convenient and very secure," giggled Claudie, "..you go try getting up there!"

Bob finished off a drumstick that might have come from an ostrich, and went over to the curved blue staircase. It didn't appear to be booby-trapped or covered with landmines, and didn't have security guards or snarling dogs anywhere. It simply curled upwards in a broad sweep, narrowing and almost turning back on itself at the top. He tried to ignore the giggles and waves from Naomi and Claudie as he turned out of sight, and soon reached the first landing. There were no doors, just two featureless walls and one with a large window looking out towards Brooklyn. The next flight of curving stairs began over on the right side, so he raced up them and arrived at another landing, which also had a window and no doors. He went over to the next flight of stairs, and quickly arrived at another landing - with a window and no doors, just like the previous two. And so was the next. And the one after that. And also the one after that. There was even a scuff mark against one wall that was becoming remarkably familiar.

Most of New York could have heard the penny drop as Bob finally realised he was caught up in some freakishly bizarre time and space odd-ball scenario. He prepared himself for an embarrassing return to the floor below, and went back down the solitary flight of steps to arrive near Naomi's desk - just in time to be laughed at.

"Aww, poor Bobs!" laughed Claudie, "That's Naomi's Security Glitch, and how! You go up the second flight and find that you're.."

"..back at the top of the first flight, yes that's pure genius. How did you manage that?" he asked, embarrassed and impressed at the same time. Naomi put on her weediest voice.

"Those nice fellas in Spatial Dynamics sorted it for me. They can be so good to damsels in distress.."

Bob figured that damsels like these were highly unlikely to ever find themselves anywhere near any distress.

"If we decide to let you get up to our floor, you'll see there's a few normal doors in a normal corridor, just like in a normal apartment block. One of the doors is yours, and the big one at the end leads to the building we live in. It's a straight link to our lobby at 417 Park Avenue - a Park Avenue address right by Central Park! Saves walking nearly forty blocks - and how nifty is that?"

"Veee niff-teee!" confirmed Claudie.

Half an hour later when the food had been taken away, Bob yawned his way up to the first landing and touched the scuff mark with his key. Nothing happened, just as expected, so he estimated a point three feet above it and pushed. The hidden door swung open and he walked into a fairly short corridor just like Naomi had described. Four white doors faced each other, and one that looked like a standard front door was at the far end. It even had a letterbox, no doubt put there for a laugh. A few small half-tables stood against the walls, trying to support sprawling varieties of house plants. Another year-free collection of calendars hung along one side of the cream walls, and a small series of Manhattan etchings each with a small clock beneath them ran along the other. All in all, it wasn't too weird. Except for one door.

Most of the door, its frame and part of the wall was covered in manic scrawl. The words "Bob's Room" had been neatly written in a thick black pen near the top, and then been crossed out and replaced by "Bobs's Speakeasy" in blue, which in turn had been replaced by "Bob's Room" again. This was heavily scribbled over and "Jazzbo Bobs's Swagger Patch" was written underneath - which had a line through it. This continued down the door until Bob's name no longer appeared anywhere, and a scripted argument was in full flow.

Nearer to the floor the handwriting had deteriorated into scrawl, scribbles and stick-people. It finished with a wavy and smudged "Stop writing on the door CLAUDETTE", which was answered by "Well you are as well NAOMI". The last line, "Now look what you made me do," was written on the carpet.

The handle gave a friendly click and Bob stepped into a room that sent a shiver down his spine. It was the same size as his bedroom back home, the bed was in the same position next to the window, a bedside table stood by the headboard, and the wardrobe and a desk were in the right places as well. Of all the weird things that had happened in the previous few days, this was the weirdest by at least four lengths. This was suddenly very personal.

Although the layout was the same, the decor was strictly 1920's. A tassled lamp stood in place of the lava lamp, and a rickety Victrola 6 turntable was where the mini hi-fi ought to be. A row of books and crime novels next to another Radiola box took up the space for the tv. Bob sat down at the table which in Barton would have been a desk with a computer on it. He pressed a key on the black Underwood typewriter, piercing the air with a loud and very clean 'thwhack'. A bold and precise letter 'a' appeared on the sheet of paper.

"This is on the eerie side of.." Bob's whisper trailed away as his attention was drawn to the posters on the walls. The pop princesses and various actresses had been replaced by their long-forgotten counterparts. Amongst the array of unrecognisable faces, one or two stood out as being familiar and felt almost like friends. Lillian Gish smouldered from a publicity shot, the female robot from Metropolis looked out as impassively as ever, and Charlie Chaplin shivered in the Klondike snow for The Gold Rush. But that wasn't the weirdest thing by a long way. Bob couldn't believe that all the actresses had badly drawn beards and moustaches. Even Chaplin hadn't avoided the artist's pen. A thought-bubble floated above his head in which he was confessing that he wasn't in the tiniest bit funny. Except for the handwriting, it practically matched one that Andie had done a week or two earlier.

"This is too.. top-level weirdness by at least a.. uhh." Words failed him and he took a moment to just lie down on the bed and try to shut everything out.

Three hours later a loud knock on the door woke him up, and it opened as he flicked the table lamp on. Naomi poked her head inside.

"Bob? How do you like your room? Pretty darn gee isn't it? There's even records as well for you. Anyway, I thought I'd let you know that we're finally calling it a day now - so if you need us we're only next door-ish, so just knock. Actually, you can wander through anyhows 'cause we're in apartments 963 and 963a, but it doesn't really matter which one 'cause there's no wall between them. Oh, in case you don't know, there's a kitchen and a bathroom on this corridor, but don't go in the room opposite this one, whatever you do."

Fear sparked Bob's brain into life.

"Why? Is there a vortex or some kind of dimensional catastrophe going on in there?"

"No, no. It's full of Claudie's washing. Long story, quite funny, don't ask. Anyway, it's been a big day for everyone, so night-night."

She gave a wave and the room fell back into silence. He clambered over the bed and leaned against the window sill, looking down 199 floors to the city below. Or maybe 198 floors, he couldn't decide. Either way, in the dark it didn't look so real, and much to his relief didn't have such a high Head-Spin Factor. A blanket of tiny lights flickered down below, and reached far away, mile after luminous mile. The East River offered the only interruption, winding like a huge black snake through the city, but even that was dotted with smaller lights making their way slowly to and fro. Bob took a while to sit and watch.

Just like he did at home, he left the curtains open and lay in the moonlight thinking about anything and everything, mostly linked by thoughts of Andie. As normal, just at the point where he was falling asleep, he remembered something he needed to do. This time, he had to fill in his new diary. Agatha would be bound to ask him about it and he didn't want to get on the wrong side of her. He scribbled down anything he could remember, and crawled back to bed.

Bright and early next morning the berserk high-pitched clanging of alarm bells filled Bob's room with sheer unadulterated panic. He sat up quickly, sure that if the building wasn't on fire, the rest of the world must be. He desperately looked around in the blinding morning sunlight to see where the noise was coming from, and soon clobbered the bells on the top of the alarm clock. It fell over and landed with a deserved thunk on the floor, where it gave a few defiant clanks. Even the loathsome bleeps of his evil clock at home were preferable to that manic din.

He wandered down to the office and followed the sound of voices and the inviting aroma of coffee into the kitchen. Naomi and Claudie were already looking over a collection of newspapers.

"Ooh, breakfast with Bobs! You'll have to help yourself.. we don't have a butler yet," said Claudie, sounding slightly more awake than Bob felt.

"Post's Grape-Nuts Flakes? Catchy name," he said, reading a boring cereal box and already missing his Crunchy Munchy.

"Hmm. Don't get excited though, because it's got no grapes or nuts - just a flaky mush," said Naomi, and took out a new pad to start planning the day ahead.

"Now then.. first of all we'll get you gift-wrapped in the most darb garb, and then perhaps linger a while in just one or two shops down on Ladies' Mile.."

"Yeah Nay, but you'll need to find a lady first!" interrupted Claudie. It was too early for anyone to be having a good laugh yet, but Bob made a valiant effort.

"..and then we're off to The Plaza for lunch with Madame Agatha, so you need to be very smart Bob! They're strict in there."

By nine o'clock they were in the Department Of Time's corridor, and Claudie finally managed to lock the reception door. It looked surprisingly complicated, and seemed to involve swearing at the right time. After her fifth failed attempt, Bob had wondered if his key would be as good at locking doors as it was at opening them, but decided against trying to find out until Claudie was a safe distance away. A very, very safe distance.

Naomi opened one of the other doors in the corridor, rather than going out through the main door. It lead into another corridor, which contained a further dozen doors all identical to each other and each giving no indication of what lay beyond. After a quick word with Claudie, she chose the tenth one, which lead down two short steps and out onto Fifth Avenue. Bob stood on the sidewalk and looked back at the insignificant, ramshackle door they'd just come through.

"Don't even think about how, just be happy that it does," said Naomi cheerfully, and lead the way into the busy morning.

In little over half an hour Bob had been totally decked out at Bauman's Attire - a stifling store with a stifling name, and he hoped they would never open a branch in Barton. His clothes were deemed big-time suitable for a nifty Flipper in New York, and then he had to go through it all again for ones that were 'sench for a sharp Rube' in Arizona. That would have made him feel good, if he had any idea what it meant. Instead, he felt terminally embarrassed, but knew that he wasn't really in any position to argue. Apparently, a few odd-fitting suits with razor-sharp creases and also a chunky-weave jacket were essential for any self respecting lady's man. Strangely, all the clothes were a bit too big for him, but it was eventually pointed out that he needed the extra space for concealing the blue bags around his waist, because that way he'd stick less chance of losing them or forgetting them. Bob couldn't help but be impressed with how quickly they had come to know him.

The rest of the gloriously sunny morning was spent touring the kind of shops that ordinarily he would never, ever go near unless he was with Andie, and he quickly decided that she would love most of them. She'd probably really like Naomi and Claudie as well, and he felt sure that they would like her, which made the whole morning feel a whole lot better.

Bob had been awarded the title of 'Official Sherpa' in recognition of his expertise at bag-carrying, and was getting to know parts of Fifth Avenue and some of the side streets quite well as they made their way backwards and forwards. They finally wound up at Bloomingdales on Third Avenue, and still hadn't been anywhere near Ladies' Mile for Naomi.

The store was huge, and felt bigger by the minute. After combing four floors they arrived in the European Fashions Department, where they left Bob alone in the formal waiting area near the Mademoiselles' Fitting Rooms, with the difficult task of staying with the bags. A perky sales assistant automatically handed him a cup of coffee, and he pretended to flick through a newspaper. The time had come for a meeting with Bagshaw.

"Hey Bagshaw.. Bagshawww.." he whispered to the book, cunningly concealed behind the open newspaper. His Lordship wandered into the frame, trying to light a pipe.

"Morning, Sah! Where on earth are we?" he said through a cloud of black and white smoke.

"Bad news. We're in one of the Ladies' Fashion floors at Bloomingdales - there's so many of them! But that's not entirely important right now. I need to know what a Flapper is, and a Sheik and a Sheba as well. Oh, and a Clara, a Forty-Niner, a Grummy, a Lollygagger, a Sockdollllager Mutton, a Six Cylinder Dingledangler.. and a whole load more as well. I started writing them down, but I reckon some of them can't actually be spelt. Any ideas?"

"Hmm.. wait here, while I consult with my reference files."

Bagshaw put his pipe down on a table which Bob had thought was just a stray line. He returned a couple of minutes later, clutching a few sheets of paper and looking very pleased with himself.

"Well, according to a Sear's Catalogue who I once spent a year next to, a Flapper is, and I quote: 'A rectangular device made primarily of canvas, measuring three feet by two, secured above a bed to keep the occupant of the aforementioned bed pleasantly cool during hot, languid summer nights. Its modus operandi is a simple series of strings and pulleys, controlled by a servant or reclining owner'. What will they think of next? And for that people paid seven of your American dollars! Ye Gods the world is ever more preposterous. Now then, a Sheik, as far as I know, is the head of a Middle Eastern land-owning tribe or family, generally in possession of many camels and wives. As for the rest, I have absolutely no idea whatsoever. And there you go. I trust that helps?"

Bob despaired.

"That's great, really great. Bagshaw, when we get back to my time I'm introducing you to dad's Encyclopedia Britannica, all three billion volumes, and.."

Claudie appeared in an explosion of colour, making a film-star entrance from behind a long pink curtain. She'd either gone completely mad or had simply taken too many things into the fitting rooms. She wore a gravity-defying random collection of half-on half-off clothes, topped with a canary-yellow cloche hat balanced precariously on top of a scarlet one. Even her shoes were different to each other, but it all seemed to make sense to her as she stood before a ludicrously tall mirror analysing each item - all while swinging the longest necklace Bob had ever seen.

"Hghghallo, Meesta Pres'dent.. whooo, me? Si, one would be honayred.. gratzee, gratzee.." she said a few times to her reflection, curtsying, scrutinising and altering different clothes each time. Bob suspected she was discarding the ones that didn't match her accent. She stepped over to him on her way to consult with Mme Babette, the store's Fashion Advisor.

"Bobs, whatever Nay's got on, say it's the bee's okay? She's not rolled for straight lines, and Lu-Lus need those haych vees. Lean on the trés pohsi-teeves, y'follow?"

Bob tried not to look blank, and failed.

"Curves, curves, curves," she whispered to him, as if that helped. "Okay, just say it's all copacetic, and that'll do fine.. practice while I'm gone. Kohh-pahh-ket and you know the rest."

Naomi emerged soon afterwards, with a black fur coat draped over an unbelievably long white evening dress. Bob could see that she wasn't suited to the linear things in life, and her figure - which in Bob's era would stop men blinking - denied her the authentic straight-line Flapper look. She groomed the white ostrich feathers on her minute hat, and small-stepped over to the mirror.

"Just pretend, Bob," she said while trying a new pose, "that you're the military leader of a rich European country, who's planning on getting up to all kinds of war-type things next winter. And also just pretend that you're going to attend a Something Ball in a week's time in the capital city of your country, okay?"

"Ja, ich bin ein crackpot," said Bob with a salute.

"No, pretend Italian. Now, imagine I'm me, dressed like this. Would this outfit make you want to stand somewhere like.. I don't know.. the top of a long flight of marble stairs near the ballroom, if I was wearing it and started speaking to you? Just pretending."

"Oh yeah, definitely. I'd even stand there holding a tray of knives and a hot drink, too. And scissors. Right on the edge of the top step."

"So you wouldn't necessarily notice someone in a hurry who might get too close and possibly bump into you?"

"Not a chance."

"So, if say, Claudie came along and gave you a real wallop.."

"I wouldn't know what had hit me.. but I'd know exactly what I'd hit, all the way down. Every single step."

"Hmm, that's good, very good.. but black's not really me, is it? Wait there for a bit.."

Two entire hours crawled by before they finally emerged back onto the streets of Third Avenue and started filling a taxi with bags, hat boxes, shoe boxes and more bags. They travelled a long way up town to meet Agatha for lunch, and on the way Bob had a very odd guided tour of buildings which Naomi and Claudie felt were important. Naomi set the ball rolling.

"Look there, Bob! That's where my Granpa used to have a bakery! It burned down one night. Everyone was very sympathetic, though - even the fire crew said it smelled lovely."

"Aha, Bobs! That clothes store is where Naomi got pinched once for stealing! The exact spot's right by that sloping tree."

Naomi looked annoyed.

"I wasn't properly arrested and I wasn't stealing, I wouldn't ever. They were having a big Buy One And Get One Free sale, and when I was queuing up I decided that I didn't really want the scarf I was supposed to pay for so I went and put it back, which left me with the free one. You can't buy something that's free, so what was I supposed to do? Anyway, I would have been fine if the cop wasn't so mean to me. Sometimes I'm unlucky beyond belief, I really am."

"Unlucky?"

"He wanted my name and all that, but I thought he was just making a move, you know like looking for a date. So I gave a friend's name and address instead, but it turned out that she was his niece. Now that's unlucky in anyone's book. He was so cross with me.."

Bob's mind began wandering as Naomi and Claudie rapidly worked their way through countless stories and laughs, using more Flapper-esque words that meant absolutely nothing to either him or Bagshaw. After a few streets had drifted by, the taxi stopped for a while to let a tram roll past. Claudie poked the side of his head, and pointed to the scruffiest tramp in Manhattan.

"Looky Bobs, there's my Uncle Dethro, sleeping on that bench!"

"Death Row?"

"Yeah. He should have been named Jethro, but the Priest had the worst hangover imaginable, plus a split lip from a wedding the day before. Anyway, goin' back a while, ol' D was the most successful fella in our family. He ran the habso best chicken farm in all of New Jersey. His secret was the Chicken Magnetiser."

"Chicken magnet..?"

"Catching chickens for market is real difficult for chicken farmers. Chasing them's easy enough when they're just eggs, but once they get those legs and wings it becomes moocho tougher and that makes harvesting difficult. So Dethro developed a feed for them which made them easier to catch."

Bob looked at the whino, who was being licked by a passing mongrel. The dog quickly stopped, choked in disgust, and licked the pavement a few times before running away.

"Keeping this in English, was the feed drugged or something?"

"No, it contained iron filings. Then he designed a magnetic pad the size of a rug which had decoy chickens stuck onto it. So after he'd fed his chickens, he'd get them to run around and then once they ran over the pad - he could just walk along and pick them up! The boff was a genius."

"What went wrong then?"

"Two things really. First, he had a metal leg which meant he was stuck on the pad more times than the chickens, and second, he plain hated chickens. So he sold the idea and retired off'uh the profits."

"Wow, he must have done really well for himself."

"Yeah, he did."

"So why's he asleep on that bench?"

Claudie waited for a long moment.

"Because he's tired," she said, as if Bob was a complete idiot.

She even kept a straight face, and for a moment Bob's brain tied itself in a knot trying to figure out if she was telling the truth or delivering some kind of joke. Naomi was hiding behind her hands, barely containing her laughter until Claudie fell apart. Bob was set to join in without really knowing why, but he was suddenly distracted.

As the taxi turned into a long parade of brownstone houses, an open-sided truck caught his attention. It looked completely out of place, parked in such an expensive-looking area. And then maybe it was the sunlight or maybe it was his imagination, but in the space of one blink Bob was almost sure it jumped backwards a few inches and then instantly forwards again. If he'd been more certain that he'd seen something odd, he would have mentioned it - but instead he joined in with the laughter about Dethro until the taxi pulled up outside the Park Plaza Hotel.

CHAPTER FIFTEEN
Boffins and Dibbs

For the first time since he arrived, Bob saw a place that he could recognise. Dense layers of trees marked the southern border of Central Park over on the other side of the road, which he proudly pointed out to Naomi and Claudie - who were more amused than impressed. He played along with the fake cries of amazement, but as he followed them towards the lobby he was struck by the contrast and difference that just a day or so had made in his life. It was hard to believe that just 24 hours earlier he had been anxiously walking along the same huge road that everyone else knew as West 59th Street, searching for Lexington Avenue and feeling like he was being a dismal failure of the worst kind. Looking at Central Park from the steps of one of Manhattan's finest buildings, he was starting to feel like the city was his, or that he was the city's, one or the other.

The feeling didn't last too long as they were quickly guided through a series of tall and extravagantly decorated corridors to the even taller Palm Court restaurant. A pianist in a slightly lowered central section played something light and classical, accompanied by a violinist who seemed oblivious to everyone around him. Bob wasn't entirely surprised that Aunt Agatha would choose somewhere like this for lunch. He made a Mental Note in capital letters to never, ever, ever suggest to the older Agatha back in Barton that she ought to visit his favourite restaurant for a meal, at any time of the day. The heaving Lots'a Hots'a Pots'a Pasta didn't quite compare.

Two waiters finished adding the final touches to a table in a corner of the room, and drew three of the four chairs out from under it. They opened the private patio doors and the tablecloth swayed slightly in the warm breeze, the cutlery gleamed and the glasses sparkled in the bright sunlight, and it was all completely wasted on Bob. He sat down feeling ravenous, hoping the chef knew a thing or two about chips.

"What to drink, Bobs? How about a tall Budwine?" asked Claudie while changing her white Shopping Gloves for her even-whiter

Lunching Gloves.

Bob didn't find the prospect of drinking a combination of lager and wine very tempting at all, so after a moment's rapid search for any excuse, he managed to find an abysmal one.

"I think that it'd have to stay on the table for a few years before I can drink it, and by then it might be a little flat. Don't you have age limits for drinking in America?"

"Yeah, nobody's old enough. It's called Prohibition. Mind you, you wouldn't know it in most places," she said, and laughed. "Don't fret Bobs, Budwine's a fruity, not a hoochie. You'll get the idea."

"How about Coke?" Bob suggested, pointing to a placard near the bar which had a pleasingly familiar logo.

"No, no, Budwine's far healthier. Try it! Dame A's fond of it with crushed ice, so it must be bearable. I wonder when she'll turn up because.."

Right on cue, Agatha arrived in the restaurant to a wave of compliments, in an understated cream and white outfit that seemed to define 20s elegance. She eventually sat down at the table after being sidetracked at most of the other tables on her way over, and gave a despairing look.

"Phew! I trust you've all had a productive morning? And I see you're dressed for business now, Robert?" she asked, inching her swooped white hat backwards.

"Err.. yes, I've been seriously garbed, apparently, and I could blend in anywhere - I've got a wardrobe a chameleon would be proud of," Bob replied, with a nervous laugh. Agatha looked pleased, and therefore Naomi and Claudie did as well. The head-waiter arrived, carrying an armful of enormous cards.

"Et voila, les menooz, pour Mme Agateyrr, laideez, and ah muzsyewr," he said, proudly presenting a menu to each of them. He mentioned something quietly to Agatha and then backed away to wait for approval.

"How disappointing," Agatha sighed, "It appears the gazelle's off. Never mind, never mind.."

Bob disappeared behind his huge menu, and found that it was written entirely in French, or possibly Martian. Either way, he couldn't make any sense of it and had no idea what to order. He opened his jacket, raised the compendium slightly, and whispered.

"Pssst, Bagshaw.. Bagshaw.. what can I order? I don't understand any of this! What's foreign for pizza?"

"Oh, are you fine-dining today? Excellent! If you take a look at the Cuisine Section commencing page 230 you'll find a chapter dedicated to elevating one's eating standards, but I suspect you have very limited time for perusing this book and a menu, so I suggest you take the safe route and opt for soup followed by a left-sided steak. Can't fail, old boy."

"A left sided.. what difference does it make?"

"The well-informed diner should know that cows invariably stand with their left sides towards the sun. It's their way of monitoring what time of day it is. By the time they've turned to face the opposite direction to the one they started off facing, they know it's time to go back to the barn. The great benefit about this kind of behaviour is that the meat on the left side is considerably more tender than the meat on the right side. Therefore it is always advisable to be 'side-specific' as you Americans might say, when requesting a steak. Now, make sure you ask the waiter for anti-clockwise vegetables.."

Bob shut the book and ordered chicken.

"So Bob, what do you do at the future-school where you're from?" asked Naomi, appearing genuinely interested.

"Nothing special, really. There's Maths, Geography, Chemistry, Heimskringla Chronicles, Monarchial and Non-Monarchial Nordic Studies, Viking Exploration.."

"That's a bit Scandinavian for an English one, isn't it? Don't you ever think it's odd that.." began Claudie.

"I'm quite sure there's a perfectly good reason," said Agatha, in a 'drop-it-Claudie' way.

"..and I've got an Ynglinga Saga test on Wednesday. Part of it's in Norwegian, which always makes things a bit tricky."

"Is that because it's a difficult language to learn?" Naomi asked, fending off a puzzled expression.

"I don't know," said Bob, "Norwegian's not on the syllabus till the Fourth Year."

Naomi searched in vain for another question, and gave up with a smile. One of the waiters returned midway through the main course, and handed a silver plate to Agatha. She opened the note on it, and excused herself with a subtle sigh. Bob was nervous enough about the world's predicaments without the Guardian Of Time being unexpectedly called away from lunch.

"Is that something serious? Should we all be back in the office?"

Claudie shook her head, and Naomi answered.

"Oh it'll be nothing. That kind of thing's always happening. She can never have two minutes to herself. There's always someone who's forgotten how to breathe or climb the stairs or something like that. Believe me, if it was important we'd be back there already."

The lunch was put on hold for a while, and Bob felt the time was ideal to do some fishing.

"Well how about you, Naomi? What do you do for Aunt Agatha, or can't we talk about.. that kind of thing here? Classified stuff.."

Claudie answered before Bob had finished.

"Oh don't worry about talking, this is one of our places! I'm tellin' you, nothing unimportant happens here and Agatha's been coming since it was the old Plaza, and some folks practically live in the bar," she said, pressing another air-button towards a group of people perched on a row of tall chairs. "As for Nay, she's been here a year and is a certified Level One Administrative Assistant, no less. First step on the road to Trainee-ship, etcet."

"And what about you, Claudie?" added Bob. Naomi took over.

"Well she's been here a year and four months, and is a Level One-And-A-Bit Administerrative Assistant" she replied.

"Indeedy, I get the 'And A Bit' because I do all the hard work. The last thing Naomi filed was her nails."

"You cheeky.. shuffling papers doesn't count as work, and you wouldn't even do that if someone didn't keep putting them there."

"Anyway Bobs, once we've passed the Level Two Assessments, we get that ageing slow-down thing, but that's not for another three years at least. But once we've got it, hello Manhattan!"

Once the laughs had died down, Bob had a serious question.

"How does it all work then? I mean, like what other departments are there, apart from Spatial Dynamics, whatever that is.."

"Well.. there are twelve major Departments back at the Lexington Building, which allow the day-to-day existence of the world, its occupants and the immediate universe around it to operate smoothly - without the general public, that's Outsiders to you and me, being aware of its role. Our department is the second largest and the second most important, behind Spatial Dynamics. That one's huge. It's responsible for, and I quote, 'The smooth co-existence of perceivable and non-perceivable realities'. There."

Bob looked from Naomi to Claudie, hoping for a little help - a sure sign of his desperation.

"In other words Bobs, they make sure everything around you works. Like if you walk into a brick wall, you don't go through it. It's all to do with.. err.. atoms and molecules and stuff interacting and that kind of thing. They have so many theories to sort out all the time. Nothing works without those trés specialle Spatial types figuring out how and why first. They leak simple stuff to smartie Outsiders every now and then for a laugh, and see what they make of it. Some do quite well, like that Henry Eisenstein."

"No, wasn't he an Albert? I'm sure he was. Albert Einstone.." added Naomi.

"That's right Nay, Albert Einstone. What a funny guy, really funny. Jeez, don't I just always get names wrong. Anyway, the Spatial Dynamics Department have more sub-departments and special offices and Research Centres than you could shake a real big stick at. We spent a day with the Perspective Office last week."

"Perspective Office? What's that for?"

Claudie finished off another glass of wine and discretely swapped her glass for Naomi's, knocking the empty one over in the process. Naomi stood it back up and took over.

"Those boffins work out why things look smaller when they're far away, and bigger when they're nearer. Sounds simple, but it's a real headache. They sussed out the principles ages ago, and monitor them.. and.. do stuff.. so it doesn't go wrong. Don't ask me. Look around you Bob, it's working right now!"

Naomi waved her fingers close to Bob's face, and then moved them back a few times.

"Occasionally they mess up in a big way, so some unlucky schmoe slips through the net, and then ooops - you've got another victim of Irrational Perspective Disorder."

"Irrational what?"

Naomi filled the glasses to the levels they were at before Claudie had drained them all.

"Imagine someone starts walking away from you, but they don't get any smaller. They stay the same height, no matter how far off they go. Well, by the time they turn around and start walking back, they're going to be huge when they reach you, aren't they? It's an irreversible condition, so they have to be monitored and observed, regularly. A few years ago, one of the trainees devised a way to herd them all together into Observation Zones, without any of them realising they were being herded, of course. I think they called it 'Basketball' but I'm too scared to go and see."

Bob nodded, for no good reason.

"Then there's the Department Of Nature, who keep an eye on climatic conditions, seasonal continuity, and what's growing everywhere. They have a sub-department for plants, which is the one I wanted to join but the waiting list's 137 years too long. Boooring. And then there's Outer Existences, which is a strange one."

"Spooky spooky spooky.." said Claudie, covering her eyes.

"And how. They're a bit creepy there, a bit too shiver'n'quiver for me. I don't know exactly what goes on, but they have to deal with freaky Supernatural Beings & Bi-Planar Existence, like everything from rampaging poltergeists to little-bitty fairies. It's all a bit mad and off-limits for almost everyone, and they can't operate without Spatial Dynamics and Time - but they wanted to be a department on their own. I think everyone just likes to keep them happy.. very wise move, probably. Then there's Colour, Sound, and Taste. Those three departments are inter-dependent - and run by triplets. Three Guardians who all look the same! No-one ever knows if they're talking to the right one, not that it matters, 'cause they haven't got a brain between them. All they do is argue about the most trivial things. Mind you, when they get it right, they really get it right, but they don't bother very often. You know when you look at something and think, 'Oh I bet that tastes gorgeous', and then you try it and it's foul and makes a squelchy noise? That's cause those three were either arguing or having a laugh."

Claudie giggled to herself and took over.

"There's the Communication one too, a real dumb bunch of monkeys who keep dreaming up ways for people to mis-understand each other. Utter spanners, the whole yardfull. They're meant to do it the other way round, but all they ever do is make life more complicated. Rumour has it, okay, a few years ago Madame Agatha threatened to wind the clock back and stop one of their top guys from ever being born. I don't know what she got all heat-up about, but she sure squared one big uppercut on him. Problem solved."

"Yeah, we don't mention that.. so where are we now Claudie?

That's eight isn't it? Okay then.. umm.. the Department Of Historical Artefacts. They're the ones who work out ways to keep everyone off our trail."

"They keep.. how do they do that?"

"They make sure that there's enough interesting stuff buried in the ground to keep folks wondering where it all came from. Sometimes they turn on the style, big time - they won so many awards for Tuten-whatever.. that fella's tomb in Egypt. A real boffin thought that one up! But I think some of the small things that the Ossification Studio make are more effective. One of their juniors got transferred to another department for dropping his wallet next to a Tyrannosaurus skull they'd buried somewhere in China. It nearly caused a national panic when it was dug up, so we had to help sort it all out. Took ages. You'll have to visit their studio, 'cause they make some crazy stuff that can't ever get used. Really funny.."

"That's nine," said Claudie, and drained the last few drops from the wine bottle.

"Use a glass, Claudie, like Madame Agatha said to, y'know think classy. So, nine down? See over there, Bob - there's that lead-head who runs the Department Of Health. I can't believe any species on earth has survived this long. Don't get me started on that bunch.."

Claudie took over.

"And that leaves the Department Of Ruvvelatee.. Revitalisalise.. Sleep. Talk about the 'old school tie' brigade, eesh. You ever wondered why you can't get to sleep at night, or why you wake up feeling dead? It's 'cause they're useless."

"That's eleven, I think.." said Bob, who'd been trying to keep track.

"Is it? Oh yes, there's just one more to go. That'll be Gravity of course, won't it, Claudie?"

"Ugh, those dibbs in Gravity," she said, flicking her glass to make it 'ping' until she giggled. Naomi moved it out of her reach.

"See Bob, if you can't do anything else, join the Department Of Gravitation. Most of them can't even spell it. They only have one thing to worry about - 'Make sure nothing falls up!' I mean, how difficult does it get? You wouldn't believe the trouble we've had with them. Take last year, there was a trainee who wasn't too switched on who allowed a Category 'A' Technical Inversion Oversight to happen. You know what that means? It means a few hundred miles away in Ohio some golfer guy Bobby Jones goes to tee off in the Open. The ball stays still, and the rest of the world moves instead. The entire planet shifts nearly 180 yards in a big swoop, then bounces against the ball till it finally stops in a sandpit. I'm not joking, four or five billion people fell over. Twenty six countries got wiped out! It took Madame Agatha and seven other departments nearly a week to fix that one - you've never seen her so livid. And you'd never guess who'd been kickin' laughs with that particular gravity-goof just the night before?"

"Well he seemed perfectly alright when I left him.." said Claudie, and they both dissolved into a mass of giggles. After a couple of minutes they were pretty much back to normal. Claudie leaned her chair a long way back, and pointed at Bob.

"But Bobs, being vee serious now, you must always, always ALWAYS be nice about the Spatial Dynamics crowd. It might just be office rumour-ola, but that Guardian and a certain other Guardian were.. kind'a 'close' many moons ago.. if you catch my drift. And bearing in mind he parks his job for 200 years at a time, and a certain someone else intends keeping her job for a very long time too, they might just get 'close' again, if you know what I'm saying, if I was saying anything.. which I'm not.." she said, and suddenly sat upright again, with a look of innocence on her face.

"Well, I return at last, everyone. The fools we have to put up with.." said Agatha, and sat down with a smile - until she noticed the cold remnants of her lunch. A waiter instantly hurried over with replacements for everyone, and Naomi moved the conversation back to safe territory, with a slightly nervous wobble in her voice.

"So as I was saying, everyone, did you know Ingrid's just had a baby? Apparently he looks just like his father!"

"What, fat, ugly and bald?" replied Claudie.

"Yeah, and he's only happy with a bottle!" Naomi added, and even Agatha laughed.

Bob was enjoying lunch too much to be bothered by the scale of what he'd been finding out. It all seemed so normal, and he was beginning to fully understand why Feiya had been so insistent on keeping things simple and not asking questions. Trying to analyse and understand everything all at once would have blown any fuses in his brain that hadn't been blown already. Eventually, Naomi moved even further into safer areas.

"I'd love to know what styles are hot in your time, Bob! I just can't imagine, I'm sure!"

"Uhh.. can't you try the Mirrors? You could sneak a look couldn't you? Take a front row at the catwalks of err.. Paris or wherever."

"No, alas Naomi could not. Personal interests are not the function of the Mirrors, and would be very difficult to explain at an Inappropriate Usage Tribunal. It's best to walk a narrow line, tiresome as that may sound. How about desserts, everyone? They look divine.."

After a subtle prompt from Agatha, Claudie waved for the Dessert Waiter to hurry over, and he quickly arrived pushing a tiered silver trolley loaded with calories, calories and more calories, all with extra cream. Despite all the ooh-ing and aah-ing, only Bob ordered anything - desserts seemed to be just a feel-good ritual for the others.

"How did you two get involved with becoming Trainees then? I don't expect your jobs are easy to find out about.." asked Bob between mouthfuls of the official World's Greatest Cheesecake. Agatha handed her teaspoon to him, so that she could try some.

"Well," said Claudie, "if you have some kind of vee spesh ability, you're off to a flyer. But not me. I used to deliver flowers to reception for Madame Agatha's office - I thought it was just another big company. And then I asked if there were any jobs going and she said there were because some people weren't around anymore, so I started to do things like typing stuff, and the rest just followed. But Naomi's a special case, aren't you Nay?"

"I'm very special!"

Agatha looked to the heavens in despair.

"Here's an example. I can tell what kind of tea you're drinking just by looking at it. Go on, order some brewskis, everybody order some brewskis.."

Agatha beckoned a waiter over, while Naomi covered her ears and quietly sang something tuneful to herself. They ordered four different teas, and Claudie whispered to Bob, from behind her hand.

"Whatever she says, just agree - let her have her moment or we'll be doing this for weeks.."

The teas soon arrived, and Agatha was called away again by a group of very affluent and over-dressed executives types who were obviously having an all-day meeting near the bar. That brought the lunch to an end, and the three of them took the long route back to the office via two complete tours of Ladies' Mile. Bob felt fit to drop.

A brick-sized portion of cheesecake was not a good idea before spending an afternoon struggling beneath a mountain of bags.

Back at the office, Bob grew more apprehensive as the afternoon drifted into evening, and the prospect of going back to Arizona was weighing heavily on his mind. He couldn't even face the arrival of the Evening Buffet trolley. Naomi sensed his growing nervousness, and handed him a crossword magazine as he headed towards the stairs on the way to his room.

"Everything'll be fine Bob, you're no dummy and if things get pretty bad you can always come back here, I think. Madame Agatha shouldn't be too livid, I expect - but don't count on that. So don't get too stressed by all the responsibility that you're carrying and just try to put the horrible seriousness of the situation out of your mind - well, at least until tomorrow, in which case you'll need to have it right at the front of your mind, and.."

"..thanks, Naomi. I'll do that."

"Oh yes, I nearly forgot. Have you seen these? Crosswords. You have to be so switched on to do them, though. I thought you might have a restless night ahead of you, what with everything and all, so if you try tackling a few of these I really guarantee you'll sleep like a sleepy thing that's been up for far too long! Zuzzin' in no time."

"Oh thanks.. that's great" he said, trying to give the impression that she had really helped him. He carried on up to his room, and lay on his bed feeling more stressed than Naomi had imagined. After a few minutes the door opened while the person knocking on it was still knocking on it. Claudie stepped into the room, and closed the door firmly and quietly behind her, before shuffling around in her not-as-small-as-it-looked black handbag.

"Quick convy on the hush, Bobs. Here, take this.."

Claudie pushed something very cold into Bob's hands. He looked down and saw that he was holding a compact silver gun, and almost dropped it.

"You're joking? You reckon I'll be shooting people? I can't shoot someone - besides, I'll get arrested and then fried or hanged or something a whole lot worse!"

Claudie tapped her nose and pointed at him.

"Image Bobs, image! Hayshakes just like you will see a gun. You know what I see? I see the niftiest ciggy lighter in Tiffany's, that's what I see, courtesy of Louis C Tiff himself. Well, a cousin of his, anyway. Well he said he was his cousin.. anyhow, you see the handle? It matches the Tiffany Blue of those darb bag-things for the Mirrors! If you're going to take someone for a ride, do it with style. So I'd say you're a bit more prepared now, aren't you? Put your image way ahead of your feelings and you'll be fine, really you will. Oh, and last of all, just remember the most important thing - always, always watch the green, okay?"

She winked and disappeared around the door, leaving Bob sitting on the bed turning the lighter over in his hands. Claudie had just moved herself a little higher in his All Time Weirdest People list. When would she ever need something like this? And more to the point, when would he?

He looked out across the city as the warm evening gradually grew darker, and tried not to think of situations where he'd need to convince someone he had a real gun. And then he tried not to think of the next day, which was bound to be a million times tougher than he expected it to be. He hadn't got a clue how to find a Mirror, and for all he knew he could spend the rest of his life looking for it, never mind the other four afterwards. All he was sure about was that he had to do everything to avoid any Troubler-weirdos, and if he was caught by one or more of them.. well at least he could light their cigarettes for them.

Bob stood at the window. If the QE2's anchor chain ever got tangled up with itself, the ensuing knot would be nothing compared to the one he could feel in his stomach. He sat down by the typewriter, and the perfect relaxation-therapy popped into his mind. Three months had passed since Christmas, which meant the school's ban on him writing any more scripts for Drama Class would soon be lifted. Considering that Jefferson Hortney-Flowt had left hospital two whole months ahead of schedule and had even returned to school, the ban could be over inside two or maybe three weeks. Jefferson had been moved down a year of course, but that was for his own good and shouldn't really count against Bob's literary return.

Drama classes made up for all the lessons which Bob couldn't stand. What he actually liked about them was that he could sit back and watch all the people who usually ignored him, as they wandered around a stage saying the words he'd made them say and doing the things he'd made them do.

Bob sat in front of the typewriter and thought of Jefferson, and laughed to himself. If money could buy brains, Mr and Mrs Hortney-Flowt would have had a real genius in the family. Instead they had Jefferson, a lumbering oaf who had always found Andie to be an endless source of amusement. So last November, Bob gave him the lead role in a potentially hysterical play entitled 'Escape From The Asylum'. In hindsight, it should have been called 'Trapped In A Mangle' but at least it had made Andie laugh. The ban followed, but it was worth it - after all, Jefferson wasn't rude to Andie any more.

So Bob stared at the typewriter and thought for a long time. He decided to create a daring tale of bravery and village idiots, large boils, timeshifts, and a knight with a magnetic chicken - and plenty of disease and even more boils. He carefully picked at the small oval keys and typed the title of his new epic, immediately deciding that words looked better on a real typewriter, even if the spelling didn't.

BUBONIC SPLAT: A historical tale og Medieval Sorcery adn Pagan Tyranny, by Robret G Taylor.

He sat at his table while the world outside grew darker, typing and typing, no longer noticing the sharp clacking of the keys against the paper, filling page after page. Shortly after one o'clock he finally felt like going to bed. Bubonic Splat had rounded the day off well, and he felt sure it had all the makings of a Trygvason Comedy Classic which would be performed to rapturous applause for years and years to come. Probably.

CHAPTER SIXTEEN

King Olaf The Useful

Bob's alarm clock flew across the room and bounced off the wall at 5.30am precisely. The quiet light of early morning soon made up for the clamouring bells and a few minutes later he was ready to face the day ahead. He nervously dressed in his Arizona clothes, took a few deep breaths before opening the bedroom door and stepped out with real determination to face whatever challenges the day might hold - and immediately fell over a bag. He stood up rubbing his knee and read a note that had been stuck to the door.

'Morning to you, Bob! Don't trip over the bag, you might hurt yourself. You have to put your ordinary clothes in it and take it with you so you can change when you get back to Barton. Forgot to mention that last night, oops. And Mme Agatha says you're to take all the Encapsulation blue bags as well, as you don't know which Mirror you'll find first, but I said you'd have thought of that already because it's so obvee. Left some cereal in Clau's Kitch. Attaboy Bob, go get'em! (the Mirrors, not the cereals, although the cereals are an important way to start your day). Naomi. x'

A happy face was drawn after the 'get'em'. Feeling particularly stupid, Bob went back into his room and took all the blue bags from his wardrobe, wrapping two under his shirt, and folding the other three into Naomi's very-1920s rucksack. Considering they felt so tough, the bags were incredibly thin and had a strange texture like a cross between aluminium foil and cotton. Then he left again, checked the note and sighed as he went back in to put his Barton clothes into the bag as well. He took a moment to think hard about anything else he might have forgotten, and then finally went downstairs.

He survived another bowl of cereal-mush and soon found himself staring at the panel of buttons next to the department's main door. A note had been stuck alongside it, with the words 'This one, Bobs!' and an arrow pointing towards the button marked 'Ground'.

The door quickly opened and Bob tried hard not to think about how he was able to step straight out into the huge reception hall. He noticed that a new plant had replaced the strangled one, and there were two or three times as many people milling around as there had been on the afternoon when he had arrived. Somehow, he wasn't surprised to see so many faces at such an hour of the morning, because nothing about this place could strike him as being odd anymore. A cool morning breeze ushered him across block after block all the way along Lexington Avenue, accompanied only by Bagshaw's occasional snoring.

Naomi stood in Agatha's office, and looked through a gap in the long, laced-net curtains with a pair of binoculars. She watched him walking up Lexington until he was too far away to see.

"Why couldn't we just take him back to near where the portal is? You wouldn't have to know where it is.. and it wouldn't be any trouble especially in your car, and it'd be a whole lot safer for him, wouldn't it?"

Agatha was quiet for a long moment.

"It's good for his confidence, Naomi. Now, I'm sure you have work to be doing?"

At 7.30am precisely, Bob arrived at the steps of The Ansonia feeling pretty good with himself. He'd survived countless street crossings and run the gauntlet of Columbus Circle again, and survived intact. He would have felt incredibly good with himself rather than just pretty good, had there been many cars around. Even the trams weren't doing very much. However, watching New York starting to build its momentum for another energetic day had been a remarkable experience. Looking along the near-empty avenues and streets and seeing almost nothing at all from one side of Manhattan through to the other except for a few cars, delivery trucks, and the occasional horse-drawn cart was bizarre. Those very roads would soon be dense with a million busy lives, but in the quiet before the storm Bob felt a real privilege in being there, almost alone. The feeling was the exact opposite of being alone anywhere else.

He quickly crashed back into the real world - two or three steps into The Ansonia's reception he knocked a tall ashtray over with his rucksack and sent a loud metallic clatter echoing throughout the hall as it hit the marble floor. A combination of ash and sand spread out in an arc over at least six of the vast black and white squares, and a disgruntled porter began walking over with a broom.

Bob was aware that a broad-shouldered security guard at the foot of the stairs was watching like a hawk. A tagless key and no reservation in the hotel's guestbook was highly unlikely to get him past this line of defence. The guard stepped a little nearer, and a knot returned to his stomach, bringing a few friends along as well. Nervously, Bob walked up to the reception desk and stood before an important-looking man, who was cleaning his glasses.

"Hello, are you the receptionist?" he asked. The man hardly moved.

"No Sir, I believe I am not 'the receptionist'. I am the Senior Concierge," he replied, and slowly looked away. He took a deep breath and sighed loudly, before slowly turning his head to look back at Bob. "And I am a very busy Senior Concierge. In what way do you hope I may help you?"

"Err.. I was here the other morning, and then I left but didn't check what room number I'd left from, and now I have to get back up there."

The concierge said nothing and began cleaning the other lens, briefly pausing to stare at Bob in an 'Are you still here?' manner. Bob tried to be far more convincing.

"The room should be in the name of Agatha someone. Maybe Taylor, because that's my name.. but Great Aunt Agatha might be on my mother's side, not my dad's.. and she might have got married as well, I'm not really sure. Oh, and the 'Great Aunt' bit probably won't be written down.." said Bob, feeling like he was using a large spade to dig himself into a hole.

"How unfortunate, Sir," the concierge said with a sigh, and began polishing his pocket watch. "Would Sir care for me to see if a room is held under the name 'Agatha'?"

"Yes if that's okay - I'm sure it'll be there. Somewhere up around the top, probably the 14th floor or higher 'cause I lost count."

The security guard grinned and leaned against the desk, while the concierge opened a large wine-coloured book, emblazoned with 'Ansonia Residency Status' on the front in narrow gold lettering. He ran his finger down one list, and then another.

"Alas, no Agatha has deigned to grace us with her presence. I trust Sir is now content to leave?"

Bob figured that however the word 'Angst' was defined in a

dictionary, even if the meaning was preceded by the word 'very' a dozen times, it would still be an understatement.

"Okay, but before I do, could you help me get the phone number for Number One, Lexington Avenue?"

"I will even do it for you.." the concierge offered, and laboriously moved his hand a few inches to pick up a black telephone. He made no attempt to hide the fact that his forefinger was pressed on the receiver.

"Ah, hello imaginary Operator. I am in need of the phone number for a person by the name of.." he raised his eyebrows and looked a long way down at Bob.

"Agatha.. Agatha.. oh yeah," he said, and immediately realised how stupid he must look. Henri dropped the phone back into place, and a dreadful sinking feeling stretched the knot in Bob's stomach all the way down to his feet.

"Does Sir know of any other names, preferably complete with surnames, or is Sir soon to be rejoining the world outside?"

Trying to save a little dignity, Bob pulled out his official King Olaf Trygvason notebook from his inside pocket in an attempt to look as if he was the kind of person who kept a notebook crammed with names. He held it upright so that the concierge couldn't see that it was practically empty except for a strange drawing of a trampolining polar bear who was wearing a woolly hat, courtesy of Andie.

"Oh my word, Sir!" exclaimed the concierge, staring at the cover of the notebook, "You're a member of the Trygvason party? If only you had said!"

Bob looked up with an expression resembling a rabbit who had just noticed rapidly approaching headlights.

"Err.. yes, that's right. I'm with the Olaf Trygvason party. Is that more helpful?"

He missed off King Olaf's title in order to appear even more important than he had just become. After all, a king's friends wouldn't refer to him as 'King' all the time would they? They'd be on first name terms, like real mates.

"Ahaa, yes indeed! We so rarely see anyone from the Trygvason entourage. Such undemanding guests. Please refer to my good self as Henri - I personally will accompany you up to your floor, if Sir would permit one?"

A hint of apology had crept into his voice, but was soon replaced by the false charm of a professional crawler.

"Yes, that's err.. entirely okay, thank you" replied Bob, now fully understanding how a lottery winner must feel. Suddenly it occurred to him that for the first time ever, all those endless Nordic Saga lessons might actually come in useful outside the school. Before the concierge could close the residency book, Bob wanted to enjoy the moment.

"Henri, do tell, is Geira around? Or maybe Gyda's dropped by? It's been so long.." he said, and raised his eyebrows in a hopeful way. Some heavyweight name-dropping could only help his new image, and King Olaf's first two wives were pretty good names to drop. The fact that they had both been making snowmen in the sky since the 10th Century meant there was little chance that they had been ordering room service recently.

"No, I don't believe so.." he flicked through the residency book again, and then opened a slightly larger one.

"No, I don't see them. It's possible that they are here but I fear I wouldn't recognise any of the party. As I say, your associates are very private people. Shall we go now, Sir?"

Henri located a small white drawer labelled Trygvason Group on the wall behind him, and removed a slender silver key which bore a striking similarity to the one underneath Bob's shirt. He felt a warm glow around his neck and against his chest, which slowly began getting warmer and warmer.

The security guard pressed a button outside the lift and the small dial above the doors soon pointed at the word Reception. They opened with a sharp 'ting' and the concierge gestured Bob inside. The interior was huge, bright and filled with mirrors which made it seem even larger, and Bob would have been thoroughly impressed if he hadn't seen the Lexington Building's alternative. They steadily trundled up to the sixteenth floor, and then stepped out into the lobby. The bank of security doors looked impenetrable, which made Bob feel even more important. Henri tried fitting the key into one of the central panel's locks, and made a self-conscious laugh as he failed.

"I'm sure this is the right key.. normally these doors are opened by the Trygvason residents for our staff.. do bear with me.."

Bob figured this was a good opportunity to make an even bigger impression.

"Confidentially, Henri, there's a special knack to it. Allow me," he said, calmly. The key felt warm as he took it from Henri, and instantly became unbearably hot as it touched the lock. The doors immediately folded away into the walls , and Bob tossed the key back before it burned his fingers. Henri didn't seem to notice any heat at all, and handled it as if it was perfectly cool. He looked puzzled and held it out towards Bob again.

"It's okay thanks, I'll get a spare key from one of my.. family, now that I'm back up here, thanks."

Henri loitered for a moment, and then held his hand out for a tip. Bob cringed as he realised he still didn't have any American money.

"Here you go, have this," he said, and handed over an unused biro. To Bob's surprise, Henri seemed less than impressed and walked swiftly and silently back to the lifts. The doors sealed the floor again, and Bob breathed a sigh of relief.

After twenty minutes of wandering around trying to find where the diamonds on the floor were, by pure luck he eventually stood outside Room 963. The pale blue door opened as soon as he touched its handle, even before he'd taken the key from under his shirt. The friendly warmth of the apartment welcomed him as he walked in, and he took a moment to sit down in the suite's living room and have a think about what he was supposed to do next. That didn't last long as his mind soon began wondering about Andie again, and if she'd ever get to come here - or even believe a single word if he told her about everything. Then he started wondering why the entire floor was booked under the name of his school. Hopefully the Great Aunt Agatha in Barton would be able to offer an answer or two.

The clock in another room began lightly chiming eight o'clock, and Bob took a deep breath and started walking towards the wall. The small circle appeared and quickly expanded into the elaborate archway. He kept on walking towards it, took another deep breath and then a big step towards the blue staircase. The tuneful chimes quickly faded away and..

CHAPTER SEVENTEEN

Back to Arizona

..were replaced by the steady ticking of the grandfather clock at the far end of the upstairs hall at Number 107. It carried on from the exact second when Bob had left.

"Three minutes past five. And still Sunday as well, of course.."

The door to the Master Bedroom closed solidly behind him, and looked as if it had never been opened. He wandered over to the end window to prove to himself that Barton was still there and was still being the same old Barton, as if he'd never gone away. It was, and a seagull continued on its flight along the cliff tops, unaware that anything at all had interrupted its journey. Bob almost began wondering if anything had actually interrupted anything else, but soon figured that Feiya's First and Second Laws were more important. Keep it simple, and don't ask questions.

Further along the road and far beyond the seagull, Bob could just make out The Coffee Pot, perhaps. There was so much he wanted to tell Andie, and more than anything he wanted to take her back to New York. She'd love that, and she'd have a great time with Naomi and Claudie. He stood outside the Arizona Portal, or the Not-The-Master-Bedroom door as he preferred to call it, to think about going round to see her before doing anything else. A loud and intense hiss pierced the air a few feet away from him, and he nearly jumped through the ceiling. Startled, he twisted around to see Jinx at the top of the stairs with her back arched, staring straight at him.

"Okay, okay.. I won't mention it to her, I promise. I'll go to Ar.."

He turned back to face the Arizona door, and found that it was already open. Without pausing to think, and therefore not allow himself any time to become even more nervous, he walked into the bedroom and stopped just before the wooden table in the kitchen, back at the farmstead.

He wandered over to the window and looked at his watch in the dim light to find out the time and location details, but the day was still on the wrong side of the dawn for him to read any of its small panels yet. Instead, he took a moment to work out what he actually knew. He knew it was 6am on the morning after he'd run away from the hotel, and somewhere out there was the Salesman loon - and maybe a few more loons as well, who would soon be a little annoyed to find that he had left town earlier than planned. So therefore he would have to be extremely careful while looking for any bizarre Mirror-related happenings taking place.

Even though it wasn't really light enough to be looking for weird things outside, he knew he had to start sooner rather than later. He slung his rucksack over his shoulder and took a nervous wander around the other downstairs rooms, expecting to find psychos behind every door and around every corner. All the rooms were empty except for a few piles of planks and scatterings of tools.

"Hardly worth getting worked up about, really.. fancy a tea, though," he said loudly, to see if Bagshaw had woken up yet. He responded with a loud snore and a mumble.

Bob set out onto the dusty track, hoping that one or more of the Mirrors would be lying on a road-side table below a large sign saying 'Mirrors Here'. The air carried a strong and acrid smell, which felt as if it had some warmth underneath it. Bob remembered that when he was leaving Arizona there had been the faintest of burning smells, but even now he still didn't think anything of it, because farmers around Barton were prone to burning things whenever it suited them. By the time he reached the main road, he didn't give it a second thought, and stayed close to the hedgerows and trees in case anyone less-than-friendly was on the look-out for him. The ill-Agatha's words '..they're onto you..' kept running through his mind, which didn't help him to fend off a whole new collection of knots and stressed-out butterflies in his stomach.

The burning smell became increasingly powerful as he neared the town and by eight o'clock, when he branched off the main road, the reason why became apparent. The entire population seemed to be up and about already, and Bob walked through the crowds of townsfolk to try and find out the cause of all the commotion.

Suddenly his legs refused to go any further. He stopped in disbelief, staring at the gnarled remnants and blackened walls of The George Washington Hotel. Everything was gone except for a few charred bones of the building. Smoke still drifted upwards from dozens of hidden fires, and lines of exhausted helpers passed buckets of water along to dampen down the stubborn embers. Gradually the voices of the people around him began to form into snippets of sentences and conversations. Their tone and emotion ranged widely as he walked through them.

"..twelve missing that they know of, maybe thirty, forty more.."

"..and I heard there was a whole family in there.."

"..and she saw a real oddball theatre-type leavin' after dark.."

".. jus' took two hours round midnight an' it was all gone.."

"..no chance, no-one had a chance, it ain't real.."

Bob felt sick. Really sick. He could feel his heart beating throughout his entire body. The only way he could get himself walking again was to breathe deeply and repeat, "Aunt Agatha can sort this out, she won't let anyone die, she can sort this out, she won't let it happen.."

He slowly managed to look away, and walked over to the Cornucopia to think about what to do next. Bagshaw yawned, and started to show signs of waking up.

"I say, Bob old boy, that's a rather uncomfortable smell.. burning and whatnot. How about keeping a glass of water in here next to me, just in case?"

The top pocket of this jacket was much deeper than his usual one, so Bob pushed a couple of handkerchiefs into his Distressed Toff pocket, wedging them underneath the compendium to raise it enough for His Lordship to see what was going on.

"Oh no, there's been a fire - and we're at that dashed Cornucopia again. What a dreadful start to the day.."

Bob peered down at him, and tried not to comment on the Victorian night-cap that Bagshaw was wearing. It even had a small pom-pom.

"Don't worry, Bagshaw. You won't get toasted and you're not going back in there. We're only here to look for a Mirror, that's all. Like all that stuff Aunt Agatha was talking about yesterday, remember?"

"No, no not really. Do recall plenty of talking, though. Didn't follow too much of it.."

The sky was growing cloudy, and Bob took a small amount of comfort from the prospect that it might rain sooner or later.

"That's pretty desperate.." he thought to himself, and leaned against a post to try and work out if he was blending in better than the day before. His clothes looked more appropriate, but he was far too slick for his own good. Naomi and Claudie had done a decent enough job for late 1920's New York, but for Back-of-beyond-ville in 19-whatever, he looked like an apprentice gangster. Despite the chunky-weave jacket, he'd already had a few odd looks off people, and decided that the hat might have to go.

He checked his watch for some idea of location. It was 8.24am precisely, he was on MAIN STREET in A TOWN and was on a BUMPY SIDE WALK. It was an impressive piece of technology, even if it was pretty useless.

He stayed behind the post and scanned the buildings and crowds of people, looking for anything even a little bit strange. Apart from the destroyed hotel, there was nothing particularly out of the ordinary and he wondered if the whole day was going to be wasted. And then he froze.

As if from nowhere a tall man with a tall black hat wandered out to join the crowds further down the road. He calmly looked at his pocket watch, and began to walk away. But then he stopped, almost as if he sensed he was being watched. His expression changed from smug triumph to one of grim concern and he looked around, agitated. Bob crouched down and ran into a side street, looking for an open doorway to hide in. A familiar and very irritating voice pierced the air.

"Hey you therrre, weren't you here yesterday? From the thee-ayytre, actin' all puh-culiar around an' abouts, an' up at the Town Hall too?"

The woman from the day before, who had briefly resembled Andie's mum, stood accusingly before him. She stared intently at his face, and Bob could see other people stopping to look at the scene she was making. Drastic action was needed, and nothing could be more drastic than his French accent.

"Parrrdonez moi?" he curled, and politely tipped his Fedora to her. "Qu'est ce que vous parlez? Au coin de la rue et mon arbre, uhh.. je voudrais une demi-tasse de café et umm.. et la voiture de mon oncle est une rouge Peugeot. Ne Porsche pas pour lui. Merci?"

Bob pretended to be counting on his hand for the last few words, to add to the effect. The woman looked tired and mistaken.

"Well.. y'sure looked like the fellah t'me."

Bob shrugged in a Gallic way, then turned and hurried along the side street, racing one way and then the other in a frantic search for a safe refuge, and all the time wondering if Salesman had actually seen him. After half an hour of constantly moving around and not achieving anything at all, he arrived at the worksite-end of a partially built street which lead out onto the Town Hall Square. He clambered through the windowframe of a semi-constructed bare-wood building and scurried up a ladder to its first floor. He needed a moment to sort out something resembling a new and improved plan.

As he crept from one window to another, looking for anything odd outside while trying not to sneeze in all the sawdust, he stared in amazement beyond the trees, over at the Town Hall. Not the entire building, just one of the upstairs rooms. He was almost sure a bird had tried landing on the panelling above a window and gone straight through it, perhaps. It was at least a hundred yards away and he could easily have been wrong, so he decided to wait for confirmation. A lifetime seemed to pass by before another bird had a nasty surprise. Bob felt like cheering as if England had won the World Cup, but restricted himself to a small Bagshaw-approved "H'rahh."

He quickly checked the street below for any tall people in hats, and left the house to walk around the outer-grounds of the Town Hall twice, taking the long route and moving from tree to tree. There didn't seem to be any weak points in the building that would allow a discrete entry, and if anything, access was becoming highly unlikely because more and more people and security staff were arriving, which was odd. But that wasn't the weirdest thing of all. On both occasions when he had been in line with the suspect window, even though he was forty or more yards away, he could see his breath as if the entire grounds were in the depths of winter. It happened to everybody who crossed the band, which was probably the width of the room behind the window, yet no-one seemed to be aware of anything strange happening. Even their conversations briefly descended into gibberish, and also went unnoticed.

Bob moved further around, and looked out from behind a broad oak tree at what was happening. A white truck with Borden's Catering written on its side arrived with a loud splutter, followed by two much larger vans. They pulled up in a line alongside the building, and a dozen smartly dressed staff clambered out of the back, stretching and looking slightly the worse for wear. Luxury travel probably hadn't caught on yet, Bob figured. They began unloading stacks of boxes and trays that were piled high with plates, fruit and carefully wrapped parcels, so Bob crossed his fingers, hoped that there must be a grand civic event happening, and decided to try and get involved.

He ran across the East Lawn and was soon in the midst of the frenetic comings and goings of the waiters and chefs. A man who looked as if he ate more than he ever served was ticking off a huge list while staff showed him their tray-loads of vegetables, fish and raw meat. His red face went through every emotion as the procession of food passed before him on its way to the kitchens. Bob strolled up, and put on his most aloof English accent.

"Hello? Could I be of some assistance, sir? One happened to be passing herewith.." he lorded.

"Say wha'? Look kid, you can be a tray mule or a plain old go-fer mule, 'cause I need plenty of both kinds a'mules. You know anything about doin' either?"

"Well.. yes, actually I do. I've just moved on from the.. err.. internationally renowned McDonalds' Dining Establishment. I believe I can handle trays ra-a-ather well, if I do say so."

Even Bagshaw didn't speak English in quite the way Bob had just managed, and only a few bad foreign actors playing English people on tv could ever hope to get close. However, the important goal of impressing the fat man had been achieved.

"Innt'rnational? That's good. Go an' get yuhself uniformed from Vin over there an' you can be on Hordurrves and the like. Hey watchit, yuh sleepwalkin'.."

The man's attention was taken away by an over-burdened waiter who was making a monumental clattering noise behind him. Bob went off to find Vin, and was pointed in the direction of the thinnest man he had ever seen. Vin said nothing and simply reached into the bottom of a linen basket, threw him the first jacket that came to hand, and pointed towards the kitchens.

The jacket would have looked generous even on a yetti. That wasn't such a bad thing, as it was so large that Bob decided he didn't need to risk leaving his rucksack anywhere. He moved it around to his front, did the buttons up on the white jacket and patted his new pot belly. He caught his reflection in a mirror and tried not to laugh. After all, gaining a few excess pounds was preferable to looking like a hunchback.

For the next hour or more as the rain started to pour down outside, Bob dragged chairs to dozens of tables, continually looking for an opportunity to break ranks and sneak upstairs for a thorough search. Approaching midday, the large man who seemed to be in charge of everything started ringing a bell, and announced to the waiters and chefs that the guests were arriving, and that Stage Two was about to commence. For a moment Bob looked around in the same way that he always looked around at school whenever he thought everyone except him knew what was going on. Just for a change, most other people hadn't got much of a clue either.

He was handed a large tray of hors d'oeuvres to carry, under strict instructions to make sure that everything was eaten. Bob took the tray and loitered near the spacious entrance and reception rooms, watching the State Dignitaries arriving along with railroad people, mining executives, and according to one of the other waiters, anyone else with mountains of cash to pour into a new town. As the rooms filled up with two or three hundred people, Bob was beginning to wonder if he was ever going to get away, and realised that clearing his tray would be a good start. He sneaked four hideous thingies into his mouth, and instantly regretted it. The guests would definitely have to eat the rest, and they were more than welcome to them.

He scanned the growing crowds of people to spot someone who looked as if they needed a small piece of toast with a dollop of gunk on top, when his eyes fell on yet another black top hat. His heart almost stopped as he saw the tall spindly figure of Salesman across the room, walking almost unnoticed through the chattering throngs of people. His penetrating black eyes were set directly on Bob, and a vile grin curled at the corners of his mouth.

Bob put his tray down on the nearest chair and dodged around dozens of groups of important people, then ran out into the grand entrance hall, closing the doors behind him. He turned around and looked in despair - for the first time in two or three hours, absolutely nobody was around. He shuffled under his jacket for the compendium, while a clock somewhere chimed a long, ominous note.

"For whom the bell tolls.. most dramatic!" said Bagshaw, as Bob brought him out into the world.

"Bagshaw, we have a problem. Psycho in pursuit, with evil intent!"

"Ah, evasiveness required.. the most obvious thing to do would be hastening up the stairs, or exiting the building.."

"Good thinking! Which d'you reckon?"

"Neither! If it's obvious to you, it'll be obvious to him, so do the least obvious thing - try the third door over on your right, by that table. Wonderfully obscure and unpredictable. I tell you, a similar thing did the trick in Naples. There was a large basket.. or a turtle.."

"Later, later.." whispered Bob, nudging past the table in his hurry.

He silently shut the door behind him, flicked the light on and cringed. Two dense rows of coats and jackets ran either side of the narrow box-like room, which couldn't have been any longer than twenty feet. There wasn't even a window at the far end. He knew he didn't have enough time to go back out and find a better place, so he hid his jacket and rucksack behind the coats in one of the far corners, and crawled behind the row of coats into the other. He curled up and tried to convince himself that he was in the best place possible, and after two long minutes, he very nearly started believing it.

The handle gave a click and the door slowly creaked open, and two hard-edged footsteps came inside, followed by another long creak and another very definite click.

"Oh, did mine eyes deceive me?"

A light voice slithered through the air, making Bob's skin crawl.

"Was that a haunting once again? No, no.. nothing's to haunt as nothing's deceased.. oh, I do believe a rat-child is somewhere.. where does frightened vermin hide and cower? Sewers? Nooo. Shadows? Perhaps, perhaps. Corners? Ah, maybe corners. They do tremble and shake in corners.. does this one?"

Bob's mind raced in desperate circles as Salesman began furiously ripping coats from their hangers, hurling them onto the floor.

"Come-to-play, come-to-play.." he snarled with every wrench, spitting out the last word each time.

Bob had no ideas and no defence. Could he find the lighter in time? Could he make a run for it? Could he try and put up a fight against such a loon? More questions came with every heartbeat. Coats started landing closer to his hiding place, sending tremors through the weak cover that hung in front of him. Suddenly the door clicked - or maybe it didn't? Bob couldn't be sure. Salesman carried on hurling coats to the floor in his growing rage, and the ones resting against Bob began loosely rocking and shaking as he drew nearer and nearer.

Another click. The door opened just a few inches and a voice carried through.

"..oh yes sir, allow me to place your raincoat in.. hey! What.. what are you doing? You can't do that! Security, security!"

Salesman cursed loudly as the waiter raised the alarm, and three huge security guards burst into the room and flattened him against the floor. His head was level with where Bob was sitting.

"A rat! A rat! I was chasing a filthy rat creature.." he protested, trying his best to sound convincing. A slow and heavy voice, which Bob recognised as the large security guard who had spoken to him before, now sounded very, very angry.

"You crazy or somethin', huh? Seein' rats everywhere? Yuh breakin' an' enterin' an' that makes yuh uh piece uh.."

A gap opened up in the coats just wide enough for Bob to see Salesman's eyes burning straight back at him. He gave a small wave as Salesman's head was jerked upwards, and then breathed a huge sigh of relief as the wailing protests grew fainter and fainter. The waiter came back into the room and carefully hung all the coats back up.

"Those crazy folk're getting everywhere these days.." he mumbled, and eventually left.

Bob rummaged through the coats to retrieve his rucksack and jacket, and was struck by his all-time greatest-ever moment of inspiration. If the owners of the coats were to find anything missing from their pockets, Salesman would be the Number One Suspect and could easily be required to 'assist the police' for a while - and that might allow Bob a free run back to the farmstead. Agatha could probably trace who was missing what, and sort out giving it all back later on - or something like that. Total genius, and he allowed himself a mini Mexican Wave in celebration. Claudie would approve of such cunning, he thought to himself.

The first coat had a huge wallet loaded with banknotes. For a moment Bob wondered if this really was such a good idea, and quickly decided to worry about that later. After fifty or sixty coats, he was truly amazed at what people kept in them. He found the most incredible jewellery, wads of money, a few loose gems, handfuls and more handfuls of change, and more than a dozen shining pocket watches as well. He put them all into his own pockets until there was absolutely no room left, and then filled up the rucksack. It soon weighed at least a ton and made him look twice as fat as before, but hopefully that wouldn't matter.

He very slowly opened the door, and looked out into the wide entrance hall. Two new security guards sat outside, on the steps to the building, so Bob took a chance. In a bid to look like a genuinely-genuine waiter, he picked up a few glasses that had been left lying around and waited nearby until he saw them stand up and walk just out of sight. He ran up the stairs as fast as he could (without jangling too much) and slowed down on the first floor to acknowledge a couple of Officials who were on their way down, lost in conversation.

The stairs ended at the third floor, which was different to all the others. It wasn't only missing people, it was also missing carpets, wallpaper, furniture and any signs of daily use. Bob walked along empty corridor after empty corridor looking out of the windows to try and spot where he had been standing in the morning. He stumbled against a huge wooden box that was blocking the entrance to one corridor, spilling most of his coins like a Las Vegas slot machine. Rather than leave any trace of being there, he spent a few stressed minutes picking them all up.

The entire corridor ahead was full of upturned chairs and plenty of junk, as if someone had very deliberately, and very badly, tried to block it off.

"Ahaaaa.. a clue perhaps, Dr Watson.." he whispered to himself.

"This isn't where we're staying, is it? A tad unkempt for my liking.." asked Bagshaw, "Haven't seen a hotel this distressed since.."

Bob began to clamber over the mess, wondering which of the six or seven doors the Mirror might lie behind, and then he started wondering what he'd do if they were all locked - or perhaps sealed with a dimensional clever-thing, or something worse. And then his heart froze.

Someone had stumbled out of the door at the end of the corridor.

CHAPTER EIGHTEEN

The First Mirror

The person, very overweight and carrying a large object, faded away into nothing. Bob stared and wondered what on earth he'd just seen. Then the figure briefly appeared again, only this time much nearer and outside a different door, pushing at it before fading away, and then repeating the action in front of the next door along. The image grew fainter as it moved further down the corridor until it appeared at the furthest door. Strangely, it seemed to look back up the full length of the corridor for a moment, staring straight at Bob for a few seconds before throwing itself against the door. That one must have opened because the figure fell straight through it. This sequence happened twice more, and Bob realised he was looking at himself doing the things he was just about to do.

That made his brain overheat for a moment. If he could see that the far door was the only one he could get into, did he need to bother trying all the others? And if he didn't try them all, how could he have just seen himself doing so? He gave a whimper of confusion. Rather than set a world record for brain-numbness, Bob scored a few hundred Feiya Points and simply followed the series he'd just seen, and half-heartedly tried each and every one of the doors.

"Quelle surpris, quelle grand.." he mumbled as he found they were all locked.

The final door was falling very slightly in and out of focus, matched by a varying, high-pitched whistling noise. This had to be the right one. He reached for the handle, and wondered if he could look back and see himself watching himself. He stared back towards the start of the corridor, but no matter how he tried, there wasn't anything strange or time-shifty going on over there at all.

"Weird, weird, weird.." he mused as he distractedly tried the handle, and found that it was completely rigid. Unlike the others, it wouldn't even turn a little bit to either side, so he patted his rucksack-belly and stepped back to give it the kind of heavyweight shove that should knock it right through the other side of the building. But as he ran towards the door, it edged open slightly and Bob saw that it really didn't need the kind of sumo-slam he was about to deliver.

He landed on the floor of a small room, and managed to bring down a tall shelving unit lined with tools, tins, nail boxes and dozens of pots. He lay under the mess, praying that nobody had heard the racket and that he hadn't damaged anything important. Or himself, for that matter. He slowly crawled backwards from under the fittings and kneeled in the doorway. Beyond the framework of the shelves, just beneath the window on the far wall, lay something very strange.

A filthy canvas had been partially draped over a long, shimmering oval, which was perhaps four feet in length. It was sending flashes of intense silver light out through the gaps in the oily material, which trembled slightly against the Mirror's surface. Bob closed the door and unfurled one of the middle-sized Encapsulation Fields, making very sure not to touch the Mirror with his hands.

"It's the Immediate Past or Immediate Future, Bagshaw. Look at this rag," he said, keeping it well away from the bag, "There must be some real idiots at work here.."

"You don't mean us, do you? Strictly between you and I, old boy, I haven't the first clue what's going on - could you offer anything?"

"Uhh.. no, actually, but it should start making complete sense really soon, though. I hope."

He carefully slid the bag further over the Mirror, gently working it along the curves while trying to ignore the slow-motion blurs that his hands were leaving behind, and trying even harder to ignore all the ghosted images of himself falling in through the doorway. He could even hear his footsteps echoing and fading along the corridor, and flinched as the shelving unit toppled over again. He drew the dark strings together at the end of the bag, and watched spellbound as the bunched end merged into a sealed unit. The time-altered images and sounds faded away, leaving Bob sitting in silence.

"I think I did it.. I actually did it.." he whispered, too relieved to be scared for the time being.

"Excellent show!" applauded Bagshaw, "Now then, where do we take whatever it is?"

"Umm.. anywhere but here," he said, and ditched his waiter's coat, put his rucksack on the right way, and carried the Mirror out into the corridor. It was almost too heavy and he wondered how he'd handle the large Present Mirror, if he ever managed to find it. Worries like that could wait for later, though, and he stopped to look for Salesman through nearly every window as he made his way back to the staircase. He crept down the first flight feeling paranoid that somebody would appear and start asking questions, so he took a look for another route on the second floor.

He soon found a doorway marked 'External Steps, Maintenance Only' which obligingly swung open, and he stood at the top of a staggered flight of stairs that lead to the West Lawn. For a heart-stopping moment he looked down at Salesman, who was standing only yards away in the grounds having a heated argument with the security guards. Bob hurried back inside and came to a halt midway down the main stairway.

A huge commotion had broken out somewhere downstairs, and was rapidly growing louder and nearer. It crossed Bob's mind that perhaps taking all those wallets and valuable things was, after all, a bad idea. He stumbled and jangled his way back up the stairs and tried to find somewhere to hide, or even better, another flight or two of external steps. But every door seemed to be locked, and he had to pause for breath by the time he reached the third floor again. His entire jacket made a din as he gave his newly-titled Aristocratic Partner-In-Crime pocket a quick shake.

"Hey Bagshaw, any big ideas? I'm up to my neck again - real hefty spot of bother!"

"Oh, you are telling me! Outside there lies a true bounder, and downstairs are an indignant mass who would not take kindly to a heavily burdened young chap making a hasty exit. I suggest that you set course for the roof."

"Right! Is that 'cause old buildings have some kind of alternate way down from there, then?"

"How should I know, old chap? It's the only place I can think of where nobody's after you - so it's got to be worth a look, hasn't it?"

Bob couldn't argue with logic like that, and eventually found an unpainted door with 'Personel.. Perosnnal.. Staff Oonly' hand-written on it. He cheered when it opened, and hurried up its narrow staircase to a small landing which ended with a solitary, imposing door. The awkward handle took a long time to give way, and Bob froze for a moment before opening it. Voices were coming from below, somewhere behind him.

"Strewth, 'ark at that lot.. I dunno, like they're ever gunnah miss a few notes and some fancy-Clancey jewellery.. we'll get blamed an' all, you wait.. swear I'll lynch the thievin' creep m'self.."

Suddenly Bob's pockets felt very heavy indeed. He pushed the door open, quietly closed it behind himself and messed around with the loose lock until something went 'cla-clunk'. Then he ran through the sparse Staff Room and over to a short series of steps leading to yet another door. He desperately twisted the handle, but the door wouldn't open. He threw every ounce of his strength into it, pulling the handle further round until it began to bend slightly, but it still wouldn't give an inch. The voices started to drift through the other door, and a key loudly rattled and grated in its lock. Almost in a panic he put everything into a final twist and turn of the handle, but there was still no response. Bagshaw gave a polite cough.

"I say, Bob? Might I suggest pushing the door, instead of pull.."

Bob, the Mirror and around $15,000 in cash, deeds and jewellery fell out onto the Town Hall's roof before Bagshaw had even finished his suggestion.

"Hoorah and so on, Bob! I did suspect that we might be facing a Canadian door, you know. Push not pull, even with a handle on the left, and all that. Remind me to tell you about those one day.."

"Cheers, Bagshaw.. you can tell me a few times."

Bob quickly wedged the door shut with a few stray planks, and dragged some heavy tins of foul-smelling black gunk up against it as well. He gathered up his bounty and then scurried through the puddles from one broad chimney stack to the next. Keeping a low profile this high up wasn't easy. Bob had a quiet laugh as he looked out from one of the raised triangular corners of the roof, and down to the statue of Halden J Kolvereid III. Salesman was being lead away by even more security guards, and receiving a good lecture from a collection of fuming women. A group of smartly-dressed and very indignant men looked on, shaking their heads. To make things even better, Bob found a metal step-ladder between two insignificant sections of the building, leading down in a gentle zig-zag all the way to the ground.

Despite a few wobbles and close calls, he reached wet terra-firma without falling off, breaking his neck, or even worse - dropping the Mirror. A few feet away, a box-like van was making a dreadful racket as its engine hauled itself into life, and Bob wondered about trying to hitch a lift to the farmstead. The prospect of spending two hours lugging a heavy Mirror through constant drizzle wasn't in the least bit appealing. He spent a couple of minutes weighing up the pros and cons, and decided he had to walk it. Getting involved with too many people was bound to be another bad idea, so he started off in more or less the right direction for the main road. The skies began clearing a little and the sun started shining, and the day looked like it might turn out to be a good one after all.

Even though his arms and legs felt like they could fall off at any moment, Bob kept out of sight by staying on the other side of the trees and bushes, although it was far muddier and messier that way. A few cars passed by, horses and riders would trot past and even a few carriages clattered by as well. All of them were probably oblivious to Bob being there. He kept a wary eye out for freaks and weirdos, and practiced a few lines as he went along, before reaching the cow again. He pointed a finger-gun at the loner.

"Go ahead moo-punk, make my day.. you feelin' lucky?"

The cow stared back, and carried on slowly swishing her tail and lazily chewing. She didn't look very scared at all, so Bob kept on walking and walking until he arrived on the track leading up to the farmstead. The journey had taken a lot longer than usual, but that was fine by him. Agatha would be pleased, Feiya would be pleased, Naomi and Claudie would be pleased, and even Jinx might give a purr of approval. He felt like Field Marshal Someone, returning from a great campaign and..

..and then he felt like he'd been struck by lightning.

Salesman sat very casually on a rocking chair, hidden out of sight to the side of the house where he wouldn't be seen until the last possible moment. He tipped his hat up and grinned over to Bob. His reedy, snake-like voice was just strong enough to be heard.

"Ah, little one.. we meet again, do we not? I was growing tired passin' the time waiting here for you. Reasoned I might need to come lookin' but you've saved me the inconvenience. Oh, and have you heard? I believe the town may well be needing some more security staff soon, how about that? Seems the last few have.. relocated. Found employment elsewhere, guardin' the Gates of Heaven, maybe Hell, who's to say? I expect you know the townsfolk are needin' a new hotel too?"

He laughed to himself as he stood up, steadily buttoning his long black jacket and not taking his eyes away from Bob for a second. His skin look even more pallid than before as he stepped into the bright sunshine, straightening his narrow tie.

"Ah, I see you've wrapped my treasure! How protective, and how well-informed you must be. You do know all the right people - or should I say 'did' know? See, you may choose to hand over that which does not belong to you, or I might resort to harsher means of persuasion. Be a shame, wouldn't it? Which'd you prefer?"

He walked with long strides towards Bob, and stopped just in front of him.

"Now, you care to play along?" he said, and appeared to hold out a hand for the Mirror, but instead he cuffed Bob hard across his head with the other hand. His sickening grin returned as he slowly removed the heavy rings from his fingers, one by one. Bob lay on the ground with his head reeling, watching Salesman pick up the Mirror, dust off the dirt from its bag and lay it on the chair by the house. He gave the door a hard kick with his boot, which made no sound at all.

"Portal's a cleverness, ain't it? Well, in some ways it is, but in other ways.. it ain't. Makes me think to myself, maybe we're not too dissimilar, you and me? See, there's some of us have our individual means for gettin' around, don't we? None's perfect, but what is?" he said, rubbing his hands and stepping backwards from the doorway, almost admiring it. "Mind, y'gotta be clever to be playin' with time, gotta be clever, one step ahead, two steps ahead.. as many damn steps as you can take ahead! But that's not for you to be too concerned of, though - seems as your playtime's over. Oh, a real shame.." he laughed, and started walking back towards him.

Bob's head had started to clear a little, or at least enough for him to be aware of Bagshaw shouting something.

"..the lighter-contraption the young lady gave you.. must be a good time now if ever there was one.. hello? I say, the lighter.."

Bob pulled Claudie's lighter from his inside pocket, and pointed it towards Salesman, while rubbing his aching head in an effort to get his vision straight enough to look him in the eye. He figured that if he ever saw Claudie again, she would have a good laugh at this prime display of bluffing. Salesman looked more amused than scared.

"Oh, a man of hidden talents! Is that little trinket yours? I wonder, dare you actually pull the trigger? Could you do so - without even understanding why? Ah, I doubt that. You're a child playing in grown-up games. A mere child.."

Bob held the lighter as steadily as he could, and despaired to see that it was shaking more than a jelly in an earthquake. He tried desperately to think of something to say or even do, but no great Hollywood epic of a plan appeared. He shuffled backwards enough to try and stand up, but Salesman moved closer and pointed a twisted finger down at him.

"Do you have the slightest idea who I am? Do you?" he shouted. His reedy voice grew louder and more aggressive with every step until he was close enough to wrap his bony fingers around Bob's arm, pulling him almost upright.

"Do you even know what lies around you? Not a damn thing! You know nothing, nothing of what you are involved with, and I care nothing for your involvement! This is no game, child - you're a pathetic, small fish drifting amongst very large sharks and the time's come for you to be devoured!"

His voice had reached a screaming crescendo that terrified Bob almost as much as the look of evil and insanity that had completely taken over Salesman's features. For a long second he looked as if he was actually going to bite Bob, but instead his eyes narrowed into black slits and he tightened his vice-like grip while drawing a knife from inside his coat.

Bob pulled the lighter's trigger hoping to at least inflict a nasty burn or perhaps an uncomfortable blister before dying. Instead, Claudie's lighter made a ground-shaking blast that lifted Bob off his feet and blew a hole through Salesman's thigh. A burning gap immediately opened up in the barn, large enough to drive a tram through.

For a long, long moment Salesman stood transfixed, and looked into Bob's eyes with an expression of complete shock and disbelief before collapsing on the ground clutching the injured part of his leg. It wasn't a pretty sight, and Bob was pleased to be lying down already.

"Oho, bravo! Bagged one there, haven't you? And you've only damaged its leg - that'll fetch a good few guineas! What is it?" shouted Bagshaw, absolutely delighted and looking for his monocle.

Bob dropped the lighter in shock, and then quickly picked it up again. There was a very good chance that Claudie hadn't been telling him the entire truth when she called it a 'nifty ciggy lighter'.

Describing it as a 'Miniature Ground-to-Air Missile Launcher' would have been a little more accurate. It was still hot enough to leave red marks on his fingers, but he didn't care.

He ran over to the rocking chair and struggled to pick up the Mirror. He meant to put the gun away, take out his key to open the door, and then drag the Mirror inside - like any normal person would. But instead, he noticed that there was still a dense plume of smoke rising from the gun's barrel, so he looked into it and suffered one of those moments that had plagued him throughout his entire life. Every now and then his body would get a split second ahead of his brain. Usually that would involve harmless things, such as letting the Thompsons' dog take the first lick of an ice-cream - only to realise just as the lick started that perhaps dog-slobber might spoil it a little. But this time Bob out-did himself by a long, long way.

As his finger reached the point of no return on the trigger, he realised that he didn't actually need to know if it would fire again, and he definitely didn't need to know what the bullet looked like. Another huge explosion ripped through the air and a streak of unbearable heat roared past him, less than an inch to the side of his head. An enormous hole appeared in the verandah, and part of the half-ready first floor lost an entire wall. A sudden loss of feeling in his legs made him sit down for a moment.

"You worthless, evil runt.. I'll find you, I'll hunt you down.. oh I will damn you to Hell.. where you belong! You filthy.."

Salesman was screaming and ranting over to Bob, wrenching him back into the real world. He looked over at the sprawled figure writhing only a few feet away from him, and had absolutely no idea what to do. Shoot again and finish this deranged freak? Run away and just keep running? Or go back to Agatha and ask her what to do? His heart was racing and he was in a whirlwind of confusion. Somewhere amidst all the chaos he could hear Claudie's words, 'Image, image, image!' becoming stronger and clearer in his mind.

He stood up, whispering the words to himself. He pointed the gun down towards Salesman's head, and walked over to him.

"You messin' wid me?" he asked, trying to keep a steady voice, "I said, ARE YOU.. MESSIN'.. WITH ME?" he shouted at the top of his voice, playing out a movie role worthy of an Oscar nomination for Best Shouty Idiot, as he stood over Salesman. Incredibly, Bob saw genuine fear alongside the hate in his eyes. He kept the gun firmly pointed in more or less the right direction, and slowly walked back to the doorway, which rattled open as he drew near. He managed to pick up the Mirror and stepped into the farm house. His heart pounded in his chest as every part of him screamed to just run for the portal. Somehow he resisted, still whispering "Image, image.." to himself. He stopped in the doorway, and turned around in the coolest Terminator style he could manage. He noticed the black top hat had rolled a few feet away from Salesman, who was beginning to crawl towards it. Bob pointed Claudie's lighter.

"I'll be ba.." he said, and lost the final word in the roar of another enormous blast.

The hat disintegrated in an explosion of earth and stone, leaving behind a ditch-like rut at least thirty feet long, which Salesman couldn't help but roll into. Bob picked himself up off the wooden floor, reached for the Mirror, and ran for the portal.

CHAPTER NINETEEN

Jinx

He emerged from the bedroom of Number 107 running and stumbling at full speed, and realised that a series of tall windows were getting very close, very quickly. Fortunately he collided with part of the thick wooden framework in between two of the broad panes. After a moment spent trying to get his breath back, he looked around for useful things that he could block the doorway with. A couple of raids on the downstairs rooms provided a few small cabinets, cumbersome chairs and some useless tables which he piled up against the door. They wouldn't stop any really determined loons from getting through, assuming the farmstead's security didn't hold out, but they might cause them to have a few goes and maybe receive a few injuries in the process.

He left his rucksack at the top of the stairs where he wouldn't forget it, changed into his Barton clothes and hurried out onto Lincoln Drive, cursing himself for not bringing his bike when he and Feiya had arrived earlier. The journey felt like it took forever.

Feiya was sitting behind the desk in the reception area, anxiously stroking Jinx who was on the table. She sipped pensively at a steaming mug of coffee and looked stressed, dangerously over-caffeinated, and more than a little unstable - still, that was a big improvement on the last time he'd seen her. He leaned the blue bag against the desk near to Jinx, and felt like an all-conquering hero.

"You won't believe what.."

"Is that so? How fascinating.."

"I just shot the freak who.."

"Oooh, did you? Goody goody goody.."

"..and he'd burned down.."

"Well he's very bad then.."

"..and I've blocked the port.."

"Well lah, deee and also daaah.."

Feiya didn't seem even remotely interested in Bob's escapade. She was far more interested in the bag and shuffled it onto the desk where she ran her hands around its edge. Jinx stared at it briefly, then at Bob, and then combed her ears with a paw before fixing her eyes back on him.

"Does Jinx ever blink?" he asked, unnerved.

"No frame! Unbelievable. It's the.. Immediate Past Mirror.. well that's okay - to start with."

Bob tried to stir up some enthusiasm from her.

"One down already! That's good, isn't it?" he said.

"It would be good if we only needed one Mirror. As it stands, we only have one and that means we don't have four. Therefore we don't have five."

"Oh. Well, how about a coffee then?"

"I've already got one, thank you. Jinx'll come and get you when the time's ready for your next excursion so until then, you go home and don't do anything stupid. And you do understand that you're not to breathe a word to anyone, don't you?"

"Yes, I know, I know.."

Bob turned to go, but was struck by something odd.. but what, exactly? He almost asked if something had changed in the reception since he'd been away. Maybe the paintwork had a few new cracks in it, or maybe it was a shade or two different.. or maybe the desk was angled slightly the other way, or the pattern on the floor ran left to right, not right to left.. but whatever it was eluded him. He decided to let it go, because Feiya didn't seem to be in the best mood for vague nothings. He had almost reached the front door when a much larger thought landed on him, and this one couldn't be ignored.

"Are Naomi and Claudie here?" he called back.

"I'm not at liberty to say, for reasons of securitable..ness. You have to go now, bye bye."

"But.."

"Talky talky talky talky talky all the time!"

"Uh, Fey, maybe you should put more milk in that coffee?"

She drained the mug and struggled with the large bag up the stairs, while Jinx remained on the desk and kept on staring at him.

Bob picked up his bike from outside Pierpont House, from where he had left it a very long time ago - or at least, it felt like a very long time ago. According to his new old watch, the time was 6.15pm precisely, he was on MARINE DRIVE in BARTON ON SEA and was ON A BIKE. He free-wheeled along the road and gave a small triumphant cheer when he could see The Coffee Pot ahead, silhouetted against a very impressive orange and yellow sunset. He decided to call in and see Andie.

The café usually stayed open until whenever Andie's mum felt like closing for the day, which tended to be very early at this time of year, so Bob went around to the side and rang the other doorbell. Her mum let him in with her usual friendly welcome, put the kettle on and went back into the lounge. She was having her official 'Tea & Telly' time, and very little was ever allowed to interrupt those sacred sessions. Not even World War Three, or The Coffee Pot turning into a raging inferno, or the cliffs collapsing all the way back to Scotland.. nothing would disturb Mags' quiet time.

"Andie's upstairs, so when you go up be a sweetie and take her a cuppa, would you? She's got her nose in a book about something or another for a test which I can't even begin to pronounce.. you know, I wonder about that school at times.." she called to him, stopping in mid-sentence as the adverts ended.

Bob soon made his way up, carefully trying not to spill anything from either mug. He nudged Andie's door open and was greeted as always by Princess Diana, who was smiling a perfect smile from a perfect black and white world. Different rules applied here, compared to Bob's room. Andie's posters were untouchable and in her own words, definitely unmoustache-able, especially the carefully chosen gallery of pictures which Diana laughed or sashayed her way through. Andie's latest display of Official Favourite Pebbles dotted the window sill, leading to a new lightning-fast computer and a big tv that her over-indulgent dad had bought for her when she'd had a particularly nasty bout of flu last Easter. Bob stepped carefully between all the Very Important Things (teddies, cd's and books, mainly) which covered just about any available space.

"Brewski for the Sheba? Special Delivery Missus - who ordered a tea? C'mon, I haven't got all night.."

She looked up from her thick 'Ynglinga Saga: Volume Two' as he put the mug on her desk, and smiled at him as he carefully sat down on her bed, nestling between Robert The Moose and Mrs Penguin. He'd never had any secrets from Andie, and more than anything in the world, he didn't want to start having them now. Predictably, his mind went completely blank now that a good moment had appeared, and he had no idea at all how to start. She turned away from her desk and faced him.

"Hello you," she said, "I think I'm brain dead.. really flat-lining. I've been reading this all day and I can't take any more. I'm not sure I really care how much land King Onund once cleared away.. is it nice outside, or a bit dismal?"

She caught her reflection in the dresser mirror and quickly tried to put her hair back to its usual style.

"It's pretty good actually," Bob replied, wondering if she could read lips in a reflection, "The sunset's looking just like a movie one. Do you fancy seeing if the world's still out there?"

Andie nodded, so they went to one of the tables outside to finish the tea, and tried to establish what King Onund did, why he did it and where he did it. And when, of course. They quickly gave up and drifted away for a walk towards the golf course where they sat under their usual tree, which was the best one for looking out at the sweeping coastline. From this distance, the beach looked a whole lot nicer than it did close up. Neither of them said anything as the sun cast the final colours of the day across the sky, until Bob decided to take one of his giant leaps.

"You know Jinx, that weirdy black cat? She's totally beyond freakishly bizarre. She's way off the scale."

"How do you mean, DoLittle?"

"You have to take my word for this, okay? It'll sound ludicrous, but that's only because I can't think of a way to make it sound like anything other than Billion-Carat Psychobabble. This really is award-winning Babb. That cat, Jinx, lead me off to Aunt Agatha's other home on Lincoln Drive, which isn't a real home, it's a series of doorways through time!"

"Yeah, I thought so.." she said, nodding and slyly tapping her nose.

"Really?"

"Oh I give up with you, Bob. But carry on anyway.."

"When Aunt Agatha decides to nip down to the shops for some groceries, she doesn't have to go to the BreezyEezyBuy to fill her trolley up. She could come back with.. I dunno.. stuff bought from the market stall that Julius Caesar's dad used to run, if she feels like it! I'm not joking, she can go anywhere! I've lost track of how much time has gone by since I last spoke to you, but I've been to a nameless town way out in Arizona, people are now trying to kill me and I've actually shot someone, and then there's New York as well, all since lunchtime today! Oh, and the universe is in big trouble as well. And this is the really amazing part - I have a book that talks to me!"

Hopelessly failing to control his trembling hands, Bob gave her Dr Buntz's book. Andie didn't look too impressed.

"This talks to you, does it? Well fancy that.."

She turned the book over a couple of times, flicked through the pages and had a good look at the portrait of Lord Philliponte Bagshaw-Philliponte.

"Nice coffee stain. Can anyone else hear this apart from you?"

"Nope, just me. I know this sounds like something from the dark side of Planet Weirdfreak, but it's true. That bloke who translated the book actually speaks to me, because of something to do with the Aid And Beneficiary Rules which are meant to help whoever's doing the time travelling!"

"Oh, those rules about time travel, I should have known.." said Andie, emphasising 'those'.

"Yes! I can choose three things to speak to once I've travelled through a door-kind-of-portal-thing, and then they can speak back! It's amazing, but I don't understand why. It just works like that."

Andie tried to fold a crease out of the cover, and made the corner section fall off.

"So.. if no-one else can hear your book chatting away, you must hear these voices in your head?" she said, pushing the triangle into her sock and hoping that Bob hadn't noticed.

"Err.. well I suppose so. Is that bad?"

"No, no I don't think so. I suppose the time to worry is when real people would rather speak to the voices in your head than speak to you. That'd be bad."

"Right.. that makes sense. Well anyway, I've met Aunt Agatha's younger version of herself in 1927, and made a couple of new friends who you'd really like and who aren't getting any older, and I've got a whole floor of a huge hotel to myself. And nobody anywhere has a clue about it."

"Me included. Still.." she said, and touched his nose in the way that a vet would check a dog, "..yes, at least you've got your health."

"Andie, I know this is really insane and the only reason I can deal with it is by not thinking too much about it, but I need you to believe me. I can't prove any of this to you until the next few days have been sorted out, and if I actually get through them I'll be amazed. But I really do need you to believe me, especially you more than anyone, because.. uh.. that's.. I.. you.."

Bob hovered on the brink of saying something very, very deep. For a moment the thought crossed his mind that he'd been telling Andie the most ridiculous and unbelievable story, and therefore he should have no trouble ending it by saying the most simple words of all, straight from the heart. That bit would surely be the most believable part for her.

But his brain suddenly called an immediate and all-out strike, and he found it almost impossible to find any words at all to try and convey whatever it was that he was trying to find the right words for. His brain finally rolled over and played dead. Instead of delivering a few lines that would wipe the floor with Shakespeare or Keats, a huge knot started forming in his stomach and was soon joined by its big brothers and a few hefty cousins. He was going to need a lot of time to figure this one out. Andie looked as if she was going to say something, but her attention was suddenly drawn away.

"Oh look, here's that Jinx cat again! You must smell like a tin of cat food, Bob. I didn't want to be the one to tell you, but it's true.."

Jinx strolled nonchalantly past Bob and rubbed her shoulders against Andie's leg.

"See? She likes me, don't you, you like me! You're so gorgeous and sweet, I just know you are.."

Andie stroked her and made all the appropriate noises that people make when a cat chooses to grant plenty of attention.

"Aren't you just so beaut? Yes you are! We were just talking about you.. and uh.. about.. aren't you.. lovely.."

Andie's expression changed slightly as if she was distracted, and her voice drifted up into a series of mumbled, aimless words.

"..we were.. sunset.. just.. ju.."

She carried on stroking Jinx, who now appeared to be oblivious to her affections and had turned her intense eyes up at Bob.

"..we.." mumbled Andie.

Jinx moved away, making sure her slender tail passed through her hand. Andie was staring transfixed at a point somewhere between herself and the cat until Jinx threw a hiss over her shoulder back to Bob, and slowly walked away with her head high in the air.

"Andie? Are you alright?" Bob reached over and pushed Andie's knee a little.

"Hmm?" she said dreamily, before snapping back into life.

"Oh look, over there Bob! There's one of those black cats again! Did you know they're supposed to be lucky? I wonder if she'll come over here? Aw, I don't suppose she will though, they only seem to follow you. Shame.. now then, why did we come out here? The sun's almost gone already. Umm.." she paused, looking very confused, "..did you want to talk to me about something? King Onund and all that stuff?"

Bob realised that he'd been given a demonstration by Jinx.

"Oh, no, nothing really.. it looked like a nice evening and I just fancied some cloud-watching in a decent sunset, that's all."

"Well that's okay for a while, but we could both do with a half-decent mark on the test, and as for the presentation.."

CHAPTER TWENTY

Bob & Andie's Secret Place

Monday 16th March

After a restless night Bob woke up way ahead of his alarm clock, and stared out of his window to watch nothing in particular. Even by the time he got up he was still trying to figure out what day it felt like, but that didn't matter too much by the end of his second bowl of Crunchy Munchy. It was a tempting thought to take a few boxes back to Claudie's Hot House and raise the standards a little. That would be one way of putting time travel to particularly good use.

Shortly afterwards, he stood at the bus station with Andie and found himself viewing everywhere and everything with suspicion, just in case a Mirror might be concealed somewhere nearby. He made a Mental Note that between The Coffee Pot and the bus station there probably weren't any at all. By the time the bus wheezed into the station, the morning was starting to look as if it was becoming one of those half-way days. Not cool or fresh enough for spring, but not warm enough for summer. In Andie's terminology, it was a perfect Sprummer day.

Up until the time Short Pudgy Kid had boarded, Bob was frustratedly trying to weigh up the pros and cons about whether or not to wake her up in order to tell her about everything again, now that there was little chance of a certain cat being around. But he decided against it, not just because she had mentioned feeling incredibly tired after Jinx had left her the previous evening, but also because he didn't want to risk anyone, not even the bus driver, overhearing them. The issue was finally decided for him when the coach started filling up. There was no way he felt like risking any attention from the Psycho Fifth loonies, who all stumbled along the gangway looking as if they were on new, untested medication.

He knew he'd made the right decision as it was a particularly rough journey, and one unfortunate Junior received a brand new haircut which was very unlikely to ever become trendy. So Bob was going to have to bide his time and wait until lunchtime.

The Headmaster, Father Yarri Flüggensohn, was the latest in a long line of Norwegian Headmasters, and was possibly the most excessively Norwegian of them all. After nineteen years in the role, he still hadn't quite got the hang of the English language and very few of his words were ever understandable, unless they were repeated by his secretary, Miss Gudbrandsdal, who always spoke very quietly indeed. By Trygvason standards, he was still a new boy and his portrait had not yet been added to the formal Gallery Of Headmasters outside the hall, for such an honour was only granted after thirty years of service. Bob suspected that Old Yarri would easily stick around long enough for at least two or three portraits, despite how ancient he already looked.

The school assembly was a particularly drawn-out and tedious one, and Bob wondered if the Headmaster was trying to set a world record for Talking Without Breathing In. He had spent over twenty minutes recounting a historical story full of olde Norse rhetoric that explained why the following day was going to be a school holiday. Of course, it was pure coincidence that the day-off coincided with the Headmaster's birthday. Each year there was a different battle or event to be commemorated on March 17th, as if historical figures in days gone by happily sat around waiting for that magical date each year before giving their historians something to write down. In this case, the grand event to be heralded was Smalsarhorn Day. Apparently, one year short of the first millennium, heroic King Olaf Trygvason had climbed to the top of the Smalsarhorn mountain and fixed his shield at its very peak, and without realising it had justified a day-off for a few hundred grateful pupils a thousand or so years later.

As Father Flüggensohn's clipped, monotonous voice continued its assault on the captive audience, Bob noticed that Andie, standing beside him, had started breathing a little louder. He looked at her with an equal combination of admiration and bemusement. Occasionally, she could somehow manage to sleep through an entire assembly while standing up. Once she even managed to keep her eyes open, only giving herself away with the smallest of half-snores. Bob gently nudged her as the historic saga staggered to its conclusion.

Father Flüggensohn left the stage to the brief applause of one embarrassed First Year, and complete silence returned. The Deputy Headmaster, Mr Nordkapp, took over.

"The following pupils have earned Linguistic Misappropriation Detentions this week.."

Bob cringed, and waited for his name to be read out. Mr Nordkapp had introduced a new policy of Non-Offensive Socio-Verbal Awareness a few months earlier. This involved posters being placed all around the school listing expressions and words that pupils were not permitted to say, in order to avoid causing distress or offense to anyone. They ranged from the most obvious terms of abuse to the incredibly obscure, and Bob had a lunchtime detention lined up for Thursday, for reading one of the new posters aloud. His defence that 'the ones at the back couldn't see' didn't stand up for very long.

The rest of the morning dragged by even more slowly than the Smalsarhorn tale, not helped by the fact that Bob was eager to get back home to search for the Mirrors, but even more so because he wanted to let Andie know what was going on. And lunchtime would be the best opportunity, in their Secret Place.

The Secret Place was discovered around a year earlier, while Bob had been killing time one afternoon at the school. The annual Open Evening granted the afternoon off for the students, who would then return in the evening to guide their parents around the classrooms and various exhibitions of work. But during the afternoon, a few students always stayed behind. These were either the very keen types who would be putting up stands and displays for school clubs, or preparing rows of test-tubes and monitors, or perhaps rehearsing Nordic Saga plays. The other sort were like Bob.

He was there as a form of punishment. In his case, he was obliged to spend the Open Evening demonstrating a low-tech physics experiment in order to make up for 'Not applying due care and attention while in possession of expensive equipment'. In other words, he had dropped something heavy during a Physics lesson which had refused to go 'bleep' ever since.

The strings and lumps of plasticine took less than half an hour to find and set up, and Bob's dismal Gravity Demonstration was ready for public performance a long way ahead of schedule. And that left him stuck at school feeling unbelievably bored. His parents were working so he couldn't get a lift home, and the school bus had done its re-scheduled run an hour ago, which meant that there was an entire afternoon to kill. He left Physics Lab 3 and went for a wander.

Nowhere could be quieter or lonelier than an empty school on a grey and rainy day. He crossed the playground, hoping to find anyone remotely friendly still around, but it was deserted. He reached some of the newer buildings which had been added onto the original school over the past century and wandered along corridor after corridor, noticing the kinds of things that could only become apparent when no-one else was around. In this instance, as he entered the Science Block, he acknowledged that someone had done a very good job of all the newest repair work. The style was old, the bricks looked old, even the smell was old - and nobody could possibly spot the joins. It looked as if the Upper Sixth had never blown a hole through Chemistry Lab 2's wall.

He reached the Biology end of the Science Corridor, and in a moment's weakness while passing the first lab soon found himself roped into helping scrub down a heavily stained dissection bench. Whatever had been cut up recently must have been pretty annoyed about it, and put up a really good struggle. However, Mrs de Nante, the Senior Biology teacher soon left Bob on his own to start and finish the job, claiming that she had important business to attend to elsewhere. No doubt this involved a coffee, a magazine, a settee and Drama Of The Day on the radio. So Bob found himself alone, with only a bucket and a small piece of sponge for company. Ten minutes of pure boredom later, the sponge had disintegrated into a yellow mush so he began opening the drawers behind the teacher's desk in a half-hearted attempt to find another one. The search became more interesting as he stumbled upon confiscated items, which increased in age and danger towards the back of the huge drawer. It was like taking a brief trip through the school's history of mischief.

Right at the back of one drawer were two keys held together by a loop of worn string. They were rusted and very old, which raised Bob's interest levels sky high and he immediately started to hunt around to see if they might fit anything. After drawing a blank on the entry door to the other two labs, then another blank with the storage rooms, window locks and even all the cupboards, he was beginning to feel that the keys were grim and rusty for a good reason.

Rather than return to the horrible task of cleaning the bench, he wandered along the main Science Corridor until the old building imperceptibly took over again. He reached the narrow side-corridor which was tucked away behind the final lab. There was one room here which nobody ever went into and most people had no cause to even notice. One key snugly fitted its lock, and after a scraping clunk and a hefty shove, the door opened just far enough to allow Bob to quickly squeeze inside.

The room was so compact that it wouldn't take much of anything to make it absolutely full. A few piles of faded old text books stood gathering dust, and a series of broken tripods, gas cylinders and other damaged laboratory apparatus lined up against the side wall. The frosted window at the far end of the room allowed in just enough daylight to enable him to leave the dangling lightbulb switched off, which gave him a feeling of secrecy and subterfuge that only James Bond could understand. Probably.

A dark blue door which had once probably blended in with a long-gone colour scheme stood on the other wall close to the window. The other key fitted it with a push, and after another toe-curling rusty clunk, the door obligingly opened.

Bob found himself at the foot of a small flight of very narrow and dusty wooden stairs. He pulled the door fully open to let in as much light as possible, and took a moment to work out that he was probably somewhere behind the school stage, more or less. His shoes slid a little in the layers of undisturbed brick dust on each of the dozen steps, and eventually he stood in the murky light at the top trying to see what was ahead. He could just about see a very narrow passageway, but it quickly disappeared into complete darkness as the door behind him swung shut.

He waited a moment. Nothing barmy or crazy came running at him, and maybe nothing was likely to, so he decided it was probably safe to fish out his house keys from his pocket and twist the Mini-Light keyring into action.

The cramped passage went on for a series of twists and turns, down a few short steps, before ending at a vertical step-ladder. Bob nervously climbed the metal rungs, expecting to emerge in the middle of the stage, or maybe a busy road - or even worse, the staff room. He reached up and pushed against a small trapdoor, nudging it upwards just enough to look out into yet more darkness.

The weak orange glow from his keyring wasn't helping too much, and Bob climbed through the trapdoor and began carefully walking forwards using the wall on his right as a guide. Judging by the painted panels showing huts, vikings and bodies, this definitely had to be the back of the stage.. somewhere. He leaned against a flat tree to have a think. Suddenly a column of light broke the darkness ahead, and the massive stage curtains separated slightly. He froze, trying to think of a plausible excuse as to why he was there.. but nothing came to mind.

"Marvellous.." he thought, squatting down for a moment and hoping that there might be a Bob-shaped theatrical prop lying around which he could hide behind.

Muffled footsteps and the voices of teachers and students passed by on the other side of the curtain, and Bob decided that in the absence of a brilliant excuse, a brilliant hiding place was called for instead. Unfortunately there didn't appear to be one, until he noticed the sharp light catch the rungs of a lighting-ladder running up the side of the stage, which quickly disappeared into the darkness above. He ran over to it as quietly as he could, climbed a few steps upwards and figured it reached all the way into the ceiling, which was a very, very long way to go.. and thoroughly unappealing.

Shadows passed across the open section of curtain, and a couple of Fourth Years hurried inside and went over to the furthest part of the stage where they began to open the curtains - so Bob began to climb. After forty five increasingly nervous steps, he reached the top of the ladder and was faced with the completely dark entrance to the area high above the hall. He looked down, which was a bad idea - not simply because of the height but because he noticed just how useless the safety cage around the ladder was. Its huge gaping holes wouldn't stop a falling hippo (assuming one ever managed to climb up that far) and the sections that were still complete had jagged dents poking inwards.

The stage was in full light now, and a herd of First Years were starting to put chairs in place for the Headmaster's evening address to the pupils and parents. It was possible that even if someone did happen to look up in Bob's general direction that they wouldn't notice him, but he didn't fancy taking the chance. From the weak light of his keyring he could see that ahead of him lay a narrow walkway of planks, and countless supporting struts and beams which held the hall's ceiling panels in place.

As Bob nervously walked into the semi-darkness along the wooden boards, he noticed that for the entire length of the hall, there were gaps every few yards where the stage spotlights were attached. And if he balanced precariously he could even see the place far below where he and Andie stood for assemblies. His head started swimming for a moment as he realised just how high up he actually was, and he had to make himself keep on walking and ducking under the beams. As he approached the far end, he passed through a gap in a wall of dusty boxes which stretched far out to either side of the building. Immediately beyond them was a properly floorboarded area, most likely intended for some heavyweight storage many years ago. Bob settled down and waited until long after the Hov had grown quiet again before returning to his trapdoor, and eventually the Biology lab.

By the following lunchtime, this storage area became Bob and Andie's official Secret Place, a refuge from the rest of the school and a place where lunches and bad mornings always seemed better. After a couple of weeks they had smuggled up a few baggy cushions, a delicatessen's worth of food and drinks, plus emergency batteries for the low-glow torches - and most daring of all, at Andie's insistence, they'd managed to 'acquire' a thick old curtain from the stage, to act as a carpet.

And one year later, this is where Bob thought he'd be able to tell Andie about the new turns his life had taken. But first, Andie had some unfinished business.

She had crawled along to one of the openings in the floor, and was carefully looking down in between two spotlights. Her prey had been spied. Fifty feet below, Dertha Lynch and her menagerie of barely-human friends sat eating their lunches, throwing the occasional morsel into a victim's hair. Andie had gathered a deep pyramid of dust and fluff together, the kind that seems to be attracted to neglected areas around electrical objects - and the spotlights had attracted it by the ton.

She gave Bob the kind of grin that a demon would grin, one who had just thought of something particularly demonic to do which no other demon had ever dared to think of before. He crawled over to her, and raised his eyebrows in an 'I despair with you' manner. Over the next few minutes Andie patiently flicked, nudged and blew the entire pile of dirt very steadily down onto the group below, avoiding their suspicions by taking her time.

"Softly, softly, catchy Monkeeeees" she mouthed to Bob, and had to hold back her giggles as the girls far below started sneezing. The cloud of near-invisible dust quickly became so bad that they had to get up and leave. Andie laughed as she watched them coughing all the way out of the hall. Revenge for the detention had been served so Bob and Andie settled down with their lunches behind the boxes. He flicked on the band torch, which was about a foot wide and gave out a gentle white light instead of the usual bright yellow kind. This was much easier on the eyes, and more importantly, it didn't reach too far either.

Andie looked to be deep in thought while Bob pondered a subtle opening line about Agatha, but she soon set the ball rolling.

"I think I might get that blue top on Saturday, rather than the green one. It's been annoying me since I didn't try it on, you know."

Bob remembered Naomi's eagerness to know about fashionable things in the future, and that seemed to offer a good enough chance to pull the conversation in the right direction.

"Oh, uh good idea. So.. speaking of fashion, what big names are around today, who've been around for ages? Like way back in the 20s for instance?"

"You're asking me about fashion? You?" she said, emphasising the 'you' part. That was definitely a bad sign.

"Why on earth do you want to know about that?" she laughed, more in surprise than because it was funny, "I mean, you do well to get everything on the right way round in the mornings, and sometimes you wear odd socks - and you did that three times last week. And how many times have I re-done your tie? You have things to tell, don't you," she said with a slight wag of a finger.

"That's just it, I'm not sure how tell you. Every time I so much as think of telling you about all the new people and places.. that second rate 1950's B-movie monster called Jinx appears and gets all weird and then leaves."

"Huh? That's stupid beyond belief, and you know it. You just like having a secret with your new friends."

Bob could tell he'd annoyed her, and thought hard for a reply that wouldn't involve being mauled by Jinx, or even worse, by Andie.

"However.." she added, much to his relief, "..you could prove your point, couldn't you?"

"I could?"

"Yes. If you start telling me exactly what's on your mind and a black cat turns up in here of all places, completely out of the.. black, then I'll know you're into something weird in a big way, won't I? And if nothing happens, you'll have said everything and then I'll be clear about what's bothering you. Win-win then, isn't it?"

Bob was always pleased that Andie could think straight, and for the millionth time in his life he was glad she'd made something difficult become something simple. She unwrapped three of The Coffee Pot's finest Roast Mediterranean Specials and unscrewed the cap off the flask.

"Well yeah, that makes sense. Here goes then.." he began.

Suddenly footsteps began clanging up the metal ladder and Bob switched the torch off. He and Andie went into Emergency Procedure One which involved crawling over to the side of the floorspace, keeping low behind some carefully placed boxes which allowed a view of the metal caging of the entrance. The curtain-rug with their things on it gradually followed, and was wrapped up like a bag of old stage paraphernalia by the time Mr Wilkes appeared.

Bob and Andie lay very low, and edged further into the gap between the end of the boxes and the start of the wall. This was definitely not the right teacher to be found by. He was a large, gruff and intimidating ape-like man with a notoriously short temper. If the right authorities knew about him, he could be a living exhibit at The Natural History Museum, instead of being a Gym teacher. School Rumour Number 4,287 claimed he was sacked from his previous job after the bodies of three teachers, eight pupils and a dinner lady were found behind a cricket scoreboard. Other rumours said the bodies were found under the tennis court and the floorboards of his house, and the remaining rumours were obviously too made-up to be taken seriously.

He stepped onto the boards and called down, "What light switch a'you on about? There's not one or anythin' up here!"

He cursed a few times trying to find the switch, and eventually a series of weak lights glowed along the roof's apex, extending all the way to the far end. He took a few steps into the gloom.

"There's nowt up here but beams an' piles of nowt!" he called back. He then grunted in reply to whatever had been called up to him, and slowly clumped his way nearer and nearer to the boxes. He passed within five feet of their hiding place, and began laboriously looking around for whatever was so important. At the same moment that Bob was wondering if he'd actually hidden the band torch, Mr Wilkes picked it up.

"Useful if them lights go out.." he muttered, and put it on the top of one of the boxes. It fell off straight away, and clattered over towards the side of a large box - and lay inches around the corner from Bob's head.. and a stray battery rolled even nearer. To make a bad situation worse, Andie was trying to fend off a sneeze, which was highly likely to be one of her ground shakers. Bob was convinced that one of them had once registered on the Richter Scale, but Andie had always insisted that was pure coincidence with an earth tremor. This was not looking good.

Mr Wilkes cursed, cursed again, and then produced the kind of noise that under normal circumstances would have made Bob laugh himself into hospital. Even the undefeated Class 3B Digestive Disorder Champion, Duncan McGuffley, would have been impressed. Mr Wilkes laughed to himself, and Bob tried desperately not to give in and crack up. Instead of picking the torch up, Mr Wilkes gave it a kick so hard that it ricocheted off a side-beam and stopped at the edge of the gap by a long row of spotlights. Luckily for Bob, he didn't want to retrieve it. Instead, he trudged around for an eternity, muttering that there was still "..nowt o' that varnish up 'ere..", and finally began making his way back towards the ladders.

The horn for the end of lunch sounded, and Bob knew that a really good chance had gone. The lights went out and Mr Wilkes made his noisy way down to the stage. Bob relaxed, and was about to mention that the coast was clear to Andie, but she could hold back no longer, buried her face into his shoulder and delivered two enormous sneezes.

"Thanks, I really needed that.." she said, rubbing her nose.

"The honour was all mine," he replied with a sigh, "Look, I'll tell you tonight then, okay?" he added, and they hurried back to their Form Room.

The presentation in the afternoon went fine for the most part, and Bob made a careful Mental Note of certain people who needed teaching some respect. A few new characters would be added to Bubonic Splat, and one or two new props would be needed.

Eventually the four o'clock horn signalled the end of another school day, and they headed towards the entrance of the main corridor. Andie stopped midway down the steps.

"Hold on - it's Monday today!" she exclaimed.

"Monday? How about that. Oh.. yeah, I remember. Can't we leave it just this once? It's more important to tell you about.. other things, before the bus gets here."

"No. It's your fault they think he's haunted, so it's your responsibility to check up on him."

Bob sighed as Andie lead him back inside, and they hurried towards the Gym changing rooms. In two respects, Andie was quite right. Melvin The Haunted First Year wasn't really haunted, and secondly it really was Bob's fault that everyone thought he was - the Psycho Fifth in particular. Back in September, rotund Melvin came to Bob's attention by falling over a lot. His shoes had the wrong sort of soles for allowing the wearer to stay upright on the highly-polished tiles of the Classics 1 Corridor, especially if the wearer was in a hurry to get to a room which he couldn't find. So on the first four occasions that Bob saw him, Melvin was always running and falling over, then running some more and falling over again, and so on along the entire length of the corridor. Each fall made an increasingly laugh-inducing 'smack' sound against the floor's tiles. In Bob World, this was comedy at its very best.

But the icing on the cake was Melvin's sticky-plaster. Every day the plaster was in a different place. His ear one day, his nose the next, then his forehead, then the other ear, then his chin - it was always somewhere new. Around that time, Bob had seen a documentary on poltergeists and ghostly presences, so he figured that the original plaster on Melvin's head had been thrown away a long time ago, and had come back to haunt him in the same way that the long-deceased Barron of Noerst had come back to haunt the creepy Noerst Manor in Latvia - just not quite so scary, and a lot less likely to be turned into a movie.

On the last occasion that Melvin had tried to hurry along the corridor, two passing members of the Psycho Fifth noticed that Bob was laughing uncontrollably, and stopped to find out why. Not far away, Melvin was trying to stand up again, and had fortunately succeeded. Bob knew that if he told the Psychos that Melvin and gravity didn't get on very well, the poor First Year wouldn't live long enough to see the end of the corridor, so he changed the reason to one he thought was harmless.

"That plaster on his head keeps moving.. it's like he's being haunted by an Elastoplast.." and then Bob started laughing again. So did the Psycho Fifth, but unlike Bob they soon decided an exorcism was called for. This involved taking Melvin to the boys' changing room and suspending him by the back of his underpants from a clothes hook. This manoeuvre had become known as 'Doing A Melvin' in his honour, and the Psycho Fifth knew that on Mondays Melvin The Haunted First Year had Gym to end the day.

Bob pushed the swing-doors open. Melvin was in his customary place three feet above the floor, attached to a coat hook on the central bench. His arms were folded, and he looked surprisingly untroubled.

"Hi Melvin. Come on, I'll help you down.."

"Oh it's okay Bob, they haven't arrived yet. I got some friends to put me up here.. see, if I save them the trouble, they might not bother any more. I'm wayyy ahead of them.."

"Ah, good thinking. You have a military mind, young sir. Well if there's nothing I can do, I'll be off then?" said Bob, with a salute.

"Cheers, Bob. See you next week though, just in case?"

"Yeah, of course!"

Bob grimaced as he went through the doors again, wondering if there was still enough time to get to the park for a word with Andie. He explained to her why he'd left Melvin in mid-air, and her look of disapproval had worn off by the time they were making their way along Father Magnus Road towards the Vidar Park. If it hadn't been a part of the school, Vidar Park could have been landscaped into a picturesque addition to Ringwood's forest. Instead, it was usually last on the school's priorities for development so although it wasn't Amazonian jungle yet, it was slowly and surely getting that way.

They wandered about twenty yards into it, well away from the stragglers who were walking home. Bob checked the area for any signs of a weird black cat. Nothing. They stood on the other side of a wide oak tree, out of sight.

"Okay Andie, about that Jinx cat? You have to promise that if you see her you won't stroke her, touch her or do anything, no matter what, okay?"

"Hmm.. okayy, I promise," Andie replied.

"Right then, here goes. Great Aunt Agatha's house on Lincoln Drive is a time portal and.."

Jinx launched herself from the branches above and landed on Bob's shoulders, immediately digging her claws so far into his face that he couldn't even cry out in pain. Over and over the small dagger-like claws re-attached themselves to a different part of his neck, and his hands were ripped to shreds as he tried to knock her away. She scratched wildly as if she had a dozen sets of claws. The excruciating pain became so intense that Bob knew he was either going to pass out or go mad. And then the scratching and tearing stopped as suddenly as it started. Bob felt Jinx leap from his shoulders, and heard her hissing as she ran into the undergrowth. He fell to the ground and after a few trembling moments dared to look at his hands.

No scars, no scratches, no blood. Nothing. He touched his face, and felt no pain at all. Both his ears were still where they should be, and the top of his head wasn't even missing. He stood up, feeling his heart pounding, and looked over to Andie who was calmly staring at a point somewhere between the two of them. She raised her head to look at him, blinked slowly and then rapidly as if she was waking up, and looked around at where she was.

"Andie? Are you okay? Can you see there's something weird going on here?"

"Something weird?" she said, puzzled, "Weird about what? We've come all the way to the park, which is a nice thing to do for a change, but I don't see why we're here. I mean, the bus'll turn up in a few minutes and if we don't hurry we'll be sitting right at the back, and you know what that means. Now come on, Freaky Deaky, we ought to be hurrying back. Chop chop.."

Bob tried to hide his troubled feelings on the bus back to Barton. Andie seemed fine though, but he could sense from a few of her tell-tale signs that deep down something was troubling her. He began wondering if she could remember the things they were talking about at lunchtime. Maybe she thought he was turning into a headcase, or perhaps she was wishing he was someone else. That last thought turned a day which hadn't been a particularly good one into a day that was guaranteed to become an abysmal one. As the journey wore on, more questions started plaguing him, most of them involving fine examples of who Andie should be with instead of him. As the coach wearily pulled into the bus station, he decided that Jinx had a lot to answer for. A short while later his mum arrived to pick them up from outside the car park, and by the time he dumped his schoolbag in his room he was feeling truly awful.

Dinner was a burnt mixture of peculiar things which may well have been recognisable a day or two earlier, and his parents' intellectual jousting certainly didn't help either the dinner or his mood. His father sat at the table and began reading the Obituary column in the local paper.

"Oh, I see old Mrs Gryffen's died. Remember her? Used to own that New Age oddity shop for years. She was hit by a car doing seventy miles an hour on the A35. Shame.. says here she would have survived but she was doing almost a hundred herself, at the time. Still, she'd hung on for weeks. How resilient."

"Almost a hundred? That's how old Mrs MacFarlane was. Hmm.. we have to sort a card out, it's her funeral on Tuesday. You know, Robert, she was so ill for so long that she built up an immunity to absolutely everything that medical science could offer her. Even De-Oxymologuptase.."

Bob's mum made the mistake of pausing to think, and his dad gleefully jumped in.

"..Acercubal Benzylate-Substitute. She came off that months ago of course. She'd been on HPZ4 since then, because the company who made it were taken over by the Schniffelheimer Corporation of Munich. They're German, Bob, very big since 1984. Autumn of '84, I believe. In fact, they've just been taken over - by the Travel Bite Lodge, of all people. Would you believe it?"

Bob's mind began to fill with a thoroughly impenetrable fog of boredom and self-doubt. Suddenly the phone rang, and he felt sanctuary had arrived. His dad answered it at the end of the third ring, as always.

"Hello, the Taylors' residence.. no, no, we have adequate window insulation and insurance. Yes, both here at our domicile and also at our business location, however I would consider changing for a local firm. Where are you based? Oh, that's far too far away. Have you a regional franchising policy in operation? You haven't? Well is there one planned? No? Well don't you think there should be? They're simple to initiate.. let me have a word with your manager.. yes, put him on.. yes, I'll wait.."

Bob cringed and began walking up the stairs, lost in the latest video by a glamorous trio who were riding high in the charts, Por Que No-ing their version of a hit from last summer. He switched his brain onto auto-pilot and did a third-rate homework, while Charlie Chaplin wooed Paulette Goddard in the background.

The film ended as Jinx began making a din just inside the front garden.

CHAPTER TWENTY ONE

Eugi in Manhattan

Bob arrived at Number 107 feeling thoroughly miserable, and didn't particularly want to do anything. Jinx disappeared from the window as soon as he cycled into the driveway, and he found her sitting outside the master bedroom, sniffing at something interesting in the carpet and generally behaving as if nothing had happened. That in itself was irritating - but throw in the prospect of Andie dating every unworthy-male-creature in the school, while he was to spend however long being chased by homicidal Troubler-loonies and trying not to destroy the entire universe - and that just made everything feel so much worse. Bob felt he'd earned the right to sing the blues. He decided not to, though.

His barricade was still in place and looked like a big shambolic mess, the kind that would win an Art Award if someone famous had done it. Significantly, it didn't look like anyone had tried to break through, which was a big relief. He put on his Arizona clothes for his return to New York, while wondering if Agatha would be annoyed with him for stealing enough money to open up his own bank. Actually, he was amazed and also embarrassed at how much he'd taken. All of his pockets, most of the lining and every available inch of the rucksack were crammed with notes, coins and things that sparkled. Without the motivation of Troublers chasing after him, the rucksack had suddenly become harder to shift than a beached whale.

"Good thing Aunt Agatha didn't need a beached whale, 'cause I'd never get one up the stairs.." he mumbled to himself as he awkwardly slung it across his shoulders and almost fell over. Somehow, taking things from the past didn't really feel like stealing and Bob classed it as 'Financial Archaeology' - and Agatha would hopefully go along with that particular Case For The Defence.

He found Bagshaw in the newly-titled Slumbering Lordship pocket of the jacket, and decided not to wake him for the time being. Besides, he felt a little bad about having left him alone for a whole day, and made a Mental Note in red Mental Ink to always leave him in the library. He staggered to the Master Bedroom and stepped over Jinx.

The suite in The Ansonia hadn't changed since he last saw it, and he had to take a moment to figure that it was only 6am on the morning after his last visit.

"Ohhh.. six in the morning.. again?" he moaned to himself. He'd only just finished one day, and really didn't fancy another already. He stood near the window and took a quick look through his diary, to brush up on what he'd done 'yesterday'.

"Carried bags for Naomi and Claudie, lunch at the Plaza.. aha, stayed overnight and then came here early.. so today's the day after that? I was hardly here for it.." he whispered, confusing himself.

He wandered along the Sixteenth Floor corridors until he managed to find the lobby, went straight into an open lift and then out of the silent hotel and into the sunshine of another summer's morning in New York. He felt tempted to drop into Gerstle's Café and leave a huge tip to the woman who'd been so nice to him a while ago, and even stopped for a moment outside to weigh up the why's and why-not's. He decided it was probably wiser to off-load all the money at the office first and come back with a tip later.

The long and leisurely walk back to Aunt Agatha's lifted his mood completely. The quiet streets began to show more and more signs of life as he went from block to block, and by the time he could see Gramercy Park in the distance, New York was alive and kicking, and he felt surprisingly good. And he could really do with a coffee.

He walked through the busy entrance of the Lexington Building feeling like he belonged there, and navigated his way through the clusters of smart-set people and went straight up to the receptionist, who greeted him with a smile.

"Mawwwnin' Mistuh Bawb! You wan' Madame Aaagathuh, don'tchoo? Well you jus' go rydonup, she says you c'n do that now."

Bob suddenly felt very tall indeed. A few important-looking managerial types stared over to him, raising their eyebrows as he walked past on his way to the elevator. Feeling a little shorter he walked all the way back and asked her which floor he needed. The elevator soon opened and he confidently knocked on the reception door at the end. It hadn't been shut properly, and swung open.

Naomi sat on her desk, carefully buffing a shine onto her nails.

"Morning Bob! How're you? And how did you get on with everything? You're not supposed to tell me anything at all though, until you've seen Madame Agatha.. but in a nutshell?"

"Well, I was supposed to be barbecued the other night and then I shot someone the next day.. and I nearly had a close-up look at a small missile, and then I figured I'd come back here for a coffee.. and I'm so loaded I could buy at least three States and still have enough left over for a bag of pretzels! Oh, and I got the first Mirror, so hooray and all that. It's the Immediate Past one, I think. And the presentation at school went fine, more or less," he said, taking off the rucksack with a heavy thud.

Claudie wandered by in mid-yawn on the way to her desk, holding a coffee and reading the back of a magazine. Bob felt a grin coming on.

"That's some cigarette lighter you gave me! I bet it's great if you're trying to give up smoking. What happened to the tiny flame?"

Claudie had a strange laugh that was somewhere between very friendly and utterly evil. Bob couldn't quite tell where, though.

"Oh, my mistake Bobs, maybe that was the one for cigars? I wonder how that happened.." she said, laughing, "Just remember to be vee careful with it, and let me know if it needs a top-up. You didn't lose it did you? Only we go back a long way.."

"No, but I nearly lost my head because of it. That nearly went back a very long way."

Claudie laughed again and Bob sat down in front of Naomi's desk, next to a coffee mug labelled Bob's Hot Java-Pot. Music drifted from the radio and he started feeling that he was now officially on the road to getting the Mirrors, and that Agatha would undoubtedly be pleased with him, and once Andie would find out about all of this, she'd be pleased with him as well. So for the time being, he felt pretty good. But then Naomi started talking to him..

"Do you have loads of friends back home Bob? I bet you miss them, what with being here and there and all over the place all the time, don't you?"

"Uhh.. no, not really. I wouldn't call many of them friends, hardly any of them actually. They're okay if I get them laughing, but it isn't always easy. Y'see, I don't live anywhere near the school, so it's like I have to get to know old friends and new ones again after every holiday, and I don't really see them much outside school anyway. Actually, I never really see anyone except Andie."

"Who's Andy? A real buddy, huh? I bet you get up to all kinds of wild scrapes!"

"No, she's.. she's just a girl I know.. you know."

Naomi stopped in mid-buff, and eyed him intently.

"No I don't know, 'you know'! C'mon, tell now! Speak to Nayo-meee!" she said, pointing to herself on the last syllable.

Bob knew he was blushing - it was almost as if part of his brain was completely out of control and wanted all the world to know it.

"There's not much to say, really. I mean, you'll be asleep inside a minute, honestly."

Naomi pointed a finger at him.

"Speak, or.. or I'll have to ask for that coffee back. Your choice."

The day had suddenly taken a turn for the embarrassing worse, and he could feel himself being swept further and further out of his depth. He wondered if he could just go out of the office and come back in again.

"Okay, okay.." he surrendered, determined not to say too much. "Umm.. well, she lives just down the road from me, and I suppose I've always been like her brother, and I expect I probably always will be, most likely. See, my mum and her mum were expecting at the same time, and that's when they got to know each other. So I had to be Andie's friend back in nursery, just to make sure that she had a friend and we've been.. friends ever since, and that's it really.. really, that's.. it."

Bob could tell from Naomi's expression that she wasn't going to let him off the hook that easily. She raised her eyebrows, prompting him to go on so he ventured a little further, self-consciously stepping into dangerous and uncharted areas.

"Well.. her hearing's not too good which hasn't ever bothered me, like it's just part of her and that's no big deal, and I don't even notice it but sometimes kids tease her, or they just aren't as nice as they really ought to be, even in small ways.. and the small ways can be the ones which hurt her the most, and.. you know.. that hurts me. So I try to make her laugh, or make her feel like there's someone there for her all the time and that she's.. really special.. and I never take a wrong step - well, I try not to. So she probably thinks of me like a brother, doesn't she?"

"Oh, I wouldn't be so sure about that.."

"Well she seems to like getting attention off some of the other boys, which annoys me 'cause they joke behind her back or even if she's near by, because they know she can't always hear them.. and I never know if I should.. you know.. tell her.."

Naomi edged nearer, and leaned forwards.

"Mmm.. tell her what?" she said, almost in a whisper, "That they make jokes, or that you-are-in-lurrrve, sweety pie?"

"Luhh.. luff? I am not! No way am I not in.. lu.. that word that you said! Or a sweety pie, I don't think she'd ever call me a.."

Bob knew his Blush Factor Rating was almost qualifying as a new personal best, and therefore a new World Record. Claudie suddenly took an interest and began scooting over in her chair. Bob cringed and struggled to wipe the smile off his face, but the more he tried, the more firmly-set it became. This was not good.

"Hey there, you two! Who's in love? Did someone mention the 'L' word without consulting me first?"

Claudie pulled her chair close enough for her knees to be touching his, and he suddenly started to feel like the world was coming to an end a whole lot earlier than Agatha might have feared.

"Habso, Claudie!" pined Naomi, "Bob needs to tell his sheba Andie that he loves her but he hasn't a clue how or even when to say it! Doesn't your heart just break?"

The Blush-ometer exploded and Bob squirmed like a World Champion Squirmer who'd just worked out a whole new series of Special Moves.

"No.. I was.. I was just sitting here going red.." he said, sensing that if he went any redder he'd start glowing. Claudie briefly placed one of her fingers firmly against the tip of his nose down to his chin.

"Shh! Listen to Auntie Claudie," she instructed, while Naomi nodded in agreement, trying to look serious. Bob knew that putting up a fight was useless. Even a huge Russian tank loaded with enough explosives to obliterate a small country wouldn't get him out of this. Claudie allowed an agonising moment of silence to pass him by before moving her hand away.

"Now then, listen good. Years ago, my Gran'ma Maisie told me when it's the exact right time to tell someone that you love them."

"Really?" said Bob, immediately realising that he might have sounded a little too keen. He tried to tone it down.

"I mean, not that it matters though, because I'm not.."

Claudie put her finger back over his mouth and briefly gave a stern glare. Despite Agatha's best efforts, Bob had never realised until then just how intimidating a pair of eyes could be, and tried to convince himself that this was simply because Claudie's were a very, very dark shade of browny-greenish-grey-blue, and had nothing to do with the fact that she was reading him like a book. She gave a slight cough.

"Ahem. The best time to tell someone that you love them is before somebody else does. There you go! But you don't need to know that, do you Bobs?" she said, tilting her head a little.

Her phone began to ring and she propelled her chair back over to her desk, grinning like the Cheshire Cat. Bob was vaguely aware of Naomi laughing about something beside him, and maybe Bagshaw was saying something or another, but none of that mattered in the slightest because now the whole world probably knew that he was.. he was in.. he was in..

"Mr Bobs? Hello over there? Mr Bobs, Madame Agatha will see you now," Claudie announced theatrically, bringing Bob back down into the office with an almighty crash, "And Bobs?" she whispered loudly, "For heaven's sake, don't blush so much in front of her, she hates that."

Bob nodded, and dragged the rucksack through a barrage of giggles into Agatha's office.

"Oh dear me, Robert, are you ill? You look as if you're running a temperature of at least 150. There are strains of algae living inside volcanoes who must feel cooler than you do."

"Huh? Oh I'm fine, sort of.. yes," he floundered, and quickly moved on. "Yes. Anyway, I came back to tell you I found the weird Immediate Past Mirror, and you were right - it did cause loads of weird things to happen around it, major weirdness actually, but not to me for the most part. Really weird. And I've got a whole load of money and stuff, and it's not mine but there's such a good reason.."

Agatha raised an eyebrow in approval, and rocked her chair backwards.

"Tell me everything, but try and limit the use of the word 'weird' - it's beginning to lose its meaning.." she said, looking towards the window while drawing a thin gold necklace through her fingers.

Bob took his place on Agatha's side of the desk and decided to stare at the floor and just keep talking, while also trying to keep track of how red he was. This meant that he gave a very, very detailed account of his return trip to Arizona, and also became extremely familiar with the small spiralling patterns on the carpet.

"Excellent Robert. That was just the kind of report on your activities that I need. Well done. I hope my two Assistants get you equally embarrassed the next time you drop round."

Agatha threw a toying smile straight at him as she leaned a long way back in her chair.

"Ah, first love! What greater joy to call one's own, when finds a heart.."

Bob sat in silent agony and stared intently at a bird gliding in wide circles far away outside, while Agatha drifted off into a rhyming world of rambling whimsey. By the time she'd laughed the prose to an end he knew he'd started blushing all over again, and was relieved to see that there was the tiniest chance that she might not have noticed. She was grinning and writing on one of her many pads instead.

"Empty out your borrowed riches into the.. fifth drawer down in the azure desk over there, and we might sort it out when all this is over and done with.."

Bob opened the long drawer and tipped all the money and jewellery into a huge collection of even more money and jewellery. Before he could ask her where all of it had come from, Agatha carried on with her instructions.

"..and in the meantime, this is a list for you. Assuming that you have found the only Mirror from Arizona, you have to block that portal properly, just to be sure. I doubt any Troublers would be able to come back before the Alignment, but we just don't know what they can do, or how they can do it. I find it's always better to be safe than dead, so you must buy these specific things from these specific stores, in exactly the order that I've written them, understand? Even if they sell everything in one place, you must not buy anything more than you're supposed to. You can start after lunch and when, and only when, you've got everything you may head back to the portal."

She handed Bob a flamboyantly written list of basic items ranging from nails and hammers to planks and glue.

"Have a word with Naomi and she'll give you some money for everything, and hopefully you won't need to revisit.. Arizona again."

For just a split second Bob thought Agatha was going to mention the name of the town, but he must have been mistaken. The moment passed, and he had more important things to bother about - such as facing Naomi and Claudie again.

Claudie was on one of her phones, dispensing more valuable advice.

"Listen, Caz bunny, you have to understand that you can't change a man. Well, not emotionally of course, but you can physically. Bones break, and that's the only way they learn.."

Bob shivered and gave his list to Naomi, carefully avoiding eye contact. She hummed her way through the items, added a few extra roads onto his map and then shuffled around in her slender shoulder bag looking for her purse. She groaned when she found it was empty except for a couple of quarters and a few mints, so she bent down and opened one of the lower drawers in her desk. Bob's eyes almost popped out. It rolled out at least four feet more than it should have, and contained rows and rows of different currencies. Each pristine bundle was neatly bound, labelled and dated. There was one gap.

"Oh no, we've run out of proper Now Dollars already.. Claudie have you been in here again?"

Claudie pressed the phone against her shoulder.

"Huh?"

"I said, have you taken all the Now money again?"

"That depends. Did y'see me?"

"No.."

"Then it wasn't me," she said, turned her chair around and went back to her conversation.

Naomi rooted through a couple of smaller drawers and scraped together a few dollar bills and a handful of change.

"Okay, there you go. The Bank Of Naomi is now closed due to a complete lack of money. I hope you're happy, Valentino!"

A knock on the front door was soon followed by the arrival of a spectacular lunch. This made the excessive buffet of the evening trolley look like mere leftovers from a Dickensian poor-house. The first of the multi-tiered silver carts contained what Bob presumed to be the starters. A huge shining soup terrine, masses of exotic delights each nestled in different salads, alongside piles of odd pastries and a whole collection of small silver containers. The other trolley was covered in upturned silver dishes, most of which were sending out wavering trails of steam.

"Ahh, today must be Overseas Cuisine day!" explained Naomi.

The aroma was exactly how Bob imagined Heaven should smell, and he switched his brain off for a lunchbreak. He had no idea what time it really was, either now or in the future, but he did know he felt far hungrier than tired. Claudie took a carefully-prepared tray of plates and dishes through to Agatha, and returned a few minutes later to the sound of someone hammering loudly on the reception door. They all hurried to see who was making such a noise.

A huge bouquet of flowers stood outside, supported by a pair of legs. Somewhere behind it, or more accurately, beneath it, was a porter who was struggling to stop it all falling apart.

"Sorry f'rr kickin' y'door," he said, and tried to read from his card. "Deliv-uhhry for Mzz Claudette.. uhh.. surname I can't make out.. from a gent in a big car called Mortimer. You have to sign please, if y'don't mind.. you there, kid - you'll do."

Bob took the folded delivery slip from the porter's other hand, and seized the moment to give Claudie some of his own advice.

"Claudie, never trust a man who gives a name to his car, especially one like Mortimer."

"Well lookit me I'm laughin'! Ha, ha, and another mighty haaaah. Morty's very nice actually.. I think. Which one was Mortimer, Nay?"

They carried the bouquet into the office and managed to get most of it onto Claudie's desk. A pile of books and magazines immediately slid onto the floor, followed by a few dozen of the flowers. As Bob picked them up, he noticed a bright red journal with a cartooned front cover. A girl in a tassled red dress was in mid high-kick, stretching her impossibly long legs and arms through huge musical notes and millions of champagne bubbles. Bob picked it up, as if it was a priceless work of art.

"Wow, look at this! 'The Sench Flapper's Almanac, From The Enlightened Pen Of Felicity Chancer' - do you think this would be useful for Bagshaw to learn something from? He knows as much about this place as.. well, as much as I do."

Claudie exploded with laughter.

"Oh, I'm poppin' a cork! I-am-popped! That is just wayyy too much - Lord Bags and Lady F!" she laughed, taking the compendium from him. She put it into her top drawer along with the almanac, closed it firmly, and cracked up with more laughter. Naomi explained why Claudie seemed incapable of speech.

"Learn something, Bob? He'll learn everything. Felicity Chancer

225

IS the Flapper Queen, and her newspaper columns are the habso foundation for the whole fashion, social, dance and party world! No joke, Manhattan's entire scene hangs on every word she writes, and most of our friends would rather starve if they can't dine where she does, or go naked if they can't buy what she says is IN - and Claudie really did do, a while back. Starve, that is. Anyway, Lady F will put him on the right track in a big way!"

"Really? This is all so weird.." said Bob, scratching his head and looking over at Claudie, who was still laughing. Naomi joined in, nodding in agreement as they wheeled the carts into the kitchen.

The three of them sat around the table talking and joking their way through any number of courses while Bob told them all about Arizona. Cheers, giggles and a few ooh's and aah's peppered the tale, especially the part about Claudie's lighter. Having a laugh and being able to talk everything through without feeling like a complete loon shifted a little of the weight from his shoulders, and Bob started to feel like a real part of the team.

"Which side of your family is Madame Agatha's?" asked Naomi, while chasing the last melon-ball around her silver dessert bowl.

"Subtle one, Nay, just how we rehearsed," said Claudie.

"Umm.." Bob wondered aloud, "I don't know, but I wish I did, especially yesterday at the portal. I'm sure she was on my dad's side for a while, and then my mother's, then it changed.. again.. but I'm always wrong about that, apparently. I learned years ago not to ask about anything. What's her surname?"

"No idea," shrugged Claudie.

"No, nor me," said Naomi, "Odd though, isn't it? I've never heard her mention sisters or brothers, and get this - not even Sandrine in Higher Admin could think of any, and she's been around here since like for ever and knows everything. Almost."

"You blabbed Bobs to her? A's going to wipe the floor with you!"

"No, I said to her that we were thinking of throwing a big birthday party for Madame Agatha this year - a tiger of a one, with a big list."

"Ah, that's clever.. I'd have been proud of that," said Claudie.

"Are you two trying to give me another stomach ulcer? I've got enough to worry about.." Bob joked weakly, and poured the coffees, "..but do you know why the name of my school should mean anything? The entire floor with the portal is booked under it, and until the concierge knew that was mine, he was treating me like something you wouldn't want to step in. Now he thinks I'm royalty!"

"King Laughy Trig-Someone's school which isn't in Norway?" said Claudie, her voice rising through the sentence.

"Yeah, King Olaf Trygvason School. My folks say it's a mad-house that ought to be somewhere like Oslo, and the only reason it must be good is because the fees are a bit steep. What's the big deal?"

"Well, Madame Agg says anyone who's anyone went there, you know. But apart from you and her I've never met anyone who's even heard of it.. does Andie like it there? I bet she does, but only 'cause of you, schweety-pie, ol' hunny-bunny.." she said, fluttering her eyelashes. Bob noticed that she had a look in her eye, the kind that could easily lead back to the 'L' word. A small clock chimed near the sink, giving him the chance to escape.

"Well, look at the time! I think I need to be off now because this shopping list's longer than a fat orangutang's arms. Do you think Bagshaw's had long enough with Felicity?"

Claudie grinned, and went to search through her drawer. She soon handed over the compendium, managing to look both mischievous and serious at the same time.

"Let me know how those two neckers got on, Bobs! I wonder if books can get hitched? Well, that's my Bizarre Thought For The Day out of the way.."

Her Agatha-phone rang, and she soon began rooting around in a filing cabinet for something, while talking to Madame Agatha as if whatever she was doing really was 'no trouble at all'. Naomi started picking her way through the flowers on the desk.

"C'mon Bob, you be good for Andie. If you find it hard to say something to her, you can try other ways instead," she said, and handed him a rose. "Here you go, I'm sure Claudie won't miss one."

Bob didn't go too red as he put the flower into his inside Floral Communication pocket, and surprised himself by feeling really good with the entire world.

"Madame Agatha, Nay," called Claudie, gesturing for her to go through to the office. They both gave him a small wave, so Bob took his rucksack and made his way out onto Lexington Avenue.

Agatha stood by the window, looking through a small pair of binoculars at Bob as he headed off in the wrong direction. Naomi stood at the desk, and waited for a few long minutes to be spoken to.

"Something concerning you, Naomi?" Agatha said, still looking through the window.

"No, no there isn't. Well.. yes there is. Those things on his list are no different to what he could buy anywhere, and there's nothing special about those shops either. They're not even ours, are they? And the map's all over the place as well."

Agatha turned to face her.

"Yes, but he doesn't know that. And he won't know that, will he?"

"I don't understand why, though. Surely someone might try and kill him if they know he's here? You said he's been spotted already."

"Oh, I'm sure they know he's here, and I suspect they might even be watching every move he makes, outside of these few rooms. I don't believe they're foolish enough to harm him, though. Have a seat."

Agatha pointed towards a low chair in front of her desk, and turned to the window again.

"Although we can't track him, we can track the watch that you fetched for him, at least while he's in Manhattan. What do you think might happen if he gets killed between here and the portal?"

"I don't know. That's an awful thought.."

"Yes it is, in a way. But let's assume someone pulls a trigger, or even drives a little too near him. His watch stays in one place for a little too long, we become concerned, and thus we put certain of our own wheels in motion - officially. Regardless of who does it, we'll be able to find out where, when, who and how, won't we? You and I will trace everything about them, and then we'll have a direct link back to the Troublers within these very walls - at any point either now, or in the future - and perhaps the future may change? I expect they already know that, so he really should be quite safe. But they might get impatient. And if they do, we can.. deal with them."

Naomi tried not to show her anger.

"How can you dare say that? He's your family.. well, he will be one day.. oh, you know what I mean."

Agatha sat down, slowly.

"I'm saying, Naomi, that it's in everyone's best interests that if he meets with an unfortunate incident, it should happen here where we can find out who did it and who they're connected to. You need to realise this is not just one person that we're talking about. As I've explained to you already, in Robert's era the entire structural control of the Guardianship is threatened. Do you know what that actually means? You must have seen enough in your short time here to realise what that jeopardises - would you stand by and see a shift in power to an unregulated and unaccountable ruling body? Of course not. I've seen this organisation grow out of a past which you could never imagine, and I won't allow it to fall back again, regardless of who I.."

Agatha took a moment to regain her composure.

"None of us are indispensable, and none of us are irreplaceable. And none of us, not Guardians, not you, and not even.. we aren't more important than the system we're part of."

"That's still awful.."

"In a way, you're right. But one day you'll realise why you aren't right. You can go now."

Naomi stayed where she was, and bit her lip.

"Can I ask something, first? You've.. you never mention your family," she said, looking at the floor, "..especially not sisters or brothers.. and unless they were top-level like you they would have passed away a long time ago, which makes your link to Bob go back more generations than he knows about.."

"I said you can go now."

"Don't get me wrong, I'm not saying he isn't really related to you.. I mean, he's got your eyes for a start, and your nose as well, but maybe you could let him have a family tree, or as much of one as you know? You've changed his whole world, and his life's on the line because of.. you.."

Agatha stared Naomi into silence.

"Tread very carefully, Naomi," she said harshly, "You may go."

Bob had emerged onto Lexington Avenue and into a sunny, noisy and very busy afternoon. All the buildings of New York must have been empty, because it seemed like everybody was out on the sidewalks, hustling and bustling in every direction. He wondered if a law had been passed that made everyone change office buildings at this time each afternoon.

He didn't have too much trouble finding the first store as it was only two blocks away. He scribbled Claw Hammer off his list, and for another few minutes carried on feeling pleased about life. But then somewhere along the way he must have veered off the map slightly, and no matter how much he thought he was getting back to Lexington to start over again, he seemed to be getting further away.

He decided to take a break to sort himself out, and stepped into a friendly-looking diner filled with shining chrome. It was noisy and full of laughter at one end, so he chose a table in the empty section and pretended to be reading his compendium.

"Pssst.. Bagshaw.. I'm lost! There's no avenue numbers or street numbers down here - they've all got normal names instead, and I can't make any sense of Aunt Agatha's map! I have to buy things and get back to.."

Bagshaw was leaning on the frame of his panel.

"Howdy.. matey Bobsy.. chappy m'laddio.. and no mistake then. Have you met Muss Flippity Saucer? What a luvvuly girl, oh what a luvvaly, luvvaly ever such a nice girl she is too she is, like a champagne bubble with legs.. but a musch, musch better figure though.."

"Bagshaw, you're sloshed! Look, I need to know if you remember being in New York - you said you'd been here before, remember?"

"..oh show me the way to go home, ahm tired an' ah wanna go to bed-duh.. come on, join in Bops, you musht know the wordles.."

"Bagshaw, try and pull yourself together, can you? I need you to think about when you were last here!"

"Who, me? Well don'you worry, Bobert, I new Know York like the back of my hands, both of them. Where 'bouts there are you t'day?"

"I'm in a kind of diner place called Auster's, somewhere on Cannon Street. I've given up trying to sort out where that is."

"No no nooo, don't you be there of all places. You'll be knocking back those egg-creams aaaalll day long, ol' chap. Oh, those egg-creams.. go out and then left, and don't stop till you get to the gates of Buckingham Palace, and give my regards to.. ah, whichever one of them's home today.. uhoh.. falling over.."

Bagshaw dropped out of sight, knocking the table and the rubber plant over in his panel, and soon began snoring loudly. Despite Bob shaking it upside down, nothing re-appeared.

Bob left Auster's and crossed over an endless series of roads, all with names instead of numbers. The tall buildings cast short shadows as he wandered through the glaring sunshine, and he rapidly began to feel useless, a First Class Idiot. His map made less sense every time he looked at it.

If the names of the nearby shops and hotels were anything to go by, the vast stretch of water just beyond the next road was the East River and therefore he was completely, hopelessly lost. The top question in his mind wasn't to do with his whereabouts, but more to do with trusting anyone enough to ask for some help. He wandered for a while longer trying to go north, and sat down on the steps outside the huge Municipal Building next to an askew roadsign for Centre Street. He stared at it for a while, wondering what to do.

Big cabs with yellow and black panels continually pulled over by the kerb, and one or two even called to Bob in case he needed a lift somewhere. Then a brilliant idea sprang into his mind. These cab drivers should know where he ought to go, and even if they didn't, they might have a map of the city which he could take a look at. And more importantly, if they seemed even a little bit creepy-weird, he could just dart into a few buildings or narrow places where cars wouldn't be able to follow.

"Fool proof!" he declared.

Now that he actually needed one, he found most cabs were busy or happy to ignore him. However, two had been parked for a while further up the street, so Bob casually meandered over to them, just like a normal person probably would. A passenger climbed into the back of the first one while Bob was speaking to the driver, and it immediately set off and left him in mid-conversation. The second one was still standing a short way behind. There was no danger of this one doing the same because there was no driver in it, so Bob sneaked a look through the side window for anything resembling a map. It was empty except for a forgotten glove on the back seat and a carpet of cigarette ends on the floor.

But hanging from a nail inside the driver's door was something far more interesting. A dented compass with a brass handle hung on a nail, from a loop of frayed string around its neck. Bob decided that his situation justified taking a risk. He opened the front passenger door, and for an embarrassing moment expected a wailing alarm to start dragging everyone's attention to him. Surprisingly enough, that didn't happen so he carefully kneeled in the footwell and reached across the driver's seat. The nail fell off, and the compass went with it. Bob grabbed it off the floor, left a few biros on the seat as a form of payment, closed the door and very, very casually walked away as if he was just a completely normal person having a completely normal stroll. It lasted for no more than a few steps, and he quickly broke into a run until he felt like he was closing in on the sound barrier.

He slowed down a block or two later and eventually felt safe enough to stop, so he sat down on the step of a clumsily-fixed doorway next to a cake shop. His hands were shaking as he held the compass for a closer look. The actual compass section was about two inches wide, cracked and encircled by a band of worn-down brass. It sat at the end of a heavy brass handle that must have looked very impressive once, but its engravings were now worn with age. There had been something inscribed along its length, but only the first three letters of the first word remained. Bob was about to speak, and then wondered how to start a conversation with a compass - a nameless one at that, and one without any pictures to answer back. He took a deep breath.

"..err, hello Mr E-U-G?" he said nervously, carefully reading each shallow letter in the sunlight, "Can you hear me? I really need you to help m.."

A gruff ashtray voice interrupted him, and seemed to come from somewhere within, or maybe around, the head of the compass.

"Huh? It's Yeww-gee, an' who's you? You ain't Amboig, so who am I dealin' wid? An' what's dat stinkin' smell?"

Bob figured Mr Amberg must have been the cab driver, not that it was important any more. He had a quick think for what to say back.

"I'm Bob, and that smell is just fresh air. But look, I'm incredibly lost but I don't trust anyone enough to ask for help. Long story."

"Hey, I'm right with you. What I don't know ain't gonna hurt me, so just say where we're headin' and we'll get there.."

Bob started feeling as if he'd actually had a lucky break.

"Do you know your way around here, then?"

"Do I? What are you, a wise-crackin' funny-makin' Mr Hee Hee kinda guy? You spend as long as me in a cab, and you know where everyone's goin'. You also know they're business, an' sometimes they don't like sayin' much, jus' like you. So what line of work you into? You runnin' numbers, dealin' in the fallin' down juice, pushin' this an' racketin' that, or what? You gotta be the youngest hood.."

"No, no, I'm no-one dodgy, I just travel around.. a lot. Secretly, like incommunicado, I suppose. So I need you to be an.."

"..all-seein' an' a nuthin'-sayin' accom-pliss? Yeah, gotcha. Say, don't tell me no more, I don't need to be knowin'. So where's we headin' for?"

Before Bob could reply, a man wearing an apron (which might

once have been white) appeared in the bakery doorway. He handed a huge loaf down to him.

"Hey kid, you have this okay? Now you take care o' yourself, and don' you be 'round here any more, not till the doctors get you head sorted out, okay? I don' wan' no trouble, but if you come by here again, you'll see.."

Bob stood up, obligingly twitched his head a couple of times like a proper loon, and walked away. Somewhere behind him he could hear the man saying, "Yeah, is okay, he gone now, crazy joe-schmoe.."

Being lead around Manhattan by a real expert poking out of his top pocket (which seemed to give Eugi a perfect view of the world) allowed Bob to buy all the other items on Agatha's list within half an hour. The price of the final item in the final store perfectly matched the amount of money Naomi had given him, which meant that she was either a devoted DIY enthusiast or her Weird Factor had just leaped higher by a frightening amount.

Eugi offered instructions all the way along Broadway, pointing out some of the more dubious places which were never likely to appear on any of the usual sight-seeing tours. As they reached Columbus Circle the bags were getting heavier and the journey was starting to drag. After a break to pick at the loaf and feed a frenzy of pigeons, they arrived back at The Ansonia. Bob returned a friendly wave from the concierge, and took the elevator.

"Thanks for all that help back there Eugi, I'd still be wandering around looking over my shoulder every five minutes."

"So you get tailed every now and then - like who don't? Ah, I was sick of bein' in that cab anyhow. All day long the noise, the shoutin', the same ol' cussin' and so ons. Like they ain't even funny cusses ee-thuh. An' the smells! Oh Lord high above.. the smells! I ain't no doctor but smells like that ain't right.."

The lift gave a soft judder as it reached the sixteenth floor, and Bob started to make his way to Room 963. It didn't take him very long to be on the wrong side of the building, well and truly lost again.

"This is.. a guided tour of the floor, Eugi, so that you know where everything is," he bluffed as they arrived at the doors by the lifts again. Bob meandered his way to the right room a few minutes later, and it all impressed Eugi. Apparently, it was 'one classy joint'.

"Eugi, I'm putting you with a friend of mine who might not be too talkative just yet.. so try to speak quietly.."

Bob took the snoring compendium from his pocket, and carefully put the compass next to it in his bag. He stepped into the archway, and arrived back at Lincoln Drive.

After some intense redecorating, the entrance to the Arizona portal was hidden behind a new covering of boards, dozens of nails and a few securely-hammered chairs as well. Bob looked proudly at his DIY handiwork, and then piled the cabinets and other items against it. No-one could possibly get through that doorway unless they were using some kind of enormous medieval battering ram, and very few places sold those - especially in old Arizona.

"Fingers crossed that I don't have to go back.." he thought.

He put on his usual Barton clothes again, and headed over to the stairs. Jinx sat on the top step, blocking his way.

"What? I've done everything for the time being, and now I'm going to tell Feiya about Manhattan. What have I done wrong?"

Jinx stood sideways along the step, and arched her back. She seemed to be looking over at the room that lay near the staircase, which, technically at least, was behind the newly-blocked bedroom.

"Oh.. I get it. Straight on with the show then? I'm not whingeing, but do you know how long I've been up? I wish I knew - and my brain's already on overtime from yesterday.."

Jinx showed no sign sympathy, so Bob picked up his rucksack and warily stepped past her to the drawing room. The door opened with the slightest of touches, and he looked into yet another room that didn't fit the dimensions of the house. His heart started to pound, and he half hoped it would be just an ordinary room which didn't lead anywhere. The latest moment of truth had arrived.

"Imagine the viewing figures this would get.." he thought.

Rather than simply going straight through, he tried taking a look instead and rested his hands on either side of the door's frame. He leaned his head inside first, as far as he dared to go..

CHAPTER TWENTY TWO

The America

..which made no difference at all. He was sucked in and landed face down on a pale mauve carpet.

Bob raised his head and looked around. The drawing room had gone, replaced by a new room which was a little smaller than the one at The Ansonia, less ornate, and far more modern. The table and chairs facing him looked like they had been designed by a mathematician - sharp angles, broad curves and sweeping lines of symmetry running everywhere. Three large, corner-less square windows and a long row of drawers ran along the far side of the room, well beyond the table.

"Strange.." Bob thought, as he realised that the carpet and the whole floor felt as if they were vibrating slightly. A very low and steady humming sound seemed to be coming from.. pretty much everywhere.

Bob got to his feet and looked around. He was in a split-level lounge, with two or three doors down on his level which could all be tested later on, maybe. A few steps lead stylishly up to the higher level, where long royal-blue settees lined two of the walls, with a multi-layered glass coffee table in the corner which looked even more expensive than the one in the parlour at Lincoln Drive. A few copies of The New Yorker, Vogue and some foreign newspapers lay spread out across it, so he cast his eye over them. They were all from May and July of 1954. The style of The New Yorker's cover illustration had changed, but the style of the title hadn't and Bob felt pleased that some things were, in their own way, timeless. It was like finding a common link between the decades, a minor symbol of stability and continuity between The Ansonia back in the 20s, and wherever he was now. He held up a copy and looked at the cover. A woman on a guided tour of a huge creepy cathedral tower had just noticed a gargoyle flying away - but no-one else in her group had seen it. Bob laughed and felt as if he understood how she felt.

"That's life.." he thought as he dropped it back on the table, and immediately began wondering how barmy he was becoming, now that he was feeling an affinity towards a magazine.

Etchings of Manhattan by people Bob had never heard of hung on the walls, so he took a moment to look at them and scrawl down their names in his diary. One or two like those would go fine in his room back at Barton.

"Pennell, Nevinson, Dar.." and then his attention was drawn to one in particular. Four women dressed in very 20s fashions walked along a lamp-lit street, and three of them were vaguely recognisable - at a push. Bob grinned and read the title.

"Shadows on the Ramp.. 1927.. M Lewis.."

He wrote it down in large letters in case he might stumble over a print somewhere. His spidery scrawl was now completely illegible, and made him realise that he'd been up for far too long.

A pair of glass doors lead through to a spacious conservatory, and beyond that lay a wide verandah overlooking miles and miles of very calm sea. This was impressive. Bob slid the doors open, and walked out into the fresh early morning breeze. He leaned against the shiniest wooden rail he'd ever seen, and checked his watch. Just as he expected, the hands made a near-vertical line to show 6.05 am precisely. The date read August 14th 1954. In the panel underneath the face in customary tiny letters was SS AMERICA, followed by THE ATLANTIC, and below that came LOVELY BALCONY. Bob had a quick think and decided he knew nothing at all about 1954, even less about liners, and as for the ocean.. well, it was wet.

He looked ahead to the angular bow of the ship, and let the passing waves draw his gaze back along its elegant lines until he was looking down at the white water surging out from the side, forty or fifty feet below. The ship seemed to reach back for a mile or two, but was probably nearer to a couple of hundred yards, give or take a cabin. He sat down on the recliner and spent a few minutes just watching the broad waves rolling by, feeling the ship rising with the swell of the sea and then serenely settling back down. If his reason for being there hadn't been so serious, he felt like he could quite enjoy being on a cruise liner. A seagull flew alongside the ship for a while, effortlessly matching the America's speed, gliding just a few feet away from the verandah. Bob had seen gulls flying around Barton countless times, but he'd never been alongside one as it actually flew before. He watched, captivated as it soared and dived effortlessly on the wind.

A few hours later the steamed blasts of the midday signals woke him up in a way that his alarm clock never could - unless it had been plugged into an enormous amplifier and strapped to his head. He looked around to see if the ship was sinking or falling apart, and by the third long blast he stared far up to the towering front of a winged red, white and blue funnel.

"How American does it get?" he said to himself, and figured that if his heart ever recovered, he really ought to sort out a plan of action for the day ahead. The final signal managed to wake Bagshaw.

"Whass.. whuh.. who?" he said, rubbing his head and wincing.

"Relax, Bagshaw, it's midday that's all. And in case you missed our arrival, we're on a liner called America. How about that?"

"Well I never! I hope she's a big old girl like The Great Eastern. Magnificent, she was, and so safe.. 'fraid I'm not too sure about boats, never really trust them," he said, missing both eyes with his monocle, "Sailed to Alexandria back in '78 on the way to a diplomatic posting in India.. or maybe '62.. anyway, diabolical weather! Got blown so far off course we turned up in Quebec of all places, months and months later. Ohh, I felt dreadfully queasy. Sometimes think the ground's still moving like that deck.."

Bagshaw's reminiscing was curtailed by a very, very excited Eugi.

"Well excooze my interruptioning here Columbus, but holy smokes did y'hear that! I never heard a horn like that before! You gotta get one of those kid - ain't nobody gonna be stoppin' in your way if you got one of those. Jeez, speak to the Captain an' find out what he wants for it! I'm tellin' you.."

Listening to Bagshaw and Eugi while lounging around on a very comfortable chair and watching nothing but occasional dolphins and white-capped waves drifting by wasn't going to get a plan worked out, so Bob wandered back into the cabin. Seeing it in full daylight, the word 'cabin' wasn't quite appropriate anymore, because Agatha's quarters were more of a floating apartment complex, with a vast number of extensions.

He left Andie's rose in a spare vase on the conservatory table for the time being, crossed the living room and went down to the other living room - and nervously turned the handle of the heavy pine entrance door. The key around his neck glowed with a comforting warmth and the door slowly opened up, revealing a narrow corridor with just one direction to go along. Bob put Operation Wander About A Bit into effect.

The corridor passed by a few doors, and eventually lead via a series of steps down to another corridor, past some round windows looking out to sea, and finally a passageway lined with paintings of old cities. The door at the end needed opening like a proper door, and Bob was amazed that he was actually required to turn his key. He put it down to very impressive security. As he stepped into the First Class lounge, he held Eugi in a handkerchief and pretended to blow his nose, to hide the fact that he was talking to a compass.

"Eugi? Hey Eugi, are you taking all this in? I could do without getting lost on this thing - it's like a labyrinth and if I have to start running I can't afford any wrong turns or red lights, if you know what I mean.."

"Ah no probs, this tub ain't big enough to lose nuttin' in. Show me a plan or somethin' and we'll be fine.. an' go easy with dat nose, okay? It don't sound too pleasant from where I'm sittin'.."

Bob kept away from the pre-lunchtime crowds and stayed firmly against the walls as he crept around the lounge.

"Are you quite sure this is a ship, Bob? Looks more like the Ladies' Area of the club in Kensington.." said Bagshaw, who was quite enjoying himself. He was right though, because the America's main lounge didn't look particularly ship-like at all. The chairs were all big, curved and looked very comfortable, the decor was either floral, chrome or varnished, and the balcony running high around the lounge looked like part of an elite hotel. There were no string hammocks, no white-bearded officers, and not even someone walking around saying 'Arrrr Jim Lad!' with a parrot on his shoulder. Still, Bob kept a very edgy look-out for someone else who was tall and deranged, and now possibly with a serious limp. For the time being, the only people around were casual holiday-makers, who didn't look at all threatening.

After a few more paranoid minutes of wandering into bars, lounges and an unexpected trip through the Tourist Class dining room, Bob finally stumbled across a framed series of the ship's plans, intended to help out lost passengers. Eugi had them all figured out in no time, and they headed out onto the deserted Promenade Deck. The hundreds of passengers were having lunch in the various restaurants, and the aromas carried on the air to Bob, who felt like sneaking into the next restaurant and dining like a king.

"Mirror first, and then nosh later," he told himself, and started wandering again.

The America's Promenade Deck was enclosed, running like a broad corridor along either side of the ship, which meant that there was no real wind to carry away any footsteps made by unwelcome guests. And that was perfect for someone listening for those kind. His feet made strange 'skwumff' noises on the non-slip tiling as he walked the length of the ship, and he felt convinced that he was giving himself away with every step. He slipped his hand into his pocket and held onto Claudie's lighter, and paused at one of the support-struts to try and listen for any other footsteps. But he heard nothing, just the soft sounds of the ship moving slowly through the waves. He carried on walking, and soon reached the front end of the deck, and found that it was just as quiet and deserted as well.

He ran as carefully as he could around to the other side of the ship, and for a moment thought he saw someone stepping into a doorway at the end, but his view was immediately obliterated by a loud and raucous party of a dozen or more passengers. Bob returned their cries of 'Ahoy there, boat buddy!' and casually walked into the next doorway along, just like a real holiday maker would.

More varnish and chrome. Whoever decorated the corridors and lobby areas on this ship must have had a good friend at a varnish-and-chrome warehouse. It was everywhere. He walked an aimless path inside as he searched for anything weird happening, or maybe anyone suspicious or weird doing something suspicious or weird. Eugi was getting bored.

"Where're we goin', kid? If someone wuz onto you, they could just sit down an' wait fuh you t'turn up 'cause you're just here-in' an' there-in' an' then goin' back again all the while. If you wanna go somewhere, jus' say 'cause there ain't no charge outside a cab."

"Okay.. maybe there is somewhere.." Bob said, unconvincingly.

He sat on the stairs and stared at the loop-patterned flooring, taking a while for a think. And then another. He eventually decided that it was time to try out Bob's Theory Of Repetitive Numbers.

"Okay Eugi, here's the plan. I'm looking for Room 963. I don't know what's there or who's there, but there's a chance it's someone I need to speak to, yeah?"

"Now I like that. For a moment I was gettin' all messed up with the backwards and forwards stuff, but now there's a place t'be goin' and I like that. So Room 963 it is then. You wanna see the sights, or you in a hurry?"

They took the scenic route, and just over an hour later they arrived back on the Promenade Deck, at the entrance to the section where the rooms began with a gold number nine. Bob now felt like he had a good sense of what was where, and was even starting to think that there wasn't a Mirror on board - but he decided to hold back on a final judgement for a while yet.

"957.. 959.. 961. They've stopped, Eugi. There's no 963?"

"An' I'm tellin' you there's a 963, else I wouldn't uh come all this way. It's somewheres 'round here.."

Bob looked around. The cabin doors had come to an end, leaving two plain staff entrances and a First Aid room. The first staff door was locked and looked exactly like a staff door should look, so he crossed the corridor to try the other one - and stopped for a moment as his key glowed strongly. There was another door beyond the First Aid room, at the end of the corridor. How could he have missed that? He was sure it hadn't been there a moment ago. He walked up to it, and the key around his neck began pulsing with heat.

"An' here you most certainly is!" announced Eugi, as if doors always appeared out of nowhere.

This one was different to all the other doors. Instead of being solid wood, its top half had a cut glass panel made up of large diamond shapes, and the lower half was entirely frosted glass. Bob took a look through the top part, and peered into a softly lit side-room which contained just a single chair and small table, with an open book on it. The walls were completely featureless other than a couple of triangular light fittings, and that was it. What a monumental disappointment.

His key glowed again, so he half-heartedly tried opening the lock with it. Even though it was by far the wrong shape, the door opened for him, and did so in the most bizarre way he'd ever seen. It drifted towards him, fading away as it passed through him - or as he passed through it, to reveal the ordinary small room beyond. And then the whole room faded away as he tried to step inside, and he found himself at the start of a winding corridor full of doors and paintings.

"Are you still taking all this in Eugi? There's a whole load more new streets up ahead."

"Oh yeah.. I like findin' nuw terrahtreey once in a while!"

Bob followed the sharp turns of the corridor passing door after door, most of which had strangely abbreviated titles on them, and past portraits of indecipherably-named people. And then suddenly Eugi coughed.

"Room 963 sir! That's a buck thirty, an' have y'self uh nice day! Ha hah.." he said with a laugh that sounded like someone shaking a bucket of wet gravel.

A cold sweat broke out on Bob's forehead as he checked the numbers on the door. He knocked, nervously, and waited for a reply. He counted from ten down to one, and tried again. His key glowed intensely and the door slowly swung itself open to reveal Feiya sitting in a chair across a lounge, pointing a huge double-barrelled shotgun straight at him.

"So you're finally here!" she snapped, "How did you get in?"

Bob tried to think of something to say, but found the gun a little too distracting. Feiya raised it more towards his chest.

"I've been hearing your footsteps for the past few days and I was wondering when you'd show up. This entire area is pass-protected and visually blocked to Outsiders, so that makes trespassing difficult, doesn't it? And that door you just opened was light-sealed as well."

"Fey, it's me, Bob.. oh, you don't have a clue do you? Put that gun away and I'll stick the kettle on.."

"How about you stop talking? I ask the questions and you don't, and then maybe I won't redecorate the wall with you. Now who the hell are you and what are you doing in here?"

Bob couldn't take the situation too seriously. Somehow, knowing Feiya without her realising that he knew her was really funny. And as for the 'redecorate the wall'.. he held his hands up like a bad actor in a very low-budget made-for-tv crime caper.

"I'm Bob, and.. I've bought a fluffy toy mouse for Jinx to play with. Madame Agatha says the Little Beastly One likes them. It squeaks."

The gun clicked into readiness as Feiya prepared to inadvertently cause a Secondary Existence Dilemma of the fatal variety.

"Okay, okay. I'm Bob, and your Madame Agatha is my Great Aunt Agatha. I'm from quite a few years in the future and I've come here to retrieve any missing Eternity Mirrors which are on this ship, but there might not be any at all here. The Andromedan Fault has something to do with it all, and your locks don't work because of a key which you gave to me, years from now. Oh, and for some reason I don't exist, so no-one knows I'm here except an older version of Aunt Agatha and eventually an older version of you. And maybe a younger version of Aunt Agatha as well, but I'll have to have a think about that. How's that sound?"

Feiya thought for a moment. She pointed the gun up towards Bob's head.

"Where's Jinxy's toy?"

"Incredibly, that's the bit I made up, but the rest is all true, honest. Can I put my hands down?"

Feiya nodded.

"Close the door then. We'll talk some more. And I'll have a coffee. And just the tiniest sprinkle of sugar. Frothy milk, too."

Bob soon emerged from the kitchen and sat down on what must have been the all-time comfiest chair ever. This chair could set the industry standard for Aaaah Ratings. He sank a few inches into the padded soft white leather and tried not to stare at the oh-so-1950s version of Feiya. She was a vision in pastel green, buried somewhere under a voluminous flared skirt with thousands of knife-sharp pleats, and fronted all the way up to her neck with a long row of white buttons. The gun didn't really go with the ensemble, but Bob thought he was better off by not mentioning that to her.

He opened his diary and carefully picked a short path through the details about why, where, when and what had been happening. Despite his best efforts, he didn't confuse himself too much. Feiya gradually became less intent on shooting him, and had even lowered the gun from his head. It now just pointed at his feet.

"So Bob, you're telling me that somewhere on this ship is Madame Agatha's personal Holiday stroke Business Portal?"

"Yeah, it's up at the.."

"No don't tell me! If she wanted me to know, she would have come down here and just knocked on my door and told me herself! I don't know about it for a reason, not unlike none of the others who don't know anything about it.. neither."

"There's others on board?" asked Bob, trying hard not to look bemused by her triple negative.

"Well of course there are," she said, stretching a few vowels on the way, "My Relevant Clothing sub-department alone occupies half this deck. I've probably got the largest mobile wardrobe on earth! And there's a couple of dozen admin types and Event Recorders, plus a few other minor drones and the rest are Vicinity Observers. Maybe forty people, all in all."

"Wow, you really know how to pack for a holiday. You are on a holiday, aren't you?"

Feiya finally gave a big genuine smile. She stood up and hurried across the uncluttered room to a pine cabinet on the wall which made Bob's eyebrows drift upwards into cartoon-character territory. She re-attached her heavy rifle onto a panel next to three other bigger rifles, which stood alongside a collection of pistols and shotguns. Two enormous Samurai swords hung to the side of them, and a row of unpleasant knuckle-dusters and small silver javelins ran the entire width of the cabinet. There was a pretty good chance that she wasn't on a normal kind of holiday.

"I'm on a Decade Strata Voyage, which if you haven't heard of one already, is a way of experiencing life at lots of different levels, or 'strata' you see? Every time I get off the ship in a new port, I'm someone new. New name, new clothes, new me! That's what the others are here for - they enable it all to happen, subject to Madame Agatha's approval of course. There's plenty of string-pulling to be done in preparation for my arrival, and it's all immediately wiped from the history books as soon as I'm back on board here! Of course, the relevant Outsiders have to be expecting whoever I'm supposed to be, and then they have to forget they ever met me when I've gone. They get an Appropriate Memory Replacement thing. I'm the only one who doesn't know what's coming up, except for the occasional visit here and there."

Bob noticed a curved Turkish blade poking out from behind one of the cushions on her settee, and wondered if anything like that was behind his. Feiya closed the cabinet, hurried over and began hastily rearranging the cushions to cover it up, and gave a small laugh.

"I was cleaning that.. don't worry, it wasn't covered in blood or anything. Just a precaution."

"You need that stuff?"

"No, not all the time. In Monaco I was a famous soprano having a night out with the upper echelons of European aristocracy, which was great - I won a fortune at the casino! Had to give it back though..

and in Civitavecchia I was Argentina's Minister of Agriculture on a formal visit. That took some studying and there was even a small State Welcome for me on that one. And then in Barcelona I was immediately arrested for being a.. lady of expensive virtue, if you know what I mean. That was embarrassing, I can tell you."

"Well it would be.. why does all that happen then? Do Naomi and Claudie have the same treatment?"

Feiya flopped down onto the settee, and something heavy dropped onto the floor, behind it.

"Aww, there goes the flanged battle mace again.. darn it," she said, kneeling over the back to look at whatever had embedded itself in the floor. "I spent ages stitching that thing within easy reach, just here behind the.. you know, Bob, you should be glad I chose to point the gun at you instead of just launching that thing your way, 'cause in olden times, the Mongols.."

"Oh I say, Bob, she's such a livewire! Why didn't we come here first? So spirited.."

"Not now, Bagshaw.."

"Hey kid! If she's fuh real then we're in hot water an' I mean hhaych-oh-teee HOT.. so like turn on the charm or buy her a drink, jus' do anythin' that's nice.." said Eugi, impressed and more than a little nervous.

"Yeah.. uh, Fey, I was wondering about Naomi and.." he repeated.

"Yes you were," she said, leaving the mace where it was, "They don't do these yet. I managed to pass my Stage Two Tri-Committee Assessment first time, so I'm a quarter of a level ahead of them. Only eighteen more and I get to be Madame Agatha's official High Assistant Of The First Order! All this travelling around the world is just a stage of the training, and it's really educationing..able. So I get to spend ten years travelling almost all of the time and that way I have plenty of places to experience, rather than just see."

"And get arrested in, I expect?"

"Yes, but I'm getting used to it. It's preferable to being shot at, though. I hate it when that happens.."

"Ah, well who wouldn't?"

Bob had the kind of idea that should have made a lightbulb appear above his head. Now he could move the conversation into safe Fey-friendly territory.

"Have you brought a camera with you? I bet you could get some great photos from all over the place.."

Her face lit up, and she disappeared through a white door into her bedroom. She emerged dragging the first of two huge boxes, both of which were crammed full of photographs.

"There's hundreds there, Fey - how far into this Strata voyage thing are you?"

"About three weeks, nearly four. I do like cameras. I'll be snapping the Statue of Liberty tomorrow!"

An hour or two drifted by as Bob happily worked his way through the pictures and further into Feiya's good books. A small clock gave six melodic chimes and she suggested that they ought to go for an early dinner, before the restaurant-bar would become too full.

"You see, I can't order Room Service because the room isn't officially here, and the powers-that-be in New York haven't got around to supplying us with a proper secret restaurant yet," she explained to Bob while dragging the boxes back.

After half an hour Feiya was ready to go, and they took another half an hour to find the special passageway to the restaurant. Eugi didn't take kindly to having his advice ignored, and Bob was glad that Feiya couldn't hear what he was saying. As they made their way around the decks, crew members and occasional passengers gave friendly 'hello's and a few barely-concealed flirtatious looks.

"Won't they all get used to seeing you around? If you're going to spend ten years without a real cabin on the ship, plus you won't be getting much older, wouldn't a low profile be better?" asked Bob.

"Nah, they think I'm new every day! They forget me after every time they see me, which would be a bit of a blow to my self-esteem if I didn't know that it wasn't their fault."

Eventually they crossed through the First Class Smoking Room, and eventually found a short corridor with a gold 'TR' written above it. Bob had to do a double-take as he neared the sign at the end.

"The Trygvason Restaurant - By Appointment Only," he read, scratching his head.

"It's a Norwegian name, apparently," said Feiya. "Restaurants always go for odd names, don't they? In Malta I was in one called.." she chatted, as they hurried up a few densely-carpeted steps.

They arrived in a cleverly laid-out room containing a dozen or more tables, a long bar at the far side, and a small lounge area off to the left. Masses of tall plants and painted mermaids broke up the harsh lines and metallic sheens of the decor, and leant the room a peculiar dream-like atmosphere. Bob heard music playing in the background and pinned it down to Harry James, and immediately started wondering where it was coming from. There were no cd's and probably no tape-decks in the 50s, and nobody would ever try playing vinyl on a liner. Information like that was probably classified, so he gave up wondering and followed Feiya to a pleasant window table in a small alcove.

"You should feel honoured, Bob. Hardly anyone's allowed to just wander in here, it's all got to be booked and cleared days ahead. Most folks don't bother, they just use the ship's normal restaurants, but I think you'll be much safer here. Not 'cause of the food, but 'cause you're amongst friends. Except them, they're embarrassing beyond belief," she said, with a subtle hitch-hiker's gesture.

A group of the loudest and most pretentious people Bob had ever seen occupied the large table in the centre of the room, and were working their way through a random collection of dishes. A colossal man wearing The Tie From Hell (complete with matching jacket) clicked his fingers, loudly.

"Hey there, garston, attentseeyohne requested vwa-lah! Bring me a better wine than this Chateau Drainpipe.. yes now! We want a bottle that wasn't filled-up yesterday!"

He lobbed the empty bottle to a waiter, and then noticed Feiya and Bob. He prompted his pack to wave to her, and she waved back while pretending to be in a deep conversation with Bob. Undaunted, the man and his equally wide wife came over to the table.

"Good evening to yourself Faynuh," he said, almost without slurring, "Have we a new colleague here tonight, or only a passin' acquaintance? We haven't been introduced.."

Bob felt a knot in his stomach. Agatha hadn't given any cover stories for him to throw around, and this didn't seem to be the kind of person who'd let anything sneak by. Feiya seemed ruffled.

"Hello Mr Tiber, this is.. Abner, who is a friend from.. uhh.." she stumbled, and paused.

"Gee ahhhm shurrrr pleeez-duh tuh meet yew, Surrr.." said Bob, at precisely the same moment that Feiya finished her sentence with the word "..London."

The man wiped his greasy black fringe across the top of his head and looked suspiciously down at Bob. Apart from having terrible fashion-sense, there was something else about the man that wasn't quite right, but Bob couldn't figure out precisely what that might be. Feiya decided the best way to counter Mr Tiber's suspicion was to confront it with even more suspicion. Weird suspicion, at that.

"This is important, Mr Tiber - have you seen anyone on board who's Peruvian, about five feet and one inch tall, very hunched, and has greyish hair? And a lisp? Perhaps acting worried, as well."

"No, I'd remember a someone like that.. why do you ask?"

Her plan hadn't quite worked. He wasn't supposed to ask a question back.

"Oh, no reason, we were just wondering, because.. Abner found his wallet!"

Bob cringed while Mr Tiber looked stone-faced at her.

"You could tell all that from a person's wallet? You're quite the detective, girl! Perhaps you should consider a different line of work, one more suited for your.. obvious skills?"

The woman beside him gave a shrill laugh and her red cheeks turned crimson.

"Oh Earle, you're such a tease! I'm sure Fayurrrnuh is feedin' you a line for being so nosey!" she said, and patted her husband's arm. "Now you and Abner have yourselves a lovely evening, unless you want to come join us? There's room aplenty at the Tiber Table, and you just come right on over, if you do!"

She gave an over-bearing grin and offered a finger-wave as she guided Earle back to their table. He sank a glass of the replacement wine and burst into laughter.

"Who's that walrus?" whispered Bob.

"Ugh, he's one of the pedantic drones from Admin. He's in charge of three people and thinks that he's some kind of all-powerful god. He only got the job because the interviewers couldn't stand him applying for it over and over again. He drove them nuts. Forget him, he's a waste of space and it's time to get some dinner, I'm ravenous.."

Mr Tiber kept glancing over during the meal, eyeing them both as if he genuinely expected them to start causing trouble. Bob figured he needed to give the right impression, which in this case would be to look as relaxed as possible and show that he felt right at home. He put on a friendly-but-serious expression and called a waiter over, aware that Mrs Tiber was watching closely.

"Ah.. Heinrich, could the chef rustle up a speciality? Where I'm from, Les Pois de Robérrr are a must. Have you heard of them?"

The waiter looked to Feiya, who shrugged.

"Here you go, I'll write down the recipe.. it's a delicate blend of semi-puréed pois, or 'mushy peas' if you like, which are hand-crafted into a shape similar to a tennis ball, then dipped into a light mixture of flour and milk plus a few other essential ingrédients, which is the 'batter' as we say, then they're deep fried for a bit. And very classy they are too - European royalty thrive on them. Don't worry about doing any now, tomorrow evening'll be fine, really."

He handed the list to the waiter, and felt very pleased that he had made his subtle mark on the culinary world. An hour later, Mr Tiber's party were finally standing up to leave and as they reached the foyer, Feiya leaned over to Bob.

"See? They've forgotten us already! They're such.."

All seven turned around and waved as they reached the steps.

"Damn it, why should they care less who's here?" she said, hiding her words behind a smile.

By the time the coffee arrived, the restaurant was empty and Feiya was feeling more talkative about the events of the previous few days.

"There isn't that much to say really. For the last day or so there's just been lots of footsteps going up to my door, and nobody was ever out there when I'd take a look. And then it got worse this morning - someone was knocking on the door continually, the same few knocks over and over again, every single time. Driving me nuts. Once they even happened while I was holding the door open! I thought that I was either going mad, or that maybe something really unexpect..able was going on. And then when you did the same series of knocks earlier on and then actually opened the door, I was ready to send you right back from where you came! Was I ever annoyed.."

This was a good sign, and Bob breathed a sigh of relief.

"This is the kind of thing I'm looking for! I think that means there's a Mirror somewhere, 'cause it sounds like the future and past have been getting all mixed up. I might be stretching things a bit, but the Mirror might have been in a room near yours - above or below, maybe. I suppose they've moved it out of the way by now.."

"I could go and start hunting around everyone's rooms? I'd get armed to the teeth first, but no-one would ever know, of course.."

"No, you shouldn't get that involved. I'd really like to tell you everything but I don't understand a fat lot, and besides, you gave me a lecture in Barton about not thinking too much. So if you landed yourself in big trouble with big Troublers, you might make things more dangerous for yourself now.. and for both of us in the future, as well. I mean, what if one of them killed you? Major headache."

"Honestly, I can look after myself! I want to know what's going on and what I can do to sort things out - a bit of responsibility wouldn't go amiss every now and then. Or maybe you don't trust me?"

"Of course I trust you, but the problem is that you exist, and that means you're traceable. So if they're watching they might be able to find out everything that you do, and therefore I'd say we're both better off keeping it all under wraps, like.. err.. like it's classified."

Bob felt pleased with the way all the logic had fallen into place, and wished it could happen more often. He finished off his cappuccino and noticed that Feiya had gone very quiet. They left the restaurant, and this time followed Eugi's directions back to the hidden door at Feiya's corridor.

"Well you know how to get here," she said, "..so drop in when you need a hand or you have something minor enough to tell me about."

Bob could see that she wasn't happy about doing very little.

"Okay then, I'll be around at some time during tomorrow. But when I knock on your door again, try not to go for your rifle, please? I'm not selling encyclopedias or kitchen things, you know.. well, not yet, anyway. And if you still want to redecorate the wall with me, I'll bring a couple of brushes and some paint - but it looks fine how it is.."

"Well, no promises," Feiya laughed, and Bob decided she wasn't likely to turn barmy or launch a concealed deadly weapon at him. She went through the bizarre door to her room, and Bob followed Eugi through the quiet corridors and heaving bars to Agatha's suite.

The night was still warm, so he went onto the verandah and sat down on the recliner. He stared out into the endless night and moved from star to star thinking about how much Andie would be sure to love the America. He decided that once all the Mirrors were back where they ought to be and everything else in the world was back to normal, this would have to be the very first place to bring her. Apart from New York, maybe.

CHAPTER TWENTY THREE

Fog

Bob woke up shortly before 4am and shivered. Falling asleep outside was a bad idea on a ship, unless it happened to be moored somewhere in the Caribbean, probably. However, the America was nowhere near there so he hurried into the pleasing warmth of the conservatory and then into the living room, which was even warmer. He flicked the first switch that he found in the darkness and the entire room filled with a soft golden glow from dozens of small pin-point lights hidden in the ceiling.

He sat down in a high-sided chair, intending to sort out some kind of plan that would not only locate the Mirror, but also involve staying alive long enough to tell both Feiyas about it. But at that time of day, the last thing his brain wanted to do was start working. Three switches poked out of the mahogany panelling next to him so he tried the middle one, and faint classical music drifted out from a speaker, somewhere in the room. He tried the left one, and a series of subdued grinding noises similar to the coffee machine at The Coffee Pot briefly mingled with the music, until a small panel next to the switch opened up to reveal an elegant red and black glass cup full of steaming coffee.

This was impressive, so he tried the right switch. Nothing happened for a while, and then the chair slowly reclined a few inches and seemed to adapt itself to him. This was no way to start the day, and Bob vowed that if he ever had to have an incredibly early start to a day ever again, he wouldn't do it this way. But for the time being, he'd suffer Agatha's luxuries while trying to sort out what to do next.

He finished off the frothiest coffee ever, and had figured out the best possible way to spend the next few hours. He'd walk around the ship going wherever Eugi suggested, while keeping an eye out for weird things. Granted, it wasn't the most complicated of plans, and Bob knew it was so simple that it could've been thought up by a hibernating tortoise, but that didn't really matter. He was feeling far more awake now and completely ready to take on the world, and it was only.. 5.30am. Bob despaired with himself for dozing off and making the day start an hour or more later than it should have done.

"Okay Eugi, we need to find something that's fallen into the wrong hands, so we have to go high and low, and turn this joint upside down.."

Bob felt that the best way of talking to Eugi was to try and keep everything like an old gangster movie.

"What you sayin' thayre? This joint's a ship, ain't it? We turnin' a ship over? Jeez, who annoyed you? Still, if that's what you wanna do.."

"No, I mean we go all over the place looking for anything a bit out of the ordinary, that's all. Before everywhere gets busy.."

After an hour of creeping around the sleeping ship and finding nothing even slightly strange and absolutely nobody scary, Bob was beginning to feel concerned. A Mirror could be anywhere, perhaps even overboard on a raft or attached to a buoy floating miles away. Eugi, however, was having a great time. They had covered the lower decks twice, gone bow to stern on the long internal middle decks, and finally reached the upper decks again. Bagshaw woke up with a long yawn.

"Oh I say, Bob, you're up and about dashed early.. what's the occasion, or are you taking a morning constitutional? A chap should really be outside for one of those, y'know, fresh morning air and so forth. What say you?"

"Ah, sound advice there, Bagshaw. Eugi, let's head down to the back of the ship and start constitutionalising. The open-air bit of the Promenade Deck please, Eugi."

The round-end of the ship (as Eugi put it) looked out onto a cloudy morning. The huge propellers sent powerful vibrations through the deck's boards and left a broad white tail behind in the calm waters. But there was still nothing odd to be seen anywhere, so Bob reluctantly headed back inside, cutting through the circular Smoking Room and then out to the lengthy Enclosed Promenade.

The left side (or port side, as Bagshaw pointed out) contained nothing but a few deck-hands cleaning away the remnants of the day before, and a man in a peak hat asleep in one of the hundreds of chairs. He looked slightly the worse for wear, and a danger to no-one but himself.

They made their way to the front and went across to the right side of the ship, which started an argument between Bob's companions. Bagshaw claimed it was called the starboard side, but Eugi insisted it was called the 'who-gives-a-bug's-ass-what-side'. Bob stopped a few yards before they reached the open section again at the back end.

"Shh you two, listen.. I thought I heard something."

Silence fell over them, and they waited for a few minutes to hear anything. A barrage of ripping, thumping and splashing noises, interrupted only by a few high-pitched wild squeals, came from somewhere above.

"Bagshaw? Can you hear that? What do you reckon it is?"

"Oh.. that's most unpleasant, isn't it? It's almost as if something vast and unpleasant above us is causing a dreadful commotion with something else which is equally vast and unpleasant. I'm glad we're down here, and ne'er the twain shall meet, I say.."

"Thanks, that's really great. Hey Eugi? Where do you reckon that noise is coming from?"

"I would sug-jest that's uh lifeboat with sumthin' I don't like in it. If this tub goes down, you start swimmin' - don't bother rowin' that thing, no ways.."

"Hmm.. but it might be what I'm looking for, so we need to get up there for a look.."

Bagshaw nearly choked on his tea.

"Go up there? Oh wouldn't you rather consider the deck ABOVE the deck above, and we could safely make a keen observation from on high, looking a fair way down at the bother?"

"Good idea. Eugi, how d'you reckon we get to the deck above the deck above, from here?"

"Huh?"

"The one above the Lifeboat Deck."

"The roof uh the ship? Eethuh you is too dumb for words, or I ain't speaking Enguhlish plain eenuff. Listen up. There'z sumthin' woyth avoidin' in one of those boatz. You unduhstandin' me now?"

Eugi eventually gave in and lead the way to the highest stairway, and Bob stepped through a small, unlocked door marked Crew Only and out onto the vast white expanse of the top of the ship. He stood at the base of the first of the two enormous funnels, and made his way as far over to the side as he could. Feeling nervous, he crawled over to the edge and looked down at the long row of secured lifeboats below. They were suspended by powerful joists and ran almost the entire length of the ship, and were an impressive sight. Not so impressive was the drop of more than ten feet beneath them onto the emergency-only Lifeboat Deck. A dark grey border ran along its far edge and made the deck a few feet wider, which was important because, as Eugi pointed out, the floor of Lifeboat Deck was the ceiling of the Enclosed Promenade deck, and without the grey bit being there folks out walking would get wet in the rain. Bob tried to think of something to say back, but couldn't.

He looked intently at the grey tarpaulins and canvasses covering each of the white boats, one by one as he went along, trying to fend off thoughts of huge squid and freaky sea-beasts that might have come up from the depths and taken residence in one of them. And then he froze as the thumping and pounding noises returned, sending powerful tremors through his feet. Just before they ended he realised they were coming from the other side of the ship, and he'd spent the last eternity scrutinising the wrong lifeboats.

"What I would give for a brain.." he sighed, and hurried past the funnels to the other side.

He kneeled down between the tops of the joists holding Lifeboat J in place. This had to be the right one - its badly-fitting tarpaulin even looked different to all the others. The rest were clean and taut, but this one was a dark, oily, brick-red mess, like a larger version of the kind spread over the Mirror in the Town Hall. Bob stayed low, and waited for the noises to start again.

After ten long minutes had dragged by in which nothing at all happened, Eugi came to a conclusion.

"Well whutevah dat was, it must'a gone now. Prob'ly don't like people too much.. how about you take a quick look-see an' we can get outta here, yeh?"

"Indeed Bob, I agree with my observant and analytically-correct colleague. You must have scared off whatever foul and danger.. sorry, timid and harmless, occupant was here - or perhaps.."

Bagshaw trailed off and seemed to be thinking.

"..you don't suppose this might be all illusionary, do you? I'm sure that very few sea-creatures can inhabit boats, unless the boat has sunk, of course. I once ate something peculiar in the Upper Volta that disagreed with me, and it played terrible tricks with the old noggin. I swear on my word of honour I saw an elephant trying to put on my shoes - while I was still wearing them. Most distressing.. everyone thought I was mad. Wouldn't let me near a rifle for days.."

Bob wanted to believe they were both right. He stretched a leg out to one of the joists, and started lowering himself down onto the lattice-wire floor of the safety platform, alongside the lifeboat. He landed with a wobble, and looked back to where he had been, and groaned. There wasn't a hope he would ever climb all the way back up there again.

The breeze blew in, and he was suddenly engulfed in an all-too-real stench of decay, seaweed and saltwater. This was at least a thousand times worse than the lung-wrecking fumes around the back of Huddlestone's Fishmongers, the week after it was closed down.

Then Bob's heart jumped. The far edge of the tarpaulin rose as if someone had quickly poked it upwards, and he edged back on the narrow platform, holding onto one of the support poles. Whatever had gone away had decided to come back. Another movement, this time from the middle. And then another, followed by another, each one getting slightly larger than the previous one. Bob watched, unable to even blink as something that could only be a shark fin pushed the cover upwards, making a brief zig-zag movement along the lifeboat before dipping back down again. Others cut across it, and rough noises of fins dragging against the tarpaulin followed each one. Bob clung onto Bagshaw's words of wisdom.

"It's not real, it's all just an illusionary Mirror-thing, it's not real.. it can't really be happening.."

"I've had a thought," stated Bagshaw, "Why not run down to your newest lady-friend's room, borrow or rent something large from her magnificent arsenal, and then come back?"

"Yeah, an' maybe leave us wid her till yuh finished?"

"Shh.."

A moment or two went by in silence and Bob could see that he would have to release the dozen or so small hooks running along the side of the lifeboat in order to open up the tarpaulin.

"Marvellous.." he whispered, and reached across with a trembling hand to the first of the cover's eye-rings. It popped away from the side of the boat and Bob recoiled in an instant, convinced something covered in slime would reach out and grab him. Nothing happened. He waited until his heartbeat dropped back down to critically high before leaning forwards again and steadily removed the next hook.

Seconds passed by, and again, nothing happened. Bob's confidence grew in the silence, and he carried on whispering to himself.

"It's not real and I'm doing fine.. it's just a fear thing.."

He worked his way further along the side, releasing three more hooks, and then stood up. Holding the side of the filthy cover, he started to pull the next hook away, and then the next came with it.

"Okay guys, we're going in.." he said, and began to pull the cover back. And then he stopped. The lifeboat began shaking, rattling the joists and vibrating the wire mesh platform. Bob let go of the greasy tarpaulin, and didn't have time to scream.

A huge white shark launched itself up towards him, ripping the cover from both sides and clamping its enormous jaws shut just inches away from his face. Their power shook through his chest and sent air loaded with foul seawater all over him, and its cold skin rubbed like wet sandpaper against his face as it knocked him hard against a joist. He lay against the wire platform, feeling it shake and rock with the wild thrashing inside the boat.. and then complete silence fell again. It finished as quickly as it started, leaving only the sound of the ship's distant engines.

"Breath like that is way too real" he said, glad that he hadn't had any breakfast yet. He wiped the water from his face, and realised as he kneeled up that he was drenched. The Mirror had to be in there, and he'd need to take a risk of ludicrous proportions to get it.

Another few seconds of silence passed, and Bob raised himself to a crouching position, and shivered. The tarpaulin had covered the boat again, and the hooks which the shark had forced open were all firmly re-attached once more. A narrow triangular fold from the hooks he had undone revealed nothing but part of the boat's white-painted floor, which seemed to be completely dry and empty. His heart pounded as he flicked the unhooked part of the cover back, revealing a bench. A small crab scuttled along the seat, and fell onto the floor. Bob undid the next hook, and another crab ran to join its friend. Another hook gave the same result, and Bob sensed a pattern. The next hook was met by a large shark fin moving beneath the canvas just feet away, and Bob changed plan.

He crawled on all fours, almost lying down, to unhook the rest of the side, quickly shuffling away to safety after each one. The boat remained silent. Without even trying to convince himself that it was a good idea, he leaped up and threw the entire cover back.

A writhing mass of revolting sea creatures instantly began appearing in the boat, and it rapidly filled with hideous forms entwining and devouring each other in a wild feeding frenzy. Sharks and huge eels were attacked by enormous black fish, squid longer than the lifeboat flailed in the chaos, and huge spider crabs emerged from the centre of the seething mass and began crawling towards the sides. Bob was frozen to the spot and watched as the lifeboat started overflowing. The joists shook as its violent rocking grew stronger, and the cables quickly began to snap under the strain, allowing the boat to slide along its tracks towards the very edge of the ship. It came to a loud scraping halt, pivoting against the ends of the track-rails, held back only by the twisted joists which suspended it high above the grey band of the Enclosed Promenade Deck. The remaining fraught cables at either end squealed with tension.

Hundreds of weird sea creatures poured out onto the Lifeboat Deck, splattering with sickening thuds before spilling out into the sea. Bob could hear dozens of voices shouting from somewhere above, so without thinking he dropped himself down from the platform and ran through a very real layer of revulsion, and took refuge around a corner at the end of the deck.

Voices seemed to be calling and shouting from everywhere, and he covered his ears and closed his eyes to make the bedlam go away, but it was all too loud. He could hear the crew trying to ditch the boat into the sea, clanging poles and oars against the joists and its side. He had to stop them, even if it meant firing off a few warning shots from Claudie's lighter. Raising it in front of himself, he ran back around the corner shouting at the top of his voice for them to stop.

But there was nothing there. The decks were empty, the noise was completely gone, even the crew were gone. Everything had gone except for Lifeboat J, which still rocked precariously a few feet above the edge of the ship.

Bob watched a blanket of shade fall across the deck as the sun disappeared behind the black clouds gathering above. He slowly walked towards the lifeboat and noticed three of the crew's poles lying underneath it, and figured one of the deckhands must have touched the unprotected Mirror in a desperate bid to fend off the creatures. Quite what that had resulted in was anybody's guess.

A thin layer of mist slithered across the horizon and grew into a towering wall as it rolled relentlessly nearer, and within seconds the ship was shrouded in a dense and impenetrable fog. Bob slowly fumbled his way along the deck hoping to find any door that might lead inside, and was soon unable to see anything at all.

"Eugi, can you guide me back to Aunt Agatha's?" he whispered.

"Uhh, sumthin's wrong.. head's like spinnin' crazy, nuthin doin' kid," he replied, dizzily.

Distant foghorns blasted eery warnings to each other, and the America responded with her own sombre calls. Bob reached a window, and worked his hands along the glass hoping to find a door nearby, but only felt yet another protruding metal column dividing the bays from each other. By now the daylight had almost completely faded away, and been replaced by indistinct greyness. Suddenly a row of blurred golden lights blinked into life along the deck, disappearing away into the murky gloom.

Although they didn't reveal anything around them, they did prove that there was still activity somewhere on board. Larger panels of light began to appear from a few rooms further along, and Bob breathed a sigh of relief. Not everyone had disappeared.

"Could be a good sign, or a very bad one, couldn't it? Depends who's working the switches," pondered Bagshaw.

"Cheers.." Bob whispered, rather than telling him to shut up.

For the first time since he had arrived on the ship, the low hum of the engines had stopped, replaced by the most intimidating silence Bob had ever felt. Beads of perspiration broke out across his forehead as he realised that even the distant foghorns were no longer calling, leaving just the sound of waves lapping against the side of the ship. Bob shivered as one by one all the lights went out leaving him stranded beside the metal column, unable to see his hand in front of his face.

He carried on slowly making his way along the Lifeboat Deck, and soon stumbled over some stray chairs and found himself completely disorientated, kneeling in a corner where two metal walls met. He sat down with his back against a pair of warm pipes occupying the join behind him, and figured a good plan would be to sit still and wait for the fog to lift, and also to have a few words of wisdom with the fountain of all knowledge.

"Bagshaw.. do ships usually cut their engines in heavy fog?"

"Oh definitely not, old boy. You see, a ship wouldn't come to an immediate halt by doing so, she would merely slow down until she lost forward momentum, at which point sea currents would start moving her around. Imagine a shipping route full of drifting vessels - you'd get all manner of collisions, similar to that hoo-haa in the Bay of Biscay in '67, thereabouts. You'll find Chapter 24 is entitled 'Sea Travel & Drowning' and deals with them both in great depth. Do take a look, it's fascinating!"

"Well, do ships ever turn their lights off then, like for safety reasons?" said Bob, determined to find an excuse to avoid feeling ultra-stressed, no matter how minuscule it might be.

"Heavens no, that would be terrible! Drifting invisible at the mercy of the elements.. bad show, that. Why?"

"Oh, no reason. Dark, isn't it?"

"Yes, it is. Perhaps evening falls suddenly on this stretch of ocean?"

"Yeah, maybe it does.. you go have a cup of tea, Bagshaw."

Bob stayed crouched in the silence, looking out into the featureless, darkening grey bank around himself. The sound of the waves grew steadily quieter and quieter until even they seemed to become lost somewhere far away. For a split second Bob thought he heard a noise, and even stopped breathing as he strained his ears to hear it again. Footsteps? Maybe someone else was wandering around? He thought about calling for a moment, but held back.

He could hear the faint but distinct sound of someone walking, very slowly. Strangely, every second step was accompanied by the harsh tap of something against the deck. As Bob sat silently in his corner waiting for the person to come nearer and maybe even into view, he figured that whoever it was must have a stick or a cane with them, like an English gentleman, a Lord-of-the-Manor type person..

..and then he felt a wave of fear wash over him. The kind of person who would walk with a cane would be someone with a bad leg, someone who had probably met with an accident sometime whenever and was hunting down the cause. As the footsteps drew nearer he stared and squinted into the fog, desperately looking for any sign of movement or any tell-tale outline of a figure. His skin crawled as the footsteps came to a halt just yards away from him. Silence fell once more. After a few moments, a terrifying and familiar voice spoke softly, and Bob hardly dared breathe.

"What's this, I wonder? Do I smell the stench of something despicable.. perhaps vile? Where is it hiding itself?"

The silky smooth voice floated through the dense fog, somehow finding Bob and creeping all around to him. Very slowly, he edged himself a few inches lower down against the wall, until only the top third of his body lay propped against the pipes. He daren't move anymore and daren't go for his lighter, as the fear of making a noise and giving himself away was unbearable.

"Is it.. HERE?" Salesman shouted, ending with a loud swish as he lashed out with his cane.

The pipes behind Bob shook with a vicious clang just inches above his head. Another clang immediately followed, this time a little lower, and a sharp jet of steam began to escape. Scalding drops of water landed on his shoulder, soaking straight into his clothes and through to his skin. The urge to cry out and make a run for it was overpowering, but instead he edged further down, shuffling a little to the side of the pipes, keeping himself pressed against the deck and the wall. He moved feet-first, inch by silent inch, until his foot pushed against a deck chair, and for a heart-stopping moment he prayed that the minute scraping noise had been lost in the sound of the steam.

"Then perhaps it is.. HERE!" Salesman screamed.

Another clang rang out, this time exactly where his head had been seconds earlier. Bob lay on his side against the damp wood of the deck, edging into the tight gap between the deckchairs and the wall, silently fighting the stinging streams of water that ran all around him. With despairing horror he realised that his feet had reached a stack of folded chairs and he had nowhere left to go. He froze, pressing his whole body against the deck.

The gentle tapping of metal against wood came nearer and nearer in small, teasing circles before settling into a steady rhythm barely inches from his shoulder. And then the tapping stopped. He knew he had to break cover before the cane could come down again, and trembled as he desperately tried to think which pocket Claudie's lighter was in. Seconds crawled by. Was the cane raised for the final strike? Was he..

..Salesman pounded the wall three times immediately above his head, and silence fell again. Bob pushed himself into a ball behind the chairs, no longer feeling the pain of the scalding water, and waited for the inevitable first swish.

But there was nothing, nothing but silence. Bob listened intently, trying to hear any movement or sense any vibrations through the deck's boards as the fog gradually began to lighten, little by little. Eventually he could see two or three feet of deck stretching out in front of him, and nervously raised himself into a crouching position. He looked to where the sun was trying to break through the fog, almost making out a tall silhouetted figure somewhere before him. Bob could see the vague shape of the top hat, and dared to stare up to where Salesman's face should be.

"Image, image.." he breathed to himself, while frantically searching through most of his pockets to find the lighter. He pulled it from his third inside pocket, and immediately dropped it. The figure laughed quietly and faded further back into the fog, leaving Bob to fumble around by the chairs. By the time he had found it, held it close for a quick once-over and narrowly stopped himself from checking it still worked, Salesman had gone.

"You'z somethin' else, kid! Jeez, what you gonna be like in a few years, huh? That wuz close.."

"Eugi! You're back to normal again? Can you get me back to Fey?" he whispered, trying to keep his voice steady.

"An' what about the pick-up? We had a job t'do."

"Yeah, but this is weird stuff and she needs to know about it..and besides, we can't stay here because.. I err.. don't want to waste the wrong person, or.. be loosing off any rounds."

"Okay big man, take a right.."

Bob took a right and walked straight into the wire safety rail which ran around that end of the Lifeboat Deck, doubling up across the cables for a few horrible seconds while he edged himself backwards onto the deck. His life didn't so much flash before his eyes, it went hurtling over the barrier and into the sea below.

"Big yipes - are you sure you're feeling okay, Eugi? We nearly took a dive there!"

"Huh? Oh. Maybe go left a way first.. then left instead uh right.. nah, I'm still kinda mussy.. just find the door.."

Bob trod carefully along the deck, still unable to see beyond a few feet, and after a few false turns eventually arrived at a heavy wooden door which opened into a pitch black stairway.

"This one?"

"Yeah," said Eugi, as if he was waking up.

"But I can't see a thing in there - anyone could be inside!" Bob replied, hoping that Eugi might suggest somewhere else instead.

"An' the bad guys don't know that? If it's black f'you, it's black f'r anyone! Take the fight to them, if you gonna take it anywhere. Now, we're goin' down three flights.. no, two.. no, make it four.."

Bob cringed with every echoing footstep on the metal stairs until he reached the relative secrecy of a carpeted corridor. The door four flights above slammed shut, echoing like a volley of gunshots throughout the ship. He threw himself to the floor clutching the lighter in both hands, and lay waiting in the darkness for the sound of footsteps racing down after him. But there was only silence.

A few minutes later, the corridor started to grow lighter as the fog outside steadily lifted, and the hazy patches of light grey along one side became recognisable as windows. Eugi began to grow more confident in his bearings, and guided Bob up and down flights of stairs and side-routes. By the time he rounded a corner into the ship's deserted central lobby, he had begun to wonder if Fey was still on board - or if anybody else was, for that matter. He found himself staring at the unoccupied Purser's desk and neighbouring reception desk, and trying to fend off a dreadfully sick feeling.

He wandered across to the blue-carpeted staircase, the one leading up to Feiya's deck, and sensed that the ship had developed a lazy rolling motion from side to side.

"Marvellous.." he thought, and grabbed the handrail at the foot of the stairs.

The long strip-lights begin flickering and buzzing themselves back on, followed immediately by all the smaller lights. The floor shook gently as the engines started turning far below, and the whirring reassurance of the air-conditioning filled the lobby. Bob looked around as people began fading back into reality on their way across the floor and up and down the staircases. The women behind the desks re-appeared and carried on their conversations with the people in front of them, and others emerged care-free from corridors as if nothing had happened. Bob knew that if the passengers were re-appearing then the crew would also be re-appearing, and the Mirror was possibly still in the lifeboat. Square One seemed to be on its way around again.

"Slight change of final destination Eugi, we need to get back to the lifeboat, and quick!"

"Whadyuh sayin? After all that you wanna go back? If we was cabbin' this joyney you'd be payin' up front.."

A few exhausting minutes later, Bob emerged onto the very top of the ship, racing into the bright sunshine. He quickly passed the two funnels on his way to Lifeboat J's station, and his heart jumped a mile as he saw two members of the crew clambering out along the damaged joists. One was already hanging down and trying to get a foothold in the boat.. but there was something wrong about them.. they weren't dressed like any of the crew Bob had seen before.

They wore heavily marked blue over-alls and wide gardener-style black gloves that reached up far beyond their elbows. Suspended between the two of them was a dark brown length of canvas, which they cast into the boat. They both gave a laugh and a few cheers. Idiots they may well be, but they were obviously aware of what they were handling. Seconds later they both lowered themselves from the joists and the lifeboat immediately began rocking wildly on its hopelessly inadequate support cables. Bob reached for Claudie's lighter and cautiously made his way nearer, hardly daring to breathe as he silently crossed over the iron-panelled flooring.

Suddenly more lines snapped with a succession of deeply resonant twangs, and both men fell from sight as the boat swung to an even more precarious angle. Bob forgot about being silent and ran across to Station J, his heart pounding and his eyes glued to the lifeboat.

Both men had fallen from the boat, but one had managed to cling to the far side, hooking an arm around a rowlock. His other gloved hand flailed wildly in a desperate attempt to find something else to hold onto. A long solitary cable at the front and two thinner ropes at the rear kept the boat attached to its crooked joists, but the front was inching lower and lower, pointing itself towards the sea.

The man's eyes fixed on Bob, who's own eyes had fixed on the long shining crescent of the Present Mirror, which was only partially covered by the canvas. Bob felt too sick to move. The lifeboat was the last place on earth he wanted to go.

"Image, image, image.." he told himself under his breath, trying to find some courage. The lifeboat kept rocking as the man tried to scramble back onto it, causing another section of the Mirror to become exposed. Bob knew he had to do something, and struggled out along the less-damaged of the two joists. Shaking like a leaf, he lowered a foot into the back-end of the boat. A large bolt came away from the pulley, struck the lifeboat and bounced off, spinning and careering a very long way down into the sea, ending in a minute splash. Bob let go of the joist and covered the Mirror with the canvas before anything from a nightmare might start appearing again. A desperate voice called to him from the other end.

"Help me, please help me - you have to! You don't know what'll happen down there.."

Bob started to open up the largest of his Encapsulation Fields, ignoring the man's panicked cries, and very carefully edged it over the Mirror's top end. Everything was blocked from his mind. The increasing waves, the creaking and groaning of the metal and wood, the constant rocking and shifting, the wind, and above all, his own fear. After two minutes that felt like two lifetimes, the six foot long Mirror was completely sealed. Bob's work was almost done, and just for a moment, he stopped repeating 'image' and turned his attention to the excess baggage hanging over the side.

Steadily, he clambered over the benches, down towards the lower end and sat just a few inches away from the man. In spite of everything his brain was telling him, Bob decided it was time for some fishing.

"Claudie's going to love this.." he thought. He reached across and flicked the man's long hair out of his eyes.

"Look shipmate, you need help whereas I don't need help, so this can be easy for both of us. Tell me who you're working for and I'll help you out of your.. current predicament. Couldn't be easier, all things considered."

Bob tried to lean casually against the bench, in an attempt to hide his shaking hands.

"Don't do this to me! I'm tellin' you nothin' till I'm in the boat, now HELP ME!" the man screamed back.

"That's unlikely to happen, isn't it? Very slim chance I'd say."

The man swung his foot back up onto the side, with a mighty effort that wrenched the boat a few more inches lower. Bob pushed it off with a finger, and the man's grip on the rowlock slipped a little further, leaving only the top of his shoulder and one arm above the side of the boat.

"Are you going to tell me who you're with, or are you going to play with the fish?" said Bob, and pressed his foot against the man's elbow. He slipped a little more, and yelled a few words in a very foreign language, finishing in English.

"You piece of.." he snarled.

"Yeah? Send a postcard, shark bait!" Bob said, and kicked his arm away. He watched him fall, plummeting and screaming in complete silence, and fading into nothing before reaching the water.

"Blimey," Bob muttered, unable to think of anything that was more appropriate.

The lifeboat rocked and made a horrendous wrenching noise as an entire pulley flew past his head and clattered off the edge of the deck into the sea. He struggled the Mirror into a position where he could slide it over the side of the lifeboat and safely onto the top of the Enclosed Promenade deck. It landed five or six feet below, with an inappropriately gentle shoosh sound, coming to rest just a few inches from the edge of the ship. Bob half jumped and half fell from the lifeboat, scrambling to throw an arm across it before it could slide further away. The cable and ropes gave a final long, pitiful chorus, and snapped in jolting quick succession. The boat crashed into the grey part of the deck with enough force to demolish a huge section of the wall beneath. It lodged momentarily in the shattered supports and wood, creaking and squealing as its split boards dragged against the unwielding steel of the struts, before finally rolling off into the sea.

Bob pulled and dragged the Mirror back across the Lifeboat Deck and around the nearest corner at the rear of the ship, while dozens of crew members started running out from doors in the lifeboat bays towards the wrecked area.

He slowly made his way inside, and edged along one of the red-lined Emergency Corridors before stopping at the top of the stairs, aching from head to toe.

"Get to Fey, get to Fey.." he repeated, blocking everything out of his mind.

As he tried to work the Mirror down the stairs, he realised that it was unstable even though it was inside an Encapsulation Field. It had gradually changed from being too heavy to carry, and had become light enough to lift with one hand. It practically floated a few inches above the floor, before gently settling back down - and then quickly became unbearably heavy again. This made dragging it down to the lower deck more difficult, especially with passengers offering to help him carry it once he'd reached the busier areas. Nobody except Feiya should even be aware of him being on board, so gaining attention off tourists or perhaps even Troublers wasn't a good idea.

However, to the untrained eye, he was a drenched idiot who was struggling to carry a surfboard in a pale-blue bag, and that was bound to draw attention on a cruise liner.

He stood at the entrance to a busy corridor, eyeing every single person with suspicion.

CHAPTER TWENTY FOUR

Zoltan's Axe

"Eugi, is there a quicker way to Fey's room from here? I can't manage all these long corridors on my own lugging this thing, and we can't afford to be seen, either! That last bit's more important by a mile, come to think of it."

"Well ain't I surprised. Why d'you wanna go down this one anyway? All you gotta do is take that door by the lifebelt, twenty feet through another, then you an' us are almost outside her place, easy. Ee-ay an' zee-why."

Fortunately Bob wasn't caught entering either of the ship's 'Restricted Access' doorways, and stepped out of the staff door to find himself opposite Room 961. The corridor was clear and he shuffled through the strange, vanishing door into the equally strange small room, and anxiously made his way to Room 963. Feiya's door swung open on the second knock.

"Hello Fey? I did knock, but it was open.. I think," he said to the empty room, "and I could really do with a hand, pretty quick as well. It's a Great Big Mirror Situation.. are you here?"

"Yes.. with you in a minute," she called from her bedroom.

She emerged adding the final touches to a mid-morning outfit, and immediately began lowering her white headscarf to almost cover her sunglasses.

"Need to be discrete," she explained, as she hurried over to him by the door. "Oh, look at this! I can't believe you've actually got one here.." she said, helping to drag it inside the room until it briefly became light as a feather, "..and I can't believe I didn't even suspect it was on board. How atrocious."

"Shark bait.. hee hee.. I just got it.. that wuz good.." laughed Eugi.

"Not now.." whispered Bob.

"What not now?" asked Fey, leaning the Mirror against a cabinet.

"Umm.. not being in Aunt Agatha's suite. We shouldn't not be there, especially not now."

"Well that's obvious," she said, "Hmm.. we can't let anyone see us moving it, so.. I know!"

She hurried into her room and returned with a flattened cardboard box and a white blanket. After a few minutes of tearing and taping, the Mirror looked like a long white rectangle in a white sheet. Apparently, even people who knew all about Encapsulation Fields and Mirrors wouldn't have a clue what it could be.

"Hmm.." she said, looking at their handiwork, "..it's good, but it could be better. Let's see, one more little thing.."

She went over to her Weapons Cabinet and opened one of the drawers beneath the first set of rifles. Bob didn't quite see what she pushed into her handbag, but it certainly bulged a lot and swung heavily as she walked back.

Bob took one end of the Mirror and Feiya took the other, while Eugi offered well-educated guesses to guide them along some of the less well-known parts of the ship, and risk a couple of staff elevators. After a very long and nervous journey, the end was almost in sight. They reached (according to Eugi) the foot of Sub-Passage D's Stairwell, Access Point 2, and started to climb the metal staircase.

"No joke Fey, getting this was a load of trouble.. you haven't smelled anything until you've smelled shark-breath really close up. Now I think about it, I haven't smelled anything since."

Feiya laughed and dropped her end of the Mirror, triggering the walls to give a slight wave. They looked at each other as the stairway began to shake with a thunderous pounding, which was soon joined by the sound of hundreds upon hundreds of footsteps. Faint soldiers appeared from nowhere, and for a moment Bob lost sight of her as they both became engulfed by troops racing down the steps, all of whom seemed oblivious to anyone else being there. They hurried past in a mass of echoing voices before fading away into nothing. A strange silence returned.

"What was all.. that about?" Bob gulped.

"Nothing. This was a troop carrier in the war, and I doubt the Captain would want it to be one again. That'll be an 'Oops' there."

"The passengers wouldn't be too chuffed either," added Bob as they carefully picked it up again.

They soon reached the top of the stairs, cleared another two short flights, stumbled along even more corridors while the ship gave a few lurches, and staggered across the First Class Lounge to arrive at a door which Feiya had never noticed before.

"I know you don't want to know anything about Aunt Agatha's apartment, but maybe you could keep your eyes shut, or just make an exception? I'll mention it to her and she's bound not to mind, and you might even score a few Guardianship Bonus Points."

Feiya thought for a moment and then nodded towards the door, prompting Bob to open it. They struggled up the last four flights of narrow stairs to Agatha's private deck, and the unmarked door swung open long before they arrived. Feiya's eyes widened as she stepped into Agatha's main room, and Bob breathed a sigh of relief that the door closed itself silently behind her.

"Oh wow.. ohh woww.." she repeated a few times, each with a slightly longer '..oww..'

"A split-level living room! Look at all the other doors.. and a conservatory! And a verandah that's bigger than my entire suite!"

Suddenly her nerves vanished as she hurried to the upper level and then ran out onto the balcony. Bob carefully stood the Mirror by the portal, and followed her outside. She was leaning on the rail, loving the sunshine and looking out for her first sight of land in over a week. Bob joined her, pleased to be drying off in the heat, and wondered how long it would be until the Statue of Liberty came into view. He glanced back over his shoulder a few times to check up on the Mirror and held onto Claudie's lighter, just in case of any unwelcome guests, but the paranoia steadily passed. A few minutes of wave-watching helped bring them both back down to planet Earth, and Bob figured he really ought to be getting back to Barton.

"So I'll head back to my time, then. It's been really good to see you, Fey. If the police let you into America, say hello to Aunt Agatha for me? Or maybe you shouldn't, come to think of it.. or maybe you don't need to? Ugh.."

Bob felt himself rapidly sink up to his neck in another quick-sand of confusion as he tried to work out whether 1954's Agatha already knew that he'd found the Mirror, or if Feiya in Barton would remember having met him in 1954.

"Hello? Bob? Are you there? You've gone blank, all glazed.."

"Sorry.. moment of excessive bewilderment. I was trying to figure out if.. isn't there any way at all that I could just get off the ship with you, go to the Lexington Building and ask Aunt Agatha whether or not I managed to find all the others?"

"What?"

"Well, imagine I went and saw this Aunt Agatha when the ship docks, instead of going back to Barton, right? Wouldn't she already know that I've found this Mirror?" he said, feeling his brain starting to seize up, "You see, every time I get back to Barton, I'm supposed to drop off a Mirror at Pierpont House, and then head back to Manhattan in 1927 and tell the healthy Aunt Agatha what's happened. So even though I don't know if I find the other Mirrors yet, Aunt Agatha would, wouldn't she? It's 1954 now, so she'd have found out twenty seven years ago that I've just found another Mirror - I'd have told her already.. in which case.. oh my brain.."

Feiya sighed.

"You're breaking Rule Number One, Subsection Blah, Directive Blah-hundred and eleventy blah."

"Am I?"

"Yes. Keep-It-Simple-Matey. It's always underlined at least twice, in any book. You're just having a beginner's Chicken And Egg Dilemma, that's all. If one can't exist without the other, which came first and therefore how did either ever exist in the first place? Your version of that is 'Does the 1954 Madame Agatha know everything that you're doing, before you're aware that you've even done it? And if so, how? Oh, what a frightmare that one is.."

Feiya rested her head against the back of her hand on the rail and took on the expression of a Grand Master chess champion who had stumbled into a very tricky situation - such as a King and a pawn being surrounded by three full sets on a very large board. Eventually she felt capable of speech again.

"Okay, I think I've got this now.. okay. You're into a whole new ball game that doesn't follow the logic or the rules of the usual kind of past-interventions. You know why? Because the future's Madame Agatha is the one who sent you back in time to meet her younger self, to tackle a time-problem that the future-one had kind of created, so.. I would.. I'd say you're causing a Temporary Alternative Existence, stemming from your first visit to 1927. That's major stuff, even if it is just theoretical..ular."

"Ahh.." said Bob, as a dim and distant memory stirred at the very back of his mind. Agatha had mentioned something like that, absolutely ages ago. It didn't make any sense then, either.

"Shh, don't throw me off track.. 1954's Madame Agatha would have no idea she's ever met you because as far as her Official Time

Line is concerned, you haven't been born yet and therefore she doesn't know you."

"So there IS more than one of her? I thought so."

"No there isn't, for crying out loud.." she said, exasperated.

"But.."

"Again shh. Because you keep directly interference..ing with her life in 1927, there's a Parallel Time Line stemming from the future's access points.. making the Official Time Line all but inaccessible where July of 1927 is concerned. Think of it as a different route to get there. What a mess, but also what a great big huge wow! I wish I was doing all that."

"Huh?"

"Yes it is complicated, but only because Madame Agatha's the one who got you to interfere with her own life, so every time you step into the PTL and go back.. to her.. you're adding to the amount she'll have to sort out later on. D'you follow the beat?"

Bob nodded to prevent her repeating anything, and felt pleased with himself for not saying 'Huh?' again.

"Right. Let me think, let me think.. see, when you retrieve all the Mirrors, the Lines should merge - once Madame Agatha's back in the saddle again. She'll start wiping out the Troublers, probably before they're even born, and the Parallel Time Line should replace the.. the Temporary Parallel Universe..sesses and merge with the Official Time Line.. so therefore..."

"Uhuh.."

"..therefore.. all the Temporary Alternate Existences will be gone as well.. but you probably figured that already, from the 'Temporary' bit in the title. Unless they become permanent.. hmm, that's a new one. Assuming you don't wipe out the entire universe, this'll be great reference."

"Uhuh.."

"Precisely. I wonder if I'll ever actually remember meeting you? Hmm.. that needs a bit of thinking about. Well, all I can say is you'd better not blow it, Sparky, because the potential for monstrous screwing-upness is enormous."

"Uhuh.."

"Yes. Oh, how I hate all this parallel stuff.. it gets so complicated. But I ought to start reading about it, I suppose. I've got ten years on this ship to go, so I might have enough time to get my head around all that without going mad. Now don't ask me anything else because I might have dislocated my brain just now. The cookie jar's empty, no more cookies left.."

Bob could recognise a weird expression when he heard one, but quite what it meant was beyond him. And so was all the stuff before it, for that matter. Fey and Claudie would make a lethal double act.

The sunlight reflected against the white paintwork of the verandah, making a hot day feel even hotter. Feiya was loving it, once she'd had a while to recover from trying to work out what Agatha may or may not have a clue about.

"It's time to catch some rays now Bob, so enough of the brain-beating and Mirror-hauling, and on with the good stuff. Do you think there might be any drinks inside? Something really cold, chillier than a penguin's Spaldings. Mmm.."

Bob looked blank.

"Saddle shoes, they're trés chic.." she said, pointing at her feet.

Bob wandered back into the apartment and took a couple of chilled cans from a veneered drinks-fridge with enough compartments to reach the ceiling, and let his hands linger in the coolness. As he stood there with the fridge door closed against his forearms, he wondered if he really ought to be going straight back to Barton. He decided one chilled Coke wouldn't bring the world to an end, and besides, he quite liked talking to Feiya when she wasn't so tightly wound up and over-stressed. He started to cool down, and began pondering whether expensive cabins on board liners in the 1950s really did have fridges, or huge lamps disguised as tall white panthers, or even remote-control televisions and music centres. Maybe they did, maybe they didn't, but this one certainly did. A button marked 'Essentials' on the side of the refrigerator was begging to be pressed, so he did - and half a dozen ice cubes cascaded from a panel beneath it, onto the floor.

"Ohhh, too good, wayyy too good.."

He took a couple of ridiculously long glasses from a cabinet, loaded them with ice and took the drinks back out to the verandah, where Feiya had made herself comfortable on a recliner. After a few minutes of crunching her way through ice cubes while they watched long, unbreaking waves rolling by to nowhere, she decided to de-classify a file.

"All that Parallel stuff is nothing compared to the other problems you might be causing without even realising it. I could lose sleep over that, but I won't allow it to bother me that much.. no I won't.."

"Not more problems? I can hardly keep track of the ones I know about.. maybe you could draw a few pictures this time? I've got loads of biros if you need one, because I've found that in the past they were almost like money. That's how I bought my compendium."

Feiya muttered something under her breath which was lost in a sea-breeze and another ice cube.

"Madame Agatha gave me a huge book on 'Basic Level: Cause And Consequences' and no joke, it's monumentally complex beyond belief. It's one theory after another, all inter-related, and only scratches the surface of how major catastrophes were averted, or even caused, by Time & Place Intervention..ing..ism. And that's important, and you don't know about any of it.. which gets on my nerves like you wouldn't believe. So listen carefully, because this bit's important."

"If you say so. Wouldn't you rather have another drink with more ice, and in an even taller glass?"

"Yes and yes, but first you need to know why you have to be surreptal.. surreptanitious.. discrete.. in the past so that you don't mess things up in the future."

"Okey dokey.."

"Be serious, 'cause you mustn't tell this to anyone, right? It's rated Hugely Classified. A month or two ago, Madame Agatha was using the Mirrors regarding a few current political things that were bothering her. Anyway, she found that half the world would almost certainly be wiped out between 1990 and '93 by a complete rock-head called President Urguk, in the nuclear Krymsk Wars. So she did stacks of research and found out that back in 1896, President Urguk's grandfather, Zoltan, who was a young man at the time, shouldn't have received an axe on his birthday. Instead, he should've had a bike."

"Krymsk Wars? President who? I've never heard of them.."

Feiya stared over at Bob and flicked her sunglasses up. After a moment or two, the penny dropped.

"Oh right.. the wars never happened, because that bloke was never President of anywhere. You're saying that Aunt Agatha turned the clock back a few generations, and swapped the axe for a bike. How did that change anything?"

"Cause and Consequence, Bob. Zoltan had a bike not an axe, so instead of scaring people and damaging everyone and everything in sight with an axe, he rode around the nearby Russian villages getting to know folks instead. The plan was that he would grow up with an appreciation of the land and the people he lived with, and then one day he would pass that attitude on to his own son - instead of handing down the family axe and all the gains of a life of crime.

Therefore, instead of being a nasty piece of work, Zoltan's son would grow up with a similar appreciation of the world around himself, and in turn create a positive environment for his own son, Urguk, to grow up in! That way, being violent and mental would never play a part in young Urguk's life so he would never feel the need to prove himself by dominating other people. And Madame Agatha figured Urguk's quest for world domination - and all his emotional problems - were a direct result of his grandfather having had a lousy birthday present! That would have been incredible."

"Would have? It worked properly, didn't it?"

"Sort of. Before Zoltan got anywhere near his new bike, Madame Agatha pushed him under a train.. and I think she shot him a few times as well. She's like that. Anyway, there was no Zoltan, no kids, no grandkids, and therefore no crazy Urguk wiping out nations. Job done. Actually that's a bad example, but it sort of makes my point."

Bob had no idea what to say, and resorted to his First Uncertainty Principle: When in doubt, change the subject.

"New York's getting close isn't it? I'm sure I can see buildings. I can even hear cabbies swearing.."

"No it isn't near and no you can't hear anything. You're trying to change the subject, but it's important. The point I'm trying to make is that you do one action, and it might have no results or it might affect millions of other actions. It's all linked to Arefrode's Domino Theory and his Second Axiom of Prior Responsibility. He won awards for it, and piles of luncheon vouchers."

Feiya finished off her drink and looked as if she could do with another. The sun was getting a little too hot, so they headed back inside and settled into the air-conditioned comfort of the conservatory. The wicker chairs creaked under the cushions, and Feiya leaned over to the coffee table and switched the radio on. Up until that point, Bob had thought it was a toaster.

"Ooooh, this is how to travel.. Madame Agatha really knows how to do it in style, doesn't she? Umm.. what were we just talking about?"

Bob watched the petals and leaves of Andie's rose gently shaking with the engine's vibrations, and tried to remember anything that Feiya had said in the last hour or so.

"Was it dominos?"

"That's right. I didn't mean real ones, they're just an analogery.. an alagenary.. it's symbolism, Bob. Say you knock over one domino, on purpose or accidentally. Maybe it hits nothing, but what if there are millions of others leading off from that one? They all start falling over and there's nothing you can do to stop them. And when you step back through time, you increase the number of 'dominos' you can knock over by a factor of a billion per year travelled, I think - I ought to read up on that."

"I see.." said Bob, hoping to sound convincing. He tapped his chin to add to the effect.

"So what was your big question again? Something about New York wasn't it?" said Feiya, looking very puzzled.

"I'm not sure anymore. There was one about Aunt Agatha already knowing everything I've done, before I know I've done it.."

"Which she doesn't, I reckon. In a nutshell, don't go near her because we don't need any more Parallel Time Lines cropping up. See, once you've got the Mirrors back where they should be, she'll totally slaughter you for making it all more complicated. So don't."

Bob looked out beyond Feiya's shoulder to a definitely solid horizon.

"Hmm.. in that case I really ought to be getting that Mirror back to Barton now - plus there's another Present Mirror a few miles over there," he said, pointing to the skyline, "..and that means there's a Fluctuating Wibble-thing just waiting to happen which is well worth avoiding, apparently. I don't know if you'll be able to get out of this room unless I let you out, so.."

"Hmm.. okay, throw me out of this luxury.. let's call it a day then - I forgive you. Having a balcony's so cool, plus this room's amazing. But anyway.." she said, shaking her head clear, "..all you have to keep in mind is that you can't figure out what you've done so far because you can't possibly figure out what you haven't done so far. So just keep doing what you're doing, and worry about how you did it later on. Simple."

Bob felt like his brain had already packed two large suitcases and booked a hotel far away. He pushed everything out of his mind as they made their way along the stairs and passageways down to the final door, and Feiya hurried through it with a long "Byeeee." It closed with a very secure clunk.

He tried to put the suite back exactly as he found it, just in case Agatha didn't really appreciate him treating it like a home, and edged the Mirror to the portal. The wall shimmered, gently revealing four short steps leading up to a brightly-lit landing, which had a large picture hanging on the far wall. He could just recognise Agatha, sitting outside a café on a very sunny day and dressed in something casually timeless.. but he couldn't see who she was with. He tried to move around to avoid the light which was reflecting on the glass, but the more he tried, the worse it became. He gave up, and waited for the Mirror to become lighter. And waited.. and waited.. and then gave up and braced himself to carry it through..

..and immediately dropped it onto the floor outside the drawing room. Its top end collided harshly against the door which Bob remembered was the one that lead into black nothingness. Ripples spread out across the wooden panels, carrying on into the walls and across the ceiling and floor. He watched in fascination, expecting it to finish any second. But it didn't. The small waves didn't fade at all, and just carried on racing outwards. He dragged the Mirror as quickly as he could around to the stairs, trying hard not to look at the distortions which had spread across every surface of the house. Step by step he dragged it down to the front door, which had become a blur of minute undulations. He held the key towards the lock, and closed his eyes as he stepped out into the driveway, dreading the prospect of seeing the vibrations spreading across the world outside.

The front door rattled shut a dozen or more times behind him, and he waited until the sound had died away before daring to open his eyes. The same old Barton was still there. Nothing was shaking or blurring, although the elder tree was waving a little in a sharp breeze. He began the long walk back to Pierpont House, slowly taking the Mirror one laborious step at a time, except for those few moments when he could practically run with it for a few paces.. which was a bad idea, considering the risks of dropping it. After twenty minutes of arduous shuffling, he had an embarrassing brainwave, and gave Feiya a call on his mobile phone.

Two minutes later her Audi TT roared up, pulled a handbrake spin and rocked to a halt by the curb. The Mirror squeezed in perfectly, wedged onto the fully reclined passenger seat.

"See you at the house.." she called and sped off with a very loud wheel spin. The passenger door slammed closed as she threw the car into a deliberate left slide, and she raced on towards Marine Drive.

Bob kept walking and walking, and eventually flopped into the chair next to the reception desk. Ten minutes later, Feiya came down the stairs and perched on the very edge of her chair, and folded her arms tightly. He tried not to look bemused, but it was difficult to hide.

"You've noticed, haven't you Bob? I've grown another leg and a second nose since you left here."

"Eh? No, sorry, I don't mean to stare. It's just so weird. Half an hour ago I was sitting on a scorching balcony having a drink with you, and New York was almost appearing on the horizon. And now we're here and all those years have passed for you but not for me, and you won't remember any of it until.. 'the loop closes' or something like that. Maybe not even then. I don't think I'll ever get any of this."

Feiya seemed uninterested and fumbled nervously through a drawer over-loaded with papers. Bob watched her, still too amazed.

"You had a rifle and you pointed it at me, and there was a fat bloke asking questions, and you helped me carry the Mirror - you can't have forgotten all that?"

"Stop the talking. There's many laws of Parallel Co-Existence that can't be contravened, so I'm probably not aware yet that I've ever forgotten meeting you. I remember being on the America, though."

Bob's brain went into melt-down as he tried to work out what on earth she was talking about. Then he noticed something that would give her a very good prompt. He pointed across the reception to a large black and white photograph which now hung prominently between two doors. It showed the America moored at one of New York's piers, on a very bright day.

"You've put one of your pictures up - you're sure it really doesn't ring any bells?"

Feiya looked over at the picture and then back at Bob. She had a puzzled expression, bordering on the distressed.

"I felt like putting that up there. Big sin? Look, you're asking questions again, and once you start asking questions, you won't be able to know when to stop yourself. You have to keep it simple. I should've explained about the Temporary Alternate Existence possibil..isations because you could really mess me up if you keep asking questions like this, you know. Time Lines can merge and split and do all kinds of things, so don't talk so much to me, okay?"

Bob thought hard as he stared at the picture. He remembered the word 'Temporary' and 'Alternate' but that was about it. The world's lamest excuse sprang to mind.

"Maybe you did tell me about all that, I've probably forgotten.. it was a long time ago, after all."

"Hmmph. You need to go straight back home now and wait for Jinxy to come and get you again, and when she does I suggest you go back to New York and inform Madame Agatha of the latest developments. I'm really serious Bob, you're travelling a lot now and that means you might create more problems here than you can ever solve, so like I say, go straight back to New York, okay?"

Feiya flicked her hair over her shoulder and hurried up the stairs. Bob jumped as Jinx leapt up from behind the desk and sat in the very centre, looking as dignified as ever. She yawned and stared at him.

"I bet you don't look so holier-than-thou when you're eating a rat for dinner, do you? Or have you only been chasing birdies today?"

Jinx carried on staring at him.

"Okay, okay, I'm on my way home.. but could you knock next time you visit though? So much more polite than shouting, old girl.."

Jinx kept on staring until he was out of sight, and then trotted up after Feiya.

Bob slowly made his way back home and spent a minute or two standing outside the front door flicking through his diary. So much had happened since he was last at home that he'd lost track of what day it was, what was supposed to be happening in his world, and what he should be doing tomorrow at school. He gave a small cheer - tomorrow was a school holiday, which was just what the doctor ordered. He checked the details on his watch.

"Monday, 8.16pm, 16 March.. that's okay.. CORSAIR AVENUE, BARTON-ON-SEA, UGLY DOOR STEP.." and went inside.

So much time had passed for him that he felt like either of his parents would be bound to say something. They must suspect something, surely? His mum called from the living room.

"You back from Andie's already? Be a dear and put the kettle on, would you? Remember to use the left plug not the right one, or it'll turn all the lights out again."

In a way, Bob was glad to be back in mundane old Barton. No crazy sharks and slimey things trying to bite him, no tall freaks with personality issues, and no eerie fog either. Well, hopefully not - he was resigned to the fact that there was very little in life that could possibly be ruled out anymore.

He handed out the tea and went upstairs, and stood in his doorway for a while staring at a pile of homework sitting untidily on his desk. He tried to figure out how long ago he'd actually done it, but it was far too late in the day for those kind of mental gymnastics. Instead he sat on the floor against his bed, and settled down to watch a few undemanding episodes of The Simpsons. After Homer had said "D'oh!" for the seventh time, Jinx began calling outside and Bob wearily looked out of his window to make sure that it really was Jinx and not a passing stray with an urge to entertain. He watched her for a few seconds, hoping Mr Thompson would launch another boot in that general direction, but she gave no encores and merely sat on the gate post looking straight back up at him.

On his way downstairs, Bob figured he needed to avoid any potential hassle for when he returned, assuming he actually would return. He poked his head around the living room door.

"I left a book at Andie's, so I'll be back shortly. If I had even half a brain I'd be dangerous, wouldn't I?"

Bob's dad gave a loud snore on the settee while his mother hummed a reply and fiddled with the remote control.

Jinx disappeared into the night, and he didn't see her again until he wandered into the driveway of 107. He picked his bike up off the ground by the front door. The vibrations from his unfortunate Present Mirror Incident must have knocked it over, he mused. He changed into his 1920s version of himself, swung his rucksack over his shoulder and soon arrived at the start of a new day in glorious Manhattan. He sat down at the main table in Agatha's apartment, and in the soft morning sunlight began filling in his diary just in case she asked to see it - and also to brush up on what exactly had happened on his last visit.

"So, yesterday here, yesterday yesterdayyy.. got lost, found Eugi, bought planks and stuff.. oh yeah, Bagshaw sloshed.." he laughed, and then wrote down a vague outline of his time on board the America - without actually mentioning the ship's name, of course.

He made his way down to the reception, and strode out into the busying city. Eugi offered a long and very scenic alternative route to the Lexington Building, and pointed out the homes of the rich, the famous and the corrupt along the way. There seemed little difference between any of them. Bagshaw happily noted everything down, and even managed to supply a few of his own fond memories from his previous visits - but Bob didn't have the heart to point out that the Eiffel Tower was missing because the French preferred to keep it in France.

He waved to the receptionist as he went straight over to the lift, and pressed button 198. The corridor soon appeared, and he sneeked a very quick look out of the window at the end, but it still caused his stomach to turn upside down. Trying hard not to appear queasy, he knocked on the door marked Reception and waited for a reply. And waited. And then waited a little more. He gave the lock a careful tap with his key and walked into the deserted office. The only sound, except for gentle ticking, came from Claudie's muffled radio which didn't encourage him to hang around. He wandered over to Agatha's office, and the door opened for him. Her room was also empty, and Bob felt a knot spreading all through him - maybe the Troublers had struck, everyone was dead.. or.. or.. maybe they were just in a meeting or out somewhere - in which case Agatha might have left a note for him like his mother usually did. He cast an eye over the back of the door, the tops of chairs, the sides of cabinets, and every inch of wallspace. Then it occurred to him that maybe her desk would have been a good place to start.

A small white calling-card sat perfectly aligned in its centre, alongside her gold pen and a lethal-looking letter opener. Bob sat down in her unbelievably comfortable chair and rocked a long way back a couple of times before picking up the note. In Agatha's elegant handwriting, it read:

'Good thinking, Robert. Now kindly remove yourself from my chair and look straight ahead..'

Bob looked up to see the door to the Blue Time-Shift swing open, so he hurried across the room and stepped through.

Agatha was standing by a dark-wood desk in the Mirror Room, writing on a pad while talking calmly on the phone. Judging by her clothes, Bob wondered for a moment if she'd gone mad, but gave her the benefit of the doubt and decided that a black kimono with gold embroidery must have been perfectly trendy in the 1920's. The swooping narrow hat topped with long peacock feathers did look a little odd though. Her eyes were thinly veiled behind a short band of netting that probably ran around every hat she wore, and she casually glanced over to him. Her conversation ended with a slight frown, so Bob tried to sound as positive as he could.

"Morning Aunt Agatha! You look very.." he strained every cell in his brain to finish the sentence.

"..she looks very Oriental, indeed," whispered Bagshaw.

"..very Oriental indeed, today. I expect that the stores will be full of those before too long. You're way ahead of everyone!"

"If you had any idea who gifted this to me you'd probably say I was even further ahead of everyone - or a very long way behind them, depending on your view-point. The Empress who donated this to my wardrobe had a lot to be thankful for, and I so rarely accept money. Nice though, isn't it?"

Agatha gave a twirl, and the acres of shining material caught up with her a few seconds later. She raised her arms out, and the gold ends of the sleeves still touched the floor.

"See? Perfect fit.." she declared.

Bob felt relieved to see that she was in a relaxed frame of mind.

"I'm hoping you have some news for me?" she asked, pointing her right leg straight out in front of herself in order to scrutinise a jewelled black slipper.

"Huh? Oh, yes I do. I found the Present Mirror on board a ship called the.. I'd better not say.. and it's back in Barton now. The Mirror, that is, not the ship - I haven't a clue where the ship is. And when I said 'now' I don't mean 'now' now, but 'now' in the future. Talk about tricky.."

Bob's tale was interrupted as Agatha sat down cross-legged on the floor, and beckoned him to do the same. She pointed to a spot very closely in front of her, and as he sat down he could feel that she was staring straight into him. She closed her eyes, and spoke very softly. Even with her eyes shut Bob still felt like she was looking right through him.

"Clear your mind Robert.. we're going to calm all your inner turmoil, release your fears and doubts, cleanse the very essence.."

Bob liked this. Her voice was as soothing and as gentle as a summer breeze. However, Eugi didn't quite understand.

"Holy smokes, what's dis dame hootin' about? Pour another drink 'fore she gets any stupider - jeez what a low number!"

Agatha pressed her finger against the pocket where Eugi was. She said absolutely nothing, and Eugi apologised very carefully.

"Oh.. uh real sorry your Madameshipness Majesty. I didn't know you was you, I was thinkin' you was like someone else, you know, like not.. uh.. you. You carry on wid the head-emptyin' and I'll sit here nice an' quiet. Real quiet. An' nice, too. You see if I do. Jus' here."

It made sense to Bob that Agatha could talk to whatever she liked, and in whichever way suited her. She began speaking again, steadily lulling him into the most relaxed state of mind he'd ever been in. He felt her voice carry him from a scorched and barren desert to a beautiful oasis, a place of wonderful serenity and tranquillity where everything inside his heart and soul were in perfect balance. He felt Agatha could see and understand everything about him, even the things he couldn't find words for. And that was fine, wonderfully fine. At long last, Bob felt safe.

As he spoke about the Present Mirror, he kept his eyes closed and felt like never opening them again. Feeling protected within Agatha's re-assuring voice, he managed to talk her through everything without once feeling his heart start to race or any knots appearing in his stomach. After a few minutes, or maybe a few hours, he reached the point where Bagshaw mentioned how Oriental she was looking today, and Agatha drew his story to a close.

"You've done very well, Robert, I'm pleased. And your two travelling-companions were equally pleasing to me as well. Now, let me have Claudette's lighter. Weapons are so crude, aren't they? I'm sure you can do far better without that particular crutch to lean on."

Bob couldn't quite sense if he handed the gun over to Agatha or whether she simply took it, but either way he felt better that she now had it. He stood up to stretch his legs, and wobbled. How Japanese people managed to sit like that for so long was a total mystery to him.

Agatha seated herself at a writing table next to the Mirrors, and opened a thick leather-bound journal the size of a newspaper. She began writing lines and lines of strange symbols, lost in deep concentration. Ten minutes drifted by and Agatha didn't show a trace of emotion as she slowly closed the journal.

"It's a bit quiet in the office today Aunt Agatha - I was worried for a moment when I arrived. Are Naomi and Claudie off trawling the shops for this week's finest?"

"That's a fair guess, but no, not exactly. Look.."

She ran her fingers along the side of the Present Mirror and then the Distant Past Mirror. Naomi and Claudie slowly appeared in both Mirrors, where they were at a social gathering in the tree-lined grounds of a fortress, or maybe a stately manor.

"I'd say they could pass as 17th Century noble-women, wouldn't you, Robert? The Relevant Clothing Department were very pleased with their outfits and I can see why, now. It seemed like a nice day for a visit.. so I thought 'why not, it'll do them good'. Change of scene, and so on. Very important."

Bob watched as they demurely made their way down a wide series of stone steps to the lower grounds, where they joined a crowd of bona-fide ladies of 1692. Claudie opened a decorative fan and partially covered her face, mimicking the others as they blended in.

"What are they doing there? Averting a major catastrophe, or changing something that happens years later? Like what Arefrode was on about?" asked Bob.

Agatha breathed a quiet laugh to herself.

"No, they're a long way from any unaided interventions yet. For the time being they're just visitors. We allow trips to safe-zones for those who choose this path so that they can broaden their horizons without putting too much strain on their.. let's say 'grip on reality'. I take it you've encountered the Fourth Floor?"

Bob stared blankly, and slowly nodded as he remembered the unhinged Mr Alfons. He forgot to change his blank expression.

"Okay Robert, I'll rephrase it. In the ordinary outside world, if you travel a lot, you see a lot. You meet a lot of people, and you gain a greater appreciation of the way they live, their religions, their environment, their priorities and so on. Therefore, you're more able to hold an informed opinion. Now if you expand that principle so that you can visit anywhere over the past few hundred years in order to see what happens, why it happens and who made it happen - well, I'm sure you can appreciate that there's an awful lot to 'get your head around' as you might put it?"

"Uhuh.."

"So.." Agatha continued, gesturing with a broken pencil towards the Mirror, "..there's my two fluttering their eyelashes at the First Duke of Monaertskrieg, which could create a whole lot of trouble."

"What, you mean he might lop off their heads?"

"No, HE won't but I might, when they get back - they're only supposed to be observing and learning, not flirting. I despair.."

Bob was granted a coffee, and then headed back into Manhattan to return to The Ansonia. He went as far as the end of the block before something caught his eye, and he made a Mental Note (more of a Mental Billboard) to get hold of some American money next time.

"Pedro?" he read from the round yellow label, in disbelief.

The small general store on the corner had a pile of hand-crafted Pedro Flores yo-yos sitting insignificantly in its window, almost hidden beside a strange contraption for cleaning carpets. They practically jumped out at him, and he stared at the name for a while, remembering why Andie always called her favourite yoyo 'Pedro' regardless of which one of them it happened to be. According to her vast knowledge of Yo-yology, the craze really took off in the late 1920s, and the ones he was staring at were a kind of Holy Grail for all Stringers.

"I'll get some of them for her.. no, I'll get her ALL of them," Bob said to himself.

"Odd choice of gift for a lady there, surely?" enquired Bagshaw.

"Yeah.. but they'd be for Andie. A few of those should make up for me being such a weirdo these days."

"Oh, I see. Don't allow your hopes to run away with you, though. I found that well-intentioned gifts don't always have the desired effect. I once brought three Nile alligators back for an enchanting young lass in Windsor - and not a word of thanks. Never saw her again, in fact. Or the alligators."

"I'll cross alligators off the list, then."

"The Nile variety. Others might be fine - you just never know with the fairer sex, bless them all."

"Hey like are we goin' or stayin', yuh yak-yak pair uh.." asked Eugi, and they set off again for the Ansonia.

CHAPTER TWENTY FIVE

Smalsarhorn Day

Tuesday 17th March

Bob woke up to a bright and sunny morning in Barton, and felt relieved that the day was an official school holiday. Geography, Maths, Physics, Nordic Studies and the other ones.. the day would have been far too tedious and snoozeworthy after all he'd been through. Assuming there wasn't too much mad-cat nonsense, he could have the entire day with Andie, and that made everything so much brighter. He crawled out of bed, dressed and wolfed down two bowls of Crunchy Munchy before heading off to the newsagent for Andie's mum. Buying a paper gave him the chance to confirm beyond any question that he was definitely, exactly, precisely where he should be, and all on the right date as well - and reading the headlines and the sports pages helped him to feel like he actually belonged somewhere.

He wandered back from the newsagents along Sea Road, aiming for The Coffee Pot - at long last. According to his diary, he had seen her only last night, on Monday the 16th of March at 5.33pm, when she had left his mum's car after they had been picked up from the bus station. Bob felt as if at least two months had gone past since then, and that a whole lifetime had gone by since they had been wandering around the shops in New Milton just three days ago. As he drifted around onto Marine Drive and noticed the rainy mist shrouding the Isle of Wight, he tried to work out how many days he had actually been through, and gave up very quickly. It was all too confusing by an upside-down mile.

He stopped for a moment and looked up into the ranging spread of The Snowstorm Tree, and tried to reach up and see if he could grab any of the lower branches. He was a lot closer than last year, but still couldn't quite manage it. The tree didn't actually cause snowstorms of course, but the general idea was the same. A few years earlier when Andie's grandfather was still alive, he used to take her for long rambling walks on Sunday afternoons with Lady, his big old Alsation. Every April this particular tree would wake from the winter covered in masses of pink and white blossom. So for two or three Sundays her grandfather would be able to reach up and shake the branches while Andie waved her arms, spinning around and around, becoming hidden in a swirling snowstorm of blossom.

The first and only time Bob saw The Snow Storm Tree in action was back when he was eight, just a month or so before her grandfather became ill. They were all on their way back from a particularly long and meandering walk on one of those bright spring days - the kind that never stop looking like morning. Bob stood back and watched them having fun, and for the first time in his life he could see how two people could really enjoy the same thing, but for very different reasons. Initially he could tell that Andie loved the blossom cascading wildly all around her, laughing and losing herself in all its colours and fragrance. But then he looked at her grandfather, who didn't seem to mind about not getting covered in it. His tired eyes were bright, caring, and alive with how happy his grand-daughter was, and loving how something so simple could be so magical to her. And as Bob carried on watching, he could also see a longing in her grandfather's eyes, a longing for a distant childhood, that care-free time when he too could become lost in worlds of magical wonder. Bob could tell that somewhere inside this grey old man there was a child who was dancing and laughing in the blossom with Andie.

And ever since then, for the past few springtimes Bob had tried to reach the lowest of the branches and see if he'd grown tall enough to shake them.

"Next year should be fine.." he thought, and patted the tree trunk a couple of times before carrying on to The Coffee Pot.

Andie had almost finished loading the huge dishwasher in the kitchen with countless plates and cutlery from the first breakfasts when Bob arrived, and immediately gave him a quizzical look.

"Hi there, you. What's up? You're looking all troubled. Or are you waiting for a sneeze? Oh, you haven't stepped in something, have you? Mum'll go crazy if you've brought it in the kitchen again.."

Bob knew Andie could read him like a large-print book with enormous pictures, but how on earth could he actually tell her anything? He decided he'd just have to really go for it, regardless of any injuries that might be inflicted on him by a certain cat.

"No, no, nothing like that, don't worry. I'm just having more cat problems - I'm seeing that black one everywhere again, and I don't get a moment's peace."

"Well, as problems go, it's not quite a James Bond kind of problem is it? They'd never make a movie where he's hunted by a black cat that likes him. Bad box-office. Changing the subject completely, you know what would be a really good idea today?"

"Let me guess. Does it involve going back to This Miss for another look at a blue top-like top?"

"Perhaps.. I mean, if we happened to be in New Milton, it'd be a shame not to have a look, wouldn't it? So if you give me a hand with a few things here we ought to make the five past ten bus, so here's a cloth and there are some tables. You don't have to, of course.."

Bob took the cloth off his head and set about doing some serious cleaning-up. An hour or so later they arrived back at The Coffee Pot and Andie's new top met with the approval of her mum and also a party of pensioners who had stopped by for coffees. All was right with the world, for the time being, and they were soon heading back along the quiet road towards Corsair Avenue. At the precise moment that Bob wanted to start telling Andie again, he thought he saw Jinx a hundred yards away, near the curve where Marine Drive joined Sea Road.

"Hey you," said Andie, giving him a nudge, "I saw you flinch there. You get all bothered too easily. She's just a cat, that's all, and I can't imagine what's so wrong with her. Granted she's weird and not very friendly, but she is just a cat - and you could always buy a dog. A big one."

Bob felt sure that Jinx really was further along the road, so he nonchalantly guided Andie on a small detour through a quiet back-road instead, where he thought it might just be safe to try telling her a few things, once again. The street was empty, and after a nervous glance around, Bob began.

"Okay, Andie, here's what's bothering me. Jinx is a weird cat who leads me to 107 Lincoln Drive, which is a time-portal thing that my Great Aunt Agatha created and when I told you last time, Jinx turned up and made you forget - so I told you again, but she didn't rip me to bits when I thought she had, and you'd never believe where I've been since last night!"

He finished the entire sentence in one breath, and turned around twice looking for any rapidly approaching black blur. Nothing.

"I see.." said Andie, "I'd say you were going crazy, but that's too ridiculous to be crazy, so maybe you ought to carry on. I may have to use the word 'mental' a few times when you've finished, though."

Bob was leaping around on cloud nine. This was better than he'd ever hoped. They stopped walking and he started telling Andie everything in more or less the right order, but he only got as far as the first visit to Arizona. In his relief and enthusiasm, he hadn't noticed a strange rustling in the tree outside Number 15, very close to where they were standing.

Jinx landed on his shoulders, and he spun around in circles trying to throw her off before she could start inflicting any damage. Her small claws started digging into his skin as she started teaching him another lesson, but this time she had some help. Andie kept calling to Bob to stay still while she blitzed him with stinging blows from her yo-yos, hitting him full-on every time. The pain of the scratching was compounded by the nickel-plated bombardment.

"Andie, Andie cut that out! You're getting.. ow! You're getting me! Aim.. for the lousy cat.. damn it!"

Andie carried on with her barrage, striking Bob with tremendous thwhacks and cracks, over and over again. He fell to his knees, feeling like he'd been bruised everywhere. Jinx leapt onto the pavement, and raced behind a row of parked cars. Bob didn't know where to hold first. He started with his head and then his ribs.

"Andie, what the hell is wrong with you? Are you trying to kill me? Did you hit that mangy bag once? Try it with your eyes open, God that hurts everywhere!"

Andie exploded.

"I did, I hit her every time! She wouldn't let go and I kept trying but she was holding on and moving and don't get cross with me like that!"

And then Bob found out just how bad he could feel. He had actually lost his temper, he'd shouted at her, and now he'd actually made her cry. She began hurrying down the road, wiping a hand across her eyes. He picked up her yo-yos from a hedge and underneath a car, and started to run after her. He knew calling was a waste of time, as she'd probably ignore him even if she did hear his voice. He was going to have to catch up, and think of something very,

very good to say.

As he came to within a few yards of her, she suddenly stopped and put her hands to her mouth as if she'd seen the most horrific sight in her life. She was staring into the road, looking at Jinx who was whining over and over again, as if she was taunting Andie in a bizarre way. Bob was glad Jinx had chosen to sit in the road, especially as a large van had just turned into the street.

Andie had no idea anything else was around. All she seemed to be aware of was Jinx, and she bolted into the road holding her arms out towards her. For a split second Bob felt the entire world freeze as he realised that Andie couldn't be seeing the same thing he was seeing. His feet slipped as he started running towards her, and he knew he probably wouldn't make it in time. He grabbed a tall wheelie bin and hurled it into the path off the van, making the driver snap out of his dreamworld and slam the brakes on. Bob threw himself on Andie as the van skewed and screeched to a halt, barely two feet away from him. The air filled with the stench of burnt rubber and the driver's curses. He reversed, swore some more, and drove off loudly.

Jinx was gone, and Andie realised she was holding nothing. Tears poured down her face as she looked up at Bob.

"Where.. where did the baby go? She was crying, and sitting here.. and she was in the road.. crying.."

Bob wasn't really up to offering answers. Every emotion pounded through him as he helped her to her feet. He put his arms round her, giving a self-conscious hug.

"I'm sorry, Andie, really sorry.. I didn't mean to shout at you, I wouldn't hurt you ever, you know that don't you? Always believe that, okay? I have so much I want to tell you, and I just don't know where to start. There wasn't a baby there, it was that damn cat playing tricks, just like with the yo-yos. It's all so complicated.. I know - we're going to go where she lives, right now, okay?"

Andie nodded and folded her arms defensively. Bob wiped a final tear from her cheek, and they started walking back towards Marine Drive. After a few minutes Andie felt like talking.

"I believe you, Bob. And I didn't know I hit you, not even once, really I didn't. I wouldn't do that. I got her really good every time," she said between sniffs. Bob nodded and buried his anger at Jinx and the others deep down inside, and found it hard to think of anything to say all the way to Pierpont House.

A few minutes later they climbed the steps leading to reception, and Bob stormed ahead as Feiya came down the stairs. She sat at her desk and sipped a coffee, while Jinx settled on a new table that had appeared in the corner of the room. Bob leaned across and tried keeping his voice just below shouting-level.

"What are you sick freaks playing at? That fur-lined ball of hate just tried turning Andie into road-kill! I'm seeing Aunt Agatha right now, or you can shove those Mirrors so far up.."

"Hmm.. a nasty auto accident? That does sound a little heavy-handed, I agree. But there you go."

She seemed completely untroubled by his rage, and turned the page of a magazine on the desk. Bob was incensed.

"Let me see Aunt Agatha. I'm not leaving here until you do. No time-travelling, no New York, no nothing."

Feiya calmly opened her Appointments book, and ran a finger down the page.

"Nooo, you're not down to see her at all today. Bye, then."

A moment of silence hung between them.

"If I leave here without seeing her, I'm going for good. Forget all this weird stuff, it's your own fault not mine and you have no right to try wrecking Andie's life. You over-privileged freaks let this mess happen in the first place."

Feiya stared at him, and finished her coffee.

"Firstly, no we didn't just let it happen, and secondly you were told not to bring anyone else into this. That was your decision entirely. You should be more careful what you say and who you say it to, and now would be a pretty good time to start, wouldn't you agree? Hmm? Hmm?"

She opened the Appointments book again, and wrote down:

'11.53am Madame Agatha to see Andrea?'

Then she gestured for Andie to come closer to the desk.

"Can I have your surname please?" she asked, smiling up at her.

"Yardley," replied Andie, returning the smile. Bob was bemused by all the unexpected friendliness and wondered if he'd managed to miss an important bit somewhere.

"Thank you. And do you have a middle name?"

"Yes, Tallulah. T-A-L-L-U.."

"It's Jennifer," groaned Bob, and then watched in disbelief as line after line of unmistakeable handwriting slowly appeared underneath

Feiya's question.

'11.53 - Appointment confirmed. Andrea J Yardley meeting'

'11.58 - Andrea to meet Operatives N & C for Assessing'

'12.30 - The afore-mentioned to be Listed & Inducted'

'13.45 - Duties decided by F'

Jinx arched her back and ran up the stairs.

"Aha.. here we are. You are due to see Madame Agatha at 11.53," said Feiya, as if she'd overlooked the details before.

They all turned to the clock. The large face showed that the time was 11.51 precisely. Nothing was said while the hands slowly made their way to 11.53, at which point Feiya sprang back into life.

"Right then, Andie, up you go - last door on your left and do be very polite. Oh, but if any others are open, don't go near them. That would be a bad start, very bad."

Andie waved regally to Bob as she walked around the desk. For the briefest of moments Feiya felt something quickly brush against the back of her hair, but dismissed it. Bob grinned.

"You can go off now Bob, she'll be fine. She's part of the clan, just like you. There are some interested others who will bring her up to speed, and then at long last I get someone to help me. Not a bad day at all! A Mirror would have been nice, but I'll settle for an Assistant. No, a Primary Helper.. no, a Private Secretary.. no, a Formal Perso.."

The prospect of having an assistant seemed to boost Feiya a great deal. Bob saw that for the first time since Sunday, some of the tension in her eyes disappeared and for a moment, she even looked a little relaxed, like the girl on the America.

"There are Interested Others here? So Naomi and Claudie are definitely upstairs? That's great! Can I see them? I mean, would they remember me or would all that Parallel Co-Existence gumph get in the way?"

"Got it in one, Bob. This is the wrong time to be asking them questions that might or might not have unexpected results for you. On top of everything else, one or more of them might know things that you shouldn't be aware of, or perhaps they might not know the things that you shouldn't be aware of. Do you follow? You'll see them eventually, but we have to sort out the Mirror issue first. Believe me, all this is nice and simple for you, but not for them. They're doing unpleasant..able and dangerous things with those

Mirrors, and I don't envy them one bit. They're so unstable."

"The Mirrors, or Naomi and Claudie?"

"Yes."

Bob felt a cloud of confusion descending on him, and managed to string a final thought together.

"Can you tell me when Andie will be out?"

Feiya looked up at the clock, and seemed lost in thought for a moment. She shook her head, slowly.

"No, but I'm sure Jinx will let you know.. bye bye, for now."

Bob walked back home with a lot to think about. With every few steps he changed his mind as to whether or not he'd done the right thing. As soon as he started feeling good about not hiding anything from Andie, he immediately felt awful, convinced that he had done something really stupid and probably wrecked her life.

As he lay on his bed and stared up at the ceiling, he knew he'd crossed a line that couldn't be uncrossed, and he had well and truly roped her into his mess. Every few minutes he took a look outside for Jinx, but she didn't show throughout the entire afternoon or the evening.

After dinner he had a minor brainwave. While Buster Keaton was moving house, Bob decided to put Bagshaw next to a huge copy of Time & The Finite Universe, which had been given to him as a birthday present a couple of years earlier. He reached it down from the ever-expanding row of books on the Really-Ought-To-Read-These-One-Day shelf, blew the layer of dust from its top edge and leaned it next to the Compendium Of Modern Knowledge.

"Pay attention to.. uhh.. Professor Weurgenströmme.. Bagshaw, 'cause you have no idea how useful you need to be. It's not just me who's going to be confused from now on.."

CHAPTER TWENTY SIX

Bugsy and the Buffet

Wednesday 18th March

Bob thumped his alarm and the bleeping finished barely a second after it had started. The night had been long and restless, and he sat up in bed feeling nervous.

He couldn't face any breakfast, and got into his dad's car totally convinced that Andie would be having the day off. She'd probably need more time with Feiya, or even Agatha. His stomach grumbled as the car pulled up outside The Coffee Pot, and he watched as Andie shouted 'bye' from the side door to her mum. That was a good sign. She smiled on her way over - that was an even better sign.

Neither of them said much on the way to the bus station, because the world really didn't need Bob's dad to get involved. However, as the Volvo drove away from them at the station, Andie caught Bob completely by surprise. She was bubbling over.

"..and Naomi and Claudie, they're just the best ever! We had such a good time and we were just talking and talking and I didn't get home till so late. Mum wasn't too pleased so I blamed you, so remember it was your fault in case she mentions it. Actually, you'd better write it down somewhere 'cause she was pretty miffed, I can tell you. Fey dropped me off in her Audi and it is so awesome! She says I can drive it all over the grounds at Pierpont in the summer.."

"Huh? But what about all the time travelling stuff? And that bit about the Mirrors having to be back here by midnight tomorrow? Don't you find that a bit difficult to get your head around?"

"Uhuh. Who wouldn't? But like they kept saying, tomorrow can be a long way off, which is true isn't it?"

Bob was happy, relieved, and above all, utterly dumbfounded.

"And all those weird departments? Doesn't that bother you?"

"About as much as it bothers you, I'd say. Look, neither of us knows enough to even begin thinking about any of that, so therefore it's not something to be thought about just yet, is it? Anyway, they said we'd both spend a while in the departments sooner or later, but until then we shouldn't even try to get stressy about any of it. Softly softly, attrapez la petite minkey. You should know that. They do."

Bob picked one of the simpler questions from the hundreds that were running through his mind.

"So how are they all, then? I'm not supposed to see them in case I mess up something to do with Parallel somethings.."

"Parallel Co-Existence and Temporary Alternative Time Lines. Yeah, all that's very awkward especially for Fey because she sees you so much. The lines can cross over so she gets vague memories of you appearing and disappearing in her past.. and that's not easy for her. As for the others, well Naomi's really nice and she tried bleaching some of her hair last week but it went a bit wrong - as if she hasn't got enough to worry about.. and Claudie's such a good laugh and holds a grudge like you wouldn't believe. Oh, and Jinx is still iffy - but that doesn't matter 'cause I feel so good having new friends like them."

"I was thinking more along the lines of 'have they cracked up yet'?"

Andie made her Wednesday yo-yo sleep for a few seconds before bringing it zipping back to her hand.

"Oh.. no, they're alright despite you, I think. You're not doing anyone's grip on reality any good at all, but that's nothing new," she laughed, "..and not really your fault. Everyone's pleased with how you're doing though, and so am I - but imagine keeping all that to yourself for so long! You could have told me earlier, you know."

Bob almost apologised, but Andie was laughing again.

"Anyway, they're all under a lot of pressure, and on top of that they're not too happy because they're ageing a bit but that's down to all the Mirrors not being there. Madame Agatha's the one who's suffering the most and that's Numero Uno at the top of their list of Things To Get Stressed About."

"There's a list?"

"Uhuh. It's really long. Equal top is trying to keep the two Mirrors stable, but I didn't understand anything about that apart from it's scary-dangerous. Fey doesn't do Mirror stuff, and said something really funny about it but the others didn't laugh much."

"It's hard to imagine Fey being funny - she's always so freaked."

"Oh, that reminds me, she says you absolutely have to give me your diary so I can catch up with everything. Actually it was Naomi's idea, but Fey agreed and Claudie found it hysterical for about three seconds, and then had no idea why she was laughing. They must have seen what your handwriting's like?"

The bus pulled into the station as Bob handed over his diary. Fortunately he hadn't committed any of his more poetic thoughts of Andie to its pages. The journey was loud, chaotic and for some of the Juniors it was highly distressing, but for Bob it was by far the best journey ever. He knew he'd taken a big step, and was so relieved that it had been in the right direction. Andie mentioned more and more snippets of the night before, and Bob was pleased to find out more about the three people who had become so important to both of them. Agatha was a big worry, though. Apparently she had been barely able to speak to Andie during their brief meeting, and even then had only nodded approval before allowing her through to see Naomi and Claudie.

The morning crawled by, minute by heavy minute, until lunchtime finally arrived and they quickly made their way up to their Secret Place. Page by page they talked through Bob's diary, and although the weight on his shoulders didn't lift by very much, it had at least moved around a bit. The freedom of being able to talk without the fear of a certain cat going berserk was wonderful. Andie was disappointed that Jinx was still being cold and unfriendly, but that was the only blot on the landscape, and all things considered, it was a pretty minor one.

Bob was all set to end a glorious day watching the sun setting at The Coffee Pot, and talking with Andie about everything all over again. However, she was due to see Feiya for some more First Step Training, and as she pointed out, he was supposed to be at home waiting for Jinx to turn up. Some rules, she emphasised, really shouldn't be broken. So Bob found himself falling asleep through a Marx Brothers film, unable to fend off the tiredness of the previous few days. The film had run through once, and Bob woke up as Groucho started singing 'Hello, I Must Be Going' for the second time.

"Now this would be way too predictable for that cat to turn up," he thought.

Right on cue, Jinx started wailing outside and Bob guessed she would probably be somewhere in the general region of the gate post. He picked up his rucksack, hurried down the stairs and as he reached the front door remembered that he had to go back up for Bagshaw.

An entire day spent with Professor Weurgenströmme could only have been a good experience for His Lordship. Excited but very nervous, Bob skidded his bike to a halt at Number 107 and went in. The door to the Master Bedroom was already opening.

Manhattan was all set for another magnificent summer's day, and Bob took a few minutes to look through a gap in the net curtain of one of the tall windows, out at The Ansonia's part of the city and think of his last visit. Agatha in a black kimono, Naomi and Claudie on a visit, the priceless yo-yo pile.. and his mind immediately started wandering back to Andie.

"Eugi, would you have a think and let me know some good places where me and Andie could go, here? She might be able to come along some time soon, which is brilliant, isn't it?"

"Ayndee? Hmm, let's see.. places for a skirt tuh go, right? Sure, I know the bestest, classiest, sure-thing kinda places you evah saw. If you weren't such a mush with her she'd be here now. Hee hee, dames huh? They ain't so easy t'deal with, not like hoods or low-lives. Gotta be nice to 'em, gotta be nice.. an' by that I don't mean be a mush."

Bagshaw felt obliged to step in.

"Oh I say Mr Eugi, au contraire, young Bob isn't a 'mush' at all. He's conducting himself as a gentleman should, and not rushing his lady friend. Such behaviour ought to be encouraged, and I for one applaud his dealings."

"Whuh? Applaudin'? Liven up Lord Val-ennn-tino - if His Royal Mushness, Prince Mush of Mushdovia here don't get busy with the Boardin' Pass, the Good Ship Ayndie's gonna set sail! Dames don't stick around for no time before goin' off some place else - with some other bozo in tow who ain't no mush. Hey, she might'a got her eye on someone else already, in which case it gets real bad for this Mush-meister. I seen it before. I'm telling you kid, make like that ol' Shakespeare guy with the talking, an' she'll be your piece of.."

"Thanks Eugi, I'll try and remember that. And you too, Bagshaw, much appreciated and so on. Now how about some cross-towning? I'm supposed to be going to Lexington, not sorting out.. other things."

Bob couldn't believe that a book and a compass had managed to put his head in a spin. He didn't feel like saying much for most of the journey, because he was completely pre-occupied trying to work out if he was being hopelessly slow with Andie, and then he started thinking again of who she '..might'a got her eye on'. There happened to be quite a few candidates, all of them with foul personal habits, major personality flaws and many other disgusting problems that medical science could never hope to put right. And apart from all that, Bob knew that none of them could ever, ever care enough about her, even if they tried. And no matter how much he tried, he couldn't think of any way to let her know that. Well, at least no way that was likely to happen. He kept on walking and thinking, and didn't even notice that he'd run the gauntlet of a stirring Columbus Circle.

By the time they reached the huge intersection where Broadway - and perhaps the rest of New York - crossed Fifth Avenue, Bob felt well and truly out of step with the world. He needed a moment to catch up with everything, including himself, so he sat down beneath an elegant sidewalk-clock and stared across to the bizarre pointed face of the Flatiron Building. It looked like the prow of a great ship, breaking through the right-angled grid of the streets. Somehow it was ridiculous and magnificent at the same time. He watched the morning getting itself well underway as more and more cars pounded over the tramlines, roaring as they weaved between each other and the dozens of trundling, overloaded vans.

As he dug himself a little deeper into an emotional hole, he suddenly remembered that Bagshaw had been chatting to Time & The Finite Universe for ages the day before. Over the previous two years, Bob had made at least half a dozen attempts to read all about Finite Whatever-theory, and failed on every occasion. In fact, the text on the back cover was still a huge challenge, and even the picture on the front looked like it was the wrong way up. He was glad for an opportunity to take his mind off things, and tried talking to Bagshaw without moving his lips, to avoid any embarrassment.

"Hey, Gagshaw, how did you get on yestuday yith Kruhessor Yeurgenshtröne? Can you start exklaining any ug this tine-trahulling stuhh yet?"

"Come again?" said Bagshaw, and Bob repeated himself properly.

"Oh, Professor Weurgenströmme? My, what a fascinating lady Gunnel is! We were talking for hours and hours!"

"Well?" asked Bob, hopefully.

"Well what, old boy?"

"Well how does all this work? How can we be back in the summer of 1927, surrounded by people who are all living their lives as if 'now' is really 'now' - when in fact it's already happened?"

Bagshaw had a think for a while.

"We're back in the summer of 1927 are we? Well fancy that. To me 1927 is forwards, old chap. Quite a few years in fact. These people are living their lives as if, like you say, now is now, even though from my point of view, 'now' hasn't happened yet, and from your point of view, 'now' happened a long time ago."

Bob was relieved and impressed that Bagshaw might actually know something useful.

"Well, that sounds pretty good to me Your Lordship.. carry on, I'm all ears."

Bagshaw continued, sounding very authoritative.

"Well, it appears that you've gone backwards, I've gone forwards, and everyone else meets us in the middle, the 'middle' being the point in time where we both meet regardless of the distance in time travelled by either of us. Professor Weurgenströmme taught me something very important about all this time and space business, you know."

"Brilliant! And that is?"

"And that is that I don't understand any of it. She was talking and talking and talking. Might just as well have been blowing up balloons. I would have been as flummoxed at the end as I was at the beginning, but after ten minutes with her I had no idea of what a 'beginning' or an 'end' might be anymore. In some ways, could you be a little more careful about who my neighbours are in future, or whatever I mean by 'future'.. oh, I believe I've gone light-headed again.. do excuse me.."

Bagshaw removed his monocle and wandered somewhere beyond the frame, rubbing his forehead. Bob left the compendium poking up out of his re-named Confused Aristocracy pocket, and drifted past the final few blocks to Lexington Avenue.

Minutes later he stood outside the reception door up on Floor 198, and gave a few knocks. There was no answer. He knocked again, a lot louder this time, and there was still no answer.

"Ah, they must be on another day trip.." he thought to himself, and started fumbling for his key, but stopped when faint rattling sounds came through from the other side. The door opened very slightly, and an arm poked through it. The hand at the end slowly gestured for him to be quiet, and then withdrew back inside. The door opened a little more, and a very pale Claudie appeared in the gap. She squinted through bloodshot eyes at him, and looked very ill.

"Yawning morning Claudie, it's me, Bob," he whispered. She mumbled something as she turned away, and staggered back over to her desk where she curled up on the chair. A cream silk dressing gown wasn't quite what Bob expected to see her wearing.

"Are you ill? Maybe you should see a doctor?" he said, closing the door quietly. She raised her head just enough to move her mouth.

"Bit of a.. late night. Think a few bubbles.. might'a disagreed with me.. or got trapped in my head.." she whispered in short breaths, and slowly turned her chair to face the window. Luckily for her, the blind was drawn.

"Oh, right. Is Naomi here yet?"

A weak moan came from underneath the other desk, so Bob made himself useful and went into the kitchen to put the kettle on.

A loud and enthusiastic rapping shook the front door. After calling each other's names for a while, Claudie threatened to throw up if she had to answer the door again, so Naomi gave in and crawled her way slowly across the floor. She opened the door and bleerily peered up into the toothsome smile of an unbearably cheerful man.

"And good morrrning!" he sang down to her with a joy and sincerity that filled the office, "Do I have a delivery for you today! Here is your dayy-lee post and other assorted papers, and also a feeeyew packages from a colleague of Ma'mm Ag'tharr! They do need signing for.. is she available, perchance?"

He stopped talking, and his expression suggested to Naomi that he was expecting a reply from her. Her expression to him suggested that there was no chance of him getting one.

"Fret not, Miss. I assume that you are a sig-natoreee? I have a list of suitable names, yours may be one," he said folding over the top sheet on his clipboard. He smiled at her as if she was five years old.

"Uh, I'm Naomi. I sign for things all the time. Where do I do it for all these then?" she said, trying to stand up straight while the first of the boxes was deposited just inside the door. She was starting to feel more awake and the annoyance in her voice was becoming clearer. The man handed his clipboard to her and she took it over to her desk, gladly letting the door swing closed. His foot stopped it from shutting in his face, and whistled for the porters to start shifting the boxes in from the Postal Floor.

A long, pitiful moan escaped Naomi. Over forty items were listed by code numbers, all requiring her signature in at least two places. One of the delivery men opened the door again and four others came through, each carrying armfuls of boxes. The man began announcing each box's special code to the room with unbearable enthusiasm, and Naomi scrawled her name by each one. She handed back a blotchy counter-signed sheet, and the man bid her an infuriatingly cheery farewell.

"Aw, go chase y'self, Zeebert," she muttered, pushing the door closed behind him. A vast and unsightly collection of big wooden boxes had been spread randomly all over the room, and she opened the kitchen door for Bob to see them.

"Wow, Naomi - what have you ordered?"

"Nothing. This is a gift from some bunch or another trying to get Madame Agatha to intervene for them, or to have a sneaky look into the future for investments an' that kind of dumb thing. We get them almost every single week. Now we have to catalogue everything, declare it all to a million authorities, get things signed in triplicate and then return them all to whichever barrel-full of meat-heads sent them. Drives me scat."

"More of a bribe than a gift, then? On a better note, I've made some coffee and a load of that Grapey-Nut goop-sloop 'cause you two look like you could do with some. Do you want honey or cinnamon on the top, or a few strawberries.. and should I warm it?"

Naomi wobbled a little.

"Nuh oh.. gonna.. thu-throw.." she stuttered, and ran past a stack of boxes and into another room. Claudie giggled then immediately moaned and held her head.

Agatha entered the room and looked at the boxes with the kind of expression that could sink an entire fleet of battleships - and then send the sea into retreat. Bob thought she might explode, but instead she merely tutted lightly to herself, shook her head in despair and smiled a 'good morning' at him before returning to her office.

He handed out the coffees, put Agatha's on a small silver tray, and went into her office. She was finishing a harsh conversation on the phone, presumably with the sender of all the boxes. She noticed his concerned expression, and laughed to herself while pointing for him to take his usual chair.

"People never, ever seem to learn. If I'd kept all my 'gifts' since becoming Guardian, I'd need every building in New York to store them all. The latest collection will be out of here once my two able assistants are back in the land of the living.. whether they realise they're back in it or not," she grinned.

"They do look a tiny bit unsteady, today.."

"Oh, don't feel sorry for those two, they love life here, that's all. Claudie's a born Flapper and Naomi's.. well, she's getting there. I feel she'd have preferred the 1860's.. anyway, they make me laugh when they've taken a step too far, not that I allow them to know that. Still, they're having fun."

Bob was surprised.

"But I'd have thought this Guardian Training was serious stuff? Back home I'm only doing dull school work, but I'm surrounded by school books all the time, and loads of past exam papers and reference stuff that's nowhere near the school syllabus. My dad wants me to be one thing, my mum says something else, everyone else has got a better idea and I'm right in the middle without a clue what I want to do. Every single day's meant to be really serious."

Agatha's brow furrowed slightly.

"Well, commit to nothing until the time's right for you, and no-one else can say when that time is - that's for you to decide and I assure you Robert, you won't get it wrong. You must re-draw the line if you don't like where someone's drawn it for you. I know that's not easy to do, so just try to bear it in mind for a while, and dare to allow yourself a good time. But only when appropriate of course."

Bob wasn't used to anyone speaking to him like this.

"I don't think I'd know a good time if it ran out and bit me."

"Hmm.. you have to put your foot down every now and then. I'm aware that's easy to say, but you really must do it occasionally - or in my case, all the time, but that's different. You need to escape from the pressures that others burden you with, especially at your age, so you simply must have some fun when you can. You know why?"

"No.."

Agatha fixed him with a look that was a long, long way from being a frightening one.

"Because if you're never a child, how will you ever be an adult?"

Bob tried to think of something, then anything.. then nothing.

"I don't know."

"Precisely. Everything in its time, Mr Taylor. Now then, give those two a hand shifting the new boxes into one of the outside rooms -

300

Claudie knows which one, and you should be finished in time to be my guest at a luncheon appointment. It'll be very good for you."

"Really? What's the occasion?"

"No great concern of yours. For the most part, it's a social gathering for certain Departments and Members, which we have every two or three weeks. It stops some of us getting chained to our desks. But I'd like you to be there, because I want you to let me know if you recognise anyone, so you'll have to mingle and look at faces, mannerisms, shapes, anything."

"Anyone? From this time, or when?"

"You're looking for people you might have seen in shops, on streets, in windows, on boats, anywhere. And I mean anywhere. They might have no significance to you, but could mean an awful lot to me. Now then, go and see if the waking dead have actually woken up, would you? Those boxes could easily start to annoy me."

An hour or more later, Naomi and Claudie were in a slightly better state and were even properly dressed for the day ahead. The boxes were soon packed away into a room beside the door which lead onto Fifth Avenue, and Bob wasn't at all surprised that everything fitted perfectly.

"So Bobs, you're off to a Posh Nosh then? You're honoured, big time. We've only been to one, ever since we started here," said Claudie, faking a sad expression. Naomi looked indignant.

"Well we'd have been to a lot more if you hadn't told every fat person there that President Coolidge was going to tax waistlines."

"So I was wrong about that.."

"And you started that rumour about the Fields & Hedgerows Administrator and her Assistant as well, didn't you?"

"Nuh-uh, I did not. Okay I did, but only because she'd said that I.."

"And as for the Head Of Floral Co-ordination.."

"Oh c'mon, you agreed she was mutton dressed as pig, and any.."

"Umm.. hello?" interrupted Bob, "..I'm going there to look for people I recognise, so that Aunt Agatha can do some research, and we're off any minute to be early - apparently, it's always better to see who's arriving, than be seen arriving."

"Sounds fun. Some of those people, eesh, they'll bore your booties off. Do you want another ciggy lighter? You could really pep things up a bit - I've got a new one which I haven't tried out yet. The guy said it'll light an iceberg - is that the cat's best pj's or what?"

"Uhh.. yes, with matching slippers as well. But I'm likely to toast myself if I go anywhere near it, thanks, so I'd better.."

The three of them jumped as one of the doors opened and Agatha suddenly appeared in the corridor. She carefully finished pulling on her black driving gloves, checked herself in a mirror and decided the top button of her slender ankle-length coat needed to be undone. She beckoned Bob to follow her back through the door, amidst a round of goodbyes. Naomi and Claudie remained in the corridor, both feeling uneasy.

"So Bobs is on the social circuit already? His diary says he's hardly met anyone so how can he be looking out for other people, Nay? What's the story?"

"I think it's the other way around. Madame Agatha wants other people looking at him and I bet she'll be watching everyone's reactions like a hawk - an odd glance here, a double-take there, she'll see everything.."

Agatha opened the door again, and fixed them with a glare.

"Allow me to interrupt. I want you both to follow us down to the entrance, and then you immediately return here. Naomi, you return via Staircase One, and Claudette by Staircase F. I want us noticed."

They both nodded, wondering if she had heard anything that would result in either of them being roasted, and followed her into the Department's main corridor where Bob was waiting.

"And this time," instructed Agatha, "..do synchronise footsteps properly. Image, ladies, image," she added before pressing the button marked 'Ground'.

Silence surrounded Agatha and her entourage as they walked through the vast reception hall. Bob had never seen anywhere so busy, and yet so unnervingly quiet. Conversations evaporated as people nodded their greetings, and a brave few dared to speak an acknowledgement. Agatha ignored them all and slowly strode across the shining mahogany section of the floor, making a deliberately firm cla-CLACK sound with each step. Each one echoed, perfectly matched and strengthened by Naomi and Claudie. Bob, who had never seen anyone command respect simply by their walk, tried not to destroy the effect and stayed a long way behind - on the carpet.

Agatha elaborately pointed at the appropriate staircases for Naomi and Claudie to return through, much to Bob's bewilderment.

She waited at the end of the covered way for him to catch up, and the two of them rounded the corner outside the building and walked a few yards along Lexington Avenue. The scary, all powerful, God-like Madame Agatha imperceptibly changed back into Not-Quite-So-Scary-Anymore Aunt Agatha. She looked at Bob and a small laugh escaped her, and for a split second he thought she was going to say something about the people in reception, but instead she unfurled a hand towards her car.

"And before us, our carriage awaits! Impressed, I trust?"

The gleaming white Bugatti Royale simply oozed class, standing majestic and proud in the morning sunshine. The broad black arches above the front wheels flowed in an elegant wave all the way around to the back, where they merged seamlessly just inches above the ground. The long bonnet, crowned with a small silver elephant above the shining radiator grill, stretched further than could ever be necessary, and looked all the better for it. Bob was speechless, and walked all around the black, white and chrome masterpiece with his mouth hanging open like a hungry basking shark. Agatha stroked the nearest of its many headlights.

"It's so lovely today, we won't be needing the hood, thank you," she said, in a tone more suitable for a much-loved pet.

The sleek, jet-black canopy silently wound itself back, concealing itself beneath the black lid of the boot. Bob could tell there was perhaps something a little different about this car - for a start, there was no chauffeur inside making the roof disappear.

"They only made seven of these. This, however, is the eighth. One day I'll explain that, but for the time being, we're due for some fun - if that appeals to you? It's your decision. Fun or sensible?"

"Fun sounds good to me.." replied Bob, wondering what someone like Agatha regarded as fun.

"Excellent! That's your first line re-drawn. See how easy it can be? Now sit back and enjoy the ride because this beauty goes!"

The driver's door swung itself open for her, and Agatha eased herself in with enough grace and elegance to shame a princess.

"Oh, Robert? I'm afraid you'll have to climb over the door on your side. There was a teeny incident in Moscow, and now it doesn't open on Fridays. It gives more character, I like to think."

Bob stepped up onto the side panel, and then fell in.

"Robert, meet Bugsy, my preferred mode of transport and most faithful servant.. aren't you Bugsy?" she said, patting the steering wheel.

"..and Bugsy, meet Robert, who is coming with me to the Garden Party.. yes, my guest.. no you will not, naughty! I want him to arrive with me.. yes, in ONE piece, thank you!" she laughed.

Bob gulped as Agatha emphasised the word 'one'. She paused for a few moments and scanned her eyes over the dashboard, trailing her gaze with a finger. Bob wasn't surprised that she took a while to look over everything - it was the kind of dashboard that could make the Space Shuttle's banks of information appear 'a bit limited'. There were dozens upon dozens of chrome-ringed dials, and almost as many switches protruding from the walnut dash. The usual assortment of gauges for speed and petrol were completely lost amongst the array of others. Bob gulped again as he noticed a large one which showed 'Number Of Passengers' which was divided into 'At Start' in blue, and 'At End' in red. Another showed 'Number Of Boxes' with a series of smaller dials around it for each store visited, another displayed 'Number Of Doors' and right in the centre was a small flashing red button with 'Never Touch This' written on some sticky tape below it.

"You see this one?" said Agatha, as she pointed and prodded a gloved finger on a dial marked 'Number Of Active Dials'. "It's a new one! It tells me how many Active Dials there are - isn't that just something else?" she laughed, adding, "Look, it says 91! How divine!"

Bob nodded in nervous agreement, and wondered if he could take a taxi instead, without offending her. He watched her flick every switch in sight, all of which seemed to do nothing whatsoever. She turned to him with a mischievous smile across her face, and twitched her eyebrows twice at him, knowingly.

"Shall we.. depart?"

She pressed one of the smaller pearlescent buttons and put one hand on her white cloche hat and the other on the steering wheel. Bob couldn't help but notice that both hands were on her hat as soon as the engine began revving. The entire car started shaking and the dials all seemed to blur into one. Either a huge earthquake was hitting New York, or this car had something belonging to NASA under its bonnet. Bob hoped for the earthquake.

"You know, Robert, this is so easy just as long as you're very, very.."

The word 'careful' was said in a pitch only dogs could hear as the car launched itself onto Lexington Avenue, and weaved its way unnoticed through the mid-morning traffic. The ends of her long white scarf billowed wildly in the air, trailing far behind the car and occasionally in front of it, as the speedometer waved wildly to and fro. As Bob rolled about in his seat in between being pulled back into the car, he figured they must be taking the unnecessarily scenic route. Some buildings went past twice, and others were so blurred he couldn't tell which they were or how many times they appeared.

Agatha looked as if she was loving every minute of it. She clung onto the steering wheel, leaned over to Bob and tried speaking through squeals and shrieks of laughter.

"Ro.. Ro-b-b-buht... it's had modifi.. modificatio.. things added.. WAHEEEYY.."

Bob couldn't reply. He always found it hard to talk with his heart in his mouth. Almost three hundred blocks later, of which sixty three were actually needed, Bugsy came to a screaming halt outside a huge mansion. Bob also came to a screaming halt, fifty yards further down the road between a thick mass of hedges and three wrecked saplings.

When the world came back into focus, he could see Agatha standing by the car impatiently waving for him to come and join her. He fell from the hedge and onto the sidewalk, and eventually stumbled a drunk's path back over to her. She was the picture of unruffled, elegant dignity, and his heart was still pounding as he stood before her, struggling to get his breath back.

"That was insane.. that was completely insane.. how can.. a car do that.. and still be in one piece?" he gasped, noticing that even the white-walled tyres were completely unmarked.

"I told you - it was the eighth one. Nothing else would do. Now come along, you're covered in unacceptables," she said, brushing twigs and leaves from him.

Fortunately, the Park Avenue mansion was set a long way back from the road, and Bob looked almost presentable again by the time they reached the towering door. A smartly dressed butler welcomed them in, and commented that "..henceforth, the other guests are surely to arrive soon," with the aloof air of an English butler.

Agatha handed her coat to a lesser-butler, and they walked out into the rear grounds where a vast buffet was being laid out by dozens of kitchen staff, and a tiered band ran through a final practice session. Agatha chose a broad swinging garden chair with a clear view of all access points to the garden, and calmly waited for people to start arriving. Eventually a steady flow began appearing, and Agatha mentioned certain individuals, while ignoring others. It didn't make any difference to Bob though, as he couldn't recognise anyone at all.

Most of them made a point of coming over to Agatha and delivering their inane pleasantries, and Bob could soon tell which were friends, and which were not so fortunate. Eventually, a friend in a tangerine dress and ludicrously wide-brimmed hat sat down and caused the chair to start rocking. Agatha gave Bob an obvious nudge as if to say, 'I didn't invite this one over..'

"Robert, be a dear and fetch a couple of drinks would you? Those frosted punches look good over there.."

"No, no.." her friend added, "..try the special stuff, their Lemon Nectar instead! Nip inside and ask for Colin or Gerrard, and say that Gyllian requires two Nectars! Oh look! Oh, I'll be back in a minute, there's Eilidh in something hideous and.. I do believe she's also with something hideous! Where did she find him? And there's that new Personnel Advisor, oh she's frightful. Adelle or something like that.. she had her birthday last week. 34 apparently, but I say she's 44 in the shade! Have to dash, save this seat? I'll be a mini-mo."

Both laughed and Gyllian hurried into the growing crowds.

"I'll go and find some Nectar then?" said Bob, noticing Agatha's laughter stopped as soon as Gyllian had turned away.

"Orange, not lemon, token sprinkling of sugar - and don't forget some ice, today's becoming a little warm. Do not bring hers."

Bob dutifully headed over to the conservatory, and found a spare waiter in one of the ballrooms in a distant wing.

"Hello.. if you're not too busy, Madame Agatha would like an Orange Nectar with ice, and her friend.. isn't having one - and I'd like anything cold as long as it's in a huge glass, like big enough to lose a submarine in. A water would do just fine."

"Muh.. Muh.. Madame.. Agatha? A drink from me? Wait here a second, I'll be so quick!"

The waiter, one of the younger ones, went pale and hurried off towards the kitchens. He returned with a portly man in his fifties, who was carrying a few gold-rimmed champagne glasses on a long silver tray.

"Must be the senior waiter-type person", thought Bob.

"Ahem.." he said, examining the rim of one glass, "I will prepare one of our finest Nectars and return shortly to present them personally to Madame Agatha, whilst you wait here for our.. 'Chef de l'eau' to bring you an iced water, assuming he is capable of rising to the challenge of preparing such a delight. Let us hope that his twenty years of service in the elite dining establishments of London and Manhattan will be of some assistance to him in preparing such an ambitious cocktail. Yes?"

Colin waited for a reply as the clock struck midday. Bob had no idea what to say, so he just nodded. A few minutes later he followed him outside and they steadily made their way over to the garden chair, but Agatha had gone and two other people were sitting in her place. Her tangerine friend arrived in a laugh, sat down regardless and made the chair start swinging again. The other people didn't seem to appreciate her efforts.

"Where's Madame Agatha disappeared, then?" she asked, looking at Bob and then the other two.

"I was going to ask you that," he replied, looking around the sea of faces.

"Oh, I expect she's off circulating already. She's very important, you know - talks to everyone at these things, or mainly everyone talks to her, in actuality. I sometimes wonder if these are organised to let people try and get her hearing their requests, like we don't have enough committees and things to sort everything out for her. That was a joke just now, so don't you tell her I said that.. oh listen to me, I can't be chatting while Nectar is going unsquiffed, so if you'll excuse me, I do need to be a-mingahling.."

She downed Bob's finest tap water, picked up Agatha's sparkling glass from Colin's tray and hurried off into the masses. The band started playing a tune which Bob recognised from a film, but he couldn't remember the name of either as he anxiously looked around for Agatha. He spent a few minutes waiting in case she turned up, and then spent half an hour wandering the grounds and some of the rooms inside, and started to feel like a fish out of water.

He went around the side of the mansion to the road where they had arrived and looked for her Bugatti, but that was gone as well. Bemused, he stood for a while in the hot sun and tried to figure out why Agatha would leave so suddenly. Nothing sprang to mind.

"Where are we, Eugi?" he said, hoping the journey back wouldn't be as far as he dreaded.

"Upper East, uh long ways from home. Got the doshes f'r a cab?"

"No.." said Bob, realising that he'd forgotten to get any money again, which meant Andie's yo-yos would have to wait until whenever.

"Best put yer walkin' boots on."

"Great, really great.." he sighed.

"Ahh, the women-folk! Who's to say what they'll ever do next?" exclaimed Bagshaw, and began mumbling and chortling to himself about a lady friend who had twice stranded him in a hostile village near Bangalore. Eugi had some advice, though.

"See what I wuz sayin' kid? Bein' all mush with th'dames, they're bound to do somethin' like this. Better get used to it kid, I'm tellin' yuh this could be y'whole life.." he said.

For the first time since he'd arrived in Manhattan, Bob felt thoroughly annoyed.

By the time he arrived back at Floor 198, the streets had completely turned his mood around and all he really needed in order to make the world right again was a good long drink. Naomi was talking on the phone to Claudie, who was exactly where she was meant to be, across the room from her. They told each other Bob had arrived, and yet managed to look as if they were hard at work. At the precise moment that he was going to ask them when, or if, Agatha had returned, she walked in through the front door with a look on her face that suggested talking or breathing in front of her was not a wise idea. Bob tried not to stare, but he couldn't help noticing a large bump on her forehead. She strode to her office and the doors slammed firmly behind her.

Naomi put the phone against her shoulder and waved Bob to come over. She handed the earpiece to him for a word with Claudie, who was speaking in a whisper.

"Careful Bobs, she's been in a rotten mood ever since she got back. Rinkier side of dink, by a mile. Changed outfits twice. Danger, danger, danger!"

Agatha immediately opened both doors again.

"Shouldn't you all be out at lunch by now?" she commanded.

CHAPTER TWENTY SEVEN

Strong Breeze, Northerly Direction

"Bob? Can you nip down and find a table for us at Pete's Tavern before they stop serving lunch? Claudie and I have things to finish off up here, and we're starving. It's only on 18th Street, you can't miss it but if you do just ask someone 'cause everyone knows it."

Bagshaw encouraged Bob to find the Tavern without any help but he eventually gave up, much to Eugi's amusement, and finally arrived about twenty minutes later than planned. The narrow Tavern was long, hazy with smoke, and very busy - every dining booth was occupied. By the time he reached the far end, he saw no sign of Naomi or Claudie and wondered if they were acting as strangely as Agatha. But then he found his attention drawn to a white poster on the very far wall..

"LOST: Slightly Bewildered Person. Answers to the name of Bob(s). Last seen looking at this poster."

Someone had drawn a frowny-faced stick man underneath a question mark, scratching his head and clutching a rucksack. The real Bob was puzzled, too. A drinks mat bounced off the back of his head and he turned around to see Naomi and Claudie waving from a corner booth.

"That was my idea - do you like it?" called Naomi.

"And I did the picture - it's just like you!" added Claudie.

Bob sat down with them, in the semi-circular bay.

"Yes, it's an uncanny similarity. It's like you took every part of my personality, and put it up there on a piece of paper - in just ten wavy lines. One day, that'll be worth a fortune, but in the meantime.."

"Glad it's liked, Bobs. Now let's order - we're both starvin'.."

"Me too. I'm so hungry I could eat a hippo, a giraffe, and all their friends as well," said Bob, picking up a tall handwritten menu.

"I don't think they do that. You might have to settle for a few grilled sandwiches instead," said Naomi.

"Okay, just as long as they're elephant ones. With a side salad, of course - nice and healthy."

"You have to be careful, Bob. Claudie doesn't eat meat anymore, ever! She might give you one of her looks.." whispered Naomi from behind her menu.

"Yep. It's a big No Go, Joe," confirmed Claudie, from behind hers.

"Really? None at all? Wow. I refuse to eat anything unless it had a face - and I'll pay extra if it had a name as well."

Naomi laughed, and Claudie tried not to.

"It's lambs that got me. Too cute. That's what put me off all meat."

"Yeah, I know what you mean. A similar thing stopped me eating puppies, and as for kittens.. I won't order them at all nowadays. Flambé, roast, grilled, I won't touch them. Too darn cute."

They all laughed and soon gave their orders to the waitress. Naomi had a joke to share.

"Okay, I've got the best joke you ever heard. Ready? My dog has no toes. No, wait a minute.. no feet.. so he can't dance.. or something like that. He's missing something and it's so f'nee, really it is.."

"Thanks Nay, I'll remember that one. So Bobs, you've been chauffeured in Dame A's Bug? You seem to have survived, too."

"Yeah, but it was only one way though, and that was a life-altering experience. I dread to think how that car works. Everything was going fine at the buffet, but then I went to get some drinks and when I came back Aunt Agatha had left without saying anything. That's why I was so late getting back to the office. Does she often do that?"

Naomi took over, while Claudie fended off a no-hoper of a would-be suitor with a glare.

"Well, we tend not to question what she does, or at least if we do we phrase it really carefully. I think she got back not long after twelve but like Claudie said, she had a certain mood about her so we're treading carefully, especially after the bad start this morning.."

"Has she mentioned the bump on her head?"

"No, and it's probably a bad idea for anyone else to mention it."

Bob wasn't listening. He was staring wide-eyed at the entrance to the Tavern, where a couple had just entered twice. The first time they came in was perfectly normal, the same as anyone else would, but then they were instantly replaced by themselves coming in again.

"Did you see tha.."

Bob pointed and managed to knock over Claudie's tall glass of special-reserve Orange Crush. It fell over, shattering and spilling its contents across the table and over Naomi, who didn't react at all. She had moved on to saying something about seeing a film, but when she reached the end of the sentence, she spoke it backwards while Claudie's glass returned back to normal, full again.

Bob looked around as dozens of people repeated their actions, and watched as the repetition became briefer as time seemed to catch up with itself. Claudie's glass righted itself for the fifth or sixth time before Bob realised what was happening. He ran out of the Tavern and into the street, and knew a Mirror had to be somewhere nearby. A stolen Mirror so near to its 1927 version - plus the other four from 1927 as well, would be causing an Unavoidable Catastrophe Thing, or whatever Agatha had called it.

Bob darted into the road, turning around and around trying to look in all directions at once as drivers swerved to avoid him. He climbed on top of a huge Chrysler parked by the kerb and managed to see an open-back truck partially fading and re-appearing as it made its way along East 18th. Buildings, people and cars dipped in and out of invisibility as it drove past. He knew he could never keep up on foot, so he leapt from the car and ran for all he was worth back to Lexington Avenue.

Bugsy was parked in a small side road, nestled in the afternoon shade of the building, still with the canopy down. Panic was racing through Bob's veins, and he hurled himself over the passenger door, landing more or less on the front seats, and began desperately flicking switches and pushing buttons to try and get it started.

"How did she do it? How did she do it? Where's the start button? Just go, would you? Move your ar.."

A wildly excitable voice answered him back.

"Woah, ee'sa you again! Like you gotta talk like dat, huh? Now whatsa-prablem 'bino?"

"Huh? Oh brilliant.. you spoke! YES! You're my third thing - that's way beyond totally cool!"

"Hokay, whatever yoo say. Where we goin' now?"

The engine revved loudly a few times as Bob stood up, leaning on the chrome and wood of the steering wheel and pointing like a General in the direction of where they needed to be heading.

"Uhh.. we need to follow a battered old truck that's turned south off.. umm.. East 18th by Pete's Tavern! Can you do.. WOOOAHHH"

Bob suddenly found himself upside down on the back seat as the car roared from Lexington and tore along Irving Place. As Bugsy slid sideways around the roadworks onto East 15th Bob clambered back onto the front seats. Bugsy was enjoying the trip, and exchanging pleasantries with the other cars around.

"Hey yoo crazy.. mindawhere yoo.. yeah an' yoo too, crayzee schmoe-joe! What's yo'prahblem, stoopid! Say hey, you're Lady Agattuh's li'l friend, yeah? I remember you, you's called.. umm.."

"I'm B.."

Bob's named gained an extra few syllables as Bugsy chose to weave in and out of traffic by using the entire road and most of the broad sidewalks as well. A loud and very gravelly voice shouted from Bob's top pocket.

"Hey, Schmugsy! Why you taking' this route? You ever driven here before? Swing a left at.."

"Not now Eugi, n-n-n-n-n-n-not now-w-w-w-w.."

Bob knew an argument between Bugsy and Eugi could only be a bad idea, especially while tearing along an endless worksite with the speedometer bouncing either side of 120.

As they went past a few buildings that Bob had started to recognise from his previous wanderings, the cars ahead separated into different lanes, revealing the back end of the truck. There was something shining amidst all the junk and canvas. Time-echoes were happening all around it, and Bob was amazed that nobody was noticing what was going on. People were freezing momentarily, other people passed through each other as they walked along, and cars vanished for seconds at a time. Strangest of all though, the contents on the back of the truck were continually falling off, but were also staying where they were. Faded images of boxes and metal poles trembled on the road for a few seconds before disappearing - and no-one paid any attention at all.

"Bugsy! The truck's ahead! Hold back a bit or we'll get spotted.."

Bugsy slowed down and followed a short way behind, taking dozens of rapid diversions along the side-streets of Little Italy before re-appearing in the line of traffic behind the truck. They followed its meandering, peculiar path back onto Broadway, as if the truck's driver wasn't entirely sure where he was going. It finally came to a halt outside the entrance of a three-tiered building that towered gloriously above its neighbours. Bugsy drove along the road a little further and turned around in his own special way, leaving Bob's stomach somewhere far behind them. He parked a few yards down from the truck, in an inch-perfect space between the front and back ends of two huge saloon cars.

A badly dressed workman stepped down from the truck, and hurried inside the huge building. Bob gulped. Even in the summer sunshine, all the endless columns, green peaks, creepy gargoyles, blackened windows and elaborate carvings made this skyscraper..

"..nightmare-spooky.." Bob warbled.

"Dauntingly Gothic, I'd say," Bagshaw corrected him.

Eugi gave the kind of whistle that it deserved.

"Well whad'ya know Bob? You ever heard'a Woolwort's?"

"Woolworths? The shop places?"

"The very same. That there's two-thurdee-three Broadway, the tallest buildin' in the woyld, the Woolwort' Building, centre of that empire, paid for by Mr Woolwort' himself - a mere thirteen million bucks, settled up front furrah big pile uh cash. What a guy!"

"So that's just offices? Not a freaky hotel or anywhere creepy?" said Bob anxiously, "Only it looks like the kind of place Dracula would move into if he ever fancied coming here.."

"Maybez he would, I never met the guy. Nah. It's jus' full of bigshots in big suits, all from big, big companies, 'cuz it ain't all Woolworts in there. An' you seein' people here? Jeez, you must be in the big league.."

Bugsy opened a door for Bob to slide out, and he crouched down behind a wheel-arch to watch what was happening. Two badly dressed workmen were using poles to manoeuvre a heavy grey canvas in the back of the truck. The strange disappearances that had been taking place around them suddenly stopped, and Bob figured that the Mirror must have become completely unwrapped during the journey, and they had at last managed to cover it properly. One of them threw his pole down in frustration, and it clanged across the sidewalk. He jumped onto the canvas and began to impatiently move things around by hand.

"We don't need to waste time with them poles, we'll do it like.." he said to the other worker, who had stayed on the road at the back of the truck. He shuffled around, loosely wrapping the canvas over twice, then held up a long black cord and began to loop it around the underside of the Mirror. The other man tried telling him to stop, but with no real commitment.

"These dopes haven't got a clue what they're doing! Not a clue.." he said, hardly believing what he was watching.

Suddenly an intensely bright silver crescent emerged from one end of the canvas and went near the man's foot. A look of panic swept over his face. The other man threw a spare sheet of the canvas over it, and they both continued the securing process. After a few minutes of swearing and shuffling, they had a small stretcher made up with a pile of dark grey and brown canvas sitting in the centre of it. After a few nervous glances around, they carried it between them into the building.

"You wait here while I'm gone, Bugsy, but if I'm not back in an hour, go find Aunt Agatha okay?"

Bugsy revved an acknowledgement while Bob wrapped the smallest of the blue bags under his shirt and discretely followed.

The building looked eerie and downright sinister from the outside, but once inside Bob thought he'd entered a noisy business-cathedral. Brass, marble and mosaics of coloured glass decorated the high walls and spanned the vaulted ceiling, and wouldn't have looked out of place as an extension for the Ansonia. The voices and footsteps from the busy hordes of ordinary people reverberated around the lobby creating a claustrophobic and intimidating chaos. Bob hurried through the crowds, trying not to lose sight of the two men. He saw them approach two elevators and enter the left one, while shouting at anyone who dared get too near them. Bob struggled from one crowd to another as a new influx of people arrived from a stairway leading from a subway station.

He started running up the staircase, and groaned as he reached the first floor. The lobby had been at least twenty feet tall and he'd taken three flights of stairs just to reach the first floor, which was not far from being another twenty feet tall.

Two floors later, Bob was breathing hard and hoping a throng or two might stop the elevators for a while. Someone did press the right button, and the doors to the left elevator were open as he arrived in the third floor entrance area. He dared follow a small group inside and stood unnoticed in the furthest corner, where he could keep an eye on the stretcher. As the compartment gently rattled back into life the dozen or so people began leaving image-echoes behind, just like he had done back in Arizona when he'd found the first Mirror.

Predictably, no-one seemed to notice, apart from Bob who also happened to notice that his key was starting to glow.

By the time the lift came to its next stop at the 10th floor, Bob was almost melting. The intense heat around his neck was becoming unbearable, and he knew he had to get out very soon. By the 19th floor he couldn't stand any more and made his way to the bell hop.

"This floor for me, please? Let me out now, would you?" he said, as the world started wobbling around him. The doors opened, and Bob stumbled out into cool sanctuary and wiped the perspiration from his face, relieved that the key was returning to normal. The doors closed, and Bob started running up countless flights of stairs again, hoping at each new floor that people would be getting on or off, allowing him a few more valuable moments to recover.

Every couple of stops Bob managed to catch a discrete glimpse of the people inside, but his growing exhaustion made him a little careless. Without thinking, he looked through a group of people and straight at one of the men in the elevator. For just a moment, the man looked straight back at him and Bob saw realisation spread across his face as the doors started to close again - and he knew he'd given himself away.

"Nitwits they may be, but ones tipped off about yourself, I suspect," said Bagshaw, who had been remarkably quiet until this point.

"Any great ideas, then?" whispered Bob, and a passing lady looked at him as if he was crazy.

"Hmm.. yes. Try preparing them a cup of tea laced with an odd red liquid. Myself and some fellows used it in the Congo for knocking out wild pigs around the camp. Worked on a lion, too. I forget the name - the name of the liquid, not the lion. And we didn't give it them in tea, I think we dipped bullets in it.. or a fat local?"

"Cheers Bagshaw, maybe do that later."

"Good show. Did you bring any teabags for them?"

"No, I didn't think to."

"And that red concoction?"

"Nor that."

"Any lions, then?"

"Bagshaw, have a lie down.."

Bob hurried breathlessly up the steps and paused at the next floor.

"Now what?" he thought, trying to take a brief moment to think of a brilliant plan. His mind was made up for him as the doors to the other elevator opened. He ran into the half-full compartment and without a clue how high the building might be, guessed a number.

"Floor 35'll do, thanks," he said between gasps.

The bell hop pressed the button, and the lift moved upwards. Everyone had left by Floor 29, and the key began glowing again by Floor 32. Bob figured he must have caught up with the other elevator, and it stayed warm for the next three floors.

"Floor thuddy-fuhive, sir!" announced the bell hop.

"Sorry, my mistake. Should be Floor 53, not 35, sorry," said Bob, noticing the panel of buttons. The doors didn't move, and the bell hop kept his finger firmly on the OPEN button.

"You have to leave now, otherwise I might start thinkin' you're just a kid ridin' around in a tall building. And that's against The Rules And Regulations, okay?"

The key started going cold again, the bell hop looked smug and weedy, and Bob's brain put all three things together. Summoning a mighty effort, he shoved him as hard as he could, and sent him flying out onto Floor 35's lobby. He pounded the CLOSE button even before the bell hop had landed, and the doors steadily closed as Bob started hammering the top button, marked 53. A few floors later, the glow returned and he breathed a huge sigh of relief.

He reached as far as the elevator would go and stepped into the empty 53rd lobby, not sure of what the next move might be. The dial above the other elevator next to him was moving again, up towards floor 55. Bob groaned, and started running up the remaining flights of stairs. His legs felt like they were full of a very dense jelly, but he ignored the feeling and kept telling himself that Agatha probably knew someone who could sort out a new pair for him. He crawled up the final agonising flight, and lay on the floor feeling a long way from being ready for action. On the plus side, at least it was nice and cool against the stonework.

He looked out across a large grey-marble area at two staircases over on the far side which lead even further up, separated by a narrow elevator. Three comparatively small windows ran on either side of the 55th lobby, and a series of waist-high ellipsoidal brass sculptures stood proudly against each wall. If Bob hadn't felt like he was dying from an overdose of steps, he'd have been quite impressed with it. A minute or two later he was almost able to stand, and steadied himself on the hand rail of the staircase.

"Mental Note: Remember not to fall down this lot, it'll take a whole week to stop.." he told himself, before wondering whether or not to go and tackle the final staircase yet. The elevator made a soft 'dinng' and the doors opened, so Bob changed plan and stayed where he was.

"..takes for ever. Damn it, what the hell is wrong with you? Can't you move or somethin'? We gotta be there an' we're late already! I ain't carryin' the can for you or no-one.."

"I dunno, it's my whole right side.. it's gettin' worse, I'm tellin' yuh Mack, it's this freakin' thing that's screwin' me up - I swear it only touched my foot for a second an' now I'm like pins an' needles right up to my neck!"

"Ah shuddup an' keep movin' you dumb.."

Bob watched as the two workmen made their way across the lobby, and stared in disbelief as the man carrying the front end collapsed near the stairs. The Mirror fell with him, and lay shining brightly against his side. The one called Mack backed away, standing just a few feet from Bob. He seemed to be scared and livid.

"Put the sheets back over it!" he shouted, "Cover it an' I'll help yuh, jus' cover it over first!" he shouted, as if it was his life that was at risk.

"I can't feel anything.. I can't move.. c'mon, help.. please for mercy's sake.. help!"

Bob had to make a move. He stood up and ran into the lobby.

"I can help you here! I can cover it properly!"

The man with the Mirror looked with unseeing eyes over to Bob. His hair quickly turned grey, his skin began to wrinkle and his body seemed to be collapsing on itself.

"What the hell is all this.." said Mack, as he and Bob watched in shared horror. Seconds later the Mirror lay resting beside no more than a layer of dust and fragments of clothing. The canvas remained undamaged, still exposing part of the Mirror which glowed with a neon silver that started to fill the room. A look of wild panic filled Mack's eyes as he turned to Bob, pointing straight at him and then at the Mirror.

"Mother of.. I'm gettin' the others! You see that? That's gonna happen to you! Oh you are dead meat, dead meat!"

The man grabbed Bob by the arm and hurled him across the room towards the the Mirror. Terrified, Bob watched as it came closer and closer, helpless to stop himself landing on it. He lay motionless, waiting for something bad to start happening, while Mack ran up the stairs shouting to whoever might listen.

But nothing happened. Bob lay on his front with the Mirror underneath him, waiting to start crumbling.. and waiting. Slowly, he raised himself up, and kneeled beside it. He slipped a hand into his shirt, and began pulling out the protective Encapsulation Field, and dropped it over the arc. The light disappeared and he sat for a moment, unable to feel any emotion as he realised how close to a horrendous death he had just been.

Slowly, and very, very carefully, he began edging the bag along the Mirror's curves, unaware for a moment that footsteps were coming from high up the far stairs - and also from down the near stairs. He drew the cord to seal the unit and realised his problems weren't quite over. Both stairways were ruled out, and the main elevator had long since departed. The dial showed it was all the way down at the 18th floor, and for a split second Bob wondered how long it might take to get back up where he needed it. Six possible exits remained, none of which were very appealing - they were the windows. Bob picked up one of the heavy sculptures and hurled it towards the nearest one of them. It bounced off, but the glass shattered, allowing him to punch through and clamber outside, dragging the Mirror behind him. Half a dozen people poured into the lobby, and raced to the window.

The ledge barely extended beyond his feet, and its intricately carved terra-cotta spikes poked into the air every few inches, but for the first few moments that didn't matter at all. Bob had the Mirror and he needed to get away from those freaks, and he soon managed to side-step along to the far end of the ledge, just a few feet beyond the last window of the 55th floor. And there was nowhere left to go.

For a short while, there was nothing but beautiful silence around him and he stood clutching the prize hard against his chest, feeling like he had won a huge victory for The Good Guys. But then the wind changed. Suddenly the most awesome wall of unrelenting power pressed him against the building, and he felt his feet rising an inch or two away from the ledge. He couldn't move, he couldn't see, he couldn't think. And then it left as quickly as it came, and he found himself standing on the ledge again, with his head in a minor spin. And he was looking down.

If Bob had chosen the windows on the other side of Floor 55's lobby, he would have been less than ten feet above the roof of the Woolworth Building's second tier. But he wasn't. Instead, he was on the side that had very few interruptions. All it had was a sheer drop of more than seven hundred feet, broken only by one or two ledges and a few bird's nests. There must have been at least twenty floors to the next narrow ledge, followed by another long drop to the next, and maybe an even further drop to the last one - but that one was the sidewalk, which didn't really count.

Bob whimpered. About one million miles below his shoes, ant-like black cars travelled very slowly along the roads, streams of tiny people made their tiny journeys, and multitudes of dots sailed to and fro along the Hudson River and the East River. He had a great view, in a way, but all he could think about was how lucky everyone else was to be doing their own safe things exactly where they were supposed to be doing them - at ground level.

His stomach plunged to the street and then bounced so high it started orbiting somewhere around Pluto, and then his heart did exactly the same. Bob knew it was a long shot, but there might be the slightest chance that Eugi and Bagshaw would be able to help.

"Hey, err.. guys? You listening? I need some help, and pretty darn quick. We're in what's known as a Monumental Predicament. Ideas now, huge ones please!"

Bob swayed as a milder wind blew against the side of the building.

"Well boss, ways I sees this, you an' trouble go together like a dog an' fleas. An' you gotta lotta fleas. Dis ain't good. Dis ain't good at all. I seen good sitchewayshuns an' bad sitchewayshuns, an' dis ain't a good one. Dis - is a bad one," explained Eugi, "See, if you go left, you gonna run outta ledge in like three inches, and even if the ledge wen' all the way 'round, you'd jus' wind up back here again. An' if you go right, it's like the same thing but the other ways 'round. An' you sure ain't goin' up cause there ain't much 'up' left up there to go up, which leaves you wid'.."

"Two distinct options, I'd say old boy!" piped Bagshaw.

"Two? Cheers Bagshaw, fire when ready."

"Rather. The first involves a hasty direct retreat to the pavement, which would take you away from the danger zone but might render you out-of-action for numerous weeks."

"Yeah, I agree wid dat guy. He's got smarts," added Eugi, keenly.

"And the other option requires the use of your flying carpet. I once saw one in the Middle East. A magnificent sight, although it was somewhat dark at the time.. think I was in Luxor.."

"Yeah! Get on one o'those carpets like he says. Those Ay-rabs got the right idea wid all that!"

"Oh thanks. Thank you both sooo much. Slight problem springs to mind. WHAT FLYING CARPET? And what gave you the stupi.."

A man in a dark glasses leaned through the window.

"Hey, dumbass! You wanna hand that over, or do we just pick it up off the sidewalk in a couple a-minutes?"

Bob didn't answer - he was too busy praying for a flying carpet to appear. A long pole emerged from the window, and began to be manoeuvred towards him. A woman leaned out beside the man.

"This can be so real easy kid, it doesn't have to involve anythin' bad happenin' to you!" she called.

Bob didn't entirely believe her, and was going to shout something back to buy more time, when a wind stronger than anything he'd ever felt blew him so hard against the wall that once again, he couldn't move. After a few long seconds it died away, and he dropped back onto the ledge. The voices of the man and woman became audible again, and they were both shouting at him.

He looked over to his side, out across the East River and Brooklyn. If he was on the inside of the building, he would have admired the view for a long time, but right now it was absolutely terrifying. However, he did notice a small balcony about twenty feet down, and just as far to the left. It would involve a jump across a truly insane gap, but he knew he had to go for it. There just wasn't a choice. He shuffled to his right, back towards the final window, to give himself something resembling a run up, while watching the pole intently as it banged and clanked against the wall, ever closer.

The bag started to slip in his hands, so he tried to lift it up and get a better grip on it. A swirling blast of wind from the east brushed him and caught the Mirror, and he struggled to keep his balance. He desperately tried to steady himself but his foot broke through another spike and for a long, horrifying moment Bob felt himself teetering on the brink of balance before starting to fall forwards, twisting in the air, unable to stop himself.

He watched in slow motion as the safety of the ledge drifted further away from him, moving further and further as a tidal wave of panic swept through him, almost pushing the ledge higher above him, higher and higher and.. it all became too much and his fear began leaving him, replaced by visions of the simple things in life drifting through his mind. Refilling shelves with special-offers at his parents' shop, Andie choosing new favourite pebbles off the beach, Stan and Ollie dancing in Way Out West, yo-yo tricks and coffee at The Coffee Pot, Andie doing nothing much, Andie just being Andie.. just being everything in the world that mattered to him.

An overpowering sensation of heartbreak and loss swept through him as he realised that he'd never see her again, she'd be on her own, and he couldn't be with her ever again. Waves of darkness and powerful light filled his mind and he began sensing that he was being carried by a tide, far away to a safe place where none of the chaos around him meant anything any more. This was the end, and maybe it had all come and gone too quickly, but that's how life could be for some people, and that was just fine by Bob. It was such a safe feeling that he hoped it would never, ever end..

..and at that precise moment the wind briefly and abruptly changed direction and a strong northerly blast threw him hard against the building, keeping him pressed against the cold stone before dropping him down, letting him fall further and further until..

"Yes? Do you have an appointment to see someone? Or are you making a delivery? Hello?"

Bob lay on the floor at the foot of a desk, still clutching the Mirror in its bag. The face of a bored secretary appeared over the edge. If this was Heaven, Bob wasn't impressed. Where were the soft fluffy clouds, the friendly angels and the gently drifting sounds of Enya?

"Yes, you down there. Do you have an appointment?" she said, in a penetrating voice.

Bob's eyes drifted over to the window he'd just arrived through. It was the kind that opened outwards from the top, so that nobody inside the building could fall out - but a very fortunate idiot could fall in. It must have been designed by a complete genius. He stood up in a daze, and stared across the desk at the secretary. She wagged her pen at him.

"Well I hope you've learned your lesson - use the elevators like everyone else in future. Now if that blue package needs signing for, please leave it here or I might have to call Security. Or maybe you're just lost? Some people do get lost in this building, they really do. Are you even listening to me? Look, the elevators are over there, so you just run along now, like bye bye and I hope your day gets better."

Her hand hovered over the telephone, and Bob wandered over in the direction of wherever she was pointing. The elevator doors were already open, and a thin bell hop watched Bob all the way across.

"Well now, look who it is! Ground Floor for you, Mr Pushy-Pushy?" he said, with a very formal tone.

"Huh?"

"This is Floor Four-dee Two. Do you need the Ground Floor? That's a polite way of saying you're to get your butt outta this building, buddy."

"Floundoor yes.. very slow, slery very slow.."

Bob felt like he was walking through a dream as he left the elevator and wandered through the building's great hallway. The modern gargoyles looked down and silently laughed, or at least he thought they did. Bugsy was dutifully parked outside the entrance doors, and his engine started ticking over as Bob put the Mirror out of sight under a white fur rug on the back seat.

"Was that-a-you up there, 'bino? Alllll the way up there, was that a-you? Up in the clouds, allll the way up thayrr? Wooohoo! I backed up three whole blocks for a view!"

Bob took a few steps towards the Woolworth Building and tried to look up to where he had been standing. He kept looking further up past windows and floors, and up, and up, and then further and then even further up until the building became too tall to see and he fell over backwards. A few passers-by saw him and laughed at what they thought was just another dumb tourist taking a Manhattan Fall. However, from Bob's horizontal perspective this was much better. He started pointing all the way up to the top.

"I.. I fell off the.. fell off the building.."

A pair of pink shoes stopped beside his head, and a friendly woman looked down at him.

"Are you okay there, fella?"

Bob looked at her and carried on pointing.

"I.. I fell off the.. fell off the building.."

"Oh, I don't think so. You wouldn't be pointing back up there if you fell all that way.. don't feel too stoopid, tourists are always doin' what you just did!"

A police officer strolled up, and looked down at him as well.

"Hey there son, it's an oh-fence to lie down in the public doh-main all day. Where'd you come from?"

Bob tried glancing at him, but couldn't take his eyes off the top of the building. He carried on pointing.

"I.. I fell off the.. fell off the building.."

"Now then, you know and so do I know, that did not happ-enn, did it son? I'm try-hing to help you. Now, how'd you get here?"

"I.. I fell off the.. fell off the building.."

The cop bent down and helped Bob back onto his feet. His head started to clear a little and he pointed a wavering finger at Bugsy.

"Thanks.. offel.. offus.. officer, this.. that's my car, so I can go now, thank you.."

The driver's door swung open as Bob walked over to it, and swung shut with a loud thunk as he sat down in the driver's seat. The officer placed a firm hand on the top of the windscreen.

"You're nat old enough to drive a vee-hickle in the state of Noo York. Please stip ay-way from thiss vee-hickle."

Eugi offered Bob some advice.

"Stay put an' tell dat Blue the truth! You ain't the one who's driving so you ain't likely tuh be doin' nuttin' wrong!"

Bob felt that such an argument might not work, and tried to think of a better one. His brain was still up at the top of the building, and the best he could do was to stare blankly back at the cop.

"Sir, it is also a criminal oh-fence to consume any alcoh-holic prohdoos in the state of Noo York. Have you at any stage tooh-day.."

Bugsy's patience had finally run out.

"Say 'bino, tell dat guy to go.."

The rest of Bugsy's words were lost as the rear tyres screamed and squealed into action, surrounding Bob in clouds of smoke and the stench of roasting tarmac. Eugi shouted a few words of encouragement as they roared onto Broadway and Bob's brain started working for a moment.

"Hey Bugsy! Hey! Not Lexington, not with this! We need The Ansonia up at.. umm.. ohhh.."

Eugi helped out.

"We gotta hit Broadway 2107 and miss all uh them STOP signs. Jeez, I hate them signs. Move, move, move!"

Bob tried to add something.

"But nice and steady, nice an.. WOOOOAHHHH!"

Bugsy ignored Bob and followed Eugi's advice, cranking loudly through the gears while explaining his plan to Bob.

"We gonna have a few li'l detours again, to throw de crazy bad guyz offa the scent, okay 'bino? With de Lady Aggatuh, no-one sees us, but with you, I dunno. So we go the long way, yey?"

Bob was in no condition to reply as he rolled around the front seats. Once again Manhattan passed by in a chaotic blur of colours, sounds, squeals and bumps. His senses returned with each jolt as the journey wore on, and he started to notice Bugsy's insane way of driving. If there was a gap, Bugsy would aim for it - and if there wasn't one, he'd still aim for it. He even had a theory, courtesy of Agatha, built upon the principle that the faster you go, the less space you take up, so accidents were far less likely to happen. Bob whimpered as Bugsy explained it for the third time, and was glad to tumble down into the footwell where he couldn't see what was happening any more. Eventually they slid to a long screeching halt, and he crawled up onto the driver's seat.

"Well here's yoh place 'bino, d'Ansonia!"

Any senses he'd managed to gather in the car were lost again as he stumbled onto the pavement. He stared in complete disbelief.

The Ansonia's impressive entrance was all but completely destroyed. The tall majestic doors were gone, leaving only splintered beams of wood hanging despondently in their place. The heavy stone column on one side had been shattered, and the ornate stonework above the doors was cracked wide open, through the middle. Officials with clipboards swarmed around while police were stopping people from walking past.

"You can go home now, thanks Bugsy.. if you see Aunt Agatha, tell her everything," said Bob in a shaking voice, as he removed the Mirror and then patted Bugsy on a headlight. With such devastation all around, nobody looked twice at the strange person talking to a car.

"Ahm off, yoo jus' call when you needin' me! Arrivederci, 'bino!" he hollered, and then beeped a few times to get other cars out of the way, but no-one paid any attention to the driverless car tearing down Broadway.

The heavy silence was interrupted only by the sounds of small stone debris falling onto the sidewalk, along with the quiet conversations of builders who were milling around and trying to assess the damage.

Bricks and stonework lay strewn everywhere, and Bob carefully worked his way up the hotel's wide front steps, stepping through the weak streams of water which were running into vast murky puddles that had spread far along the street. The reception hall looked as if a dozen bombs had gone off while a massive earthquake was taking place. The chessboard floor was buried in white plaster, the fountain was missing almost an entire side, and the ceiling was full of huge cracks allowing brief waterfalls of dust to cascade down. The huge chandelier hung at an angle, ominously swaying and creaking back and forth while being watched closely by nervous porters. Bob felt cold ice spread all over his skin as he realised the people who did this must have been trying to kill him.

He picked his way towards the stairs, and took a moment to look at the place where the reception desk used to be. All but its far end was demolished - even the large panel with all the keys was gone, and nothing seemed to be where it should be, anymore. The dancing girl no longer held her clock - only her feet and shattered glass remained, surrounded by stone and chunks of the walls and fountain.

The stairway was blocked by collapsed pillars and masses of wrecked wood, and had been sealed off with great swathes of rope and yellow tape. Bob felt sicker than he'd ever felt. Not getting back to Agatha's suite couldn't be an option, but if this was the state of the hotel's entrance, what condition would his floor be in?

At that moment, a sharp 'ding' from the elevator resonated through the lobby, and its dusty, bent-iron safety doors opened. Bob looked around, but nobody was paying any attention to either it or him. He waited for as long as he dared, seeing if anyone appeared likely to seal it off. Nobody bothered, so he waited a little longer. Then a little longer. And then he stepped inside.

If the day had been any less stressful, he might have thought twice about doing so in the middle of such carnage, but at that moment the thought never crossed his mind. In fact nothing crossed his mind until the doors began to shake themselves closed, and he watched the huge central chandelier fall with an almighty echoing smash onto the remains of the fountain. He listened as a large part of the ceiling followed it - and the elevator began climbing upwards.

Bob gulped. The strains of metal pushing against metal and then dragging against wood filled the compartment and seemed to slice through him. Every few seconds the journey came to a grinding halt as the cables screamed in protest before managing to struggle on. The floor and sides continually rattled from huge vibrations, and Bob's heart pounded wildly as he clutched the Mirror tightly, praying for the sixteenth floor to arrive.

After a lifetime the floor dial almost showed '16' and the doors began trying to open. As soon as there was enough space for him to get through, he squeezed out and immediately sprawled onto the floor - the elevator had stopped just short of the right level. For a long second Bob almost felt stupid, but didn't have time to finish the thought before a loud series of snapping sounds gave way to a tormented wrenching noise. Before he could even turn and look behind himself, the lift plunged from sight chased by thick, flailing cables. Clanging metal echoed around the elevator shaft until a phenomenal crash sent clouds of warm dust billowing up into the sixteenth lobby.

He lay still, trembling for what felt like a very long time. Part of his mind tried to figure out if he'd been closer to death now, or twenty minutes ago. Much more of this, he decided, and he might consider retiring and living in a very small box surrounded by huge mattresses, in a cave somewhere very far away.

He stood up and looked over at the stairs. The walls were completely ripped apart in places, and huge chunks of wooden pillars were missing. The entrance doors withdrew shakily as he approached, and with an ever-increasing sense of dread he made his way through the destruction and blown-apart rooms to 963 - or at least, to what should have been Room 963. There was no door, and there was practically no wall. Bob hardly dared enter through the suite's enormous gaping mouth. The large central table was lying in a million splintered pieces, chairs lay fractured on their sides, curtains had fallen down, and the rugs were just rippled masses covered in bricks and dust. Everything had been destroyed.

One remaining curtain blew inwards, and Bob could see that nearly all the windows were either shattered or missing. Fragments of the apartment crunched under his feet as he walked through the nightmare, and he finally stood before the portal. He clutched the Mirror and prayed that it would still be functioning.. and had to hold back tears of relief as the archway sprang into life.

He found himself back in the familiar and undamaged surroundings of Number 107, and set about trying to block the Master Bedroom doorway. He manoeuvered a couple of chairs in the way, and wished he'd taken Claudie's new lighter, just in case Troublers were lying in wait. Eventually a very makeshift job was complete which wouldn't stop him from going back to New York, but might cause some problems for a return journey. It crossed his mind that he would be the most likely victim of his own security trap if he came back before any Troublers did, so he moved the chairs back over to the Arizona doorway and decided to rely on Claudie's latest weapon, on his next visit.

He changed for Barton, picked up the Mirror, and nervously went down the stairs, step by step, expecting a loony to jump out at any second. His bike was still outside the driveway, and he cycled as fast as he could to Pierpont House, chased all the way by wild paranoia.

He rode up the steps, and after one of his less-memorable sliding stops, he untangled himself from the bike, a rug, a coat stand and two chairs. He put the Mirror on the desk in front of Feiya, who missed the table with her coffee mug in her eagerness to start checking it. Jinx was purring out of sight by her feet, and leaped onto the desk to avoid the hot coffee.

"You won't believe how I got this, Fey.. I chased.."

"How interesting, do stop talking."

"..up to the top and I fell off.."

"Okay then carry on, it's so VERY interesting.."

"..really high up as well, and then I took Aunt Agatha's car.."

"Look at me, on the edge of my seat. No, don't stop.."

"..and they've blown up The Ansonia.."

"I do hope you haven't finished yet.."

"..and a bloke went really old and disappeared.."

"Could I care less? Hmm, let me try.. no, I couldn't care less. Perhaps you'll carry on when I could care less? Tell you what, come back when I'm asleep and have a go then. In the meantime I'll take this which is the.. ahh the Distant Past.."

Jinx quietly meowed in self-pity, and then started purring as she licked coffee from her shoulders. She seemed to quite like it.

"But you're pleased now that you've got three of them, right?"

"Three's not five, is it? We need all five. However, three's better than two.. so yes, in a way I am pleased. And you'll be pleased to know that because there's now three Mirrors, we'll be able to get a better representation..erism of where one or maybe both of the other Mirrors might be. All we know so far is that you're going to be wandering around Turkey sometime in the 1970s. Or maybe a little earlier, in the 970s, because 9s and 10s can be tricky at times. And we're not sure if it's AD or BC, because Naomi's always had trouble with those two."

"Turkey? Give or take a millennia or two? You couldn't be the teeniest bit more specific?"

"No, but when we can be I'll go and see my Personal Assistant and inform her over a cup of tea and maybe some of her mum's caramel cake. And I'll hand your compass over to her as well - life should get a little easier for you if we give him a good idea of where you're going. My P.A. will then inform you of any developments, as and when she judges appropriate."

"P.A? Oh, you mean Andie. Fair enough. Any chance of a tea?"

"I don't know, have you got a kettle at home? Jinx might be outside your driveway already."

Bob stared down at Jinx, who had curled up on the table to get the last of the coffee out of her tail. He handed Eugi over and sensed Feiya wasn't in the best of moods, so he decided to head back home. As he cycled back, he felt as if he'd gone through a wall of tiredness. He suddenly felt too worn out to even drop in and talk about things with Andie, which had to be a sign of either complete exhaustion, or of being dead. Instead, he started wondering how long he had been up, and as always, he had absolutely no idea. He sleepwalked up to his room, watched the opening credits of something familiar and immediately fell asleep.

CHAPTER TWENTY EIGHT

Upstairs & Downstairs

Thursday 19th March, 7.15am

"So I'm off to Turkey then? Should I pack anything?"

Andie looped her Thursday yo-yo in a huge, flashing arc, landed it snugly in her pocket and looked over to the wide entrance of the bus station. There was no sign of bus-life anywhere.

"Okay, here's the score at half time. We're 3-0 up but we need 5 to be sure of victory, so you've got to go off to Istanbul. And Fey says that Claudie says that wherever the room takes you, as long as you're in Turkey, you have to head for Istanbul. If you miss Turkey completely then you're to come straight back and try another room instead. Oh, and Naomi sorted out the date. You won't be needing a toga or anything like that, but maybe some big flares and a huge fuzzy Jackson Five wig might be useful. Imagine you looking like that! I think 1973 would suit you!"

Andie laughed at the thought and Bob tried to give a genuinely amused smile, but it didn't quite work. He was too concerned that there might be tall buildings in Istanbul, maybe even taller than The Woolworth Building. He didn't like that one bit, and managed to miss what Andie was saying..

"Hello Bob? Hello-o-o-o-wuh? Anyone home?"

Andie waved as if she'd just met him.

"Huh? Sorry, I was miles away. Are there skyscrapers over there? I had the official Worst Time Ever on one. Don't recommend it.."

"Well, if it did have any, tv people would mention it like they do whenever they talk about New York, wouldn't they? Or there would be famous pictures of them - which there aren't, so you don't need to worry about that, do you? Besides, I'll take Eugi to the Library for some more research at lunchtime, and Bagshaw can come too. We'll grab plenty of books and get on the internet as well, so don't worry about your detention spoiling things, okay?" she said, tightening the string up on her yo-yo.

"Oh no.. the detention.." Bob groaned. He'd forgotten about his lunchtime Linguistic Misappropriation Detention.

"Yeah, but that's no prob. You can have them back afterwards so you'll be really well-prepared for once, like Batman with a new utility belt. I think 'Hooray for Andie' are the words you're looking for."

"Yes, in capital letters with a thick pen. That'll be such a help if those two know something.. really useful."

"Exactly, so there's nothing to worry about.. apart from today's bus. Aww, look at it! Not that one again.."

There was one particular bus which occasionally turned up for the school trip which was at least twenty years overdue for a service. The worn seats rattled, wind blew through gaps in the bodywork, the road passed by through the splits in the floor, and it provided the only occasions when everyone would cheer to reach the school.

But Bob didn't mind today. He was pleased. In fact, not too long after Andie had fallen asleep, he almost felt on top of the world. He couldn't work out how long it had been since he had last felt as good about anything as he did now. Reason Number One was that Andie didn't think he was some kind of freak, and Alternative Reason Number One was that she seemed to get on even better with his new friends than he did. The only downside was that Jinx was still being an awkward and creepy monster-beasty-from-hell, but given enough time that might change. Right now, things were good. And just to make everything even better, Istanbul wasn't famous for having stupendously tall buildings.

The morning was bound to drag by. Bob stood in the Assembly thinking about what might be lying in wait for him, then sat through double Geography wondering when Jinx might turn up, and by the time Norwegian Literature was over his mind had stumbled into completely surreal areas. He was wondering if he ought to hire a team of bodyguards or a private army to go with him to Turkey.. and the day kept on dragging as if it had dropped anchor at sunrise.

The Ynglinga Test jumped out at him just before lunch, and would have gone a whole lot better if only so much time hadn't gone by since he'd tried revising for it. The only question he was sure about was the first one - 'Name:'

The lunch horn sounded its long blast, and Andie hurried to the library with Bagshaw and Eugi in her bag to brush up on all things

Turkish. Bob went off to the Lunchtime Detention Room, which was a small one near the top of the Science Block, usually reserved for specific lectures. The room was empty, and for a moment Bob thought that he might be able to go and join Andie. But then Ms Gibben arrived, looking annoyed, cross, flustered, and no doubt a multitude of other bad moods.

"Just you then, is it? What a surprise. Sit down and get on with something then, and if I hear one word or sound from you, you'll get so many detentions that this room'll be named after you."

She finished her threat with a haughty sniff, and Bob decided to tackle the evening's Non-Nordic Geography homework. There was a pretty good chance he wouldn't be able to do justice to an essay regarding 'The Nomadic Tribes Of South Yemen: Should They Settle Down?', with two Mirrors needing to be returned by midnight.

Ms Gibben sighed loudly and scraped her chair closer to her desk. She opened the first of a big pile of books, sighed again and began marking while eating a sandwich. After a few minutes, she giggled quietly. Bob ignored her, and assumed she had found a particularly stupid answer. A few more minutes passed, and she did a snorted kind of giggle. Bob let that pass as well, but soon glanced up and noticed she was taking some very big sips from her flask's plastic cup, and her cheeks had a definite flush to them. Bob was no great expert but he figured there was either a hint of alcohol in her coffee, or more likely, a hint of coffee in her alcohol.

She filled the cup right to the brim, and moved her head down to it rather than risk spilling any. Bob propped his forehead with his hand so he could glance between his fingers to see her drain the cup. And then she drank straight from the flask, forgetting the cup completely. She rocked forwards on her seat, no longer overly-concerned about marking.

"Well Bob.. ah Bob.. Bob.. Bob-buh. How's your lovely father these days? He's such a nice man, he really is. I haven't seen him for weeks and weeks.. but whenever I have a prescription, I make sure he does it for me. Very puhfessional gentleman, your father.."

Bob wasn't sure how much more he could take. He still hadn't quite come to terms with falling off the Woolworth Building, being hassled by a shark in a lifeboat, shooting someone who could see through fog, and also causing The Ansonia to get wrecked. This was almost one frightening situation too far.

"Uhh.. he's fine thanks. And how's your rash? I hope it's cleared up 'cause I'd hate to have one down there."

"What? Well if you must know it's all gone now and my ankles are fine.. the ointment worked very well indeed, so you tell your father that from me. As I was saying, I always think to myself 'what a really nice man' whenever I see him.. such caring eyes.. and a genuine smile as well.." she added in a long breath, and rested her chin onto her hand, grinning vacantly to herself.

Bob started getting more than a little uncomfortable. This conversation was going in a very disturbing direction. Hopefully Jinx might show up and wipe it all from his memory. Ms Gibben tipped the flask upside down and held it above the cup, tapping its end for the last few drops.

"Ooh yes, a lovely man indeed. Nice. You know something? I bet you didn't know that we're the same age - how about that?"

"What? You're thirteen like me? That's incredible.."

"No you idiot, your father and me! Why can't you ever be normal for once like all the other trolls in this Nordic pleb-house? Now shut up for the rest of the detention, or uhh.. you can have.. lots more for the rest of the year. Now just you remember to say 'hello' to your lovely father when you get home, and tell him I'll be in to see him as soon as something else goes wrong with me.. else you'll get lots of detentions."

Bob nodded and stared out of the window. How slowly could this pass? Finally the clock's ticking was drowned out by the double-blast of the horn signalling the end of lunch, and Bob escaped back to the 3B Form Room. Andie was already waiting, and looking very pleased with herself. She pushed a BreezyEezyBuy bag into his school bag, and very discretely brought him up to date.

"Here you go, your two well-educated friends back safe and sound. I hope they took it all in, because I found loads of stuff! I'm pretty sure that Eugi The Compass read maps off the internet, and that Bagshaw The Book had a chat with a Classics Guide about its section on Istanbul. How good is that? And I found out stuff too. Did you know.. oh actually that can wait, it's not really that important."

"No, go on you can tell me - I bet it is important."

"Really, it isn't. Okay then. Turkey became a Republic in 1923."

"I see. That is important, but you'd have to be Turkish to know why, wouldn't you?"

"Yes. But there's something else as well. The best thing is that there are definitely no huge tall buildings. They don't like them. I had a good look on the web, especially. Too many earthquakes."

"Aha.. well that's me happy! Thanks for doing all that.."

Bob wondered if he'd missed a chance to say something a little more meaningful than 'thanks' but figured that a classroom loaded with twenty six zoo attractions wasn't the right place.

The afternoon dragged by even more slowly than the morning. Triple History. Triple lessons had been banned for a while and were still pretty rare, mainly due to one of Bob's few genuine friends. The previous June, Barney 'Gawp' Ghorpman had set a school record for staring into space. He managed an uninterrupted one hour and fifty eight minutes, timed by Bob and witnessed by many others over the course of a Friday afternoon's triple Nordic Saga lesson. He only snapped out of his dreamworld when the teacher, Mr Ekelund, fractured Gawp's skull with a hardback copy of Unusual Geometry. Mr Ekelund retired shortly after the incident, but were it not for that book, Gawp would probably still be sitting there now, thinking his thoughts and staring at nothing in particular.

Since then, no class was allowed to stay in the same room for an entire afternoon, and no subjects were allowed to run beyond two consecutive lessons. But every now and then the timetable would allow one to get through the net. In this case, History. By the end of the day, Bob was perspiring and ready to explode with the tension of waiting and waiting and waiting for the trip to Istanbul.

Andie did what she was always so good at. Throughout the day she said the right kind of things to get him to take a step away from himself, and to look at the situation from a different angle. She did her best and shone a very welcome light onto everything, but Bob couldn't shake off the sick feeling that yet another in the series of World's Biggest Exams Ever was just about to happen.

The journey home took forever, and he felt an awful knot in his stomach as his mum dropped Andie off at The Coffee Pot. He certainly didn't feel like much dinner at all, and for the first time in his life he struggled with his beloved deep-fried mushy peas.

He sat in his room and tried to take his mind off everything by watching Steve Martin pursue Daryl Hannah, just as Andie had suggested. It didn't really work, and he just felt worse. And then a question occurred to him, the kind that he would normally ignore, but at that particular moment as CD the Fire Chief climbed into Roxanne's house through an upstairs window, it made perfect sense. Why did Jinx need to be in 107's upstairs window?

Suddenly Bob felt inspired and full of enthusiasm to go for a look around Istanbul. His nerves left him, he made his excuses, and quickly cycled through the falling darkness to Lincoln Drive.

Bob looked at the house in his bike's front light. Jinx was nowhere to be seen, and apart from the spindly branches of the elder tree possibly reaching out a little further, Number 107 looked just like it always did. What difference could a cat make anyway? She was just a moody cat who had been around for a while, that's all. And how many times had she ever been at the other portals? Never. His mind was made up.

He touched the door with his key, but it didn't open. He put the key in properly and rattled it, and still nothing happened.

"So maybe Jinx is important then," he muttered.

He took the key out, and figured he might as well go back home and finish off the film. But as he turned away, the door slowly opened.

"Aha, thank you, Jeeves. Remind Jinx to get here more quickly next time, would you.." said Bob sarcastically to the air as he stepped inside. Perhaps he'd never noticed before, but this time the house felt a little cold. But maybe that was only imagination and nerves, after a day filled with too much waiting?

For just the briefest of moments as he walked towards the stairs, a blurred figure seemed to pass across the other side of the frosted glass door, over at the end of the hallway. He paused for a moment, on the first step. Maybe Jinx was moving around for a change? She had been known to do that. And besides, what was through that end door anyway? He'd never really thought about it until now, and left the stairs.

The key around his neck began glowing as he touched the door's handle, and he flinched. Had he touched the handle, or had the handle touched him? For the most fleeting of moments, he couldn't quite tell. Whatever, the door opened easily and revealed a painted corridor running to the left, across the rear of the building. It was lined with pointed arched windows overlooking the back garden, all deep set in stone. They really belonged in a church, and certainly didn't fit in with the rest of the house. The garden basked in sunshine and Bob could see acres of huge pine trees covering hillsides for miles and miles into the distance, ranging high and low, and all swaying in strong winds. A door swung shut at the corridor's far end, dragging his attention away.

"Jinx? You in here?"

Bob's voice echoed as if the corridor was about a mile long, and yet his words seemed even louder as they ended than they did at the start. He cautiously wandered along the short passageway. Before he tried opening the door at the end, it suddenly occurred to him that the sun was shining outside. Puzzled, he turned around and went over to the windows again, which were no longer arched. They had changed to the conventional rectangular kind, similar to the ones at.. at.. maybe Pierpont, or somewhere. The change simply didn't matter to him, and in a strange way it almost made sense. He stood before one of them and looked out at the very dark evening to watch a few small lights in the distance, quite unconcerned. That was precisely how it should be. He looked over at the blind.

"I expect you'll rattle back up when I'm not expecting it," he said, in a Pre-Emptive Fright-Strike.

The corridor had filled with weak yellow light from somewhere, although Bob wasn't entirely sure if he'd switched any lights on when he came in. It didn't really matter though. He went back over to the door, and peered through the grime-laden glass panel. The kitchen lay beyond, mainly hidden in shadows, but from what he could see, it looked just like a normal kitchen. He jumped as the blind in the corridor clattered loudly as it re-wound itself.

"Well I never," thought Bob, telling himself that it wasn't weird, it was entirely as expected. He went back to looking into the kitchen.

"Large stove, hefty sink, big table.. pots and pans, and no Jinx. Incredible. Possibly the most worthwhile trip I've ever made.."

He turned to go back up the corridor, and paused briefly to look out at the snow-covered trees and mountains through the shattered window panes. His breath formed clouds in the cold air as he watched rows of golden lights dancing through the night sky, miles away. Were they getting nearer, or going away? Hopefully not nearer. He tried to find a better view point, because.. he tripped over a thick tree-root and fell hard against the freezing earth and lay still for a moment, trying to remember if the floor was tiled a moment ago. He decided it couldn't have been, because the carpet of leaves felt deep and were covered in frost, so they must have been there for a very long time. Ages, probably.

He decided it was too cold to stay outside, and that he really ought to get back to the warmth and safety of the fire, so he stood up and found he was already back in the corridor. That was good, and the hallway door at the other end opened. That was even better.

For a moment he thought Andie was standing there, or maybe someone else.. but either way, she was wearing an era-defying black dress with a torn lace collar. Along with her untidy black hair, her skin looked sickly and pallid, and the more Bob looked at her, the less she looked like Andie. She stood in the doorway and stared straight ahead, as if she was unaware of him walking towards her. He stopped, a little to her left.

"Hello? ..err, I think I must be Bob, so that means.. you're who?"

She turned her head to look at him, but her dark eyes remained staring straight ahead. They soon followed the direction of her head, and stopped when they reached him. She pointed to the sunny garden outside, and her jaw dropped into a grin. Bob felt as if his mind was wading through a marsh as he struggled to put two thoughts together.

"I didn't know anyone else could be here - what did you say your name was? Mine was something like.. uhh.. I'm think it was.." he floundered, not sure who or even where he was anymore.

She ignored him, and slowly tried to mouth 'Help me'. Her desperate voice followed a moment later, but it was distant and weak, a kind that didn't belong to her. In slow motion she turned around and ran into the hallway, and Bob tried to follow her through the door, but found it was shut. At the other end of the passage, the door loudly swung open hitting the wall hard as an icy wind tore through the corridor, and the girl stumbled out of the kitchen. The hallway door remained firmly shut as Bob tried turning the handle. She walked towards him, crying so hard her shoulders shook, yet her intense laughter echoed through the entire house. She stopped just a few feet away.

For a moment, Bob felt like he'd woken up. He could actually see the corridor changing and that the sunlight had been replaced by absolute darkness again. Just beyond the arched windows people were carrying lit beacons, and shouting as they ran around in the snow, and then the windows were changing shape again and again.. and then it didn't matter anymore, because the girl was standing just inches away from him, shielding him from the madness outside.. or bringing it nearer, he couldn't tell. All her features were vague and blurred except for her eyes, staring far beyond him, burning straight through him and leaving absolutely nothing unscorched, or unseen.. bringing the slight sensation of a memory back, a feeling of Agatha being there. And then it was gone, leaving him more scared than he had ever been in his life.

She moved suddenly, and her face re-appeared as her laughter and crying raced all around him. He jumped out of her way as she reached to open the hallway door, and he saw himself walking in again to look for Jinx. The girl cried harder and ran away, out into the hall. Bob went after her and tried calling, but he couldn't make a sound or even raise a whisper. He tried again and again, until his throat felt raw and his heart strained with the effort.

The moment he set foot in the hallway, the living room door slammed shut. He ran towards it, not sure if he was looking for the girl or if he was trying to get out. She appeared back in the entrance to the corridor, hunched and distressed against the doorframe, but her hysterical laughter continued loud and breathless inside the living room. The lights began flickering as Bob slipped and staggered his way to the front door. He grabbed the handle, and couldn't quite remember how he'd opened it before. Did he need the key, or could he just turn it, or should he push, or..

Footsteps started scurrying towards him, and he turned to see her racing nearer and nearer, then fading to nothing as she reached him. A cold, cold wind passed through him and he shivered so hard he couldn't breathe. An image of Agatha fleetingly appeared in his mind again, but it was lost, drawn down into a whirlpool of wild, racing emotions. The laughter carried on, echoing through every room and every wall, merging to fill the house with a barrage of high-pitched, echoing hysteria. He forgot about the front door, hopelessly covered his ears and staggered towards the kitchen corridor again.

Suddenly, a huge door upstairs slammed with enough power to shake the entire house, bringing complete silence. Bob lost his footing midway along the hall, and leaned trembling against the wall. The icy air seemed to be cutting into him, and his clouds of breath began freezing in the air. A few long seconds later a booming voice exploding with hate roared through the building.

"WHO IS HERE! WHO DECEIVES ME!"

Once more, total silence followed, apart from the steady ticking of the hallway's grandfather clock. Bob stared at the front door as it melted into the wall.

Hard footsteps thundered back and forth across the floorboards above him, and all the doors started slamming over and over again, soon in unison with the footsteps. Plaster dropped from the ceiling, pictures fell to the floor and the walls shook as the footsteps reached the stairs. They paused at the top before bounding down in three heavy lunges. The parlour door was almost thrown off its hinges by invisible hands, and furniture clattered into the hallway as the hard, freezing wind blowing stronger than ever. Bob curled up, helpless to avoid the flying debris.

"WHERE ARE YOU! WHERE IS THE CAUSE! SHOW YOURSELF!" the voice screamed as it tore from the offices to the kitchen, heightened in its intensity by vicious pounding against the walls as it went. Bob found himself crawling towards the nearest door, which fell flat as he touched it. He managed to get to his knees and stumble into the dining room, and immediately found himself in the kitchen. The room was shaking itself apart and Bob held his arms over his ears to try and block out the sound. He climbed over the upturned kitchen table and fell into the corridor, hitting the floor hard and sliding through a shower of glass all the way to the end. The hall door stayed open until he was near enough for it to strike him into the hallway, where the walls were bending inwards with the relentless beating.

He blindly stumbled back up to where the front door should be, but the living room door, no its two doors, burst open and he fell through to find himself in the parlour, rolling towards the door to the hallway.. but instead found himself for a moment in a dark, freezing forest, running terrified to a small church, before emerging in the dining room. He tripped and slid through tumbling furniture into the living room, only to appear in the garden, lying on his back looking up to a full moon in a clear night sky, watching a huge silhouetted figure swinging an axe towards him. The moment it touched his neck he re-appeared back at the kitchen door hurtling even faster along the corridor. Again the door struck him into the hallway.

He sprawled onto his front, and stood up enough to manage half a step through the chaos. The floor violently shifted beneath him, instantly turning to frozen mud and leaves while icy branches held him back as the hall's weak yellow light began to fade, plunging the house into murky twilight. His lungs were screaming for air but he couldn't hope to breathe. The noise around him wouldn't stop, the relentless pounding wouldn't slow, and the entire house was shaking more violently with its every passing heartbeat. The branches released him and he fell against the grandfather clock by the dining room doors. It had fallen over, spanning the hallway. Its front panel swung from one remaining hinge, and Bob squinted at the darkness inside, knowing if only he could touch it all the madness would end. He reached for it, trying hard to touch the beautiful, serene night.. and felt it pulling him into its eternal depth.

How long he was falling for didn't matter to him. He suddenly felt as if he had landed against some very hard ground, or maybe some very hard ground had landed against him.. but that was okay. The insanity had stopped, and that was all that mattered. The hate and the aggression were gone, and Bob was content to stay on the ground slowly getting his breath back. He didn't move a muscle, not even to open his eyes. The wonderful, peaceful tranquillity was too good to leave behind.

The sound of waves rolling onto the pebble shore somewhere near by gently lulled him back into the world. He blinked a few times, and dared to keep his eyes open long enough to see where he was. His heart jumped as he saw Jinx's eyes staring straight back at him. She was looking down in her all-time most demeaning and superior manner, sitting so close to his face that he could feel her breath. She turned and walked away towards the road, her tail high in the air.

Bob looked around. It was night time, and he was alone. He was lying face down against the entrance drive to Number 107, and his feet were slightly caught in the lower branches of the elder tree, which had shed some of its sparse leaves onto him. Despite looking brittle and angular, the elder branches felt soft and even a little warm as they seemed to untangle themselves from his legs. He rolled onto his back and tried to decide if anything was broken, bruised or missing. Everything seemed okay, which was nothing short of a miracle. That didn't strike him as being in the slightest bit odd. Nothing could ever, ever be odd. He slowly crawled across the driveway, and sat on the damaged old curb.

For a long time he sat with his head in his hands and thought of nothing at all, just listening to the soothing waves rolling against the shore, finding some comfort and stability there. They were the same as they always had been and always would be. He didn't give a thought to which sub-department was responsible for Shoreline Audio-Interaction, or if there even was one. For the time being, the waves simply offered the same steady reassurance that they had always offered him, and the unseasonably warm breeze blowing only the elder tree was just about perfect.

For a change, Bob didn't have to fend off any questions about what was going on, or how time-travel worked, and he certainly wasn't bothered about causes and consequences anymore. Hitting him over and over again were questions like why Agatha ever chose an idiot like him to be the only person in the entire world to have been born twice, and therefore the only idiot who could do anything. How could he save anything? He'd never even managed a decent grade at school in his life, so preventing an impending universal disaster could well be asking a bit much of him. The world felt very, very heavy. The waves kept on rolling, and Bob kept on listening. After a few minutes, a quiet voice called over.

"Hello? Bob old chap? Are you there?"

The compendium lay a few feet away, with its pages fluttering in the wind.

"Yeah.. I'm here.. hi."

"Such unpleasantness, I must say. I'd offer you a cup of tea if I could. Instead there's a rather nice drawing of how to hold your cup correctly, on page 588 in the Etiquette Section. It's the best I can do, I'm afraid. Worth a look, perhaps old chap.."

"Thanks Bagshaw, I'll be there in a minute.. got something in my eye right now.."

"Ah, had a few of those myself over the years. Best to ignore them, keep the old chin up and carry on, more often than not."

"Yeah.. I know.."

Bob sat and listened to the sea for a while a longer. Miles and miles away a ship slowly drifted along, and he watched its flickering row of lights blink until they had faded away into the night. He began to feel like having a serious talk with someone, and there was only one person who he'd be able to talk to. He cycled over to Pierpont

House, and stood in the empty entrance.

"Fey! FEY!"

She appeared from one of the white doors before Bob had even finished calling her name. She put an armful of files onto the desk, and looked at him, surprised.

"Back already? I was unaware you'd.."

"Are you going to tell me what's going on - I mean ever? I went to the other place but Jinx wasn't actually there and I don't know how I'm still alive! And there's no way I'm doing anything else unless you tell me more about what's up there. It's got no rules, it's like an asylum for reality gone wrong."

"You went in without Jinxy, did you? Well you were told not to do that. Remember? What to do and not to do.."

"That's all you can manage, isn't it? Always avoid saying anything. Do you actually know anything after all these years, or do you just make the tea and tidy up for my Great Aunt? Is that all you are?"

Feiya sighed and moved some of her rings onto different fingers. After a minute or two of ignoring him, she knew his anger would be passing. She held her hand far out in front of herself, contemplated which fingers were correctly decorated, and moved a final ring from one forefinger to the other.

"I don't know why that house is like it is, but I'm pretty sure Madame Agatha does - and she never says a word. I only go up there when I have to, or when she's with me - and even then I hear noises or see the most vile shadows moving around, most times. How much did it show you?"

"Show me? It did more than that, it.." Bob shook his head, and gave up searching for the words.

"Itty bit scary?"

"Scary's close. And there was a girl.."

"No, I don't want to know. And don't ever tell Madame Agatha you saw anything - that place is as much a part of her as the Mirrors are.. but I do suppose she's more likely to tell you about it than anybody else, isn't she? Well if she does, could you tell the rest of us, because.." she gushed, stopping herself with a sigh, "..because of no reason. Now then, to recap because you've obviously forgotten, Jinx will be along for you at the right time, which means that any other time is the wrong time. So instead of annoying me, you could go home and make yourself a lovely cup of tea? Allow yourself a

HobNob, perhaps. My Immediate Junior says you like them. But before you go, you'll be wanting this. Jinx retrieved it from an unnecessary mess," she said, wandering over to the stairs.

She held Eugi out at arm's length, waiting for Bob to come across and take it. She dropped it as soon as he was within range, making him hurry to catch it.

"Stay on your toes, Bob. That way they're much less likely to get stepped on. Now, toodle-oo and also bye bye."

She pointed back to the front door and casually drifted up the stairs. Jinx came down, meowed, and even more casually went back up again. Bob despaired. He returned Eugi to his pocket, and began the journey home.

"Are you okay then, Eugi? I didn't know we'd lost you.."

"What the hell wuz all thaddabout? Jeez, don't you ever get a day off? I dunno what Union's gonna be good f'you, but y'sure need one, I'm tellin' yuh. An' what's wid that cat? Jeesh, wayy too many teeth.."

He arrived home feeling shaken and useless, so he did the only thing he could think of - he followed Feiya's advice. Tea and a pile of HobNobs. Life really should be very simple at times. By the time Roger Moore had sorted out a whole load of bad guys as well as a spy who may or may not actually love him, Bob felt a little more like taking on the world again - which still wasn't very much at all.

At the precise moment that his digital clock changed to 9.45pm, Jinx began wailing outside.

CHAPTER TWENTY NINE

Istanbul

Bob nervously approached the house, not sure what to expect. The driveway looked fine, the place was still standing, and Jinx was up in her usual window. However, he knew there was a very good chance that it would be a complete wreck, and with a growing sense of trepidation he left his bike and stood before the front door.

He tried to make himself feel better by devising Bob's Loony Bin Uncertainty Principle, which stated that the world and everything in it was so completely mad that nothing was predictable or reliable, thus all bets were off, for ever and ever, amen.

And he was right. Instead of being confronted with a bomb-site, Number 107 was just how it always was. Nothing was broken, tipped over or even slightly out of place. Even the pictures were hanging neatly in a row. The door at the far end was closed, and Bob decided that it ought to stay that way. He hurried up the stairs, double-triple-checked again that he definitely had both Encapsulation Fields wrapped round his waist, and made his way over to the right, past the tall windows and the Not-The-Master-Bedroom, to the end room - where Jinx was now sitting. The grandfather clock steadily ticked in the corner, ticking and ticking.. and ticking..

"Okay guys," he said in the direction of the book and compass poking out of his Turkishly-Essential Duo pocket, "You two haven't forgotten any of the stuff Andie showed you, have you? We're up a creek if you have.."

"Fret not, Bob! Raring to venture forth unto the great city! I was there for a while back in '71, so I don't expect much to have changed at all! I was most familiar with.."

Bob groaned.

"No, Bagshaw, it's going to be 1973, not 1873. There's a good hundred years of changes."

"Oh, n-i-y-y-nteen sevt'three is it? Oh dear.. I'm afraid we may not get any preferential treatment at certain watering establishments then.. probably all changed hands by now. Shame, shame that."

Eugi coughed and seemed keen to be going somewhere new.

"What dahell is wrong wid you tourist saps? Are we goin' now or are we stayin' put, cuz Istan-whatever shewerr ain't comin' to us!"

The door swung open, keeping a fraction ahead of Bob's fingers, and revealed the split-personality decor of the bedroom beyond. He took a deep breath, kept his eyes fixed on the bright blue chair over by the dressing table..

..and emerged into a re-assuringly luxurious hotel suite. Soft sunlight filled the room with a glow as warm as it was golden, and a clock finished chiming for the sixth time as Bob made his way across to the windows. The walls were painted a subtle peach colour, which complemented the elegant cream furnishing and made for a very calming atmosphere. He decided against going out onto the long balcony, opting to stay safely out of sight instead. He opened a parting in the tall laced curtains and peered out across a sea of rooftops and minarets, reaching high and low over the rolling landscape. Istanbul looked like nine or ten cities all crammed into one, and even the first one was probably overcrowded to start with. Meandering streets seemed to be swallowed up as soon as they started, becoming lost between the myriad shallow peaks of the buildings. This wasn't good. Even if he'd brought a specially trained team of 10,000 sniffer dogs with him, the Mirror would take years to find. He fended off a knot by saying something aimless to Bagshaw.

"So has the old place changed much, then?"

"No, not one jot! It was just like this before, hoorah! Plenty of everything, spread out absolutely everywhere with plenty more pushed in between. Wonderful place. I say, if we happen to find ourselves on a charming street, something like Amu.. no, Ayam, do keep an eye out for a dark brown wallet with eight pound notes inside it. Dropped it after a gargantuan feast in a place run by a chap called Habibe. Granted, that's some while ago but it has my initials on the front and was top-notch quality. Had the loveliest picture of my wife Sarah in there too.. we hadn't been married long. Of course, I missed the money at the time but oh, how I wish for my Sarah.."

"Yeah, we'll keep an extra-good look out Bagshaw, don't worry."

"If perchance it's not their anymore, did you remember to bring some money with you, Bob? You'll be in the most dreadful trouble without any. You'll upset the locals something dreadful."

"Money? I didn't think about that. Do you think Aunt Agatha would mind too much if I borrowed some? She might have left a few Turkish Whatevers lying around in here.."

Bagshaw and Eugi went very quiet while Bob had a look around the room, along shelves, on tables and cabinet tops. He couldn't find anything at all, not a penny - or whatever Turkish people had instead of pennies. Opening drawers made him feel like an intruder of the worst kind, and he didn't fancy the idea of wandering through Agatha's private rooms - that would be too awkward and way too intrusive. He didn't look through any of the files that were neatly stored away in the drawers and cabinets, and cheered when he found a drawer full of banknotes, all of which had plenty of noughts on them. Either Agatha was wealthy enough to buy Istanbul and the rest of Europe and Asia, or the currency simply had plenty of noughts to spare. Judging by the price of a neatly folded newspaper that had been left on one of the chairs, it was the latter.

"June 3rd, 1973. Naomi was spot on!" Bob announced, and then took a look at his watch for some finer clarification.

"Today is June 4th.. fair enough. HOTEL KALESI.. well how about that. ISTANBUL.. we have confirmation! NICE CARPET.. is it really?"

"Yes, it is rather nice," agreed Bagshaw.

"Well excah-yoooz me fuh interruptin' ladies, but ain't we gotta job to do, and ain't we oughta be doin' it? B'sides, I ain't bin here before an' I'd quite like t'be stakin' the neighbuh-hood. Find out what's where an' who's who an' what they're all doin' etceteruh. That city's out there, an' we're in here so like that Dame Agattuh says, shall we like depart?"

Encouragement like that was hard to ignore, so Bob stepped out into the corridor and closed the door behind him, making a careful Mental Note of the number.

"Room 963. Well it would be, wouldn't it?"

There was even a diamond shape in the carpet, although it was very subtle. The portraits here wcren't the formal, painted variety which adorned the walls of The Ansonia - or rather, adorned the walls when it used to have walls, Bob corrected himself. These were generally relaxed photographs, showing Agatha, Naomi, Claudie and Feiya in different places around the world, appropriately dressed in ever-changing fashions, and looking as if they were all having a good time.

"Eyes never lie.." thought Bob, looking at Agatha in one shot. She was standing next to a military leader, on a grandiose balcony. Bob couldn't quite work out what year it might have been, and he didn't recognise the flag draped before them, but judging by the uniform and the man's large moustache it must have been somewhere in the 19th Century. The middle-aged man was saluting the cheering masses gathered below, and Agatha was beside him, smiling and waving. However, her eyes were sly, narrowed.. and fixed on him. She was like a hawk in momentary hover before swooping onto an unsuspecting prey. Bob figured she was just about to alter history, and Feiya had gone along for some snaps. Or maybe she'd been part of the whole plan? He made another Mental Note to ask her, assuming he ever managed to find the next Mirror.

Bob somehow managed to lose well over an hour as he drifted backwards and forwards along the corridor, studying every glimpse into the lives and friendships on the walls. Other people were in some of the shots, but for the most part there were only combinations of the four of them, always with at least one person laughing. Jinx was noticeable by her absence from every picture, but that didn't surprise him at all.

The corridors weren't anything like The Ansonia's. For a start, there were only two comparatively short ones, and he only passed four or five doors before arriving at the retracting security doors which sealed off the entire floor. Bob figured he'd have a hard time getting lost in this place, even with his eyes closed. Seven floors later, he found himself in a magnificent, five-sided reception hall which was at least twice the size of The Ansonia's. A few garish holiday-makers sat around in small groups, relaxing on wicker chairs around wicker tables and flicking through the day's newspapers.

It seemed to be a communal reception, a kind of meeting point for several hotels. Four elaborately individual entrances stood beneath the high glass-topped ceiling, almost facing each other across the vast expanse of polished dark-stone floor. A smoked-glass archway set deep into the fifth wall lead to the world outside, and with Eugi growing ever more impatient, Bob went to greet Istanbul.

He stood at the top of the dozen or more long white steps which lead down to street level, and spent a few moments taking in the scene before him - and breathed a huge sigh of relief that there really did seem to be no skyscrapers anywhere. The roads were already becoming busy, and before he had managed three steps a man was offering him watches and aftershave, speaking badly in four different languages. Bob was convinced the man could smell Agatha's money, so he played bewildered and stupid and the man soon moved on to some better tourists.

"Bagshaw, where abouts.."

"Ahaa!" exclaimed Bagshaw, "There are the minarets of the Basilica Santa Sofia, oh, we really ought to see that! And there's a sign for the Sultan Ahmet Camii which will take us a whole day for an adequate look around, and I do believe.. yes! There are the peaks of the Suleymaniye Camii, which you simply have to see.. now then.."

"Bagshaw, we're not here to go sightseeing, we have to do some searching, remember? There's a Mirror somewhere around and.."

"Oh but the splendour, the history.."

Bob gave up. Bagshaw was too happy in his world of Turkish wonderment, and was probably better off left that way. They wandered aimlessly for a while, listening to Bagshaw's historical ramblings, and generally going in a broad enough circle to let Eugi begin to establish his major bearings. Bob saw nothing peculiar happening, and quickly felt that they must be well and truly lost. Eugi wasn't concerned in the slightest, and suddenly the hotel complex loomed ahead, much to Bob's amazement. He stood against a telegraph pole, and wondered what to do next. More aimless wandering? More drifting and drifitng..

"Well, hello there young man!"

Bob spun around to see a loudly dressed couple standing behind him, both carrying shopping bags.

"Sure as day is day this is one small world! We thought there was something odd about you, and twenty years later we find out! How 'bout that?"

His heart started pounding. The man put down the largest of the bags and took his sunglasses off, and his wife followed suit.

"Doin' a little surreptitious travellin'? Well don't you worry, we're on your side! I'm afraid it ain't right to tell you what we do, as a lot of water's flowed under the bridge since we last saw you."

Bob was stunned, and said the first thing that came into his head.

"Who are you? I don't remember meeting.."

"We were on the America, same time as you visited your friend

Fay-yarh. The two of you made quite an impression on our good friend Mr Theodore Tiber, an' he asked us to make some careful notes regarding' yourself. Your name's escaped me over the years, but your face hasn't! Know why?"

"No.."

His wife answered with the most awful, toe-curling singing.

"I got a cam-erahh, I took your pic-cha! We'd know you anywhere! You've been in our home ever since - you're almost part of the family! Welcome home, good to have you back!"

Her husband cringed, and Bob could see why. They seemed genuine enough, and if Mr Tiber was anywhere near as obsessive and pedantic as Feiya said he was, then these two were quite believable.

"Yes li'l fella, pictures and you don't age, not one bit. Now, you care to tell us what's goin' on? How you've been travellin' and not ever been monitored? These are serious breaches, and need investigating so if there's anything we can do to help you or.. well, help Madame Agatha, I want you to know that we're right with you and her, okay? She's got a 'tarnished' reputation, and needs either fencing in every now and then, or given more freedom dependin' on what she's getting up to. But us two have never objected to a thing she's done yet, and we tend to watch her back for her, whether she knows it or not, you understandin'? Now then, we know you, you kinda know us, and we all know we gotta talk, don't we?"

Bob nodded, but reserved judgement.

"Oh Felding, we're pushing him! You'll scare him off! Now then, if you want to speak to us, it's entirely up to you, okay? And just to make it easier, if you feel you want to talk then we'll be at that little caf-ayyy over there, y'see it? Its got a Turkish word above it, next to a big Cokey Coley logo? We'll be in there, and we'll have one of those apple teas waiting for you. But only if you want to come along, okay?"

Her husband cringed again, and gestured for her to stop talking.

"Amy, if he don't come along we're going to have to instigate proceedings against Madame Agatha, so he needs to be there, doesn't he?" he said, and his broader accent crept through a little as he showed his annoyance with his wife. He turned to Bob.

"Look guy, if you're involved in something, you have to talk with us. As I said, we look after Madame Agatha in ways she doesn't know about, and we need to know why she's sendin' you here and everywhere. That's not to say anyone else needs to know, but if we have to force her to tell us through the Authorities, then that's what we'll do. One phonecall and she can be slammed under Class A Restrictions inside of ten seconds. But you can prevent that from happening, okay? We're going to drop off our bags, and we'll come to you at 10.30 on the dot. If you're not in that café, we make the phonecall at precisely 10.32, you understand? And by my watch it's now.. 9.50am. Check yours."

Bob played along, and nodded again. He could tell they were trying to offer him a friendly ultimatum, gambling that he knew practically nothing about how the Guardian system worked. And they were right to do that, because Bob hadn't got a clue how it worked. However, Eugi was a little suspicious and as the couple filled a taxi with their bags, he had a word with Bob.

"Start walkin' Bob, so's we can talk. What's wid Tweedle Dumb and Tweedle Dumber? You ain't buyin' that story?"

"No, I don't think so. Well.. I mean I'm not sure. It's too much of a coincidence that they met me like that. But what if they really do look after Aunt Agatha? She'd need people like that in the background, especially in her position. I wonder if they are genuine? And I don't want her under some kind of Restriction.. and if that does happen and she can't be a Guardian anymore, how would she be able to get me involved with all this, in the future? Would I just vanish or something?"

"Whad'yuh sayin'? Try English on me."

"I think I'm having another Chicken And Egg Dilemma. I really wish Fey was here.. she'd know what to do. If I do something now that stops the future Aunt Agatha ever being able to send me on this whole Mirror chase, how did I ever get here in the first place? So do you think I'll vanish at 10.32?"

Eugi had a think.

"Naah, chicken schmicken! Forget that wise-ass hooey. I seen dis before. Those loafers are fakin' it, they're sellin' you a dud. The Bad Guys are always dumb, else they wouldn't be the Bad Guys."

"You reckon?"

"I know so. Listen up, kid. Somethin' similar happened to a guy runnin' guns down on Catherine Street. He wuz supposed to make a deal wid three schmoes, all offerin' who knows what. So he goes down to the ron-dayvoo at the right time and you know what? BLAM. Guy gets wiped and looted. Real nasty. So his driver, who's deluxe auto I was in back then, loses the plot and starts high-tailin' outta there, an' goes straight into a line uh waitin' Blues. They think he's loaded with shooters, and then BLAM all over again. Wiped worse than the other guy. Shame. Real nice car, totally wasted. See?"

"So you're saying we shouldn't go to the café, we should wander off and come back just for a look? See who's around, and see if Mr and Mrs Small-World-Isn't-It are anywhere in sight?"

"Now you're gettin' it! Walk tall an' lay low.. at the same time."

Bagshaw stopped shuffling through his Classics Guide To Turkish History reference notes, and showed that he had not only been listening, but he'd been thinking as well.

"I agree with you both, you're quite right to be apprehensive of such a dubious couple. I believe they were going to meet you at any time today and deliver exactly the same story, and then leave in exactly the same taxi-carriage."

"Steady on there, Sherlock. Why?" asked Bob, to the amusement of some locals.

"Bags. How many retailers have been open long enough for such shopping? Very few, I fancy, as they tend to rise a little later here. And how many other people are heavy with purchases? Even fewer. So unless they've been acquiring vast amounts of spice from market traders, which might I point out they had not, you caught them about an hour earlier than they would have liked to have caught you."

"Really?"

"Most so, indeed. They used the bags as an excuse to leave you once the rendez-vous was arranged, and no doubt are plotting diabolical in your absence. A breakfast appointment with people as unsavoury as your friends is worthy of being missed, so what say we delight in a little more culture instead? We could begin with the Valide Camii, which is a most charming small mosque - and you can almost see its minarets from here! It's only a hundred yards, if that. Worth a visit, and would barely take a minute.."

Bob was stunned. Bagshaw had finally said something useful, which involved all those elements which normally evaded him. Logic, lateral thinking, and long sentences. However, Bob wasn't entirely sure what to do. He was very tempted to go back to the America to find out what he really ought to do from the friendly-Feiya, and then return here again. But that would involve another day in Istanbul passing by, with the Troublers knowing he was due back. They might even try to destroy the hotel like they had almost done with The Ansonia. The more he thought about what to do, the longer the list of Possible Catastrophic Results became. So he decided to take on Eugi and Bagshaw's suggestions, keeping it simple and yet mind-blowingly complicated at the same time.

"Yeah, if that'll make you happy Bagshaw, we'll go and have a quick look but we'll be back here for half ten, though?"

"Indubitably! Mr Eugi, do lead."

Eugi started navigating, and took them through a very narrow side street lined with souvenir shops and one or two small cafés. At the very end, a trader carried an armful of clothes from the back of a van into his small shop, and Bob had a supremely cunning idea. If he was recognisable to people who may not be on his side, perhaps a disguise was called for. With a little help he put on a baggy, purple-striped shirty-shawl-thing which reached down to his ankles, and paid far too many notes to the smiling trader. He rounded it off with an unpronounceable garment that passed as a hat, which was slightly flatter and only marginally less embarrassing than a triple-tassled fez. He picked up an orange-blue one as well, for Andie not to wear.

They made their way to the mosque, and Bagshaw was bubbling over with enthusiasm. He gave a rambling history of the building, and also of the times he was thereabouts with a group of old college chums who fancied digging up some ancient whatnots.

At 10.20 they started heading back, hidden amongst a group of people who he hoped were genuine tourists. Bob decided to take his all time biggest risk ever - the kind that could win awards and would deserve vast amounts of applause if it worked. He stayed a safe distance away from the café, nestled behind a collection of thin bushes and trees which ran in sporadic lines in front of the shops on the other side of the road. He waited for a few minutes, watching what was happening, frustrated that the windows were so dark and that there was so little to see. Fewer and fewer people were going in and coming out, and he didn't spot the odd couple anywhere. He checked his watch. It read 10.28, and that meant it was time for Operation Horribly Big Risk to begin.

He crawled out onto the dusty street, ran as fast as he could across the road to the café, swung through the door and looked inside. It was completely deserted. His feet failed him as he tried to run back out and he slipped on the tiles, hitting the floor hard with his knees.

He got up and staggered back out again, through the traffic and into a mass of alleyways and junctions.

A huge explosion roared through the air, sending burning debris far into the surrounding streets. Windows began shattering as gunshots broke out amidst the chaos and confusion, spreading panic and people in every direction. Cars veered wildly from the roads, and wailing and buzzing sirens struggled to be heard above the pandemonium as the emergency crews began arriving to a scene of colossal devastation. Bob kept running while Eugi calmly suggested lefts and rights along the twisting streets. He followed, ignoring everyone around him and without the first idea where he was heading.

"I say, stop Bob! Stop now, this very instant!" shouted Bagshaw, as they neared an intersection after passing a long row of vendors.

"Stop? Whufor?" gasped Bob, leaning against a wall to try and catch his breath.

"Go back to the chap on the corner! You simply must try those Simits - they're a kind of bread, covered in sesame seeds and a light oil specific to these parts. They really are most appetising, a real delicacy of the locale! Oh it's a smell I could never forget, and.."

"Yeah kid, I seen things like that round thee uhh.. Upper West Side, and they sure do smell good tuh me! Y'gotta try one!"

"What? Are you both nuts? Didn't you notice.. there's freaks.. and you choose now to.."

A shot rang out from a long way behind and immediately sent a cloud of dust billowing from the wall, far above Bob's head. He started running again, through the bustling crowds and twisting streets, and soon found himself dashing down a long sloping through-road, exactly as Eugi suggested. A high stone wall, almost black with age and pollution ran along the end of the road. Bob was set to ignore its broadly-arched entrance and follow the main road around to the left.

"Woah kiddo, put'cha brakes on like as NOW! We need to go in there, through dat pointy archway an' by all them trees an' stuff, to thuh next archway. Then we're where we're s'pposed t'be 'cause I got the levels figured out now!"

Bob raced back to the arch, not too concerned with what Eugi meant. Somewhere in the distance the sirens were still blaring, but at least no guns had gone off for almost an entire minute.

"Oh, I say! The Kapali Carsi - or as it's also known, The Grand Bazaar! What a treat! Hurry along now Bob, we want to avoid the crowds. All kinds of wondrous wares lie beyond!"

He soon entered another high-arched entrance and ran into the most mind-boggling labyrinth of covered streets and alleyways. There were no walls, only shop fronts and more shop fronts, nestled beside even more shop fronts. Eugi kept calling out directions, as if he actually knew where he was going. Wherever it was, it would be the greatest-ever hiding place on earth. How the shopkeepers ever found the same workplace twice was a mystery to Bob as he hurried past the countless windows and growing throngs of conservatively dressed people. The locals seemed to get their shopping done before the tourists took over.

"Now then, see that big fancy drinkin' fountain? Go past it forty yards an' there's a metal cover somewheres around there that you need to be lifting up."

Bob arrived in a comparatively quiet section of the Bazaar, and stood in a dead-end surrounded by a cramped array of carpet shops. He turned around and around, looking along the dusty grey floor, unable to see anything resembling a cover.

"What cover? There isn't one Eugi! What do I do now? Do you know where we.."

"Do I know..? Uh'course I know where we're goin'. I seen Nayohhmee's maps an' then those other maps wid your lady, so I know the location and as long as no-one's gettin' on my nerves, we're all in the clear an' then we're outta here. Try a shop."

Only three of the shops didn't appear to have anyone inside, so Bob took a guess and ran into the nearest one. Dozens of rolled carpets stood to attention, lined up seven-deep against the walls, and he could feel his panic levels rising as he noticed what he was standing on. Masses of gaudy carpets covered the floor, and he would have to spend hours or even days rolling them out of the way before getting anywhere near ground level.

"No joy! I can't even see the floor! This was a bad.."

"Jeez, break out the milkshakes, kid. Relax. We're right by where we gotta be, so go try the back room. I'm tellin' yuh this is okay.."

Bob didn't hear the end of Eugi's advice. He was too busy fighting with a deceptively large doorway-curtain as he tried to get through into the next room. He finally wriggled free and immediately missed the first step of a tightly spiralling staircase, which felt as if it would go on for ever. He landed in a painful heap and lay against some very dusty old floorboards, waiting in the darkness for his brain to catch up with his body.

"Ohh.. marvellous. I can't even see where we came from. Can you guide me to the light switch, Eugi?"

"So I'm a butler now, Lord Butt-Overheels? You don't need no lights, just go touchy-feely around till you find somethin' like a big metal circle, an' then open it. Y'do that an' we're gone at last.."

Bob crawled around, patting the ground in front of him, impatient to find anything that didn't feel like floorboards.. while somewhere high above, the sound of thudding footsteps carried down into the darkness.

CHAPTER THIRTY

Darkness and Light

"Got it! I can feel a loop.. and a turny bit.. here we go!" Bob whispered triumphantly as he lifted up the near side of a rough iron dish, which was slightly smaller than a manhole cover.

He fumbled his feet towards the metal bars leading down, and lowered himself into whatever lay beyond. The cover was awkward and tricky to get back into its exact place, and Bob would have given up if Eugi wasn't so intent on him covering his tracks. He eventually worked out how to lower and twist it back properly.

"Now, wedge it shut wid somethin'!"

Bob had nothing that he could jam the crude locking mechanism with, except for Andie's hat. He worked it into the slot around the curved arm, and nervously began his descent.

"A worthy sacrifice, Bob. I doubt she would have cared for fashion so unbecoming. Find one with a nice bow, leaning to the floral.."

"Cheers Bagsh.. uh oh.." whispered Bob, losing his footing on the shallow rungs, twice.

"Wow!" interrupted Eugi, "Dis is how the whole city links up! I didn't really get those maps till now.. it's like nowhere I ever been before! I thought Manhattan wuz good for that kind'a thing, but compared to this place? We ain't even started yet."

Bob had no idea what Eugi was talking about, and began wondering exactly how far down he needed to go until he could find some nice, safe ground again. After taking almost thirty steps, he was glad he couldn't see anything - the tunnel would have looked terrifying up at dish-level, and probably still looked terrifying even at the point he'd reached. He kept taking step after step down. And down. And down. And down. The air became stifling and heavy with humidity, and as Bob counted the forty eighth step, he found himself back on solid land - and up to his knees in cold water. Millions of high-pitched splashes echoed from the constant dripping all around as he began wading in the darkness. He left his baggy Turk-shirt behind, and found that he could move more easily by not wearing a huge drenched tent. He made a quick Mental Note about that.

"Eugi, how exactly did you find a map with all this on it? We're a little off the beaten track, aren't we?"

"Don'ask me, ask dat Nayuhmee broad. She an' her gaa-gaa friends spent like hours with three mirrors-which-ain't-mirrors, tryin' to find out where we gotta go, an' that's why we're down here. There's somethin' down here that we gotta fetch, an' they got the co-oddinates pinned. An' then your skirtchase.. uhh sorry, lady-friend, gave me the low-down on the city, so you tell her she did real good. Now stop here and turn right.. yeah that's good. Keep it going.."

Bob kept wading blindly through the water, trying to put thoughts of irate Troublers armed with infra-red gun-sights out of his mind.

"Oh how spectacular! If only we could see this! I do believe that we are in the third-oldest part of the city, and very, very few people have ever been here! What an honour to be navigating these rarely-trodden routes of the cistern and waterways.."

Bagshaw carried on waxing eloquently about the pitch-black surroundings, lost in the kind of amazement that only he could become lost in, and enjoying the privilege of not seeing things that nobody else had seen either. Twenty minutes of stumbling and splashing later, Eugi pointed out how close they were getting to the pick-up, and Bob noticed a very dim, flickering glow further ahead.

"Now you gotta tread careful.. this is not, I repeat dat, NOT, somewheres you wanna go gettin' yourself damaged.."

He followed the long bending tunnel, soon becoming able to make out his surroundings in the faint light. The cistern must have been almost twenty feet high in some places, at least the same wide, and spanned by long arches. Bob groaned as he realised he needn't have been wading through the water, and stepped up onto the wide brickwork footpath instead.

He noticed dozens of other entrances to passageways as he went further along, some large enough for a double decker bus, and some barely high enough to crawl through. This was one weird place. Its Weird Factor would have to be decided later because there had been so many weird events in Bob's life recently that the Weird Factor Classification System kept on being re-gauged.

He steadily drew closer to the faultering orange glow, which seemed to be coming from an alcove on his side of the waterway, a little further ahead. How anything managed to burn in this humidity was a minor miracle - and how anyone else could ever find their way this far into the labyrinthian network of tunnels was a major one.

"Hey, kid - that's the place, an' it looks like someone's left the light on for us! Must be a nice neighb'hood after all!" laughed Eugi.

The light danced across the water to the decayed wall opposite the alcove, and Bob crouched down, staying back in the shadows to figure out what on earth he was going to do next. He spent a few minutes watching the opening to see if there were any signs of low-life. Apart from the shadows and light giving the impression that dozens of people were around, Bob didn't actually see anyone. It was time to make a move.

He walked silently with his back against the tunnel's brickwork, inch by inch, ready to run for his life at any second. He eventually reached the source of the light, and peered around the corner. One burning torch hung against the far wall, revealing a wide, empty alcove which reached back for at least ten uneven feet. A pillar stood in the middle, with a chunk of its middle section missing. Bob didn't want to think how that might have happened, and hurried over and lifted the torch from its holder.

He stooped down and stepped through an entrance in the far wall, which was framed in shattered white stone. Its short passage lead out into a huge room, or maybe a cave - it was far too large for him to tell, but fewer drips were echoing, and those that did were a long, long way off. The light from the torch became far weaker as he walked along a haphazard path made of small bricks. The remnants of long-collapsed pillars and columns lined the way, almost guiding him in a zig-zag route until he finally arrived at a bank of masonry and stonework. The way ahead was completely blocked.

"Eugi, any ideas? And before anyone suggests it, I didn't bring a huge digger, or even a spade."

"Yeah, I got an idea. How 'bout we go back like fifty buh-zillion miles and pick up the Mirror. Didn't you see it there?"

"No, I.. why didn't you say anything?"

"Cuz I thought you was headin' some place more important! Jeez, keep up! You're the one who knows what's goin' on, not me."

They hurried back until Eugi coughed in a less-than-subtle manner, near to a crumpled pile of canvas rags that were covered in dust and broken stone.

"How am I supposed to have seen that? It looks like everything else here, and anyway, you'd never have known if Naomi.."

"So quit yappin' and get wrappin' 'coz we don' wanna be here when those guys get back. Like if they see you doin' stuff on their patch.. it's all hold the press, we got bad news. I seen similar before.. not the same, uhf course.."

Bob kneeled down and put the torch to one side. Its flames had died down to a collection of glowing embers, and he squinted as he lifted the canvas away from the ground. And then he squinted for completely the opposite reason as the entire room filled with intense silver-white light from the Mirror. Huge crashing sounds of stone falling hard against stone came from nowhere, shaking the ground and sending up clouds of dust all around him. Hundreds of faint people dressed from a bygone age ran through the walls into the room, falling and crawling from unseen horrors, desperately reaching out to him, as if pleading for him to bring some kind of salvation to them. The overpowering misery of their sorrow and chilling cries resonated around and around through every inch of the cavernous room, and tore through Bob.

The suffering around him was so real and terrifying that he could barely see through his tears. He slowly began inching the blue bag onto the Mirror, steadily manoeuvering along its sides while trying to stop his hands and arms from shaking, desperately struggling to keep his mind only on what was in front of him. As the bag neared the top, the sounds and the tortured images gradually died away, leaving him alone in complete darkness. He stared at the final thin beam of light as it disappeared, and the cord silently drew itself closed.

He tried to speak to Eugi, but couldn't. He'd never felt so ravaged by emotion, and could only curl up and wait until the feelings had passed away. He'd been given a glimpse of something very bad, an evil chapter of history that had created extremes of misery within these very walls, and every victim's suffering had been shown to him. After a few minutes, Eugi spoke in the closest way he could manage to being comforting.

"Hey, hey, everythin's okay kiddo, dat's all gone an' we're all here an' we're all fine, so we gonna leave now, yeah? We ain't got time to be gettin' all broke up. Bad guys on the loose, remember?"

Bob tried to answer, but still felt like he had a football in his throat. He picked up the Mirror and hurried along the path, blind and unthinking in the darkness, doing whatever Eugi told him to do.

A few minutes later, the sounds of dripping water became stronger and Bob knew he must be nearing the doorway. He held his arm out in front of himself, and edged forwards to try and feel the wall, or preferably the cracked stonework of the archway. And then he froze. Were those voices up ahead?

"Eugi? Bagshaw? Did either of you hear anything?" he whispered in a voice that was still fraught and shaking, and hoped his imagination was working overtime.

"Why yes, I believe there are people ahead of us - chattering types. Perhaps we should join onto their group, and then we might see a little more? It's been most enthralling so far, but rather dark."

Bob felt the cold stone of the entrance, and saw the first glimmer of torchlights reflecting in the water beyond. Instead of running back into the darkness, he stayed as flat against the wall beside the doorway as he could. The half dozen voices grew louder and nearer, almost lost in the splashing. Seconds later the first of the powerful torchlights reached into the darkness, and Bob hardly dared breathe as the men stood on the other side of the thick wall, no doubt aware that someone had taken their burning torch.

Three men walked in, and stood just feet from Bob to scan the cavernous room beyond with their powerful modern torches. They moved along the path, gesturing and ordering each other around and breaking off occasionally to climb the rocky mounds before returning to the path again. Two more entered in mid-argument, and hurried to join the others.

The lights moved further and further away, and he edged back to the entrance and listened for a while, waiting for any tell-tale signs that someone might be on guard duty, lying in wait.

There wasn't a sound, other than the constant dripping. Bob took his chance and ran straight through the entrance, and immediately collided with the damaged pillar which he'd looked at on the way in. He lay on the floor struggling to get his breath, and then frantically crawled around for the Mirror. He soon found it, but only because a distant torchlight had carried through the doorway and revealed where it lay. Gunshots rang out as he picked it up, and he started running. He stayed on the brick ledges as much as possible as he raced through different tunnels, not daring to look back at the constant barrage of gunfire and shouting.

With a friend like Eugi, darkness was on Bob's side and after a long series of twists and turns he began to sense that he might be safe. The footsteps and voices had died away, lost far behind the sound of the dripping, and he stopped for a moment to get a grip on the situation - and maybe even calm down. Bagshaw, however, still seemed cheerfully oblivious to everything.

"Chaps! Did you notice the glorious stonework of the walling and columns back there? Those powerful torchlights were magnificent! Judging by the fine craftsmanship, I'd say this entire part of the great city's cistern was built early in the 16th Century, around the time of Selim the Grim. A very unpleasant sort by all accounts. Now then, I propose we might be right underneath the.."

Bob groaned, but deep down he was pleased that Bagshaw lived in such a safe and barmy world.

Gunshots rang out and Selim's brickwork cascaded down over Bob's head. Voices emerged from the echoes and he looked back, horrified as he saw that the torchlights were no more than thirty yards behind. The rising water around his ankles betrayed each footstep as he chased every word Eugi threw to him in the darkness.

"Okay kid, time t'swim with da liddul fishies. Take a left, then maybe five steps and then swim quicker than a shark who don't like water, till you can get out on the other side. Then get runnin' again, only a lot quietuh 'cause you ain't too good at keepin' it t'yuhself."

Bob did as he was told and stepped down onto a ledge, thigh-deep in cold water and tried to swim on his back holding the Mirror with Bagshaw perched like a rooftop on its highest point.

He saw the faint lights grow stronger and then heard the footsteps of perhaps three or four people go running past where he'd turned off, and relaxed a little. The water was nice and cool, and he felt like he could take a moment to try and get his pounding heart back to normal. He silently drifted through the water, and didn't really mind about being completely drenched. Then he felt something wriggle against his neck, and without thinking began splashing his legs like an outboard motor. Suddenly he couldn't care less if the freaks with guns knew where he was, because there was a chance that they might shoot whatever was in the water with him. More unwelcome Cistern Beast-Monsters started nudging against him, occasionally taking double-nudges just to make sure that he was really scared. He kicked harder and harder, ignoring the aching pains in his legs as he struggled across, thoroughly convinced he was getting nowhere.

"Okay kiddo you c'n stop about.. about.. NOW!" called Eugi as the back of Bob's head connected with brickwork. He sank for a moment, took a big mouthful of chilled Beast Slime, choked and almost threw up before realising the water was still only thigh-deep. He climbed out and stumbled up onto the next section of tunnel.

"Could I.. could I have waded across all that? Why didn't you say?"

"Like it's not enough I know where we're goin' - I gotta know how deep the water is as well? Jeez, no wonder everyone's shootin' at yuh.."

After a few more twists and turns along narrow, wide, and more narrow tunnels, Bob knew he had to stop and get his breath back. One breath would do, but two would be heavenly. He leaned against a few bumps on the wall, and noticed something. Other than the constant dripping from the ceiling, everywhere had gone quiet again. No splashing, no shouting, and best of all, no gunshots.

"Oh happy day.." he whispered.

But then faint lights appeared a little beyond the corner that he'd run around just moments earlier, and a vicious blast roared through the darkness. One of the freaks had changed guns for something very big and very nasty. Bob started running again, staying close to the walls. The water was becoming shallower, but seemed to be flowing harder against him. That could be good, or maybe unbelievably bad, so he tried not to think about it.

After ten long minutes of stumbling and falling over loose bricks, he could finally see light ahead. Unfortunately it wasn't so much 'ahead' as 'over head'. A shaft of light illuminated part of the cistern, from a street-level grill ten feet or more above. A decayed and skeletal ladder stood underneath it, looking forlorn and useless. Bob gave it a small prod, and it collapsed into a rusty heap, sending dozens of rats scurrying away into the darkness.

For the first time he could see just what a scary place he was running through. Time-worn bricks poked unevenly from the lychen-covered walls, and debris from the world above lay in huge soggy mounds which seemed to act as havens for the rats - and lots of them.

"Do keep up the tempo, old boy.. can't stand those devilish little things.. liable to nibble the old pages.. does tend to make one nervous," fretted Bagshaw, politely.

"You're nervous? How d'you think I'm.." gasped Bob as he rounded the first few piles beneath the grill.

The iron meshes were spaced far apart and he passed them every couple of minutes, each one a little higher up than the one before, bringing in more light and attracting more squealing rats.

After hurrying beneath a dozen unreachable grills, he could see that they were steadily becoming lower again. After a few more minutes, he could even reach up and touch one of the heavy iron grids, and shortly after that he could actually hold one firmly enough to try and push it, turn it, twist it and swing from it. As Bob struggled with one which felt like it ought to move at any moment, Eugi offered some good advice.

"If yuh don' find one that opens, we're gonna be down here f'the day 'cause it's a long ways back. An' I don't like that one bit 'cause it stinks down here an' I prefer air that don' stink so bad, 'coz nowadays I got standards. So don' go wastin' time on the grills that don' open, just go for the ones that do."

"Well which ones open then? Are they marked or something?"

"Like how should I know? I'm just sayin', that's all."

Bob groaned, and hurried on. The cistern narrowed so much that soon he could only crouch, and the grills became separated by a hundred yards of darkness. Far away behind him he could hear voices above the flowing water. The tunnel turned a few corners and began to widen out in all directions, and once again he reached a series of closely spaced grills. He tried three that only rattled and one that was solidly set in the stonework, so he kept on running until they were all too high to reach again, and darkness began taking over. The noises behind him grew nearer, and in the back of his mind he knew he must be very close to the end credits. He could even hear their footsteps as he ran along another series of sharp lefts and rights.

"Sounds like they gotta be thirty yards behind, forty if that. An' that's closer than they ever been."

"And?" gasped Bob, struggling for breath.

"An' that means they could start blowin' yuh limbs off with a few well-aimed shots. They got serious shooters, back there."

"Thanks for pointing that out, thanks a bundle.."

"On the up side though, ain't you lucky it's kinda dark?" he concluded, trying to sound positive.

He pulled ahead once more, and put on a final big effort into a passageway that lead towards the next beacon of sunlight. The ladder looked thin, too rusty and far too close to collapsing, but at least it reached all the way up in one piece, which was more than any of the others had done. Bob had to take a chance, and climbed the twenty or more steps. After one or two heart-stopping slips he arrived at the top, squinting up into the bright sunshine and dreading the prospect of the grill refusing to open. He nearly fell off with relief as it easily turned at least two or three inches. And then it moved some more, and then some more, until he could actually push it upwards and out onto the ground above. He hurried back down the ladder, careful to avoid the jagged half-rungs, and picked up the Mirror. The extra weight made the sides of the ladder shake with each step as he made his way back up, and it gave an unnerving sway as he raised his head out to see the glorious world outside. He raised the Mirror, carefully pushing and sliding it up through the opening.

"Whuh? Hey whass happ'niiiii.."

Eugi called out as he fell from Bob's Cistern Route Advisor pocket, and made a dull wet thud a long way below. Bob knew he couldn't leave the bagged Mirror up above the grill, so praying with every step, he gave the ladder another pounding. He reached the floor, painfully aware that at any moment everything could go completely wrong. He paused to listen. The clattering footsteps had slowed to a series of stops and starts as the gang decided which route to take, and he breathed a sigh of relief. Even so, he knew they were just moments away from rounding that final corner.

"Eugi? Where are you? You okay? Say anything!" he whispered into the murkiness, waiting for his eyes to re-adjust in the darkness.

"I'm ovuh here, an' I'm okay. But this rat ain't. Jeez, he ain't gonna be doin' much rat-stuff for a long time. No, I ain't there, I'm like four feet to yuh left, an' down a bit - yeah, lyin' on the rat. Holy smokes, take your time why don't you? These rats ain't as comf'table as you'd think.."

Bob put Eugi in a different pocket.

"Welcome back Eugi, sorry about all that.."

Then a devious sabotage plan occurred to him, and he began hunting around for anything lifeless and furry. Under normal circumstances this didn't bear thinking about, but he knew he could always shout 'God Almighty That Was A Dead Rat!' very loudly later on. In a matter of seconds, two and a half deceased rats occupied the top rungs of the ladder, and Bob climbed out into the heat of the day. The first freak to climb the ladder would be in for a nasty surprise, and all the freaks below him on the ladder would be in for a pretty unpleasant one as well.

He put every ounce of strength into securing the grill back into place, and fought back a surge of panic as five men appeared in the gloom below. Bob looked around. There were tourists everywhere, walking in the outermost grounds of a huge mosque.

"Oh, how marvellous!" exclaimed Bagshaw, "The exquisite Hippodrome! We stand before the Sultan Ahmet Mosque, known to many as the Blue Mosque, due to the bountiful Iznik tiles inside its mighty walls! Can we go there? It's been so long.." he added, admiring a series of tall minarets

"Cheers Bagshaw.. you're right, this is very, very good!" he said, as he took a look around himself.

A towering stone pillar stood just a few feet behind him, surrounded by a rope cordon. It looked very important, very impressive and very old. Adding all those things together, Bob figured he could gain some unplanned help. He tagged onto the back of a nearby tour group, and ran around to the woman at the front. The smartly dressed tour guide looked at Bob as if he'd been running through a rat-infested cistern for the last couple of hours - and so did all the tourists.

"Excuse me, Mrs Tour-Guide? What's that great big huge thing? It looks amazing and I'd like to know everything about it please!"

The guide may not have approved of his appearance, but she did approve of his question. With a little encouragement from Bob, the group wandered over and stood before the enormous Obelisk of Theodyssius, unwittingly covering the grill. The guide started delivering a very detailed story beginning in Egypt, around 1450 BC. Bob knew he'd earned himself ten billion Smug Points.. plus a Triple-Score Bonus for an unexpected last bit - heavily armed police. If a group of men loaded with guns wanted to climb out onto the land surrounding a historic and very huge mosque, Bob figured the dozens of fully-loaded police might want to ask them some questions. A worthy Triple-Score Bonus, if ever there was one.

He made his way to the back of the group, and ran off anywhere. Eugi was still a little shaken from his fall and was trying to get his bearings again, so Bob kept running through the crowds of tourists, past rows of trees, and across the wide parking area, intent on just getting away from wherever he was. He wanted to get back to Pierpont House even more than he'd wanted a soft landing when he was up on top of the Woolworth Building. Well, almost more.

A long road lined with taxis, coaches and more tall trees ran parallel to the Hippodrome, and Bob checked in his It's Not My Money It's Aunt Agatha's Money pocket. The thick wad was still there, a little damp perhaps, but definitely still there, so he headed over to the ranks of taxis. A dusty, black car pulled up at the very end, and he clambered into the back.

"Hotel Kapelellesi, and very.."

"Yeesh, it's Kalesi - get it right 'cause driver's hate that.." said Eugi.

".. oh yeah, Kalesi, the Hotel Kalesi and very quickly if you don't mind! Big hurry, big Lire!" he said in short breaths, and waved the money in front of the driver before crouching down on the back seat. If he hadn't been keeping such a low profile, he might have noticed that all the other taxis were grey, box-like Citroëns. The car turned a tight circle on itself and drove off.

The journey was hot and felt like it was taking for ever, which suited Bob fine. He was drying off nicely as the car slowly crawled its way through the kind of traffic that made Manhattan look as quiet as Barton. He glanced up occasionally to see cars, lorries, bikes, carts, people and even donkeys everywhere, all of them convinced they had the right of way. The journey dragged on, but Bob knew he must have gone a long way through all those dark tunnels, so spending half an hour or more returning to the hotel wasn't too unexpected. Every now and then the driver, a greasy and perhaps not entirely hygienic man, turned the radio down to announce the name of a landmark or an important site, and then turned the volume all the way back up. Occasionally a familiar tune would appear between all the swirling Turkish songs, and Bob felt good to hear a friendly voice. Elvis started singing Fools Rush In, and he gave a small laugh at its appropriateness.

"Have to pick that up if I ever get to Saturday.." he thought. And that brought his mind to Andie, who had been pushed to the sidelines over the previous few hours. She would love the Grand Bazaar and the busy streets, and Agatha would be sure to let them do their own spot of visiting once everything was back to normal.

"How totally brilliant would that be.." he thought dreamily, before being interrupted by Eugi who seemed to have gathered himself together again.

"Jeez, what kinda through-ways are these? An' I thought Midtown was bad! What are these guys playin' at, actin' like they ALL own the place! Kid, get the window down an' say this.."

After a long and steady section followed by steep slopes and some tight corners, Bob raised his head up to take a look at where they were. He could see a narrow street winding out behind the car, barely wide enough for two small carts to pass each other. It was walled by two never-ending rows of houses, distinguishable only by the different colour paint on their plaster fronts, and the occasional old person sitting in a doorway. The houses followed every twist and turn of the ramshackle road, occasionally merging together via a short connecting passageway above the street. This didn't look like the middle of Istanbul at all.

"Are we going to the right Hotel Kalesi? It's the one near where that bomb went off earlier on, and.."

The driver parked in the shade of a tree, in a small sandy area enclosed by a circle of houses. Chickens scattered as the car backfired before he turned the engine off. He turned around in his seat and calmly wiped the perspiration from his face, making drops fall from his industrial-sandpaper stubble. He looked at Bob, then at the blue bag, and gave a gap-toothed grin.

"You sure that's yours? Should we go see your friend Mr Salesman regarding rights? No. How 'bout you refuse to hand it over, and during the struggle you die, huh? I'll dump your worthless body far out in the sea, and hey, no-one ever knows you ever existed. But you don't exist, do you? Secret's out, word's on the street," he said, tapping his nose. "Looks like I'm the one who's gonna be takin' care of business, how 'bout that? If there was such a thing as luck, yours just ran out."

The driver got out and almost wrenched the door from the car, then began to pull Bob and the Mirror from the back seat.

In the brief moment it took for the driver to change his grip, Bob saw an opportunity and seized it. He delivered the hardest kick of his life into a region that was guaranteed to bring tears to the driver's eyes. It wasn't a great sporting tactic, but it worked perfectly. The man gulped loudly and fell to the floor, no doubt regretting the turn of events, and Bob started running.

"Eugi! Hey Eugi! A suggestion or two would do nicely.." he panted as he ran down one twisting, blind alley after another. Elderly people watched and chuckled as he ran past, smiling at the reckless energy of youth. He chose a few more corners and roads completely at random, and was soon confronted by a dead end. Three picture-postcard small white houses lined the end of the alley, complete with an old lady in a black shawl outside one of them. The Mediterranean quaintness of the scene was lost on Bob, who ran past her and up two stone steps into the only open door. She didn't seem to mind.

Something strange-but-nice was cooking in the kitchen and despite Bagshaw's suggestion, he didn't stop to find out what local delicacy it might be. Instead, he ran up the wooden stairs and emerged in a short hallway. The door to a small bathroom swung open to show a heavy-set man, who nicked himself shaving. He turned to look at Bob, who looked straight back, frozen to the spot for a split second. A woman holding a baby at the foot of the stairs started calling something, and Bob realised he had nowhere to go other than an open window at the end of the hall.

"Not a window againnn.." he moaned.

Praying it didn't overlook a huge cliff or another 700ft drop, he climbed onto the sill and then launched himself down towards a cart filled with old clothes. As his feet left the ledge, he realised that an Olympic athlete wouldn't make this jump, and even Superman with a brand new cape would have trouble. He landed a long way short of the cart, and stood rooted to the dusty cobblestones for a moment, waiting for something to start hurting. But nothing did.

"Oh my God, did you see that you two? And I think I'm okay!" he exclaimed as he turned around to see where he'd come from.

"Bravo, sir!" applauded Bagshaw.

"Yeah, y'crazy nut-lug.." added Eugi.

The man looked down from the window, with half his face covered in shaving foam and a slightly bewildered expression. He shrugged at Bob, who shrugged back before racing off again.

The heat of the day and far too much running were quickly starting to catch up, and Bob slowed to a walk. He hadn't a clue where he was, and really needed to stop for a while, preferably somewhere out of sight. An ideal place appeared two streets later.

A tall black wardrobe had been left leaning against a difficult-to-sell house, surrounded by worn out old chairs, two small tables, and piles of junk. The wardrobe actually looked as if it was propping up the entire building. Hiding inside it would be a risk, but one that had to be taken, so Bob opened the door and stepped in, tugging at a nail on the inside to make it click shut. It was warm, empty and smelled of old mothballs.

"Okay Eugi," Bob said, feeling relieved, "..where do you reckon we are? Anywhere good?"

"By my reckonin' we're miles off east, somewhere up near Taksim Square, if we're near anywhere. But that ain't nowhere near where we're needin' t'be gettin' back to, 'cause we're on thuh wrong side of thuh Golden Horn, in a rough neighb'hood outside what I prezoom is the house of a low-life. Maybez. So this ain't good, this definitely ain't good. That last mess wasn't good, but it was real good compared to this one. Coz this-ain't-good."

"The Golden what? So where do we go to get back?" whispered Bob, trying to picture in his mind how far away they might be. He quickly gave up.

"Woahh, slow down Lindberg. The Golden H is like Istanbul's version of Broadway, like it splits it in two - only it's a half mile wider, a whole lot wetter an' it's real deep too. Maybe longer.. with boats. See, it runs right across where we need to be goin' so we gotta take the bridge, that's all, or maybe a boat seein' as how it's a nice day f'that. Then once we're back over where we oughta be, we aim for the Dame's apartment. No great shakes, should take an hour or two but there's no extra charge, so why worry?"

Bagshaw liked the sound of that.

"Indeed! I agree with my exceptionally well-orientated friend. We could take in a few magnificent sights and still be back in plenty of time for tea. What d'you say, Bob old boy?"

"Can either of you two be normal for just one conversation? There's people trying to kill me everywhere! Unless we sort out a pretty good plan right now, and I mean one that's a little better than hiding in a cabinet, all of us will be swimming with the fish really soon!"

Silence fell for a few minutes while everyone tried to come up with an exceptionally brilliant plan. Bagshaw landed one.

"I have it! How about that Bugatti contraption? What was its name, now.. Budgie? Did you consider bringing him along, because.."

Bob sighed.

"Thank you Bagshaw, that's a good plan. A really good.."

Suddenly Bob felt the wardrobe being lifted up and tipped even further backwards. It clattered onto the back of a truck, and after a few thunks and bumps, the workmen decided everything was fine to go and slapped the wardrobe twice. The truck shook itself into life. Bob should have felt a knot in his stomach at this stage, but he was way beyond caring anymore. If the wardrobe had been full of snakes and was at the edge of a very tall building above a shark-infested pool while someone was shooting at a ticking bomb strapped on top of it, then he would have managed a knot. Instead, he slid and bounced around inside the darkness, counting his lucky stars.

After a very long thirty minutes, the truck came to a halt and Bob waited for the men to start moving things around. He waited. And waited. And then waited a little more. The stifling heat inside soon became too much, so he opened the door an inch or two and looked out. The truck had stopped well away from the city and any towns or villages, and had called into a dusty petrol station with a café tagged onto the side, where a small group of drivers were reading newspapers and drinking bottles of water. A few other lorries, all equally badly parked, obscured a clear view of them so Bob made his move and broke cover.

He scurried over to the beginnings of a heavily wooded area, near where the gravel and coarse sand gave way to a downward-sloping series of high-sided shingle banks, which in turn disappeared into the perfect blue waters of The Golden Horn. Bob's part of Istanbul lay just half a mile away.

"How do you reckon we get over there? I can see loads of ships but no big ferries or anything.. maybe we aim for one of those bridges - what do you think, Eugi?"

"Yeah. The one up northwards is the Ataturk one, an' the other one down south is the Galata, an' I'd say we ain't closer to either from here. That's some serious walking on a day like this!"

"I suggest the Ataturk," said Bagshaw in a considered voice. "I fear the Galata looks a little higher, so you'd have further to fall if your dubious friends turned up and encouraged you over the side."

"Thank you, thank you so much. Let's go north then.. hold on!"

Bob was struck by a brainwave of such incredible military genius that he nearly had to sit down. Instead, he made his way to the truck and slid the wardrobe down from the back, and then pushed it across to the trees. It almost went by itself along the embankment and down to the shoreline.

"This'll do. I can use one of the doors as a paddle.."

"Yeah! I like it! I ain't never, ever, never been in like a paddle boat before - this is gonna be great!" enthused Eugi. Bagshaw stayed ponderously quiet, mumbling to himself that there must be a good reason why so few boats were designed to look like wardrobes.

Bob set about battling one of the doors off, and soon launched the HMS Unsinkable out into the shallows, to check for leaks. It was both ship-shape and sea worthy, so Bob climbed in. The small choppy waves which had looked so harmless from the shore were quite menacing once he'd travelled a few yards out. At twenty yards the cabinet was rocking and taking on the occasional wave-crest, and Bob was beginning to wonder if this really was the best plan he'd ever had. The water inside rushed forwards, and the front end very nearly disappeared.

A real boat slowly arrived close by, but Bob was too pre-occupied with bailing out water to notice them. It was a sturdy white fishing boat, longer and shallower than the lifeboats on the America, and laden with nets and two sun-baked fishermen. The one who was sitting at the front end looked quizzically over at Bob, who was trying to stand up. As they pulled alongside and nudged the cabinet, he finally saw them.

"Err.. hello there!" he called, "Could we have a lift over to that side please?" Bob asked, pointing to the other bank of the Golden Horn. The fishermen looked at each other, and the nearest one spoke while the wardrobe sank a little further.

"Eh, you say 'we'? Is there more peoples in box?"

"No, err.. my mistake, just me thanks."

They helped him on board, and slowly made their way out into the waterway while the wardrobe sank unnoticed. Bob was more than happy to spend a few hours trying to cast out nets and either clean or sharpen knives. For the first time that day nobody was trying to kill him, and that felt particularly good. While they all relaxed in the shade of a small canopy and waited a few hours to draw the nets back in, he managed to hold a few mumbled and grunted conversations with Bagshaw and Eugi, without making the fishermen think he was worth throwing back.

As the heat of the sun began to fade away, he went and sat on the flat wooden panelling at the front end of the boat and tried to take in the extraordinary mixture of modern, ancient and plain weird worlds around him. The minaretted beauty of Istanbul drifted slowly by, and he made another Mental Note that this was definitely somewhere else to come back to, one day very soon. Everywhere he looked, Bagshaw offered rambling anecdotes about his own visits, and how wonderful it was to know that the great towers and mosques would still be standing so majestically after all these years. Bob didn't even try to work that one out.

Eventually the time came to bring the fishing nets back up from the sea. Bob noticed they contained no golden horns or anything even remotely similar, just masses of small fish and a few crabs. He decided not to say anything, and figured he probably just needed to go to bed for a while. The boat eventually carried into a small alcove on Bob's side of the waterway, and he climbed out onto the shore. He shuffled through his pockets to sort out a couple of billion Lire for the fishermen, but somewhere in the back streets, or maybe in the cistern, he had managed to lose Agatha's wad of money. That didn't matter too much, as he still had a good supply of the Old World's unofficial currency nestled in his inside pocket.

"Here, biros for you, and biros for you as well. Thanks a load!" he said, and saluted (prompted by Bagshaw). The fishermen looked even more puzzled than they had done when they rescued him, and offered a wave goodbye.

He made his way along a winding and dusty path, cut across a few small fields, and soon found that he had rejoined the noisy, restless activity on the streets of Istanbul. The day was taking on a magnificent early evening glow, with a richness and intensity that he had never seen before. He would have enjoyed it if he hadn't been so suspicious and paranoid of everyone. Such luxuries would have to wait until Andie could be here to see them as well, he told himself.

Eugi guided him through dozens of different streets to the Deliveries entrance at the back of one of the Kalesi's neighbouring hotels. After a series of incomprehensible detours through two of the other hotels via corridors and Fire Escapes, Bob found himself climbing up a series of parched wooden steps and onto the flat roof of the Hotel Kalesi. He really wasn't in the mood to admire the view, but still couldn't help but be impressed. And he was even more impressed with the kinds of maps that Naomi must have found using the Mirrors. Eugi had probably had one extremely long night.

He tried to run across the grey roof-top, but didn't have the energy to manage it. Eventually he climbed up a final set of steps, passed through a small cubicle full of fire equipment, and lurched down another flight into a dark corridor - which lead nowhere. There was no door, no light switch, nothing except darkness and absolutely no sign of where he'd come from. He reached the wall at the end and for a moment wondered what he was supposed to do next.

"Well go on through, we're here," urged Eugi.

"How? There's nothing here.. just a wall-thing.."

"It's not, it's a somethin' whatever.. I dunno.. just do stuff.. ask that broad when we get back.. jeesh, I'm beat f'today.."

Bob crossed his fingers and poked the wall with his key, and two doors no higher than his knees opened in front of him. Deeply confused, he kneeled down and crawled out onto the floor of Agatha's apartment at the Kalesi. He looked back, and saw the two doors closing themselves behind him. They made up the smoked glass front of a cabinet, containing a dense row of classical vinyl lp's.

"Don't think about it, don't think about it.." he said over and over again, until he felt like he wouldn't think about it.

Forgetting his good intentions about not intruding anywhere, Bob knew he had to have a shower. All day long he'd been distressingly aware of the fact that apart from swimming with rats, he'd been running around far too much in the scorching heat, and seemed to have attracted more insects than a box of doughnuts in a biblical plague. It wasn't a pleasant thought, and at long last he shook with a blast of revulsion and exclaimed to the world, "God Almighty! I picked up dead rats! Oh my God, oh-myyy-God, soggy dead.."

He soon found the bathroom, which was lavish even by Agatha's standards. Everything was marble of course, and whatever wasn't marble was either gold or glass, with shining silver anywhere else. Bob stood amidst the gleaming surfaces and figured that the bathroom alone would be worth more than most people's entire houses - or entire streets, perhaps. For a moment he felt too filthy and layered with rodent-germs to touch anything, but gave in after he scratched his head and noticed a small beetle fall onto the floor. It tried running to the door, but died on the way.

Bob showered until he felt almost human again, and Eugi spent just as long in the sink (despite his objections - few of which would be recognised in a court of law). Once they were both clean and feeling much the better for it, Bob found a robe and left his vile clothes soaking in the bath for a while. It gave him time to take a step back from the craziest day of his life - or maybe it was the second or third craziest day, he couldn't really decide. But first he was going to have to break another of his Non-Intrusion Rules. He hadn't eaten or had a drink all day, apart from a few strange things on the fishing boat.. and there was a very good chance that those hadn't been meant for eating - at least, not by people, anyway.

He tried two doors which refused to open despite his key, but the third lead into a pale blue corridor which ended in a cool and spacious kitchen. A broad fan slowly rotated in the centre of the ceiling, and he was pleased to see that the shelves and cupboards were well stocked with life's essentials - and best of all, a large fridge took up most of one corner. He wolfed down enough of everything to make up for the kind of day he'd been through, then returned to the living room with a chilled bottle of mineral water and flicked the tv on while his clothes dried. Turkish tv was a strange spectacle, but he put up with it because the remote control unit was far too complicated to figure out - even the on/off button was a total mystery, and Bob guessed it wasn't typical of Sony's 1973 range.

The remaining Encapsulation Field appeared to have survived a good cleaning. On reflection, leaving it under a mountain of bubbles in the bath might not have been the best idea ever, but at least the pervading Essence Of Rat had been replaced by Summer Peach - and Feiya would no doubt be pleased about that because the bagged Mirror, which he hadn't risked washing, absolutely reeked.

Eventually Bob stood before the part of the wall which would make the portal appear, and he watched as a white door slowly formed before him. His hand passed straight through the handle, which was disturbing for a while, so he tried walking towards the door as if it wasn't there..

..and stepped through to Number 107, leaving behind what he felt must be the second-most crazy, amazing city in the world. Andie would love it. He tried blocking the doorway with a few borrowed items from outside the Arizona portal, but only managed to make them both look awful and ineffective, despite all the advice from Bagshaw and Eugi. He carried the Mirror downstairs and out into the cold night at Barton, and began carefully cycling to Pierpont House. As he reached Marine Drive, Eugi started talking as if he'd finally seen the light.

"Hey, I finally figured all dis out! Now it all makes poyfect sense!"

"It does? Nice one, Eugi! I've had loads of trouble myself keeping up with everything, and I still don't think I know what's going on. Feel like spilling the beans?"

"Yeah. You're tryin' t'muscle in on Fat Paulo's turf, an' he's tryin' to stop that fruhm happenin' 'cause he's always been way ovuh protecahtive of that Lowuh East Side. Now, you're a smart kinda guy, so you should pack in while y'still got legs, 'cause he's one mean piece of work, I'm tellin' yuh. Fat Paulo is bad news, kid."

Bagshaw seemed concerned.

"Oh I say Bob, is that so? You really shouldn't become involved in all that rough hoodlum unpleasantness. Think of Andrea and all of your little ones! What would become of them?"

"What? What are you two.. are you serious? After all we've been through, that's what you reckon is.. I don't.."

Bob's brain felt like a pressure cooker with a blocked valve. Coherent sentences with a beginning, a middle and an end were a long, long way out of reach so he eventually settled for Feiya's First Rule, and kept it simple.

"..well done Eugi, and you too Bagshaw, I'll be careful.."

CHAPTER THIRTY ONE

Real Time

Thursday 19th March, 10.25pm

Bob arrived at Pierpont House and proudly placed the Mirror on the desk, nervously picking off the last of the dried seaweed in the hope that Feiya wouldn't notice. She put down her magazine and stared at it, wrinkling her nose at every scuff mark.

"Eww, what happened?"

"Huh? You're actually asking me? Well, loons were everywhere.."

"Oh, have you started? Sorry.."

"..a café blew up, I got kidnapped.."

"Tell me next time, I've got some blinking to do.."

".. legged it under the Grand Bazaar and I sailed a wardrobe.."

"Ooh, so do you want a big shiny badge?"

"No, but a coffee would be nice."

"And so would a Mirror in a well-kept bag.. look at this.."

She took on a serious expression as she ran her hands across the only clean section, and declared it to be the Distant Future Mirror. How she managed to tell that was beyond Bob. He had tried feeling for tell-tale signs on all the Mirrors after seeing her figure out the first one, but all he'd managed to do was pick up a few electric shocks. An elegant clock by the main door started a half-hourly chime, which he hadn't noticed before.

"So just an hour and a half to go then.. marvellous. Have you any idea where the last one might be?"

Feiya took on an even more serious look. If her eyebrows went any lower, she would have had a moustache.

"No, it's proving to be really difficult - as we get closer to the Sirian Alignment, the Mirrors behave with more unpredictable..ness. Don't get too stressed, but I think you'll be on your own again for the last one. Which is fine. I'm not stressed because I trust you.. so I'm not stressed, I'm not stressed I AM NOT STRESSED, I AM NOT STRESSED" she said, failing to convince Bob.

She reached for Jinx behind the desk, and calmed down a little.

"I'm not stressed, because you managed three without any help, didn't you? Thus and therefore, you'll be fine - as long as you don't come back without it, or get killed, of course. Then nobody's fine."

"Of course," sighed Bob in agreement.

"This could turn into a very long night if you have to keep revisiting different rooms, couldn't it? Might go on for years. But let's not think about that, because I know.. I know.. I KNOW you'll do fine.." she said, in a traumatised kind of threat.

"Yeah, so do I, I think. Where's Andie? Is she here?"

"No, there's nothing my Principal Aid can really do tonight. She hasn't been near the Mirrors so there's no chance that she's ever been observed or anything, which means she's in no danger. I said she could go home. I'll go and take this one to Naomi and Claudie, and see if there's anything at all that they've found out for you.. but don't hold your breath. I'll be down in a minute or two."

Feiya hurried up the stairs with the fourth Mirror, closely followed by Jinx. Bob sat alone, feeling more nervous with each passing minute. The front door swung open a little, and he felt a cold draught creep in. Outside, the wind began picking up and the trees surrounding Pierpont House began rustling loudly. Bob shivered, and looked at the clock again. Feiya had been gone for almost twenty minutes, and he nervously assumed the location of the fifth Mirror was still causing problems. He gave her another ten long minutes, and started wondering if Jinx was perhaps already on the gatepost outside his house. He took a few steps up the stairs, feeling tense.

"Hello? Fey? Is there any news yet, or should I just go?"

There was no reply. He went a few steps further, and dared to try knocking on a few of the doors. There were no replies, so he decided to go back home until Jinx might deign to put in an appearance. He stepped outside to find that the wind had been joined by a cold drizzle, as if a storm might be on the way.

"How appropriate.." he thought to himself as he reached the end of the sheltered driveway to find the drizzle had become heavier. He was too drained and anxious to allow himself to feel tired, and couldn't bear to go home without calling in to see Andie first. She'd make things seem better.

He rang the side doorbell, and her mum let him in. She smiled and had a friendly word before hurrying back into the lounge. Her current boyfriend had arrived and was sitting on the settee, spread out as if he owned the place, and Bob wondered for the thousandth time why she was with him. Upstairs, Andie's door was already half open and the walls flickered silently in the darkness from a wildlife programme on the tv. Bob poked his head around.

"Aha, the Snow Elk. Very misunderstood, they are. It's because they've got no concept of language, so nobody ever has a clue what they're going on about.. now, an African Tree Bear, by comparison.."

Andie switched her bedside light on and sat up with a yawn.

"Think I dozed off.. how'd you get on? I was worried loads. You had such a bad day today and everything.. I could see it was all bothering you when we got off the bus. So did Istanbul go alright?"

"Yeah, it wasn't the easiest one, but your research was brilliant.. Eugi says a big thanks and so do I. And Bagshaw as well, although I think he was in a different world altogether.. so all in all, I really liked Istanbul. By that I mean I liked the place when people weren't trying to shoot me or blow me up - that very nearly spoiled it. You'd love it there. Oh.. I didn't get the chance to bring you anything back."

"Oh please, you're hopeless," she laughed.

"Yeah.. anyway, Naomi, Claudie and your Supreme Commander have got four Mirrors now and Jinx is going to turn up sometime for me to have a look for the fifth. Thing is though, no-one can suss where that one is 'cause the other Mirrors are getting weird now, something to do with that Simian Line-up.. thing."

"It's the Sirian Alignment Thing. Claudie said that was ever so likely to happen. You'll be okay, I know you will."

Andie put her hand on his arm, sending a tingle all the way up to his brain where it settled long enough to attract a few million butterflies.

"You think so? Thanks.. you've really been you know, like you're helpful and everything.. so thanks for.. being really.. good.. at stuff."

He felt like he was staring down into a huge hole, and as he neared the end of the sentence he stepped closer to its edge. At the point where he said 'stuff', he fell in. His brain totally gave up and he lost the ability to think straight, or even speak. A Snow Elk would have made more sense, even with their famously poor command of English. Andie didn't seem to notice, or at least if she did, she hid it well. Really incredibly, amazingly well. Her brain seemed to be working fine.

"I just had a Significant Major Thought, Bob. You'll be losing time when Jinx comes to get you - why not just go up to 107 and wait outside for her instead? I'll come too, if that makes you feel better? Just let Fey know you're going to be there instead of at home, and there you go, you're ahead of the game!"

"Nice one, that'll be Plan A. But you don't have to come along if you don't want to, it's getting a bit grim out there."

She gave a glare that Agatha would have been proud of, and Bob shivered for reasons that he had no chance at all of working out.

"Ouch, that was a good one," he said, "It must have gone straight through my head and scorched the door. Shall we depart, then?"

Andie laughed, and they were soon cycling back to Pierpont House. Much to Bob's despair it was illuminated by lightning with horror-movie timing as they emerged from the driveway's fir trees. The front door was slightly open, which wasn't particularly strange, but the lights were all out - and that was odd, because even in the daytime, the lights were always on. Bob's heart jumped as he sensed a smell of burning, and hoped it was coming from somewhere else.

They nudged the door further open and stepped inside. Andie switched the lights on and the two of them stared up at the layers of smoke creeping across the ceiling. They hurried over to the stairs and ran through the corridors, trampling over Feiya's shattered pictures. All the doors were smashed wide open, and every room was filling with dense smoke. They stood in the doorway of Agatha's room as the lights flickered, and then Andie raced across to the other side of the bed.

"Where is she? An' the door! Look.. at.." she choked, "The one to the rest of the house.. where Naomi and Claudie.. the Mirrors are.."

The thick door lay in pieces on the floor, quickly lost under a wave of heavy, drifitng smoke. They looked at each other, neither knowing what to say until a pane of glass from a window shattered on the floor of the bedroom. A ferocious wind blew in, lifting the curtains and sending papers up in the air, casting them around and swirling through the clouds of smoke.

"Where's everyone? What's going on.." she screamed to him.

"Troublers.." Bob shouted through the wind, "..the Troublers!"

"Number.. 107 we.. have to go there!" she called back, hurrying across the room to him.

The lights faltered and struggled to stay on as the two of them clambered through the window and down into the North grounds.

They stood for a few moments breathing in the fresh air, recovering for a moment from the effects of so much acrid smoke, before running around to the forecourt.

The rain was falling harder and the wind had picked up as they sped along Marine Drive, taking a short detour to see if Jinx was outside Bob's home. There was no sign of her, so they raced onwards to Number 107. Waves roared and crashed ever louder against the shore as they tore along Lincoln Drive, racing and wavering in the wind and rain as they drew nearer to the house.

Even before they arrived, Bob was struck by a vague image of Jinx in the upstairs window. He paused outside the driveway, and gestured to Andie to do the same. He pointed the light on his bike upwards. There was definitely a dark shape there, unmistakeably cat-like, but it was hardly more than a shadow. Bob looked at Andie, and was about to speak.

"The front door's open!" Andie yelled, "I thought it was always shut? You always say in your diary it closes when you leave, all by its.."

The door had swung open in the wind, revealing a densely black interior. It slammed shut and then slowly swung open, and then slammed again. Bob turned to Andie, wiped the rain from his eyes, and pointed at the house.

"This isn't right, Andie, this isn't how it should be up here - it's all wrong! You go back, okay? They don't know you.. and you're only in this 'cause I.. just head home again, and I'll see what's going on.. go home, Andie.."

Andie drew a yo-yo from each pocket and loosened up with a few practice shots.

"I'd say there's little chance of that happening, practically none actually. No bets taken."

"Andie, I've seen what these freaks can do! I've seen what weird stuff goes on in this place! It's terrifying and I haven't told you about it and you haven't read about it 'cause I can't describe it! And I don't want you to cross that line and get involved, Andie. Just go home, please? I can't even begin to find the words to tell you how much I.. I.. how much I don't want you to get involved in all this. Please?"

Andie looked at Bob and tried keeping her hair off her face. She watched the door slamming and slamming, gradually wrenching its hinges out of the brickwork. And then she looked straight at him.

"How many times have you ever, ever left me on my own?" she

whispered, knowing Bob would have to read her lips to understand, "So don't you ever expect me to do that to you."

"But that's completely differ.. hey!" he shouted as she cycled through the lashing rain to the front door. She let her bike clatter to the ground and then stood beside it, waiting for him to follow. Bob left his where it was and ran to her. He held the door to stop it swinging, and they stepped inside together.

As always with Number 107, a dark exterior didn't mean there was a dark interior, and the lights were all on inside - but this time they were unnaturally bright, and the shadows they caused were stark, making everything appear far too sharp and clear. Only the steady ticking of the grandfather clock seemed to be as it should be, and its every tick emphasised the stillness and silence of the house.

A solitary, morbid chime rang out, signalling that midnight was half an hour away.. and a narrow band of intense vibration passed through the house, and the clock's hands moved two minutes forwards. Andie looked wide-eyed at Bob, and his heart pounded as they made their way into the hall. The key around his neck began feeling heavier and colder with every step.

They paused for a moment by the foot of the stairs. The parlour door behind them was closed, and so was the one to the dining room and the kitchen corridor - but the living room door was slightly off its catch. Its door rocked back and forth by less than an inch, as if it was unable to open any further or shut properly. Bob felt sick. There was something in there, and he could almost sense what it was.. almost..

..and then another vibration swept through the house, and the clock advanced another two minutes.

He knew he had to go into the living room, but he couldn't let Andie stay a moment longer in this place. He hated himself for not making her go home, even if that meant getting cross so that she would have to leave upset. He'd rather hurt her feelings for one foul night and spend the rest of his life making it up to her than let her walk further into this.

"This is all wrong, Andie.. you have to.."

The parlour door flew open, and a shining black stick cracked viciously against her head, sending her crashing hard against the stairs. She slid down to the floor, lying motionless with blood streaming across her face. Bob spun around to see a familiar tall man in black looking down at him. His evil eyes narrowed into slits, and he grinned with pure malice.

"You total f.." screamed Bob and managed just two steps towards him before feeling a gunbarrel pressing hard against his forehead. Salesman's grin widened as a knife flicked out from the silver end of his walking stick, and he pressed it against Andie's throat. She didn't respond, and her eyes stared blankly from behind a veil of bloodied hair. He looked back to Bob.

"You were saying, little one?"

His whining voice wrapped around Bob, every syllable dripping with spite, while the metal of the gun barrel felt as if it was burning through his skin.

"Leave her.. she's nothing to do with.. with anything.. just leave her," he said in short, snatched breaths. Salesman took a long, leering look down, and nicked her skin with the blade. Bob knew he could never feel more hatred towards anyone. He was burning with anger and fury. Salesman gave a small, almost undetectable laugh.

"You must be calmer, child. Haven't you learned anything? Tut tut. Now, I'm so glad you could join me, or should I say, join us?"

He withdrew the gun a little and gestured towards the living room. Another vibration passed through the house. The door seemed to open in slow motion to reveal all five of the Eternity Mirrors set up in the space where the dining room's double doors should have been. And then he felt his skin crawl at what lay further inside.

He entered the living room, forced by the gun pressing hard against the back of his head. Four chairs had been set around the large oval table in the bay windows. Feiya and Naomi sat at opposite ends, and Claudie sat between them, and Jinx lay in the centre of the table. But everything about them felt wrong. Bob looked at them for a few seconds, but they didn't move. There wasn't a single blink, not a flicker of life. They simply carried on staring straight ahead, barely breathing. Bob thought that they must have been..

"..frozen in time? Is that what you're thinking, child?" he said, stronger and more aggressive, "Oh yes, that's very good - how did you ever figure that? She chose well with you - nothing gets past your eagle eyes, does it?" he screamed, swinging his cane either side of Bob.

"I thought you'd like to see them all, one last time. But look, someone is missing - that must be.. yes! Dear old 'Madame' Agatha. Perhaps it was all too much for her.. she had been unwell, hadn't she? But don't concern yourself, I'm sure she was fully conscious right to the miserable end! Would you like to see her?" he added, bringing his face close, "Have to warn you, she ain't a pretty sight, not that she ever was. Got her in a special room all to herself.. wanna go see? Go 'bye-bye' to these three and then we'll go visit, what do you call her, 'Great Aunt'? That what she told you? Well y'better be quick, before it's too late!"

A grin crossed Salesman's face as he stood upright again. Bob tried to speak, but couldn't find his voice.

"Oh, don't you want to go? Fine, fine.. 'cause now it's your turn to.. shall we say 'retire' from the merry band of Guardians? Yes, let's say that. IT'S YOUR TURN TO.."

The black cane struck Bob's midriff so quickly and so hard that he had no idea what hit him. He landed near the fireplace, doubled up and gasping for breath, clutching his stomach. Salesman hit him again, and towered over him.

"Ah, where are my manners? What must you think? Do you know, we haven't ever been introduced, an' yet I feel like I've known you for so long. How could that be? Oh, I remember now."

He tapped his leg with the walking stick.

"That's right. Oh, you caused me such problems," he said, and pressed the cane's tip against Bob's neck, pinning him to the ground. "But you've made up for that, haven't you? You brought all these wonderful Mirrors back for me - I didn't even have to fetch them myself! No need too rely on my damn-fool inferiors! Betcha thought you were being clever, a real hero? Well no greater fool's ever lived!" he roared.

"You've ALL saved me so much trouble! A 'Troubler' with no troubles! And those three imbecilic creatures.." he gestured to the table, "..they even put four of them back together! Worried about the fifth were you? Well if you'd found it you would have had to take it from me!"

Another vibration passed through the house and he threw his head backwards, practically howling an insane, baying laugh.

"Who.. who are you?" Bob choked.

Salesman looked down, shocked that he had dared speak. He struck Bob twice before pressing the cane down beside his neck, angling it across his throat.

"Ask all you want, cause you won't ever know! I'm a no-one, a someone who learned the system, found the flaws, widened those gaps.. and jumped right on in! Nothin's foolproof, 'cause there's always fools.. I had mine, you had yours - and for now it's just us! But after midnight.. oh after midnight.." he said, rolling his eyes to the ceiling and barely able to speak with hysteria, "..my workers, my pack of dogs, they're gonna be steppin' back through those doorways, ready to worship their new 'Guardian' and.. and.."

"Wha.." Bob gulped, desperate for breath.

"SHUT UP! Enough talk, enough! Know what? I was always told, 'Never kill anyone you don't know'. Well I never was much good at listening - I've never known any! And I won't know YOU!"

Another burst of insane laughter filled the room, ending as Salesman reached down and lifted Bob by the front of his shirt, drawing him up close to his face. He spoke in a deadly calm whisper, making Bob shiver with revulsion under his cold breath.

"Been pleased to make your brief acquaintance, runt!"

Salesman threw him onto the floor, hurled the cane across the room, and grasped his hands around Bob's neck. He slowly squeezed tighter and tighter, and laughed wildly as he noticed his reflection strangling no-one in the Mirrors.

"Oh, she was clever.. that's very clever.. but who's to help you now, worthless rat-child? No-one's to help you.." he said, dragging Bob before them, laughing to see the reflection in all five.

A double vibration passed through the house, and the Mirrors shimmered blue as midnight drew four minutes closer. Salesman screamed with laughter.

"My time! My time's near upon us!" he screamed.

Bob tried to struggle, but the room slowly became darker and darker, and Salesman's words began to drift further away as the agonising moments passed by. The burning pain in his lungs gradually started to pass, and even the grip around his neck became less painful as the room began swimming in small circles. Bob looked beyond Salesman's shoulders and was almost sure Andie was standing in the doorway.

"..she's fine after all.. good.. good.." he thought dreamily, as the room and all the pain began fading away..

Moments earlier, Andie had begun to regain her senses a little. The most awesome, screaming pain ran all the way around her head, starting somewhere behind her right ear. She put her hand up to it and flinched at the stabbing sensation, and moaned at the sight of so much blood over her hand. And then fragments started coming back to her. This was the portal house, and something bad had happened - but what? She didn't know, but that didn't matter. All that did matter was the thought that if she was in trouble, Bob must be in even worse trouble. She turned her head as much as she could, and saw that she was lying at the bottom of the stairs - and that made no sense at all, unless.. unless she'd fallen down them? And if that was the case, she had to pull herself together quickly and get back up there and find out if Bob was okay. She set her eyes on the top step and began crawling up towards the darkness, trying to stand but finding that her legs wouldn't let her.

After the first few agonising steps were behind her, she sensed, as much as saw, a sudden movement through the banister, across the hallway in the living room. A tall man had hit Bob hard enough to send him hurtling towards the fireplace, and was standing over him as if he meant to kill him. But what could she possibly do to help? Somewhere in her dazed mind she knew that she had to get upstairs. But why? She couldn't remember. Nothing made sense and the entire world seemed to be spinning even worse than ever.. but she had to get up the stairs. She carried on crawling, pushing and dragging herself over every hard edge, fighting to see through her matted hair, thinking only of Bob. Her head felt as if it could split wide open with every jolting movement, and she had to stop herself from being sick with the pain.. but Bob needed her, and she had to keep going..

Another weird vibration passed through the house.

At the top of the stairs, she stopped. Now it made sense. One of these rooms could take her to Bob's Great Aunt. She looked around, struggling to know what to do next. Two doors were blocked with junk, and the others were all too far away for her to even dare hope to reach. In her mind she screamed in despair at herself. Of course it was all too much, of course she couldn't do the right thing, because she was Andie and she never, ever did ANYthing. Her eyes were burning, her head hurt like a riot was going on inside, the entire world was growing more fuzzy and uneven.. and she felt her forehead resting heavily on the carpet, and her shoulders began rocking with exhausted sobs..

..and then a narrow crack of light began stinging the edge of her vision, and she lifted her head from the floor a little, not even noticing the double vibration that shook through the house. A door immediately to her left seemed to be slightly open, throwing a bright triangle of light across the floor.. and she started crawling again, nearer and nearer, nearer and nearer..

"..she's fine after all.. good.. good.." Bob thought dreamily, as the room and all the pain began fading away. The hands were so tight around his neck, and kept getting tighter.. but what was that? He could have sworn he heard Andie's voice. What was she shouting? And where was she? His vision returned just enough for him to see her standing in the doorway, holding.. a Mirror?

"Look away, Bob! Look away!" she screamed again.

Confusion flashed across Salesman's face, and he turned to her.

"You? What the hell's a creature like YOU.." he snapped, but at the split second that he realised Andie was holding the Distant Future Mirror, he also realised that he was looking at his own image reflected in not only that one, but also in all of the five behind him. He managed to look back at Bob, and barely had enough time to utter a last damning curse before his body turned into a screaming, swirling vortex of rage and burning ashes, drawn in snake-like trails through each Mirror. Bob's world went black again for a while, and by the time he was able to follow Andie's voice back into the living room, the clock had ticked even closer to midnight. He looked up into her eyes.

"Andie? You're okay again.. what happened to you? I thought he.. you.." he mumbled, reaching up to touch the side of her head. He could have cried with joy that there was no blood there - her hair was blowing wildly and she looked better than ever, way beyond perfect.

"Shut-uuuuup.." she shouted, putting a hand over his mouth. He noticed that she was wearing Tiffany Blue gloves which felt exactly like the material of the Encapsulation Fields.

"Yes I'm okay - I went to Manhattan and they all fixed me up and I bought a Mirror and Madame Agatha back with me! She's right behind me, she's right beh.."

Andie looked around, but Agatha was nowhere to be seen.

"She.. where's she gone? She was right behind me.."

Bob got to his feet and fell over as another vibration passed through the house. They ran back up the stairs, stopping in disbelief outside the Master Bedroom. The room's interior had gone, and Agatha from 1927 was just inches away from them, up to her waist in a sea of white mist, frantically and silently pounding against an invisible door, trying desperately to get through. Bob turned to Andie as the furniture outside the Arizona portal took to the air, crashing violently from wall to wall.

"The rules still apply to her in 1927, Andie! She can't go forwards in time and get here! She's caught between now and then! And look - she can't even see us or anything!"

Andie touched the invisible barrier between herself and Agatha. She stared up at her, and seemed to be lost in thought.

"I've got it! I've got it, Bob! Downstairs NOW!"

The strong winds outside were nothing compared to the tornado now blowing through the house, and everything in the hall seemed to be moving. They took an age to stagger back to the living room, fighting through the blasting wind and avoiding the rolling furniture. The walls shook as they went through ghosted images of themselves running up and down the stairs.

Andie soon stood before the Mirrors and shouted for all she was worth through the chaos to Bob.

"You have to go through the Immediate Past Mirror! She'll listen to you! Bring another Agatha through the portal again! If the rules really do apply back in '27, she'll force the other Agatha through upstairs 'cause two of them can't be in the same place! Self Duplication!"

"Huh? Go back through one of these? But only Agatha can make them work! They're part of h.."

"Yes, but you're.. you're different! You don't know what you can do! Go back to when Agatha knows you, but before I was there - and to whenever you won't meet yourself to mess everything up! Quick, let me check your diary!"

Andie grabbed the diary from his inside pocket, and began racing through its pages. The table by the windows finally surrendered to the wind and started grinding its way across the room, knocking Naomi and Feiya like mannequins onto the floor. Bob and Andie stared in horror as the frozen bodies slowly dragged over the carpet, colliding with the swirling plaster and glass. The wind blew even harder and Claudie toppled over, becoming lost in the debris and the ghosted images of everyone who had ever entered the house. Another vibration shook through the floor, and the walls bowed with disfiguring twists. Andie lost her balance and reached for Bob, and in that one moment the diary was swept from her hands and sailed high amongst the thousands of books from the library that were swirling throughout the house.

"Oh God I'm sorry! I'm so useless, I knew it, I'm useless! Take a guess Bob, just take a guess!"

"Guess? I can't guess anything! I've never.."

"You can! Just shut-up and pick a day, you have to! I know you'll get it right!"

Through all the frenzy, the grandfather clock stood unaffected in the hallway and loudly clunked forwards another notch.

"Okay then.." he said, terrified.

Bob stood before the Immediate Past Mirror and ran his hand along the side, trying to remember how he'd seen Agatha do it. It took on a bright neon-blue glow and its hard, reflective surface changed to a gently undulating misty vapour.

"I.. I need to go to Great Aunt Agatha, The Guardian Of Time, on.. err.." he looked back at Andie and shrugged.

An image flashed into his mind of the early morning when he had left the Lexington Building, the quiet Manhattan streets beginning to stir, and Bagshaw snoring all the way to The Ansonia for the return trip to Arizona. That entire day would be clear - but what day was that? What day was.. any of them? Bob knew he had been in New York at the end of July, and remembered being in Agatha's suite writing a large '27th' in his diary. Or was it a '29th' - or a '1927'? And was that the day he'd arrived, or one of the others?

"Just guess!" she screamed, her voice all but lost in the mayhem. The clock gave another loud clunk. Three minutes to midnight.

"..okay, on July.. the 29th 1927, at.." he said, and glanced over to the grandfather clock, "..at eleven.. fifty seven, but in the morning! Wherever she is!"

He moved his hand towards the blue haze and watched wide-eyed as his fingers disappeared into a beautiful warmth that seemed to race through him. The seconds loudly ticked onwards, and nothing happened. He turned to look back again to Andie just in time to see her finishing a run up. She launched herself at him, barging him towards the Mirror..

..and the room was gone. For a split second which felt as if it lasted a lifetime, he drifted through endless clouds of intense colours, becoming a part of them, and becoming lost in them. He steadily became convinced that something had gone wrong and he would be drifting forever, but the colours began taking on definite shapes, soon merging into recognisable forms which came closer and closer to him until..

..he arrived upside down, surrounded by sharp and painful knife points which felt as if they could tear him to shreds at any moment. His head spun for a few long seconds before he finally managed to wonder where he was.

July 29th 1927 was a sunny day, and at 11.57am it was also a very warm and very busy day. He could tell he was in a bush, slowly making his way head-first towards the ground. There were masses of people milling around in the huge garden, and a band was playing somewhere nearby. He crawled to the side of the hedgerow, and realised he was back at the Park Avenue garden party, which meant Agatha couldn't be far away. He looked at his watch and felt his heart pounding through his entire body as he realised he was using up Real Time.

"A minute here is a minute back there.. oh God where is she? C'mon, c'mon.."

Then he remembered the floral swinging-chair they had sat on while watching the other guests arrive. He hurried behind the long hedge and made his way closer to the band. He could see the chair, with Agatha and himself sitting on it while people came to speak to her. Her friend in a tangerine summer dress and an insanely wide hat took an eternity before she finished waffling to Agatha. She stood up and left, and then Agatha sent the other Bob inside for the drinks.. and the newly-arrived Bob scrambled out from the hedgerow and ran across the lawn.

"Aunt Agatha! Aunt Agatha!" he called, trying to keep his voice down as he jumped over the back of the chair. He caught the edge of the seat with his knee and landed face down at Agatha's feet. He kneeled up and grabbed her arms, while she gave him her most bone-crunching glare ever.

"Agh, stop it.. there's no time to explain! I've come from Barton through a Mirror on Real Time and we have to get to The Ansonia right now and we've got less than two minutes - it's nearly midnight!"

Agatha didn't ask any questions, and they hurried around to the front of the mansion to her Bugatti. Bob threw himself onto the passenger seat, and gave the instructions.

"Bugsy! We need The Ansonia, an' step on it harder than you've ever step.. WOOOOAHHHH!!"

Bugsy cheered and took off at top speed along Park Avenue, cutting across roads, sliding wildly around corners and beeping at everything in sight. He was enjoying every second, unlike Eugi.

"Leave the directions t'me kid, 'cause gettin' us places ain't your strong point. Listen up, Mugsy - we're in a hurry here! What's wid all the roads? Take a shorty through Central Park, yuh dumb rollahskate! C'mon, hang a right here.."

They bounded through an open gateway and raced across a vast expanse of water before demolishing a series of tall ironwork fences, and then obliterated countless trees and huge bushes. The car was soon filling with branches and leaves.. and Agatha's cloche hat stayed behind, caught in the low branches of one tree.

"Robert, that was my hat, and might I point out it was a particular favourite. Have you any idea.."

"Sorry, sorry, but listen, The Ansonia - that's where the portal is, but the Troublers trashed the place! I was there just after it happened and it's a total bomb site but the portal still works so you.."

Bob was bounced into the back seat. Agatha turned around, completely unflustered and looked down at him in the footwell.

"As long as all this makes sense to you Robert, I'm sure it will to me, in turn. But my hat.."

They roared across Eighth Avenue and Columbus Avenue, and the tyres squealed and burned as they rounded onto Broadway. Bob kneeled up to see The Ansonia fast approaching, wondering if they'd even be able to get up to the room.. and then he froze. He felt as if he'd been struck by at least a dozen bolts of lightning. Absolutely nothing was wrong with it. Bob shouted to Agatha.

"But it was wrecked.. a total disaster zone.."

"Perhaps it hasn't happened yet, Robert? Maybe you've come back earlier than you think?"

Bob's brain packed in. He knew the hotel was destroyed on the day of the garden party, yet here it was, untouched. Bugsy snapped him out of his bemusement as they raced towards the entrance.

"Hey 'bino, what room yoo want, huh?"

"Huh? Oh, 963 and Eugi'll guide you, it's on the sixteenth flo-o.."

They bounced up the Ansonia's front steps with the speedometer wobbling at 100, and flattened the huge entrance doors as if they were made of cardboard. They slid sideways all the way across the reception floor, demolishing part of the large fountain with Bugsy's back end and ricocheting off two walls before battering the third and coming to a slamming, sideways halt in place of the reception desk. The huge back wall next to them shook from top to bottom and great sections of plaster began falling down from the ceiling. Bugsy had managed to demolish everything in sight, and started revving his engine again.

"Ey, jus' warmin' up 'bino, you like this? I love-a-this! Let's go!"

Henri the concierge stood at the end of the desk, behind the only undamaged section, and stared open-mouthed - first at Bob, then his beloved reception hall, and then fainted. Bugsy fired his engines twice and they took off, roaring up the stairs, and Bob looked back to the scene of destruction behind them as the car turned at the top.

"Oops.." was the only word he could think of, and immediately awarded himself an Honours Degree in Understatement.

Bugsy took almost every corner at top speed with two wheels on the stairs and two wheels on the walls, wiping out carved wooden columns, smashing into elevator doors and completely re-designing the decor for flight after flight. The special security doors to Floor 16 opened in an instant by themselves, narrowly avoiding being wrecked. Bob bounced around in the back seat as the car rattled and collided with absolutely everything in the corridors, ploughing through entire rooms and walls before rejoining the right corridor in an explosion of bricks, mortar and iron beams. He clung onto the back of the passenger seat, stunned at how Agatha could possibly retain such unruffled dignity. She looked as if she was being chauffeured through a quiet country road on a Sunday afternoon.

At last they tore into the final corridor, and Bugsy turned early into Room 963, taking half the wall and the entire doorway with him. They spun around twice in the main room, finally coming to a halt surrounded by piles of debris, right in front of the portal - neatly parallel, of course. Bob leaped over the side of the car, and the archway immediately appeared in the wall.

"You have to follow me and don't stop running no matter what, okay? You mustn't stop at all.." he said, helping her climb over

Bugsy's passenger door.

He turned from her and ran into the portal, and Agatha followed closely behind him. She immediately found herself in a large white room, surrounded by rapidly flowing streams of a dense white vapour, and recognised that she was in some kind of timeless gateway between two destinations in time, but it was a kind she had never experienced before. She stared through the mists as Bob seemed to reach the other side in a slow and solitary giant step, and saw him pass a woman who was pounding against a jet black doorway. The other woman didn't notice Bob moving past her at all, so Agatha ran as fast as she could across the white currents to find out who she was, and more importantly, how she dared to be in an Immediate Absence portal.

As she charged through the white smoke, the other woman started to turn around and almost looked back at her, and immediately fell through into the blackness beyond the doorway. Agatha was determined not to let her get away, and ran faster towards her - but instead of following her through, she collided with the solid blackness and almost knocked herself unconscious. She fell down into the mist and waited for her head to stop spinning and pounding before crawling back out to Bugsy. For the first time in at least two centuries, she felt totally bewildered - and that was a feeling she didn't like. And as for the bump..

Bob had re-emerged upstairs at Number 107, and turned around to see Andie's Agatha still pounding on the invisible door. For some reason she turned to look back into the mist, and was practically thrown from the room - and straight into him. They both tumbled across the corridor and straight into the Victorian bathroom, which fortunately didn't lead anywhere except a bathroom. Agatha looked back across the corridor to the Master Bedroom doorway and saw the vague image of a woman colliding with an invisible door, then fall down into the mist.

"What the heck.." she managed, before Bob took her hand and dragged her to her feet.

All the grandfather clocks began loudly chiming midnight through the house. Agatha had regained her balance at the top of the stairs, and the two of them breathlessly struggled every step of the way down through the ferocious winds. The stairs twisted and shifted beneath their feet, the walls contorted into a hundred ceilings, and wild spirits and time-echoes screamed and raced in the air around them. The entire building seemed to be tearing itself apart, stretching every dimension to the very brink of oblivion.

They both fell through the dipping banister rail, landing outside the living room. Andie was desperately trying to hold a chair in front of the Mirrors and screaming over to Agatha, but her voice was lost in the tumult as the chorus of chimes marched onwards, growing louder and deeper as they neared midnight. The final ground-shaking chime shook Bob from his feet, and he watched helplessly as Agatha launched herself towards the chair.

Powerful blue and white neon rays emerged with devastating claps of thunder from deep inside each Mirror, linking themselves through Agatha's body, throwing her from side to side like a puppet. Suddenly Bob felt as if every noise on earth was rising through the floor, climbing to a roaring crescendo of such violent intensity that it ceased being a sound and became entirely physical, taking him from the insanity and chaos, and into an unbearable pain..

..and then silence. Nothing but absolute silence.

Bob opened his eyes, and looked up from the floor. Mild tremors were still running through the room, and the walls were bending slightly.. but that was fine, because Agatha was sitting before the Mirrors. She turned around looking pale and very shaken.

"Andie sweetheart, that needs wrapping properly and taking back before we can do anything else.."

Agatha pointed at the blue bag which Andie had only been able to partially cover the extra Mirror with. Andie stumbled over towards it, secured it properly and slowly carried it away up the stairs. The walls stopped bending, the final time-echoes disappeared, and the tremors faded away. Bob got to his knees and looked around at the devastation, amazed and yet not amazed that only the five Eternity Mirrors and Agatha's chair seemed unaffected. Naomi blinked a few times and tried sitting up, and was soon joined by a dazed Claudie. They both crawled over to Feiya.

Andie returned wearing different clothes and holding a black shoulder bag, remarkably similar to Naomi's back in 1927. She was looking very pleased with herself. Bob was stunned.

"Umm.. how long, exactly, did you stay back there? I mean.. like both times?" he croaked.

Andie grinned and shrugged, then tapped her nose in a distinctly Claudie-esque manner. Agatha stood up and leaned close to the Present Mirror, quietly speaking with words completely unfamiliar to Bob. While she waited for the Mirrors to react, she turned to everyone in the room.

"That's about as close as it's ever likely to get. Right.. now I'm back in charge, there's a lot for us to do.. first things first, I need to check on Haken.. our Guardian Of Spatial Dynamics," she said with authority and no emotion, adding Hakenthør's title at the end for Bob's benefit. The Mirrors soon glowed brightly with a series of vertical metallic beams, drifting back seemingly forever. Agatha had obviously reached whoever she was trying to reach.

"Hakenthør? Yes, it's me - I've stepped out by fifteen point three degrees I'd estimate, so I'm a little younger and in the wrong time, but.. 1927, early August. Yes, I'm at 107 Lincoln Drive."

For the first time since he'd known her, Bob saw an expression of complete amazement spread across Agatha's face, as if she had genuinely been taken by complete surprise.

"Why am I here? Because there's been a Primary Andromedan Breach! We nearly lost everything! Any communications from this department over the past seven to eight days have been simulations from Troublers, and you need to start tracking them down right now! The Sirian Alignment has passed and I'm still in the hot seat but wildly out of Allowable Sync. There's so much to sort out - we need a Code White Re-Org Committee in place, fully attended with immediate effect, and.."

Jinx demurely wandered back into the room, ignored Bob completely and stretched up onto Agatha's lap. She hissed at the Present Mirror before stepping briefly onto the tabletop, and then leapt into its metallic light. Agatha turned to face Bob and Andie, looking as if she was barely able to stay in control of herself. She took a deliberately slow deep breath, flicked a long cigarette from its case, and started twirling it into a blur.

"You wouldn't believe the aftermath of this mess. And as for everything that's happened from 1927 up to now.. that'll be almost unthinkable.. unprecedented Parallel Co-Exis.. we have no reference for this.. oh, where do I start.. where do I start.."

She seemed lost for a moment as the scale of the problems began running through her mind. Bob, who would be the first to admit that he hardly knew anything and understood even less, figured she had a mind-blowingly difficult time ahead of her. His eyes followed Andie as she went and hugged Agatha, before carefully picking her way between the remnants of a huge bookcase over towards Feiya, who was still lying unconscious near the library doorway. Naomi and Claudie weren't in much better shape, and Bob went over to help them to their feet. Agatha, however, was in no mood for playing Florence Nightingale.

"Naomi? Claudette? Snap out of it right now and follow Jinx through here.." she instructed, pointing to the Present Mirror. Her attention fell upon Feiya.

"Ah, and she must be Feiya. Pick her up and take her straight through as well. I said now and I mean now! Time waits for.."

She paused for a moment, changed her expression, and looked across to Bob, and then to Andie.

"Oh, and well done you two, very nice work.. we'll talk later. Now go straight home, there's nothing more you can do here - well, not immediately, at least. I trust you can let yourselves out?" she said, adjusting the Present Mirror.

Bob hurried over to Andie who was already in the hallway, and decided that the walk home might just take a very long time. He was shattered, but still overjoyed that she wasn't hurt, and that.. and that.. any words were pushed out of the way as a million emotions ran through him, causing one of his Terminal Brain-Overload moments. He gave up trying to think of anything. It was time to keep it simple, and some things in life could be very, very simple. He reached for her hand as they stepped through the door together..

..but his fingers closed in mid-air as he immediately arrived back in his bedroom at precisely the same moment that Andie stepped straight into hers. That was an appropriately weird ending to the day, and all things considered, an entirely welcome one. He fell onto his bed, and was asleep before his head hit the pillow.

CHAPTER THIRTY TWO

Andie's Rock

Friday 20th March 6.15am

Bob let the alarm clock bleep itself silent, slid from his bed to the floor and dressed in a semi-comatose daze. He stumbled down to breakfast feeling worn out, and started unwrapping his birthday presents which sat on the kitchen table. A book of Inorganic Chemistry, a dictionary of German grammar, a thick volume of Tangential Manifolds (maths, apparently) and a subscription to the Scientific Comment Journal. He tried to look deeply grateful, but didn't have to try for long.

"Ooh, quiet Robert, look at this.." urged his mother.

A picture of the school appeared on the tv, so his dad turned the volume up. As always, Sally the South Today news presenter looked and sounded far too perky at such an early hour. Bob made a sluggish Mental Note to write and ask what kind of coffee did that for her, and how many mugs of it she needed.

"..Trygvason School will be closed while emergency work is carried out on a collapsed tower, which occurred last night. It's believed the oldest of the five towers was badly affected by last week's storms, and that the one last night was.. oh, Happy Birthday Bob! Why not go and make Andie some breakfast for a change? And now for the weather.."

Bob was dumbstruck. His father tutted and drew a sharp breath.

"Well fancy that, Robert m'lad. The school's closed! Lucky nobody was around or that could have been a real tragedy. I'd fully expect between one and two hundred injuries, perhaps a dozen fatalities depending on the accessibility of the Emergency Services. You'd have to add a few in case of roadworks on the way, of course.. I wonder which tower it was? They're all very similar."

His mother jumped in and raised the stakes.

"Probably that one around the side. I've always thought the lower walls looked insubstantial on that one.. simple design flaw."

Bob stared at them, exasperated.

"Hold on, didn't you hear what she said? She said Happy Birthday to me at the end! She even winked!"

His mother sighed and topped up her tea.

"Now you're just being ridiculous, Robert. You're getting over-excited on your big day, and you've still got your sleepy-head on. In anyone's book that's a dangerous combination. I'm glad you're not a brain surgeon yet, otherwise somebody out there would be in for a very big headache today.."

Bob knew there was just one place for him to be.

"I'm off to Andie's.. to tell her about the school, then. Thanks for the books and all that, I'll look at them later on, really I will. See you later," he said, taking a final mouthful of toast.

As soon as he stepped outside, the fresh morning air and the sound of the sea greeted him just as they always had done for his entire life, and he took a moment to just look around and breathe it all in. The world really was carrying on as normal, and for the first time ever, Bob felt that 'normal' was actually quite wonderful. Barton was still the same old quiet, reliable, magnificent nothingness of a half-town that it always had been.

"And long may it stay like that.." he thought, closing the door.

He wandered along Sea Road, noticing everything on his way as if he'd never walked the road before. No detail was too small, pathetic or insignificant, because everything was there to be noticed. Everyone in the entire world was having a new start, a second chance - and practically nobody had a clue about it. He stood for a few moments at the start of Lincoln Drive, just outside the carpark of The Cliff House Hotel, and looked along to the small pointed roof of Number 107, way off in the dulled blue-grey distance. No ominous thunderclouds, no B-movie lightning bolts, and no sinister crows circling in the sky above. And even better than all of that added together - there was no sign of a certain black cat, anywhere.

Major Milbank, Barton's oldest and most decorated war-hero, brought Bob back to the real world with a bright 'Good morning' from across the road. His rat-sized dog was straining on its leash, yapping at another small dog who was responding in kind. The other owner laughed, and crossed over for a dog-owner's start to the day with the Major.

Bob carried on walking to The Coffee Pot, and without breaking stride jumped up to try and shake a particularly thick branch on the Snowstorm Tree. And missed completely. The worker's hut was exactly where it had been all week, and there was still no sign of the new Scenic Bench - or maybe it had fallen down into a clay pit already? Either way, a new one might be there in time for summer, this year or next.

The white delivery van from Reg's Veggies was parked outside the Barton Deli, and Mrs Reid was pointing at a tray of something green in the back. Bob returned her 'hello' as he walked past, and let her observation about last night's dreadful weather go over his head.

Andie was standing just inside the café as usual for that time of day, and looked as tired as Bob felt. She opened the front door and the bell gave its customary tinkle as he went in. His swarm of butterflies immediately took flight, and he had to wait for a moment before they allowed his brain to work out something to say to her.

"Hiya. No school today! One of the dodgy towers collapsed last night and we've got today off, maybe longer! How good is that?"

Andie nodded, gave a relieved smile and rubbed her eyes. Her mum breezed past on her way to one of the rooms near the kitchen, pausing to plant a grip into Andie's hair.

"Honestly sweetheart, your mop grows so fast.. yes, that tower business has just been on the tv - how frightening! I'm so glad you two weren't at school when it happened - imagine if it had been in the daytime? Makes me shiver.."

"Yeah.. did you hear Sally say Happy Birthday to me at the end?"

Mags raised an eyebrow at him, and laughed until she was in the laundry room.

"Oh how subtle, Bob - you're losing your touch in your old age! Birthday greetings on the news? I don't think so.." she called.

Bob looked at Andie as if to say 'I'm serious!' but she just laughed as well. Her mum came back into the dining area with his brightly wrapped birthday gift.

"As if we'd forget! Here you go.. they're a bit odd, but Andie insisted on them. I think the school's making you as mad as each other," she said.

For a moment Bob held the present a little warily, sensing that it was shaped like a book or two, it even felt like a book or two, and it weighed about the right amount as well. He tore off the wrapping to reveal a history of New York, a book of Emily Dickinson poems, a random collection of A-Z maps, and a huge diary.

"Well that's brilliant, that is! I'm really.." the sentence was cut short as Andie's mum planted a kiss on him, following it with a hug. Bob went deeply red as he noticed that Andie had a moment's hesitation in deciding whether to follow suit or not. She settled for a quick half-a-hug, avoided anything resembling eye contact and ran back upstairs to get changed. Her mum laughed.

"Oh she gets more odd, but you know what she's like. I do laugh at times. Now then, a birthday breakfast, old man? Something easy to chew?"

Bob didn't feel like having anything at all, but went along with everything she suggested. Andie returned just as he finished, and with a little encouragement from her mum decided that spending the day in Bournemouth was a good idea.

"You might not want to go in your school uniform, Bob.." she suggested, noticing that he wasn't quite firing on all cylinders.

"Oh, right.. yeah. I'll go and.. you know.. see you later, then, Andie?" he said, as she turned her attention to a seagull standing on a bin outside.

As he wandered home with his new books, he tried figuring out why she had chosen a small hug instead of.. well, anything, really. And as for not looking at him, what was all that about? Especially on his birthday, as well. Maybe he needed her more than she actually needed him? Or not. Maybe.. maybe. It was all too depressing and brain-mushingly difficult to work out. Time-travel and saving the universe was one thing, but this was in a different league altogether.

Back home, his parents' cars were gone from the driveway so he let himself into the empty house, put the books on top of the other ones on the kitchen table, and staggered upstairs with them. Today looked like it was going to be yet another difficult one, all be it for completely different reasons to all the other difficult ones. He nudged his bedroom door open, and froze.

Jinx was curled up in the middle of his bed. Just for once, she raised her head sleepily, and looked like a normal, genuine, cat type of cat. Bob put his books down and sat on the bed a short way in front of her, dreading what else the day was going to have in store.

"For heaven's sake.. you can't need me to follow you somewhere now, can you? Even after all that happened last night? I thought we were all sorted. There aren't six of those Mirrors, are there?"

Jinx did nothing, and started licking a front paw. Despairingly, Bob opened the window to let her rush out so that he could start following her to wherever. She ignored him and started licking the other paw, instead.

"Look Jinx, I'm closing the window.. you're missing your chance.. I'm closing it.. you can't climb down the trellis.. closing.. and.. it's.. closed."

Jinx turned her attention to a shoulder.

"So you're just here for the sake of it then? At last, a social visit. Marvellous."

Jinx settled down into a furry black heap. She looked straight at him, while he re-introduced Bagshaw to Miss Dickinson. He placed Eugi on the pile of maps, and then sat on the bed next to Jinx again.

"It's alright for cats, isn't it?" he sighed, and stroked her head. Surprisingly, she didn't seem to object.

"You don't have to figure out what you want to say or even how to say it, once you've figured out what it is that you need to say. And you don't have to worry about how stupid you look when you try.. or how it would feel if the person you're saying it to doesn't want you to be saying whatever it is that you're trying to.. umm.. thing. I don't know where to start, and you wouldn't believe how my stomach feels.."

Jinx stepped up onto his window sill, knocked a deck of cards onto the floor, and then stared outside. Bob crawled over his bed and leaned next to her. She was watching Andie walking along the road towards the house.

"You still don't like her, do you? Well I do. But how I get her to know that is beyond me. I can't believe that despite everything that's happened, like all that crazy stuff in all those crazy places, I'm still the same hopeless no-one that I've always been. How come nothing's different and.."

Jinx stepped down onto the duvet and leapt to the floor, and nonchalantly strolled out of the room as if Bob had never been there. He sighed, quickly got changed in time for the doorbell to ring, and greeted Andie with a just-rehearsed smile.

"So, Bournemouth here we come, then! Shall we depart?" he announced to her.

They stood at the bus stop outside the newsagents, waiting for the

8.45am Wilts & Dorset bus. Andie showed off a couple of new tricks with her wooden Day Off yo-yo, and Bob made all the right kind of responses. Half an hour later the bus still hadn't turned up, and the conversation that had been stilted at best, had become forced and awkward. There was so much to talk about, but Bob wasn't picking up on Andie's lead-ins and she was missing all of his. Maybe his birthday was supposed to be a let-down after all the chaotic mayhem of the week? Bob figured it was better to say anything than keep on doing nothing.

"How about the beach instead? I believe it's charming this time of year, and there's a whole load of pebbles that need sending back where they came from. Or collecting, if you'd want?"

Andie shrugged, and they started walking along Sea Road towards one of the few remaining cliff paths that still reached all the way down to the beach. They hadn't gone more than fifty yards before the bus drove past them.

Andie sat with her back to a large cube-shaped concrete block which the council had dumped on the beach for a geological reason last year. Shortly after its arrival, the words "Andie's Rock" had appeared on it in black capital letters - a mystery which had remained unsolved. Bob sat a little nearer the sea, with his back to her while he threw some carefully selected pebbles at the waves. He took a deep breath, and tried saying something important.

"Y'know how uh.. sometimes someone can be like.. a friend, and then they're not almost like that, any more.. to someone.."

He stopped, and knew he was speaking top-quality drivel of the very finest grade, plus he was saying it far too quietly anyway. The noise of the waves crashing against the shingle was either a help or a hindrance, but he couldn't decide which. A couple of pebbles later, he tried starting again but only got as far as taking a deep breath. This wasn't good.

Andie watched Bob hurling stones, and was distracted by something, lost in the corner of her eye. She looked down to just by her left side, and tried to see around the side of her rock. Jinx was looking straight up at her. Her heart missed a beat and she was tempted to give Bob a poke in the back with her foot, but decided against doing that because he seemed to be in an odd, hard-to-talk-to kind of mood.

Carefully choosing each step, Jinx made her way onto Andie's lap. With a slightly trembling hand, Andie started stroking her while studying her for any signs of weirdness or aggression - but apart from smelling faintly of coffee, she seemed perfectly normal. Jinx stayed put, purring softly and apparently enjoying the attention. She rested her front paws a little below Andie's neck, before closing her eyes and settling into her arms. Andie smiled to herself, gave her a huge hug and stroked her luscious black coat.

"I know you love me really, I've always known.." she said, but before the sentence was finished Jinx wriggled free and darted away, silently disappearing somewhere far behind the rock, leaving Andie feeling shocked and more than a little hurt.

Bob slowly turned around with an expression of complete and utter dumb-struck awe on his face.

"You.. you know I do? You really know.. I do?"

Andie looked straight at him, and after an equally dumb-struck moment, nodded slowly through a huge smile. Bob laughed and couldn't hold back a grin that soon felt like it might spread way behind his ears - and then keep going until it reached Australia. He crawled over and without quite believing what he was doing, kissed her. Suddenly all heaven broke loose in his heart, and as if that wasn't wonderful enough, he saw that she was still smiling at him - so he kissed her again.

"How about New York instead of Bournemouth? Or maybe we could cruise there - I know a really nice ship.." he said, taking her hand. Andie laughed, and they stood up just as Jinx reappeared on top of the rock, looking pleased with herself. She began her familiar meowing and then scampered off towards the cliff path.

Hand in hand, Bob and Andie followed her.

THE SENCH
FLAPPER'S ALMANAC
FROM THE ENLIGHTENED PEN OF FELICITY CHANCER

SECTION FOUR
COMMUNICATION!

"HEY RUBE!
Sweetify an' hold the obvee
lollygagging! Skid-over big time
an' sockdolage a baksheesh! Lu-Lu
plus nouveaux darb drainage to
cart, so land it Lindberg -
HERE!"

Now, in this section we will be looking into one of the most essential and important aspects of Flapper Life - communication! And not just any old converating will do. So far you have developed the right image, you know the right joints to be seen in, you can shop in the right shops and you can even walk the right walk - but now you must learn to talk the right talk!

You have to be seen and you have to be heard, but let's face it, you only have to be understood by those who you want to be understood by. Your clique is your world, and those who share your world need to share your language.

So, with much study and much practice, the following phrases and words will gradually become as normal to you as they are to those around you, and thus form an unbreakable bond of communication, an impenetrable fortress of parlance, an invite-only party with a verbal dress-code.. oh you get the idea.

Example One
which is showing how
to *correctly* hail a cab

A

-alicious: added onto a word to emphasise how good something actually is.

-avous: added for the sake of it, but if someone talking to you adds an ending, you use the same one if you feel like replying. It's how it goes.

Ab: *absence.*

Ab-so-lute-ly: *ooh yes! Emphasise on "lute" depending on how much you agree with the person.*

Alchemist: *make-up store/counter, or beautician.*

Alibi: *a bouquet of flowers.*

All Wet: *no way! Context: "Ah, you're all wet!" means someone's talking baloney, rather than being soaked. Not to be confused with Wet. See Wet, Baloney, and Soaked.*

Anchor: *bank account.*

And How!: *big yes! Said when you really, really agree with something.*

Ankle: *to walk somewhere. Verb: Anklin'*

Apple Sauce: *flattery that you know is hooey. Someone's laying on the compliments about whatever, and you're either embarrassed or don't believe him/her. See Hooey.*

Ashtray: *a heavy smoker.*

Attaboy!: *hey, real well done! (It's encouragement.)*

Attagirl!: *as above, but louder.*

Audience: *friends (or anyone) who you meet when dolled. See Dolled.*

B

B L Z, got the: *temptation! Derived: Beelzebub. Like, items in store windows that should stay there, a night out when you oughtn't, a somethin' that you shouldn't. Context: "I got the BLZ's for..."*

Babe: *anyone in your circle of friends.*

Baby: *a sweetheart, or something of high value.*

Baby Carriage: *a taxi that's too small for you and all your stuff.*

Baby Grand: *a big guy you wouldn't want to mess with.*

Baggage: *an unwanted hanger-on, or still-present ex-goof. See Goof.*

Baksheesh: *a gratuitie, a tip, or a small compliment.*

Baloney: *the extended rows of raised and tiered seats in a theatre. Oh, hold on.. that's a balcony, oops my mistake. Baloney means nonsense, or hooey. Hooey's a better word - allows for more emphasise.*

Bank's Closed: *no kissing ie "Sorry, the bank's closed."*

Barney-muggin': *making out (ie the bank's open.)*

Bearcat: *a fiery girl, lots of fizz. See fizz.*

Beat It: *get outta my sight.*

Bee's Knees: *as terrific as it gets.*

Beef: *a complaint. Can also be a verb, like "..to beef.." or "..beefing.."*

Being JP: *being nosey. Derived from JP Morgan's schnoz.*

Berries 'n' Cherries: *loose change.*

Big Print, in: *important news. Can also be added to the end of a put-down for extra impact.*

Big Six: *strong guy; ref: the ads for those six-cylinder engines.*

Big Time: *used to emphasise how good or bad something is. Context: "The band were great, big time!" or "That guy's a jerk, big time!"*

Bimble: *trying to walk in heels after too many bubbles. See Bubbles.*
Biscuit: *pretty gal.*
Bite A Sam, to: *a lot of work for hardly any money. Any other word for money will do. See Sam.*
Black-lung: *middle-aged heavy smoker.*
Blotto: *way, way, way too many bubbles. See Bubbles.*
Blow: *a wild party, also means to leave. So you could blow a blow, if you felt like it.*
Boarded Up: *all confused, or ignoring someone.*
Boffin: *a real clever type, brain the size of a planet.*
Bootleg: *illegal hooch of whatever variety.*
Bottle Top(s): *any hat that looks bad, or loose change.*
Bottled: *a soda done properly (served in the bottle, no glass - it's the only way.)*
Brewski: *a coffee or a tea.*
Bubbles: *champagne.*
Business, the: *the bee's knees. See Bee's Knees.*
Bull: *a policeman or law-enforcement type, espesh FBI. See Espesh.*
Bump Off: *to kill. Also means to throw something away when it's become unfashionable.*
Bum's Rush, the: *being removed from a Hot Spot. See Hot Spot.*
Bunny: *a lost or bewildered friend.*
Bus: *a car that's way past its best.*

C

Caged: *not going anywhere due to funding crisis, wardrobe trauma or hair distress.*
Cake-Eater: *opposite of a lady's man. A sissy who's under the false impression of being a smoothy.*
Camel: *late night taxi.*
Candy Store: *a room full of rich fellas.*
Caper: *crazy escapade (usually unplanned).*
Cash: *a kiss, or moocho kisses.*
Cast A Kitten: *to blow a fuse, to launch a volley, to fire the big guns, (can be meant in a good or bad way, depending).*
Cat's Meow: *bee's knees. Also "Cat's Whiskers" "Cat's Tail" and "Cat's Pyjamas (pj's)." Other animals will do just as well, but amongst Flappers, cats are preferable.*
Catch My Drift: *do you understand what I'm saying?*
Change Earrings, have to: *excuse yourself to go to the bathroom.*
Charm Merchant: *faker who knows all the right words, lounge lizard.*
Chasing Ben: *to be in a hurry. Derived: the chariot race in Ben Hur.*
Cheque: *kiss later, not now. Context: "I'll write you a cheque..."*
Chewin' Gum: *misleading waffle. Context: "Get to the point, quit chewin' gum..."*
Chunk: *a not-so-attractive person.*
Circus Just Rolled In, the: *a load of folks with hideous taste/personalities just arrived.*
Clam: *a dollar.*
Clara, a: *a girl who looks right, buys right, talks right. Ref: Clara Bow.*
Class In A Glass: *bee's knees. Also, the finest bubbles money can buy.*
Close It: *shut-up. The manner in which this is said depends on who it's aimed at.*
Clothesline: *someone who spreads gossip.*

Clumpin': *what a lousy dancer does.*

Converating: *talking within your elite circle of likeables. See Likeables.*

Convy: *intense discussion between like-minded friends.*

Coo-ing: *to admire. The noises made when expressing admiration.*

Copacetic: *top of the range excellent, really most definitely excellent.*

Crasher: *an uninvited party go-er.*

Crate: *a sorry-lookin' car.*

Cruisin': *not in a hurry, or taking your time.*

Cruisin' An' Perusin': *in no big rush around the shops. Window shopping.*

Cuddler: *someone who likes to cuddle, of course.*

Cut A Slice: *having to wait patiently. Derived: cutting a slice of cake.*

D

-dalacious: pronounced 'da-layy-shus' and added to a word to emphasise or exagerrate.

Daddy: *a boyfriend who's had far more birthdays than his girlfriend. Must be rich, okay?*

Dame: *a high-class woman who's beyond Flapper age.*

Dapper: *a well-dressed parent on the paternal side.*

Darb: *something real good, a top-notch person or thing.*

Dee: *desirable. The duration depends entirely on the desirability of the person or item(s).*

Dented: *feelin' low, life ain't goin' your way, in big need of a laugh.*

Derriere: *someone's rear, also the end of a queue.*

Dewdropper: *a layabout.*

Dibb: *a person with no brain whatsoever. In debt at the brain bank.*

Diddle The Squiddle, let's: *to meet friends for the sake of it with no plans for doing anything.*

Dingledangler: *someone who uses the phone way too much.*

Dish Rag: *someone who's real wet. See Wet.*

Dog Kennels: *dull shoes. See Dogs.*

Dogs: *feet. Can be pronounced 'Doe-Geeze.' Also: "My dog's are barking" - my feet ache.*

Dolled: *all dressed up, painted, jewelled and ready to roll.*

Don't Know Nothin' From Nothin': *kinda dumb.*

Dot Dot: *therefore. It's an abbreviation of the abbreviation - saves a syllable.*

Double Trouble: *a friend dating your ex.*

Dough: *money.*

Drainage: *the effect of must-haves on your purse contents.*

Dry Up: *stop talkin' right now.*

Dud: *a goof who thinks he's a Flipper. See Flipper.*

E

-escent: works on plenty of words.. just have to find the right ones.

Earful: *like I've heard enough already!*

Ear Muffs: *radio receivers.*

Eat The Beat: *living to dance. Context: "Do I dance? Buddy, I eat the beat!"*

Ebrew The Hebrew: *a name for someone when you're talking about them and they're right there* *with you. Saves embarrassment, usually causes moocho laughs.*

Echo Canyon: *where someone with no brain (an empty-head, hence the echo) comes from. Context: "You can take him out of Echo Canyon, but you can't take Echo Canyon out of him..."*

Eeekabouts: *goin' nuts about something. Context: "Don't go eekabouts, but.." means "Stay calm, but.."*

Eeesh: *emphasises the down-side of a sentence. Used to begin or end the statement.*

Elbow, to: *to dump someone, to dump something, or to dump anything.*

Elephant's Eyebrows: *the bee's knees.*

Espesh: *a major step up from especially. Saves two syllables in rapid convy.*

Essential: *the crème de la crème, better than best, must have, untouchable. Note: cannot be dropped into conversation enough times. See also Sench.*

Etcet: *etcetera.*

Eyeball: *"See you.." on a date. Has to be followed by the time and place.*

F

Face Ache: *a dame plastered with make-up trying to hide the years.*

Farmer's Wife, a: *heavy-built and not too fashion-conscious either.*

Fast: *a life revolving around parties, dancing, hunting, in fact simply having fun.*

Feathers: *plenty of meaningless talk.*

Fella: *a bearable and totally inoffensive guy. A fella is quite literally 'better than no-one'.*

Fetchin': *attractive.*

Fig Leaf: *a one-piece bathing outfit.*

Finale Hopper: *someone who scrams when the bill arrives.*

Fire Extinguisher: *a chaperone.*

Fiver: *someone not big on smarts (they can put 2 and 2 together all day and **still** make 5.)*

Fizz: *spark, lust for life, energy.*

Fizzer: *someone who's always, always, kicking a laugh. See Kicking A Laugh.*

Flask: *a stewed goof. See Goof. And Stewed, as well.*

Flat Tyre: *a real Zeebert. See Zeebert.*

Flipper: *the male version of a Flapper (or as close as poss), subject to majority of friends' approval.*

Flivver: *one of those Model T Fords.*

Floorflusher: *a dancer who just won't stop. Note: can be embarrassing.*

Flour Lover: *a girl buried under too much face powder.*

Flukey: *someone or something that is a bit different.*

For Crying Out Loud!: *the only response to a truly dumb statement.*

Forty-Niner: *a man searching for a rich wife. A male gold-digger.*

Frenchman's Fancy, a: *an over-dressed woman with too much of everything.*

Fret/ernation/ernatin': *a problem. Add any ending. Context: "Go chase yourself, it ain't my fret."*

Frog's Flippers: *elephant's eyebrows, tiger's toes, and so on and so on. Also, Frog's Pond.*

G

G: *good. Pronounced 'Geeeee'. Duration depends on how good.*

Garb: *clothes with style.*

Get Hot!: *loud encouragement for dancin' up a storm.*

Get In A Lather: *gettin' all heat-up, or worked up. Note: never in public. Be cool!*

Get On The Trolley!: *listen to what I'm saying. Also, catch my drift.*

Gettin' A Wiggle On: *raise the pace!*

Gettin' Fetchin': *dressin' up for an evening, puttin' on the glad rags. See Glad Rags.*

Giggles, the: *an inability to explain what's funny while laughing a lot.*

Gigolo: *someone to be dancing with.*

Gin Mill: *a cheap-o speakeasy. See Speakeasy.*

Glad Rags: *garb to step out in, town-time wrapping. See Town Time, and Wrapping.*

Gnu's News, the: *elephant's eyebrows (and all the rest) but this relates to juicy gossip.*

Go Bust A Heel: *a prime put-down, a terrible thing to wish upon someone.*

Go Fishing, to: *chasing up some juicy info, hunting gossip, finding the facts (or something close).*

Gold-Digger: *a Smarty who ignores a man's age, his looks and all of his undesirable habits in her pursuit of a financially secure future. See Smarty.*

Goods, the: *the right look or style. Also means the truth, and also gossip in factuality.*

Goof: *an idiot, or an annoying boyfriend. Can easily be both.*

Goofy: *well and truly in love.*

Granma's Handbag: *any clothing or accessory that's reeeally unfashionable. Context: Eesh, that'll go with Granma's Handbag!*

Grub-Stake: *a dinner invite.*

Grummy: *feelin' low and dented. See Dented.*

Grungy: *real envious.*

H

H C of L, the: *the High Cost of Living. Emphasise on the hhhaych.*

Half Seas Over: *incredibly drunk. Canned, double-dented, no steering wheel, half under, juiced, splifficated, pie-eyed, piffled, prohibited, stewed to the hat, trippin' over daisies, oh this list could run..*

Handcuff: *an engagement ring.*

Habso: *absolutely. Also means - big yes, I really agree, and.. umm.. absolutely. Derived: abso-lutely.*

Hack Pack: *a pack of cigarettes. Posing purposes only.*

Hack'n'yack: *talking and coughing, usually happens to smoke eaters.*

Hard Boiled: *real hard-case, a tough guy.*

Hass: *trouble. Abbreviation of 'hassle'.*

Hay Shaker: *someone from the sticks, an out-of-towner just visiting.*

Haych Vees: *horizontals & verticals. Refers to measurements and the lie of fine clothes*

Heavin': *packed dancefloor.*

Heebie-jeebies: *spooked, or shaking.*

Heeler: *a hopeless dancer who's blissfully unaware of his/her inabilities.*

High Hat: *a snob, a nose-lifter.*

High-Tailing: *to leave somewhere in a hurry.*

Hit On All Sixes: *you're on top form.*

Honey Pop: *a drink bought by (or for) a friend when cash-flow isn't what it should be.*

Hooey: *baloney, nonsense. See Baloney.*

Hoofer: *a heeler. Essential at any social function, as they make you look really hot.*

Hot: *awesome. Better than the best.*

Hot Dawg!: *well reeeeally great! Duration lengthens for sarcasm.*

Hot House: *a kitchen.*
Hot Socks!: *almost the same as Hot Dawg.*
Hot Spot: *the best swagger patch to be in. See Swagger Patch.*
Hugs: *thanks. Note: only said to friends or those who've done a favour.*
Hunting: *the on-going quest pour l'amour.*
Hush Bunny: *a friend who can keep secrets, either due to integrity or a lousy memory.*
Hush Money: *acts of kindness (bribery!) from someone you've got the goods on. See Goods.*

I

-ify: pronounced 'if-eye'. Added to anything to make it sound better. Example: Darbify - to make something the elephant's eyebrows. See Darb. And E's E's.

I the D P!: *Ignore the Da✳n Price! Mantra to take the sting out of those must-have store moments.*
Icy Mitt: *turned down or side-lined. Someone who ignores you is giving the icy mitt.*
Iffernating: *can't decide. Also, Iffernition, Iffernatious and any others you can think of.*
In A Rut: *curtailing the socialisin' due to lack of funds. Also means stuck or dented. See Dented.*
Insured: *engaged.*
Isch Ka Bibble: *endlessly useful reply meaning "Like I should care!" or something very similar, depending on the tone of the conversation. Abbreviation: Isch Ka Bib.*

J

Jake: *everything's okay, or an average kind of guy.*
Jalopy: *a crummy old crate of a car. See Crate.*
Jammering: *everyone talking all at once.*
Jane: *any female, up to the age of 30 or thereabouts...*
Java: *good coffee.*
Jazzbo: *regular guy, worth being with.*
Jeepers Creepers: *Yikes! A more expressive version is "Jeepers big-time creepers", which is used in more demanding situations. See Big Time.*
Jerk Soda: *soda from a tap rather than a bottle. See Soda Jerk.*
Jitney: *a car being used as a private bus.*
Joe: *coffee, or a name for someone who's name you don't know (unless it's Joe, of course).*
Joe Eskimo: *anyone selling ice-cream. Context: "Hey, let's go see Joe Eskimo," means "Hey, I'm melting here so let's go ice-creamin'!" Big emphasise on the -mo.*
John D: *either a guy makin' like he's as rich as, or an oily man. Derived: oil baron John D Rockefeller.*
Juice Joint: *a better-class of speakeasy.*

K

Kale: *another one for money. Derived: crinkly green cabbage leaves. No, really it is.*
Kee-yoot: *real cute.*
Keen: *something eye-catching, kind of appealing.*
Keeps: *your own money.*
Kicking A Laugh: *habso fun. Takes practice and dedication! See Habso.*
Kicks: *more fun.*
Killjoy: *a person too serious for their own good - or anyone else's good, actually...*

L

Lacemonger: *heavy-handed dress-maker. Note: avoid at all costs.*

Land It: *to encourage someone to get to the point, to sit down, or park a car.*

Lap, to: *to drink.*

Lay Off: *get someone to change the subject, or stop doing whatever they're doing that's annoying you.*

Lead Head: *not too blessed in the brains department.*

Leg Shake, a: *a party or a big dance.*

Let George Do It: *a useful phrase to avoid doing work, especially if you actually know someone called George. Fellas called George who use this phrase are worth avoiding.*

Level With Me: *be on the level with me, up and down, straight. See all of those.*

Likeables: *your group, those worthy of being with.*

Lindburg, a: *someone going way too fast and leaving everyone else behind. Can also be sarcasm for a slow case or a dimwit. Ref: Charles Lindburg, the aviator guy.*

Line, a: *a fib, or a misleading story, as in "Your feedin' me a line, buddy!"*

Live Wire: *a real fizzer. Note: Always good to know plenty of them. See Fizzer.*

Lollygagger: *a lazy good-for-nothing loafer layabout dewdrop type.*

Long-Ways: *lying down (whether asleep, blotto, or on a stretcher).*

Longsock: *someone with heaps of money but no style.*

Lounge Lizard: *a real smoothy.*

Low Number: *a dimwit, about as useful as being dealt a low number in certain cardgames.*

Lu-Lu: *Someone with drop-dead awesome fashion sense - ref Louise Brooks. A much preferred shopping partner, good for parties, an ideal hunting companion. See Hunting.*

M

Mad As A Box Of Frogs, as: *a good friend who's a little 'unpredictable' (in a good way, though).*

Maddabout: *anything you're into at this moment right now.*

Magnetised: *attractin' attention due to awesome wrapping & dolling. See Wrapping & Dolled.*

Manacle: *wedding ring.*

Marmola: *anything that sounds too good to be true. Derived: miracle slimmin' gunk.*

Mmmmwáh!: *big fake kissy-sound. Good for sarcasm, put-downs, or even genuine - whatever suits.*

Modo, a: *someone with the looks and fashion-sense of Quasimodo.*

Monkey(s): *Anything that's not right. Context: "That's monkey talk" refers to someone who knows very little yet talks way too much. "Made by monkeys" "Done by monkeys" and so on a lot.*

Mooch, a: *someone who lets friends pay all the time. Note: avoid this sort.*

Moocho: *a lot, or loads more.*

Moonshine: *homemade whiskey, can be lethal. Note: even expensive-looking labels can lie.*

Mop: *a handkerchief.*

Mouthpiece: *a lawyer.*

Mule: *an idle or unattractive person you put up with due to their usefulness, (chauffeuring or financial.)*

Munitions: *make-up.*

Musket: *someone who shoots their mouth off all the time (usually loudly).*

Mutton Dressed As Pig: *someone old trying to dress far too young, and failing habsodalaciously. Derived: Mutton dressed as lamb. See Habso and -dalacious.*

N

Neck, to: *to make out.*

Ness: *abbreviation of necessary.*

Nifty: *the bee's, the elephant's, the tiger's etc.*

Nouveaux: *new clothes, shoes, place to go. Emphasise on "vohhh".*

Not So Good!: *err.. not so good. Pronounced with long 'n' on the "not"*

Numb Nut: *someone so dumb they can only dream of being as smart as a tent peg. See Tent Peg.*

O

-ola: niftiest ending for ANY word. Makes even dull ones more *now*. Derived: Radiola.

-osity: makes most descriptive words roll better.

Obvee: *obvious.*

Off Your Nut: *you're crazy.*

Oh Yeah?: *I doubt it. Voice needs to rise as the phrase progresses.*

Old Boy: *in Flapper-talk, a favourable term for a guy, regardless of age. Context: "How's everything, old boy?" Suggests acceptance without suggesting too much acceptance, if you know what I mean.*

On The El: *someone who's ended/thrown a sheik/sheba and is back doin' the rounds. Derived: the elevated rail lines goin' all over New York.*

On The Hush: *keep it quiet, don't tell anyone, a real big shhh, and so on...*

On The Lam: *hightailin' from the cops. Nights at a speakeasy can sometimes be brought to a sudden halt this way... See Hightailin'*

On The Level: *straight up, real legitimate, totally honest, up and down.*

On The Up And Up: *totally honest, straight up, on the level etc. Note: something can be on the level and also on the up and up at the same time, okay?*

Orchid, an: *anything expensive.*

Out For The Count: *real surprised.*

Owl: *someone who's always out late.*

P

Palooka: *an outsider, doesn't know the ropes or nothing from nothing.*

Panic: *to cause a stir (whether from new garb, or big news).*

Parade: *when you go out in new garb. See Garb.*

Park, to: *to wait somewhere, or stay somewhere.*

Parlez: *gossip. Pronounced "Par-layyy"*

Parrot's Plume: *the bee's knees, elephant's eyebrows... and the rest...*

Percolatin': *everything's running smoothly.*

Petting Pantry: *movie theatre.*

Piffle: *hooey, trash-talk.*

Pill: *someone you don't like one bit.*

Pillowcase: *a guy who's full of feathers. See Feathers.*

Pinched: *to get arrested.*

Points: *tips of shoes. Context: "She has no good points at all." This is no reflection on her, but an observation about the over-worn state of her shoes. Actually, that is an observation about her.*

Popping A Cork, I'm: *feeling really excited and pleased about something.*

Pos-i-lute-ly: *yes. Notice important application of those hyphens. Emphasise is placed on the 'lute' part depending on how much you agree with the other person.*

Pos-i-tive-ly: *same as the above, but broadens your repertoire.*

Pot Belly: *a rich boyfriend, far older than the girlfriend. Context: "Oh, look at her pot belly!" In no way does this refer to the her waistline, but is in fact a reference to the one accompanying her. She has found a pot of gold, a man who is of an age where his physique ain't what it used to be, if it ever was what it ever was. Yes indeed.*

Prom Trotter: *a college type who goes to all school socials.*

Puddle Jumper: *a real softie, a sissy.*

Put The Frighteners On: *someone wearing way too much make-up has done this.*

Putting On The Ritz: *doing something with style. 'Ritzy' is a real useful variant.*

Q

Quacker: *someone who dances like an angry duck (all knees and elbows).*

Quaint: *something hot - but was hot last month... yikes...*

Quaker: *a goody who leads a quiet life with no leg-shakes. See Leg Shake.*

Quality!: *excellent! Used to describe anything good. Note: emphasise on '-teeee' part.*

Queen: *over-dressed woman with no style. Doesn't apply to genuine royalty because any royalty is worth being seen with, regardless of fashion faux-pas.*

R

Raining Pitchforks: *a real downpour.*

Razz: *to have a laugh at.*

Real McCoy: *somethin' genuine.*

Regular: *another word for a Fella. See Fella.*

Reuben: *country bumpkin, someone who's behind the times. Note: shortens to 'Rube'.*

Rhatz!: *darn it, and other similar ones..*

Ridin' The Down-One Up: *gettin' nowhere fast. Derived: stepping on the wrong escalator. Also, Ridin' The Up One Down, depending on the dumbnosity of the situation.*

Rinkydink: *an item rendered useless, dysfunctional or embarrassing due to damage, or even worse - becoming unfashionable.*

Root: *long-standing friend. See also Square Root.*

Rub: *a dance party.*

Rummy: *a whino, a street-boozer, a sidewalk stumbler, a tramp.*

S

-ski: *some words just need a proper ending, and this fits most.*

Sams: *bank notes. Derived from Uncle Sam.*

Sap: *someone who ain't too switched on. An idiot, stumblebum, headless wonder, bottle top.*

Says You: *a polite way to express a big doubt. The 'you' bit extends way beyond its natural duration.*

Scat: *crazy, your all over the place, up in the air, and so on like that.*

Scram: *to leave.*

Scratch: *another one for money. You could always stick with saying money, but don't.*

Screwy: *crazy. Context: "You paid how much for those? You're screwy!"*

Sench: *abbreviation of Essential, also raises essentialness and saves a syllable.*

Sharp Shooter: *a worthy boyfriend, a good Flipper. Spends money as good as he dances. See Flipper.*

Sheba: *someone's girlfriend, or a stylish girl.*

Sheik: *someone's boyfriend, etc.*

Shoe-Shine: *anyone with a lousy, low-paid job.*

Shoff: *push off!*

Shoot The Hoop: *come on, go for it. A strong prod in the right direction.*

Shugs: *whatever.*

Signif: *the next step up from 'significant' (and it also saves a syllable).*

Simolean: *a dollar.*

Sinker: *a doughnut.*

Sitting Pretty: *pleased with yourself for whatever reason.*

Si-voo: *please. Vary the 'oo'. Comes from a French expression or something.*

Skate: *to leave quickly.*

Skid-Over: *hurry over here like as now!*

Skirt: *an attractive girl.*

Skirtchase: *a girl who's being amorously pursued.*

Smarty/Smartie: *a girl who's with-it. Also, a good friend to be with. Also a brainiac boffin, too.*

Smudger: *someone who dances up close.*

Snugglepup: *a cuddler.*

So's Your Old Man: *a sharp put-down. If you're annoyed by someone and can't think of anything to say, then let fly with this. Usually works.*

Soaked: *had far too many bubbles.*

Soaked With A Bar Rag: *not quite had too many bubbles, feeling tipsy.*

Sockdolager: *something major, important or exceptional that happens and causes a signif impact. Can also be a hefty blow. Extend the '-ollllllager' accordingly.*

Soda Jerk: *the guy who serves the soda from a tap, not bottles.*

Spanner: *someone who's in the way, or messes stuff up. Derived: '..in the works'*

Speakeasy: *a bar selling bubbles etc, very illegally.*

Spill: *to tell. Context: "C'mon, spill the beans, where d'you buy them?"*

Square An Uppercut, to: *any great put-down, or launching a golden fact in an argument, or delivering undeniable proof.*

Squeakeasy: *a diner with a rodent problem.*

Square Root: *a long-standing friend who lacks the necessary style etc to be seen in public with.*

Stage: *anywhere you go when you're wearing something new.*

Static: *meaningless talk.*

Steal: *a must-have item, the price of which doesn't matter. Pronounced 'steeeyul'.*

Steamboat: *a really overweight person.*

Steppers: *a pair of must-have shoes, the kind without which life would become horribly unbearable.*

Stilts: *legs.*

Strugglin': *trying hard to look like you know what you're doing when dancing to something new.*

Stuck On: *real in love.*

Sugar Daddy: *a boyfriend who no longer celebrates his own birthday but treats his girlfriend like it's hers everyday. Yum.*

Swanky: *good, in an expensive way. Applies to fashionable items.*

Swagger: *the way to walk.*

Swagger Patch: *a stylish joint to be seen in.*

Sweetie/Sweety: *depending on how you say it, a good friend or someone you can't stand.*

Sweetify: *get around to my way of thinking. Also, lighten up.*

Swell: *good, in a 'good guy' way.*

T

Take The Bait, to: *to finally get someone to understand what you're talking about.*

Taking Someone For A Ride: *leading someone on.*

Tasslin': *dancing while wearing a tassle-loaded dress.*

Tasty: *real nice, vee appealing. See Vee.*

Telegraph: *a gossip-spreader, an untrustable.. and naturally a valuable fountain of knowledge.*

Tell It To Sweeney: *go tell someone who'll believe you. Said if someone's spinning a yarn, or plain bragging too much.*

Tent Peg: *someone who must've been hit on the head an awful lot, a real no-brainer. Or a short guy.*

They: *disapproving parents.*

Tiger's Toes: *bee's knees, elephant's.. you must be gettin' the idea by now?*

Tight: *someone with no loose baggage. See Baggage.*

Tin Pan Alley: *the heart of New York's music biz. Keeps us dancing!*

Torpedo: *a hitman. Can be useful...*

Town Time: *a night out.*

Tramped: *worn out.*

Treadaway: *a nervous friend, or be careful when gossiping (Context: "Be a tread, she can hear us.")*

Turn The Dial: *getting someone to change the subject (or just to hurry to the good part!)*

U

Unreal: *real good.*

Undumb, to come: *to understand something once it's been explained. I know, I know, it should be under C or maybe T, but the U's reeeally needed padding out.*

Up And Down: *being honest with you, on the level, straight up, etc.*

Upchuck: *to throw up. Note: try and avoid doing this - it simply can't be done with style!*

Upstage: *snobby.*

V

V: *very. Pronounced 'Veee'. Its context prevents confusion with Valentino abbreviation.*

Valentino: *highly rated boyfriend. Abbreviated to 'Vee'*

Vamp: *a man-trap, someone beyond Flapper-years intent on gaining attention.*

Vined: *a secret's out, something juicy's been blabbed. Context: "Uh oh.. last night's been vined."*

Voot: *money again.*

Vouchsafe: *the trusted friend who provides any alibis for your over-cooked lovelife.*

W

Wagon: *a hideous taxi.*

Washboard: *someone boring who makes lots of unnecessary noise ie talks too much.*

Watch The Green: *don't trust him/her. Derived: counterfeit money, ie looks good but it don't take long for the ink to come off.*

Wet: *indecisive, no opinion, probably no brain.*

Wet Blanket: *see Killjoy.*

Whale Bait: *someone big and heavy.*

What's The Huff?: *What's up?*

Whoopee: *fun.*

Witness: *to observe everything about someone (or something) as if your life depended on it. Context: "Witness the Lu-Lu!!" which means everyone should make a careful note of her clothes, hair, make-up, accessories and everything. See Lu-Lu.*

Wrapping: *your clothes ensemble. The kind of get-up that takes a lot of careful planning and consideration before parading to the world.*

X

Xtras: *people around you who serve no purpose. Yes, I know it really begins with an 'e' but there's plenty of those ones already.*

Y

Yack: *high-powered convy. See Convy.*

Yardage: *the amount of material in an outfit.*

Yardfull: *rubbish, junk - and lots of it, ie the kind of stuff that fills up a back yard. Context: "That's a yardfull!" is a way of expressing plenty of disbelief. Abbreviate to yard, if ness. See Ness.*

You Slay Me!: *another way of saying "You are so funny!"*

YT: *yours truly.*

Z

Zeebert: *a dull sort who sends you to sleep.*

Zuzzin': *sleeping (snoring, mainly).*

The Sench Flapper's Almanac: Section Four (MCMXXVII) reprinted by kind permission of the Felicity Chancer Estate, NY. Images 2 - 19 withheld, 1 & 20 printed by permission.

ALSO AVAILABLE BY THE SAME AUTHOR

THE
Odessa
Stone

BISHOP ULLATHORNE
SCHOOL
COVENTRY

VISIT

THE GUARDIAN OF TIME

& THE ODESSA STONE

WEBSITE AT

www.step-through.com

STEP THROUGH BOOKS